GUARDIANS, HUNTERS, COMPANIONS. . . .

Dogs have served humans in all these roles, and have become an integral part of our society. What roles will they play in the future—on our own world, or in far distant realms?

The sixteen tales in this volume follow the many different trails our canine friends may follow, including:

"Heartsease"—The little dog had lived with far too many people in far too short a time, but he knew the time was coming when he would decide his own destiny. . . .

"After the Fall"—He'd been afraid of dogs since he was three. But was he scared enough to let his fear kill him . . . ?

"Precious Cargo"—Why would anyone pay so much to ship a bunch of dogs—even bioengineered dogs—to a distant world? That was the question. She wasn't really sure she wanted to find out the answer. . . .

SIRIUS
The Dog Star

Edited by Martin H. Greenberg and Alexander Potter

DAW BOOKS, INC.
DONALD A. WOLLHEIM, FOUNDER
375 Hudson Street, New York, NY 10014

ELIZABETH R. WOLLHEIM
SHEILA E. GILBERT
PUBLISHERS
www.dawbooks.com

This anthology is dedicated to the real life Sirius, the police bomb-detection dog that perished in the World Trade Center attacks on 9/11.

ACKNOWLEDGMENTS

"Introduction" © 2004 by Alexander B. Potter.
"Finding Marcus" © 2004 by Tanya Huff.
"Brothers Bound" © 2004 by Julie E. Czerneda.
"Heartsease" © 2004 by Fiona Patton.
"A Spaniel for the King" © 2004 by India Edghill.
"Among the Pack Alone" © 2004 by Stephen Leigh.
"After the Fall" © 2004 by Kristine Kathryn Rusch.
"Final Exam" © 2004 by Rosemary Edghill.
"Precious Cargo" © 2004 by Bernie Arntzen.
"Hair of the Dog" © 2004 by Doranna Durgin.
"All the Virtues" © 2004 by Mickey Zucker Reichert.
"Dog Gone" © 2004 by John Zakour.
"Life's a Bichon" © 2004 by Bethlyn Damone.
"Keep the Dog Hence" © 2004 by Jane Lindskold.
"Snow Spawn" © 2004 by Nancy Springer.
"Improper Congress" © 2004 by Elaine Quon.
"Huntbrother" © 2004 by Michelle West.

CONTENTS

Introduction

by Alexander B. Potter

THE TRUTH comes out. I am not—exactly—a dog person. Rats are more my thing. This fact came home to me repeatedly every time I told anyone about *Sirius: The Dog Star*. I received a variety of funny responses from the folks in my life, most taking some form of "*You*? An anthology about dogs? You've got to be joking."

My reputation as something less than the quintessential dog person obviously preceded me, and I theorize the cats in my life may have done some talking. Apparently people expected *Assassin Fantastic* from me . . . but dogs? Not ever.

Whatever the reaction, I never failed to point out that I am a lifelong, dedicated supporter of the underdog, and cats have five *Catfantastics* out there floating around the bookstores while dogs have none. Dogs have been ignored, forgotten, slighted. Cats rule fantasy with an iron claw and a self-satisfied smirk. Dogs deserve their chance to be the star.

Unfortunately, much as they understood the reasoning, no one really bought it as applied to me. The askance glances kept coming. "But you?" they said. "Shouldn't a *real* dog lover do this book?" At which time I always hastened to explain that I was born in the Chinese Year of the Dog. I am a true Dog

1

representative . . . honest, faithful, loyal, the epitome of friendship. Destined to create this anthology.

That didn't impress anyone either.

So finally I stopped telling people what I was working on, and told them I was writing a novel instead—an effective way of getting people to leave you alone and stop asking how the latest project is coming along.

Simultaneously, though, I became terribly insecure about editing an anthology focused on dogs, given my lack of dog experience and, more importantly, lack of true dog appreciation. To allay my insecurity (and guilt) I began to study dogs, research their lineage and ancestry, qualities, breeds, diversity. I read articles and Web-surfed and watched Discovery specials and bought magazines and did something I'd never done in the past—sought out actual dogs. Not only was it delightful and enlightening but also something funny, though perhaps unsurprising, happened. I met Hope—the dog who would be my dog, if such a thing were to happen. A sweet little collie who definitely knows how beautiful she is, Hope convinced me there could be a dog in my future.

So I was already starting to understand, already starting to convert, when one by one the stories came in from authors and I fell a little in love with each of the dogs I met in the following pages. Not something I ever expected to happen when I began this project. In truth, this anthology began as a gift, and a way to honor a memory. I pitched and sold the idea not because I felt personally drawn to canines but because someone important to me, who does appreciate dogs in the truest sense, suggested dogs had been slighted and should have their own anthology. From that urging, I started *Sirius* in honor of my brothers, the brother I lost when I was twelve and the brother I gained in my late twenties—Stephen and Daniel, both quintessential dog men. Stephen, who remains inextricably linked to dogs for me through a sharp Doberman and a famous bulldog and who, I believe, more than any of my other projects, would have enjoyed *Sirius* the most. Daniel, along with so much else, helped me begin to understand the root of the human/dog connection and suggested the anthology idea in the first place.

Now, as I put the stories together and survey the completed result, I realize I don't need to feel guilty about editing an anthology dedicated to dogs. The very process brought me into the world of dogs in a way I was sure nothing could. I believe creating a new convert to the mystery of the human/canine bond is a fitting result for *Sirius: The Dog Star.*

Sirius turned out to be a discovery and a joy to edit, from beginning to end. The many diverse facets of our complex relationships with dogs come to light throughout the stories—from protectors and confidantes to the most pure of friends. Each story takes us someplace new and different. From the historical fantasy of India Edghill to the new worlds of the science fiction of Julie Czerneda . . . from the unforgettable canine voices telling the stories of Tanya Huff and Fiona Patton to the only-too-human voices telling the stories of Michelle West and Kristine Kathryn Rusch.

Choose a story at random and meet an unforgettable canine character. Watch these dogs pass inextricably through the lives of the people surrounding them. Come away touched by the relationships that we may be hard-pressed to explain in logical terms, but that make wonderful fodder for rich fiction.

Finding Marcus

by Tanya Huff

Tanya Huff lives and writes in rural Ontario with her partner, six cats, and an unintentional Chihuahua. Her twenty-two books run the gamut of fantasy and science fiction, and she has numerous short stories to her credit as well. Her most recent novel, *Smoke and Shadows,* was an April 2004 hardcover release from DAW, and Tanya is currently at work in on the second novel in this new fantasy series, which features Tony Foster, one of the characters from her highly acclaimed *Blood* books. In her spare time she gardens and complains about the weather.

THE RAT was fat, a successful forager, overconfident. It had no idea I was hunting it until my teeth closed over the back of its neck and, by then, it was far too late. As I ate, I gave thanks, as I always did, that some bitch in my ancestry had mated with a terrier. If I'd been all herder or tracker, I'd have been long dead by now. A puddle from the recent rains quenched my thirst and, with my immediate needs satisfied, I took a look around.

The Gate had dumped me in an alley, pungent with the smell of rotting garbage, shit, and stagnant water. There were other rats in the big overflowing bins, roaches under everything, and a dead bird somewhere close. The bins were metal. Never a good sign.

I lifted my head to the breeze coming in from the distant mouth of the alley and sighed. Cars. It's a scent you don't forget. Mid-tech world at least. Although I could already feel the pull of the next Gate, it would be harder to find it in the stink of too many people and too much going on. Still, it wasn't like I had much of a choice.

And sometimes the low-tech worlds were worse. A lot worse. It was fear and suspicion on a low-tech world that had separated us.

Before I left, I marked the place where the old Gate had been. Not so I could find it again—they only worked in one direction—it's just something I've done ever since I got into this mess, sort of saying that the Gates are mine not the other way around. And besides, sometimes I just need to piss on the damn things.

I had a quick roll in the bird as I passed. A guy's got to do some stuff for himself.

At the mouth of the alley, I felt a slight pull to the left, so I turned. Nose to the ground, I could smell nothing but the rain. The sky must have cleared just before I showed up. Marcus could be mere minutes ahead of me and I'd never know it.

Suddenly regretting the rat, I started to run.

Marcus could be mere minutes ahead of me.

Minutes.

By the time I stopped running, I'd left the alley far behind. I knew I wasn't going to catch up to him so easily, but sometimes it takes me that way—the thought that he could be close—and my legs take over from my brain. I always feel kind of stupid afterward. Stupid and sad. And tired. Not leg tired; heart tired.

The pull from the next Gate hadn't gotten any stronger, so I still had a distance to travel. I had to cross a big water once. Long story. Long, wet, nasty story.

The made-stone that covered the ground was cleaner here. Smelled more of people and less of garbage although I hadn't yet reached an area where people actually lived. At a corner joining two large roads, I lifted my head and sniffed the sky. No scent of morning. Good. It had been nearly mid-dark when I'd entered the Gate one world back, but time changed as the worlds did and I could have lost the night. Lost my best time to travel, lost my chance of catching up to Marcus.

I dove back into a patch of deep shadow as three cars passed in quick succession. Most of the time, the people in cars were blind to the world outside their metal cages but occasionally on a mid-tech world a car would stop and the people would spill out, bound and determined to help a poor lost dog. I was hungry enough, hurt enough, stupid enough to let them once.

Only once. I barely escaped with my balls.

When the road was clear, I raced across and, although it made my guts twist to ignore the path I needed to follow, I turned left, heading for the mouth of a dark alley. Heading away from the lights on poles and the lights on buildings, away from too much light to be safe.

The alley put me back on the path. When it ended in a dark canyon between two buildings, I turned left again, finally spilling out onto another road; a darker road, lined with tall houses. I could follow this road for a while. The lights on the poles were farther apart here and massive trees threw shadows dark enough to hide a dozen of me.

As it happened, the shadows also hid half a dozen cats.

Cats are contradictions as far as I'm concerned; soft and sweet and harmless appearing little furballs who make no effort to hide the fact that they kill for fun and can curse in language that would make a rat blush. I took the full brunt of their vocabulary as I ran by. Another place, another night, and I might have treed a couple, but with the Gate so far away I needed to cover some serious distance before dawn.

Sunrise found me running along a road between houses so large they could almost be called palaces. Probably a rich merchant area. High-tech, mid-tech, low-tech—some things never changed. People who suddenly found themselves with a lot of stuff had to show it off. Marcus, who never had anything except me and a blithe belief in his own intellect, used to laugh about it. He used to laugh about a lot of things. He wasn't laughing when they tore us apart, he was screaming my name and that's how I remember him most often.

I couldn't stay on this road much longer, it was beginning to curve away from the direction I needed. But first, breakfast.

Low-tech, high-tech; both were essentially garbage free. But mid-tech—when they weren't piling it in metal bins, people in mid-tech worlds actually collected their garbage up into bags and set it out in front of their houses. It was like they were bragging about how much they could waste. A guy could eat well off that bragging.

Second bag I ripped open, I hit the jackpot. A half

circle of flat bread with sausage and cheese crumbled onto a sauce. I gulped it down, licked the last bit of sweet cream out of a container, and took off at full speed as a door opened and a high-pitched voice started to yell.

Over time, I've gotten pretty good at knowing when I'm not wanted.

As I rounded the curve at full speed, I saw that the houses had disappeared from one side of the road. In their place, a ravine—wild and overgrown and the way I needed to go. The spirit pack was definitely looking out for me on this world, but then, by my calculations, I was about due. I jumped the barrier and dove through the underbrush.

A squirrel exploded out of the leaf litter in front of me and I snapped without thinking. It managed half a surprised squeal before it died. Carrying it, I made my way down the steep bank, across a path at the bottom, and halfway up the other side. Someone, a long time ago by the smell of it, had scratched out a shallow den under the shelter of a large bush. I shoved my kill between two branches because I don't like the taste of ants and there was no other way to keep them off the squirrel—although it *was* sort of comforting that ants tasted the same on every world. Food safe, I marked the territory as mine and made myself comfortable.

Down on the path, a female person ran by. Nothing seemed to be chasing her. Running beside her was a lovely black and white bitch with pointed ears and a plumy tail. Ears flattened, she glanced up toward me as she crossed my trail but kept running, clearly aware of where her responsibilities lay. I could appreciate that. Resting my chin on my front paws, I went to sleep.

The heat of the sun was warm against my fur when I woke so I knew I'd been asleep for a while. The question: what had woken me? The answer: a sound. A rustling in the bush I slept beneath. I heard it again and slowly opened my eyes.

A small crow sidled toward my squirrel. Only half the size of some crows I'd seen, its weight was still enough to shake the branch. With one claw raised, it glanced toward me and froze.

"Nice, doggy. There's a nice, big doggy. Crow not tasty. Doggy not eat crow."

"I hadn't intended to," I told her lifting my head. "But I don't intend to allow you to hop in here and eat my kill either."

The crow blinked and put her raised foot down. "Well, you're a lot more articulate than most," she said. "Practically polysyllabic." Head to one side, she took a closer look. "I don't think I know your breed."

"I don't think you do," I agreed. "I'm not from around here."

Left eye, then right eye, she raked me up and down with a speculative gaze. "No, I don't imagine you are. You want to talk about it?"

"No." She took flight as I crawled from the den, but after a long, luxurious scratch I realized she'd only flown up into the nearest tree. "What?"

"Where's your . . . what is it you dogs call them again? Your pack?"

I'd have howled except that was a good way to attract the kind of attention I didn't want. Marcus had been the only pack I'd ever had.

"Is that what you're looking for?"

"What makes you think I'm looking for anything?" I growled.

"Well, you're not from around here. So . . ." She hopped along the branch. ". . . I'm wondering what you're doing here. You're not lost—you lot are so obvious when you're lost—therefore, you're looking for something. Someone." Crows always looked pleased with themselves, but something in my reaction shot her right up into smug and self-satisfied. "I knew it. You have a story."

"Everyone has a story." I started up the bank.

"Hey! Dog! Your squirrel."

"You can have it." Anything to keep her from following me. It didn't work. I heard her wings beat against the air then she landed on a jutting rock just up the path. I don't know why people call cats curious. Next to crows, they're models of restraint.

"Sometimes, it helps to share."

I drew my lips back off my teeth. "Sometimes, I like a little poultry when I first wake up."

"Poultry!" They probably heard her indignant shriek on the other side of the Gate. "Fine. Then I'm not going to warn you that the roads are full and you'll never get anywhere unseen. They'll grab you and stuff you into a cage so fast, it'll make your tail curl!"

I nearly got whacked on the nose with a wing as I passed. At the top of the ravine, I peered out between two metal poles and realized the crow had been right. This was another place where no one lived and the roads were full of cars and people.

I marked both posts, hoping that, given enough time, the crow would have flown off and then I started back to the den.

"I told you so."

She was still there. But, on the bright side, so was my squirrel.

"Look, dog, maybe we got off on the wrong foot. Paw. Whatever. You're on your own—and that's not the usual thing with you lot—and I'm on my own and that's not so usual for my lot either. You're probably lonely. I'm not doing anything right now. You've got a story and I'd love to hear it. What do you say?"

I bit the tail off my squirrel's fat little rump, spat it to one side, and sighed. "Do you have a name?"

"Dark Dawn With Thunder."

I blinked. "You're kidding?"

She shrugged, wings rising and falling. "You can call me Dawn."

"Reuben." With one paw holding down the squirrel's head, I ripped the belly open and spilled the guts onto the ground. "Here. You might as well eat while you're listening."

"So you'll tell me your story?"

"Why not? Like you said, you're not going away." Neither was I. Talking over the pull of the Gate might help keep me from doing the truly stupid and risking the roads. I'd never find Marcus locked in a cage. And I *was* lonely. Not that I'd admit as much to a crow. "So . . ." I swallowed the last of the squirrel and sat

down in the shade. ". . . what do you know about the
Gates between the worlds?"

I expected to startle her. I didn't.

She tossed back a bit of intestine. "I know what all
crows know. I know they exist. I know the way of opening them has been lost for a hundred thousand memories."

"It's been found again."

"You came through a Gate?"

"And I'm leaving through one."

"You don't say." She searched the ground for any bit
she might have missed then folded her wings and settled.
"Start at the beginning . . ."

"Marcus."

My beginning. Hopefully, my end.

I'd been with him ever since I'd left my mother's teat
and the warm comfort of my littermates. I remember
falling over my feet as I chased a sunbeam around his
workshop. I remember becoming too big for his lap and
sitting instead with my head resting on his knee. I remember the way his fingers always found exactly the
right place to scratch. I remember how he smelled, how
he sounded. I remember the first Gate.

I think he wanted to prove himself to the old ones in
his pack. They believed he was too young to do anything
of merit, but he only laughed and carried on. He talked
to me all the time about what he was doing; I only wish
I'd understood more. But understanding came later
when, unfortunately, he had a lot less time to talk.

I don't know how he found the Gate. I don't know
how he opened it although there were candles lit and a
lot of weeds burning and copper wires and a thunder-
storm. I'm not embarrassed to admit I yelped when the
lightning hit. Marcus laughed and rubbed behind my
ears, the sound of my name in his mouth comforting.
Then he took hold of the fur on the back of my neck
and we walked forward.

Every hair on my body stood on end and for a heartbeat light, sound, and smell vanished. If not for the
touch of his hand, I would have bolted. When the world
came back, it was different.

The sun was low in the sky—it had been mid-light

mere moments before—and we stood on a vast empty plain. No buildings. No smoke. No sign of his pack.

He was happy. He danced around and I danced with him, barking.

And then we found out we couldn't get home.

The Gates only worked one way.

I found the next Gate. And the next. By the fourth world, Marcus had learned to sense their pull—and that was a good thing because it was the first mid-tech world we'd hit and I was in an almost constant state of panic.

By the fifth, I realized that all sounds he made had meaning. The Gates were changing me. I remember the first thing he said that I truly understood.

"Well, Reuben, old boy. Looks like we'll have to keep going forward until we get home."

Only the first Gate—the Gate on the world where you belong—fights against being opened. After that, it seems to be merely a matter of knowing where they are. They recognize you don't belong and the next thing you know it's a brand-new world. Those first five worlds, when it was just me and Marcus, surviving by our wits, working together, depending on each other's skills the way a pack is supposed to, those were the happiest times of my life.

The sixth world was low-tech and we emerged into a crowded marketplace. Marcus staggered a little, steadying himself on my shoulder. By the time he straightened, the crowds had begun to scream, "Demon!" I didn't know what it meant, but I knew anger and fear when I heard it, when I smelled it, so I braced my front legs and growled.

Marcus tried to soothe me. He thought that laughter and intellect would win the day, but I knew he was wrong. If they were going to take him, they'd have to go through me.

I didn't know about crossbows then.

I learned.

It took three to knock me off my feet, but I was still snapping and snarling as they dragged us away and threw us in a tiny, stinking, dark hole to wait for the priest.

Marcus begged cloth and water and herbs from the guards. He kept me clean, he kept me alive. I don't know how he convinced them to part with such things, but that was when he stopped laughing.

I think he'd begun to realize how much I understood because there were things he didn't talk about.

The priest finally came.

The priests in Marcus' old pack were always good for a bit of something sweet and an absentminded scratch. This was a different kind of priest. The smell of anger clung to him like smoke.

They dragged us out blinking and squinting in the sunlight. Marcus lifted his face to the sky like he'd forgotten what it looked like, like he'd been afraid he'd never see it again. They said we were demons and demons had to die. The priest told us we would burn on top of a holy hill so the smoke would rise into the demon worlds and warn others of our kind to stay away. He said a lot of other things, too, but none of it made any more sense so I stopped listening.

As we walked to the pyre, I stayed pressed close against Marcus' legs because I think he would have fallen if I hadn't been there. Not that I was in much better shape.

Then we got lucky.

At the top of the hill, I felt a familiar pull and I knew from the noise Marcus made low in his throat that he felt it, too. The Gate. And it was close. On the other side of the hill, about halfway down. We should have been able to feel it all along, but I think that whatever made the hill holy had blocked it. I didn't think that then, of course, but I do now.

The way things had been set up, there wasn't room for more than one man to hold Marcus as he climbed onto the pile of wood. Why would they need more than one? He was so thin and in so much pain and even I could see that all our time in the darkness had broken something in him. When he wrenched himself free, they froze in astonishment. He grabbed the single rope they had around my neck and we ran.

They hadn't thought we had the strength to escape, you see.

They were right.

They caught us at the Gate. We'd gotten so close that it had opened and they held us so close that it stayed open, waiting for us to leave a world where we didn't belong. Bleeding from new wounds, Marcus tried to explain. The priest refused to listen. He knew what he knew, and nothing anyone could say would change that. As they began to drag us away, I saw my chance and sank my teeth into the arm of the man who held me. He screamed, let me go, and I threw my entire weight against Marcus' chest, pushing him and the man who held him back into the Gate. We could deal with *him* on the other side.

Then a hand grabbed the end of the rope tied around my throat and hauled me back.

Marcus screamed my name and reached for me, but he was falling too fast. He was gone before my front paws hit the ground.

If the priest thought I'd waste my strength throwing it against the rope, he was very wrong. I took most of his hand through the Gate with me. It took me two worlds to get the taste out of my mouth.

The crow hopped along the branch and stared down at me, head cocked. "So you got away?"

"Obviously."

"Where's Marcus? Wasn't he waiting for you on the other side of the Gate?"

"No." I scrubbed at my muzzle with both front paws to keep myself from howling. "I found out later that you have to be touching for the Gate to send two lives to the same world."

"You're looking for him."

It wasn't a question, but I answered it anyway. "I don't know if he's still by that Gate waiting for me to come through or if he's on his way around trying to get back to that world again, but, yes, I'm looking for him."

"How long?"

Rolling onto my side, I licked a fall of fur back off an old, faded scar. "This was where one of the crossbow bolts hit. It was open and bleeding when Marcus was thrown through the Gate."

Dawn glided down beside me and peered at my side. If crows knew anything at all, they knew wounds. "A long time."

"Yes. But I *will* find him."

She nodded. "I don't doubt you'll keep trying. It's a dog thing. Hopeless . . ."

My growl was completely involuntary.

"Hopeless," she repeated, clacking her beak. "But romantic. You're lucky crows are a lot more practical."

"Lucky?"

"Because you shared your story, I'm going to help you get to your Gate."

Before I could protest, she took wing, flying toward the upper edge of the ravine. By the time I'd scrambled to my feet and shaken my fur into some semblance of order, she was back. "I don't need your help," I told her walking stiff-legged past her position. "I can find the Gate on my own."

"I don't doubt it. But do you know what traffic is doing? Can you find the fastest route through the buildings? Do you know when it's safe to move on?" She stared at me thoughtfully—well, it might have been thoughtful, it might have been disdainful; it was impossible to tell with crows. "No one will notice me, but, if you're not very careful, they'll certainly notice you. Do you have a bear in your ancestry or something?"

"No."

"Pony?"

"No!"

"Marcus fiddle with your DNA?"

"My what?"

She flew ahead and landed on the guardrail. "Not important. What is important, though, is that if you hurry you'll be able to get across the road."

I gave poultry another quick thought then leaped the guardrail.

"Run fast, dog. The light is changing."

Into what? Not important. I started to run. Metal shrieked against metal. As I reached the far side, something big passed so close to my tail that I clamped it tight between my legs and lengthened my stride. Racing along the narrow passage between two buildings, I wondered just what I thought I was doing, listening to a crow.

"You're going to come out into a parking lot. Cross

it on a bit of an angle . . . Go to your left. No, your other left. . . . and you can use the Dumpster to go over the fence."

And why was I *still* listening to the crow?

On the other side of the fence, two cats hissed insults as I went by and a small, fat dog on a rope started barking furiously. I was gone before anyone came out to investigate the disturbance but not so far gone that I couldn't hear them blame the whole noisy situation on the cats. Pretty funny.

Determining this new road went in essentially the right direction, I stopped running full out and dropped into a distance-eating trot.

"Aren't you in a hurry?" The crow was on one of the wires that crossed over the street, calling the question down to me. Not exactly unnoticeable to my mind, but what did I know of this world? "Shouldn't you be moving faster?"

"I know what I'm doing," I snapped. "Don't you have a flock to join?"

"A murder." She flew ahead and landed again.

"A what?"

"A group of crows are called a murder. A murder of crows."

"Why?" I couldn't stop myself from asking even though I knew any interest would only encourage her to hang around.

Fly ahead. Land. "I don't know."

"I thought crows remembered everything?"

Dawn shrugged philosophically. "Can't remember what I've never been told."

"All right. Fine. Don't you have a murder to join?"

Fly ahead. Land. "Not anymore. I left because I'd heard all their stories."

"Stories? What does that have to do . . ."

She clacked her beak. "I get bored easily."

We went on like that until nearly full dark—Dawn flapping from wire to wire and telling me way more crow stories than any dog would ever want to know. A lot of them involved carrion. Then, as the last of the light disappeared, I looked up and she was gone. I shouldn't have been surprised, like most birds, crows prefer not to fly at night. Maybe she should have thought about that before she offered to help. I shouldn't have missed her. But I did.

As the sky began to lighten, the pull of the Gate became so strong that I knew I was close. Using Dawn's Dumpster trick, I went over another fence, finding Marcus the only thought in my mind.

Which was why I didn't notice the men until I was in the midst of them.

"Holy fuck! Would you look at the size of that mutt!"

They were all around me. Something hard hit me on the left shoulder and I reacted without thinking. The scent of so many males was too strong a challenge. I whirled to the left, flattened my ears, and snarled.

The man scrambled back. I could smell his fear. A piece of broken brick glanced off my back. The sharp end of a stick jabbed at my haunches. I should have kept running. Should have. Didn't. Now they'd closed in. Too close.

I heard a length of chain hiss past my head.

If they wanted a fight . . .

Then I heard a hoarse shriek of outrage, a scream of pain, and the circle made up of legs and boots and rough weapons opened.

"Where the fuck did that crow come from?"

I don't know how much damage she stayed to do, but she found me again where I'd gone to ground. I heard the sound of claws on gravel, looked out from behind the huge wheel on the trailer that sheltered me, and there she was. She snatched up a discarded piece of sugared bread, threw back her head and swallowed, then hopped closer.

"All right, I'm convinced, you really *do* need to find this Marcus of yours because you shouldn't be running around without a keeper. What kind of an idiot picks a fight with seven big, burly, cranky construction workers *before* they've had their first coffee? You know, if you'd tried the roll-over 'look at me I'm so cute' schtick, you'd have probably gotten a belly rub and a couple of sandwiches. Those kind of guys usually like a dog that's big enough they're not afraid of breaking it. So, you hiding under there?"

As she'd actually paused, I assumed she wanted an answer. "Yes."

"Why?"

I glanced up at the massive trailer. "Because I fit. And because the Gate's in that building."

Dawn turned enough to study the building with her right eye.

It was constructed of the big made-stone blocks. I'd seen windows and a door along the front but neither on the sides. The back of the building, where the trailers were parked, had a set of huge double doors and one smaller one with a light over it.

"So, what do you do now?" she asked.

"I wait." This close to the Gate, I was too jumpy to lie down, but there wasn't enough headroom to pace. I had to settle for digging a trench in the gravel with a front paw. "I wait until one of those doors opens then I run inside."

"And once you're inside?"

"I keep from being grabbed long enough to get through the Gate."

"I like a dog with a plan. But I'm warning you, it's barely daylight and not a lot of people are up at this . . ."

One of the big double doors swung open and slammed back against the made-stone wall with a crash loud enough to fling Dawn into the air and raise the hackles on my neck. With the barrier out of the way, the pull of the Gate nearly dragged me out of my hiding place, but I'd been stupid once this morning and stupid wouldn't help me find Marcus.

Then the other door opened and men appeared carrying huge made-things of metal and plastic and glass that I didn't recognize. I felt the trailer above me shake as they climbed up the ramp.

"Hey, a film crew." Dawn was back on the ground. "I'll let you in on a secret, Reuben—there's good pickings in the garbage outside the craft services truck. These guys never seem to have time to finish eating anything."

I had no idea what she was talking about. Nor did I care.

Two of the men were in the trailer. The other two were out of sight in the building.

My chance.

Marcus.

I was running full out by the time I reached the doors.
I leaped a cart just inside, smelled the sudden rush of
fear from the man pushing it, scrambled along a cloth
path on the floor, skidded through a room with only
three walls, found myself outside but not outside, ignored the yelling, and concentrated on finding the Gate.
I'd been in buildings before—once, on a high-tech world,
I'd been chased through an underground structure so
complicated ants couldn't have found their way around—
but nothing in *this* building made sense! The ceiling was
too high, the walls didn't reach it, and there were ca-
bles everywhere.

I couldn't find the Gate.

My claws scrabbling for purchase against a polished
stone floor, I raced around a corner and ended up in a
long hall. Three men ran toward me from the other end,
one of them carrying a net. They were all making soothing sounds, the one with the net repeating, "It's okay,
boy," over and over. I wanted to believe them. I wanted
to lay my head on someone's knee and have him tell me
I was home.

I knocked over a row of chairs, jumped a pile of cable,
and ran up a flight of stairs. The stairs ended in another
railing and a door. I threw myself against it.

The wall shook.

The Gate . . . the Gate was on the other side!

I threw myself against the door again. Someone was
whining. I had a horrible suspicion it was me.

So close . . .

Then suddenly the wall gave way, the stairs shook,
and I jumped.

A hand closed around my tail.

The Gate opened.

I braced myself for the pain of my tail being yanked
free, but it never came. Instead, the grip released and
sharp points of pain dug into my back.

This time the Gate dumped me on the edge of a
meadow. The sun was shining, birds were singing, and I
could smell both rabbits and water on the breeze. My
stomach growled and I growled with it.

Ready to move on, I turned to piss on the weed growing closest to where the old Gate had been and discovered I wasn't alone. There was a crow in the grass, lying in a parody of a nest, wings spread and feet in the air. Bending my head, I snuffled her breast feathers. Warm. Alive. The sharp pains in my back suddenly made sense.

Dark Dawn With Thunder had hitched a ride.

I glanced across the meadow, then back at her, then sighed and scratched.

I was napping when she finally opened her eyes, but the sound of her flapping awkwardly onto her feet woke me. Her wings looked as though the edges were unraveling and she staggered three paces forward then three paces back before she caught her balance.

"Rather remarkably like flying into a hydro wire," she muttered, caught sight of me and stilled. "Nice doggie. Doggie no yell at crow. Crow have very big headache."

"Crow deserves very big headache," I told her. "What were you thinking?"

Dawn cocked her head and studied me for a moment. "I was thinking you hadn't thanked me for saving your furry ass."

She was right, I hadn't. "Thank you."

"And I was thinking that I'd like to know how the story ends."

"Story?"

"You and Marcus."

"Why do you care?"

"Care?" Twisting around, she poked her tail feathers into alignment. "I don't *care*. I just hate to leave a story hanging. Gives me that unfinished feeling."

I chewed a bit on a paw, and when I looked up, Dawn was watching me.

"I was also thinking," she said, "that dogs are hopeless romantics and you need taking care of. And besides . . ." Her eyes glittered. ". . . you're certainly not boring."

"You can't go back," I reminded her.

"I'm not going anywhere until the story ends." She clacked her beak and launched herself into the air. "So, let's get a move on."

I sat and watched her fly for a moment then smiled and shook my head. She was going the wrong way. Not that it mattered, she'd learn to feel the Gates soon enough and for now, she had me. I shook, walked out of the cloud of shed fur, and trotted across the meadow.

After a moment, I heard her wings in the air above my head.

"Any sign of him?" she called as she swooped by.

"Not yet."

The pull of the next Gate was no more than a suggestion, so we had a way to travel still and Marcus could be anywhere along the path.

I could tell the crow how the story was going to end. I *would* find him.

But I supposed it wouldn't hurt to have a little company along the way.

Brothers Bound

by Julie E. Czerneda

Former biologist Julie Czerneda's science fiction has received international acclaim. Her popular *Web Shifters* series has been nominated four times for the Prix Aurora Award (Canada's Hugo), as well as appearing on the preliminary ballot for the Nebula. The first title of her *Trade Pact Universe* series made Julie a finalist for the John W. Campbell Award for Best New Writer, while her standalone *In the Company of Others* won an Aurora and was RT Reviewers' Choice Best SF of the Year, as well as a finalist for the P.K. Dick Award for Distinguished SF. She is currently at work on a new DAW series, *Species Imperative*, the first novel of which, *Survival*, is available in a DAW hardcover edition. Julie lives with her husband and two children in the lake country of central Ontario.

O PERATING manuals called it the Biointerface, shortened in use to bio'face. Those enamored of the tech called it words like loyalty, devotion, and love.

The matter of names was of some importance to those who wrote grant proposals and promoted the spread of Humans through the ranks of the First.

What anyone else called this inconvenience didn't matter at all to First Triad newcomer, Sai Vasilo Aris.

The damned dog was just another reason he didn't fit in.

"Hey, Vasi! You can't bring it with you," Baoltor yelled again, too loudly. Interested heads turned. There wasn't much to do at the staging area, and any disturbance had its merit as entertainment. Baoltor seemed oblivious to Vasi's embarrassment or, more likely, failed to read the emotion. Dains weren't the most empathic of species. Instead, he continued: "I'm not sitting in the same transport with that stinking thing all the way to Crilliton—"

"Shut up, Baoltor, and make room," Vasi ordered calmly, though he agreed heartily and would have left the beast in the field barracks had it been within his power. His hand signal, no more than a lift of two fingertips, sent the canid leaping from the muddy street into the side door of the transport, filthy paws scrambling for purchase.

The curses that followed were varied and creative, but brief. Their Triad—Vasi, Ebbet, and Medya, now splashing up to join him—outranked any of the others already crammed inside. Professor Emeritus Y Ebbet, of the 114th Siring by Raken, was on sabbatical from his duties as Chair of Concentrix Studies at the University of South Amilt, on the Queeb world for "Useful Non-breeding Citizens." His work on Aeande XII had gained widespread recognition in its first field season, so much so that any Triad he formed led all subsequent research here. And no right-minded Queeb in a position of power, even an academic like Ebbet, would tolerate public disrespect of his allies by anyone else. Vasi was sadly familiar with the quick scorn able to drip from that forked tongue, given how he seemed to fail almost every one of Ebbet's high expectations.

When Ebbet's Triad had lost its Finder in an early spring flood, the being fatally stubborn about retrieving artifacts from a supposedly dry streambed, Vasi had been pulled from his training to replace her. He'd have refused, if he'd thought it would do any good. To be unproven in the field, then dropped in as Senior Finder over all the teams on a project? Of course, Triads were professionals. His skills were undeniable, if untested. These and other platitudes from his instructors failed to console him. Vasi knew too well what they wouldn't say. Those professionals would pounce on any weakness as an excuse to send him packing.

It only got worse. On arrival, Vasi found he was the only Tidik insystem. From the moment the tug parked his transport in Aeande's Shipcity, he'd been surrounded by beings incapable of understanding the most basic signals of courtesy, let alone any higher level concepts. Every interaction was confined to the shallow meanings of

Comspeak, that bastard tongue of traders and merchants.

Why him at all? Vasi could still taste the bitterness of that ultimate insult, delivered within the first hour of his landing on this world. His skills hadn't mattered. Ebbet's Finder had been a Human, bio'faced with one of their beasts. The beast had survived its partner's misjudgment and Ebbet valued the animal's abilities so highly he'd insisted he must have another such pairing. No Human was available fast enough to suit him—but a Tidik Finder-in-training, with sufficiently similar neural physiology, was.

As easy to fly without wings as to refuse. It was accept the implant and be bound to the creature or be sent from Aeande XII in disgrace. Vasi had had no choice. Not if he wanted to ever be part of a Triad. Not if he ever wanted his chance to solve the puzzle of the Hoveny Concentrix—the single greatest mystery in explored space.

The Triads were First research teams, made up of individuals possessing the necessary skills of Analyst, Recorder, and Finder, drawn from three presumably complementary species. The diversity was deliberate. There had been too many paths taken by the myriad cultures that had formed the Hoveny Concentrix—let alone the unknown biological constraints of its mysterious members—to make any one present-day species the optimum researcher. The greater the diversity in a research team, the First administrators reasoned, the more likely it would contain some being capable of understanding whatever they found.

There was also the expectation that working in such teams would promote greater understanding of one another and so foster peace. None of the species loosely allied in this quadrant of space were technically at war—at this moment. Few, however, could claim closer association than limited trading agreements or the sharing of derogatory jokes aimed at the newcomer Humans. That might have remained the state of things, but for a mutual fascination concerning the vast civilization that had preceded them all, leaving puzzling ruins throughout their systems. The First formed almost unnoticed, an ongoing research collaboration conducted with deceptive informality by academics of all species, the name an acknowledgment of a level of cooperation that had never been managed before.

To date, the only concrete result of that cooperation was that no member of a Triad had actually killed another. Insulted, misunderstood, proposed inappropriate physical union, and found ways to brawl, yes. Still, Triads worked, and well. They were, after all, researchers with a purpose: to find out why the powerful Concentrix had failed, aeons before those now studying them had done more than mark scent and howl.

Which was something the canid appeared to be doing now. Vasi sighed, grabbing the doorframe of the transport and heaving himself inside as the multispecies' cursing renewed almost as loudly as those throbbing, mournful cries. Perhaps the animal was disturbed to have been shoved to the very back.

The instant Vasi's eyes met those brown ones, the howling stopped. He felt an unwelcome flood of happiness. It wasn't his. The canid was somehow programmed to respond this way to him; the bio'face freely passing its simple emotional reflexes into his mind. Too freely.

Damn dog, Vasi thought again, turning his back on his personal curse. The only empty seats were the last two, near the beast. Ignoring those, he walked up the side aisle to the frontmost seat behind the driver and stood waiting. The Tolian occupying the spot beside Ebbet dropped his crest and, with a sidelong look out his emerald eyes, rose and moved aside. Ebbet made an approving noise in his throat as Vasi joined him. They both obligingly slid closer to the sidewall so Medya, who'd followed Vasi, could squeeze in with them. Being a typical Brill, she didn't so much share the seat as prop some of her ample haunch along its edge.

Being a typical Brill, she was laughing. "You didn't tell us you'd taught it to sing, Sai Vasilo," their Triad's Recorder observed. "And so quickly, too."

"I didn't tell you it could pass noxious fumes out of two orifices at once, either," Vasi replied, his voice even as always. A Tidik trait, the inability to inflect speech with emotion. The slender plates on either side of his neck vibrated with frustration.

Oblivious, Ebbet blinked all six eyes in what seemed random order and chuckled. "That much we all know. Especially after it eats raw omio roots. You didn't mind my little addition to its supper, did you, Vasi? I thought you'd enjoy getting to know your new partner's specatular talent for yourself."

Vasi didn't bother to respond. Queeb humor was infamous; they had great difficulty comprehending why other species weren't as amused by bodily functions or disparaging remarks about ancestry. They had even more difficulty with the concept of reverence for the dear departed. Such interspecies' insensitivity was one reason so many Queebs worked in waste management or became archaeologists. It also explained the common saying: never tell a Queeb where your family was buried.

The transport lurched forward, obedient to a schedule that had little leeway for latecomers and a driver likely resentful of both muddy feet and alien beasts. She appeared to be taking out such resentment on her passengers. Vasi braced himself, noticing the others did as well. Still, there were sounds, several of which could be laughter; the four Triads presently on Aeande XII were comprised of nine different species, so it wasn't always easy to tell. They shared a reason to be happy, if not common ways to express it. Vasi himself eagerly anticipated a night away from slogging up mountains and digging through mud barely thawed from winter. The gleeful bedlam in the transport grew louder as the vehicle swayed into the first switchback leading down to Crilliton.

Gleeful except for a sudden yip. Vasi winced as the bio'face transferred the flash of pain. Without intending to, he was on his feet immediately, pushing his way over Medya's soft leathery thighs, his extended nails digging into the nearest seatback for support. Standing and trying to move down the aisle was like trying to slope the mountainsides of home, only without the help of skis. The transport hit a pothole and abruptly lurched to one side. As Vasi hung on to avoid landing on Baoltor's lap, the Dain scowling a warning, he smiled to himself. Perhaps more like sloping on the heels of true spring, when the hills sprouted rocks to threaten all four knee joints.

The canid seemed equally experienced at bracing itself. It had backed against the last, still-vacant seat, the front pair of its four legs splayed out to provide the most stable possible platform. The setting sun peered through the clouds and into the mud-streaked windows, beams darting here and there as the transport leaned from side to side. The light revealed the long, pink tongue hanging from the creature's gaping mouth. A streak of bright red lay amid the foam along one edge.

The wounded tongue seemed of no concern. More accurately, the pain of having bitten itself was smothered under waves of joy through the bio'face as the beast noticed Vasi's approach. It lost all sense, crouching to sway its thin body in an uncontrolled spasm of greeting, its tail banging against the seat. Having thus lost any stability, the beast was sent flying down the aisle at the next turn of the transport to follow the hairpin of the road.

Vasi grunted as the creature slammed into his lower abdomen, suddenly compressing a few body parts not meant to be so abused. As he gasped and licked tears from his lips, the beast leaped up again, apparently viewing this contact as welcome.

The creature was more practiced at the bio'face than Vasi, but he'd learned enough to force *disapproval* from his mind into its, particularly when he felt this motivated. The happy squirming slowed and stopped, the beast dropping to the floor and doing its utmost to lie on its back submissively, even as the transport swerved madly around the next bend. Vasi had to reach down and grab it so it didn't roll back into the seat support and harm itself. He might be a member of a First Triad—but this beast was more important than he was. Everyone, starting with Professor Emeritus Y Ebbet, of the 114th Siring by Raken, had left that in no doubt whatsoever.

The handling wasn't affectionate, but the creature responded as though he'd caressed it, ropelike tail banging against his boots. Vasi did his utmost to ignore the emotions rippling across the bio'face.

He turned and, grabbing seats for purchase, began

pulling himself forward again, only to halt in dismay as Ebbet's face appeared over Medya's lap. The Queeb's voice was unfortunately loud: "Finder Durgin held it on her lap during rides like this. Protected it from the bumps. Shouldn't you, Sai Vasilo?"

Vasi froze in dismay. The beast was dripping with mud and smelled worse than usual. He was wearing the only fine clothes he'd brought to Aeande XII, in hopes of finding some attractive being interested in mutual stimulation at the bar—or at least a dance or two.

Judging by the laughter in the transport, those were hopes he should abandon now.

Damn dog.

"I concur with Finder Vasilo. We should go here today." Medya's ivory-tipped finger dimpled the surface of the image displayed on the map table. "Our records of the uppermost area are incomplete."

Ebbet considered this thoughtfully, tilting his head as though the angle made some additional information available only to a Queeb's multiple eyes. Vasi would have taken it for affectation in anyone else, but he had nothing but respect for the scholar, Queeb or not. Well, respect and an ongoing sense of humiliation. How could he possibly contribute to this fine Triad, except as the keeper of that beast?

He might be smarting over last night, which had been every bit as demeaning an experience as he'd feared—including a regrettable incident involving a bodily function—but Vasi couldn't help but be excited by the red-stained area under Medya's fingertip. It was high risk. The slope indicated challenged any he'd seen on his home world, but the potential . . . he leaned closer, sure he wasn't imagining a curved outline, a suggestion of something buried, possibly a structure more elaborate and intact than any found thus far. Looking for such clues was his job, as was getting them there safely. Vasi found it hard to keep the flaps under his chin still. "The forecasters are calling for gusty winds out of the northeast, Professor," he made himself say. "Clouds are already forming on the peaks. I'd be remiss not to warn of the potential for a sudden snowfall."

"There's always potential," Medya growled. "It's spring, for Grasis' sake. One minute we're huddling around heaters, the next there's mold growing over my butt."

Vasi shuddered quietly. The Queeb roared with laughter, disturbing the canid's sleep. Its brown eyes puzzled at the three of them, then closed again. The beast had better manners than some, Vasi admitted to himself. Despite his initial skepticism, it obeyed the signals he'd been told to use and would stay curled on the floor until required for its task. Curled on the floor as close to his boots as possible, but Vasi had learned nothing would discourage its desire for such proximity. If ordered to lie by the doorway, the creature would pretend to comply, then somehow be lying nearer each time he checked until it was almost underfoot. The creature only seemed content when in imminent danger of being stepped on—or, as now, when the Triad began to move. Vasi found himself fascinated by how the sound of Medya clearing off the map table was enough to bring the canid's head and ears up to attention, its furred body tense with anticipation, eyes riveted on him.

That anticipation shivered through the bio'face—likely both ways. Vasi preferred outside and active himself and, though he had his reservations about the weather, he felt his own ears stiffen with excitement. The find they could make today? What questions might it answer about the Hoveny? How many more might it raise? He couldn't wait to see.

Three hours later, Vasi settled his hip against one walking pole and stared, aghast, at what waited for them.

Fieldwork wasn't tidy or without hazard—that's what he liked about it—but the aircar hadn't left them on a mountain slope. This was the icy tongue of a monster ready to lick them from the face of the planet. The spill of ice, wrinkled and split by black, water-slicked crevasses, groaned and snapped as it moved. Chunks larger than Medya rattled free from its face to join the jumble already damming a glacial lake.

Above? Vasi shrugged his loose hood to his shoulders and tilted his head back. The mountain's peak leered down, baring cloud teeth that ripped through what blue sky remained. It might be calm here, but the wind at those upper elevations would strip flesh from bone.

"Ah, who has the lunch pack? Vasilo, do you recall where it's packed?"

"Lunch?" The Tidik couldn't believe his ears or eyes. He must be misreading the Queeb. No rational being could stare at this—this death incarnate—and ask about food. It must be a valiant effort to shore up their spirits, so close yet so far from possible treasure.

The canid didn't need help with its spirits, busy prancing around their feet. It appeared to disregard anything higher than its eager nose, and began pushing that supposedly tender organ under a loose rock.

"I've got the lunch," Medya said, shouldering the harness for the larger of the two grav sleds. Ebbet already had the smaller tethered to his back, secured by straps that took advantage of his naturally hunched shoulders.

"Then lead the way, Finder," the Queeb ordered, pointing at the preoccupied canid. "We've no time to waste with the weather this unsettled. I won't leave a promising site to be buried under the next avalanche without at least an autosampler in place. And our Triad's marker."

"Very well," Vasi replied, abandoning hope that the Queeb was playing another trick on him. He summoned the beast with a tap of one hand against his leg, watching as it leaped forward with delight in every body part and surging through the bio'face. It sat before him, waiting for instructions.

Vasi hesitated before giving the "find" signal with both hand and thought, his uncertainty plain to read in the faint shuddering of his neck flaps, had any of his companions the perception to see it.

Strangely, the beast hesitated as well, its face lifted to one side as though it studied him, ears perked upward.

"Find," Vasi said quietly, sure his voice could carry no emotion to confuse the animal.

The canid whirled on its haunches and headed for the glacier, looking back over its shoulder as if to be sure they followed. Vasi grabbed his poles and settled his pack, then started moving. The first part of their climb would be simple enough. As soon as winter had eased,

Ebbet had hired a crew of laborers to blast a ramp up one side of the glacier's face. Gravel and debris, melted clear this spring, formed a roadway from the valley floor to the top of the ice sheet. A good, steady slope. They were all fit and trained for this—the First expected their Triads to be able to cope with fieldwork. Vasi resolutely kept his eyes focused on the happily wagging tail ahead of him, between glances at the instrumentation festooning his left arm and wrist.

He'd grown up on mountainsides and his every instinct told him this was the wrong time to be on this one. The sooner he and the beast found the suspected Hoveny site, Vasi reasoned coldly, the sooner they could start running for their lives.

Every Hoveny find on Aeande XII had been made in these mountains, old upthrust seabeds now eroded to reveal their former life as city-lined coasts. Their low altitude was a gift. Even the canid panted comfortably and Medya was able to make a running commentary of their trek into her recorder, much of it laden with cheery-sounding phrases in her own tongue, as though she too found Comspeak inadequate. Vasi thought he might ask her, when they were back in camp. If they got back to camp. The wind had tilted over the peak and was spinning columns of loose white snow, catching sparks from the sunshine. A warning.

They were now traveling on the ice sheet itself, lint on the mountain's blue-white shoulder. There was a path, beaten into the snow and smoothed by the same crew who had provided the ramp. It saved the Triad's strength for what mattered—if they found it. The orbital and aerial surveys only located possibilities. It was up to him, Vasi realized as he moved one foot carefully ahead of the other, never trusting a path he hadn't made himself.

And the canid. The beast wore boots on its feet as well today, a necessity as the sun's warmth softened the snow into a glue prone to stick and accumulate on any surface. It had only taken one such excursion without the boots to prove their value to both canid and Vasi, who'd had to use his bare hands to melt the hardened ice balls trapped between the beast's sore and bleeding footpads. The bio'face had shared the discomfort—and the easing of it.

The discomfort hadn't slowed the beast. When on the hunt, the canid was determined, Vasi had to admit. Its keen senses of smell and hearing were their guide, not as accurate or sensitive as instrumentation, but exquisitely more discerning. Humans had finally convinced the First that their beasts were able to distinguish true Hoveny ruins, with their characteristic construction materials, patterns of decay, and faint sounds of hibernating technology, from those of other civilizations.

He wasn't convinced the damn dog could find anything but trouble.

Vasi flexed his six-fingered hands around the handles of his walking poles. He should be towing a sled himself, laden with sensors. He'd packed one this morning, but Ebbet had dismissed the need for such equipment, along with three years of Vasi's training and skill, with one flick of a gloved tentacle. The scruffy beast, the Queeb asserted, was all they'd need. Since Professor Emeritus Y Ebbet of the 114th Siring by Raken was the being with a reputation to risk, Vasi could hardly protest.

Yet. The beast might work for food pellets and carry itself, Vasi thought bitterly, but if it failed to locate anything worthwhile, he'd protest, in writing, with enough adjectives to make his feelings clear even in Comspeak.

They walked, single file, the canid leading and Vasi behind, for the better part of another hour. The Tidik divided his attention between the clouds skittering by overhead and the crosshairs on the locator strapped to his right wrist, which would let him know when they were standing on the suspected Hoveny site.

Suddenly, Vasi's pole went deeper into the snow than he'd expected, and he pulled up short. The beast stopped as well, head cocked toward him. A hand signal and the canid eased down to its belly, chin on its paws. It seemed glad of the rest.

"Are we there?"

"Don't move," Vasi snapped, raising his arm to bar

both his companions. He took a step back, then another, before probing the path ahead ever-so-gently with his extended pole.

Snow crumpled away, as if he'd touched some area of rot. The resulting hole was small, but intensely dark, promising depth. "Crevasse," the Tidik said tersely. The path continued beyond, its surface unmarked and innocent.

There wasn't talk of turning back. Instead, the Triad pulled out safety lines and tied themselves together at intervals long enough to prevent all of them from dropping into the same hidden crack. Even the canid was leashed. When ready, Vasi signaled it to move forward and they continued, going around the crevasse, testing every footstep. The Tidik and Queeb planted their walking poles deeply into the snow as emergency supports each time Medya, their heaviest and so most at-risk member, followed them across any chancy area.

Midday, but the air temperature was plummeting. Vasi didn't need instruments to tell him so—he watched the frosty beard forming along the canid's jaw and a single icicle growing from the dribbling of its moist nose. When he felt it shiver, he halted their procession to adjust the warming rings strapped around its middle and chest. Its natural covering was useless in this environment, little more than short wiry hair, white with random blotches of black too small to soak up appreciable radiation from the sun. The beast, for all its lack of brain matter, appeared to understand and stood patiently, tail swaying side to side.

"We should be almost there," Medya mumbled around the nutrient tube stuck between her teeth. The cold couldn't touch the Brill through those layers of blubber and thick outer skin, but she suffered from the demands of steady movement, far preferring quick bursts of activity followed by naps. Ebbet was almost impossible to discern within his bulky thermal suit, with its broad faceplate instead of the goggles worn by his two-footed and two-eyed companions. He bounced impatiently from foot to foot. Protected like this, even an old Queeb like Ebbet could outmarch them all.

"We'd better be," Vasi said without taking his eyes

from the cliff in front of them. They'd turned parallel to the leading edge of the glacier, cutting across what would someday be a valley if the climate of this world continued to warm as predicted. "I don't want to move any closer to those—" He used his pole to point.

Overhangs of snow draped each dip and ledge along the cliff's face, beautiful and ominous. The wind played with them, pretending to carve but really building the edges out farther and farther. Gravity would ultimately win, Vasi knew. Best not be anywhere downslope when that happened.

"Storm, avalanche, or crevasse," Medya laughed. "You suggesting a bet, Sai Vasilo, or just being your cheery self?"

The Tidik felt the flaps on either side of his neck rising with fury. "You mock me," he accused, wishing his voice was anything but calm, so the others would for once realize how much he meant what he said. "I know mountains as you do not." The canid made a strange noise— a growl deep in its throat, as if agreeing with Vasi and sharing his temper. It could, perhaps, through the bio'face. An odd ally.

And, strangely, one the Queeb respected. He bent over to look at the canid, then straightened to direct his faceplate in Vasi's direction. "My apologies, Finder Vasilo," Ebbet said. "Yes, I'm aware of your expertise. It was one of the reasons I requested you for my Triad." Before Vasi could do more than blink, the Queeb continued. "The spring avalanches will bury this potential find, but I've no wish to join it. Do you feel we have time to find it and plant our markers, or should we leave now? You decide."

Medya made an unhappy sound but said nothing more.

Vasi studied the peak. The wind still whipped the clouds up and away, though he didn't doubt that could change in an instant. A cautious being wouldn't be on this glacier today. Cautious beings didn't make major finds. "Another hour, no more," he decided, splitting the difference between his common sense and his desire. "After that, this site will have to wait until melt."

*   *   *

Vasi knew they were close by the jolt of excitement through the bio'face. He signaled Ebbet and Medya to hold position, giving the canid more leash as it began coursing back and forth over the same area. The tech manual had described this behavior, but he hadn't seen it before. His own thrill as they closed on their prey would have been just as obvious to another Tidik. Vasi couldn't control how his frills opened wide, venting pheromones of hunt and happiness. The canid wagged its tail as though sensing his reaction, but didn't stop its feverish examination of what seemed only a slight bulge in the glacier's surface.

"Could be a rock outcrop under the ice, something hard enough to force it up like this," Ebbet said, his voice rising as though urging the Finder to contradict him.

Vasi consulted the one sensor he'd been able to bring, a detector discriminating enough to reveal if a vein of ore or refined metal lay beneath them. "No," he obliged, unable to make his own Comspeak anything but flat and even. "Whatever's down there isn't natural. I'm detecting traces of Barsium III." He didn't need to remind his Triad that the substance was rare in this part of space, and favored by the Hoveny in their structures.

The canid didn't need confirmation. Its tail whipped madly back and forth, surely chilling the blood flowing through the appendage, then the beast rolled in the snow as if this could somehow smear the scent it so adored into its fur—a quirk of its nature Vasi was quite familiar with, following those too-ripe fish parts thoughtfully left outside his sleeping quarters.

Still, ridiculous as the beast looked, staggering joyfully to its feet, Vasi longed to express his own satisfaction as clearly. The Queeb and Brill, patting one another wherever they could reach with rather incoherent shouts of joy, both took turns to look at him as though waiting for some sign. Vasi sighed inwardly. If they really looked at him, if they smelled the air as even the beast knew to do, they'd know this was the happiest moment of his life.

He tried. "I am honored to be present at such a discovery, Professor Emeritus. Thank you again for your

faith in me," Vasi paused then added honestly, "and for
the opportunity to operate the bio'face."

*If the damn dog had helped find a new Hoveny site,
he owed it that.*

"Grasis' glory." Medya turned her great head almost
completely around on her shoulders to gauge how far
they'd already paced away from Ebbet and their sleds,
trying to locate the outer boundaries of the site. "This
wide? Are you sure, Finder?"

Vasi studied the canid. He'd given it food and water,
and as much rest as any of them dared in this place of
hazard. It was weary, yet its willingness came through
the bio'face, a willingness to strive as long as he, Vasi,
the present center of the beast's small universe, asked
for the effort. "He's sure," the Tidik answered, gesturing
to how the canid's nose hovered about the snow, nostrils
dripping so the hairy lip below remained crusted with
ice. Its small body pulled on the leash, as though impatient for them to follow.

Medya followed, step by ponderous step, watching, as
he did, for any sign of another crevasse. "You realize if
your beast is accurate, Vasi," she said with a cheery
wheeze, "this must be one Grasis-sucking ruin."

Vasi didn't try to puzzle out her reference. The canid
had paused, nose up and working at the air. Then its
unreadable face turned to his and he felt a sudden, formless anxiety through their link. "Something's wrong," he
warned without hesitation, his neck and chin flaps snapping closed with dread.

Time seemed to stop and listen to the words, as if as
frozen as the wasteland of ice stretching on all sides. It
hardly budged as Vasi whirled around, somehow sensing
the direction of their danger. It scarcely started again
before the cliff shrugged off its winter load of snow and
ice, sending the avalanche toward them as a wall of shattered white.

There was a saying. His father had been a mountain-
eer and used to drill this saying into a younger Vasi,
day after day, trip after trip, upslope or downslope. The
present-day version fought to remember it in the dark-

ness, spitting out snow to mouth the words: "Mountains get so big because they eat fools."

Fool? Maybe. Deaf and blind, but not mountain-food. Not yet. Vasi struggled to focus. First, assess himself. Nothing broken, but he was completely disoriented. Buried, but he'd instinctively curled his arms over his face and ducked away from the onrush of snow. His arms had some room to move. He could breathe.

Joy! The bio'face filled with warmth as his return to full consciousness must have reached the canid. Warmth and pain. Vasi pushed aside snow until his left hand could reach his right wrist, fumble for the leash attached to it. He found it and pulled, dismayed as the tension disappeared. A clamp or the leash itself had given way. Waves of imposed joy and pain and fear alternated in his head, but he didn't have the heart to scold the poor creature. There was comfort for both in knowing they weren't alone.

Comfort, but what he really needed was to know which way was up. His locator couldn't help him. If anything, it added to the confusion as the indicator lights reflected from the snow, overwhelming any dim natural light that might penetrate and give the Tidik a clue where to start digging. He fought away panic, the real enemy. His environment suit would protect him from the cold. There was a distress beacon built into it. He could feel its vibration against his ribs, so it must have been activated by the force of the avalanche. But he couldn't stay buried like this, waiting for some possible rescue. He had to get out, find the others.

Hunt. Find. Not the words, but sensations rippling through the bio'face. Vasi smelled his own fear and tried to control it, concentrating on the link, sending back what he hoped was encouragement. Could the beast be free? Its body was small and light. It might have floated to the top of the torrent of snow.

Top. Vasi's mouth was dry. He bit viciously on his own tongue, tasting the sweet flatness of blood. He kept his lips closed and didn't swallow. After a moment or two, he parted his lips very slightly. The warm liquid flowed out the left side of his mouth and over his cheek, stinging the sensitive tissue lining his neck flaps. *So.* Vasi reached to his right, and started to dig his way to the surface, refusing to doubt.

Minutes or hours? He couldn't be sure without checking his wrist chrono, but didn't give in to that impulse. It would take as long as it took. One gloved hand reached up to carve deeper into what was now a tunnel the width of his shoulders, the other taking the snow and carefully pushing it back and under him, patting it firm. He inched his way farther up. Steadily, patiently. He would defeat the mountain.

He didn't battle alone. The bio'face surged with another's determination. Somewhere above him, two small paws were churning through the snow, two more shoving it back and away. Exhaustion, fear, pain. Echoes of his own or the beast's? It no longer mattered; both were sustained by their common need, to reach each other. They were brothers, bound by more than the device in Vasi's head.

The Tidik had almost fallen asleep, though still digging, when a flare of joy roused him. There was a pressure, then a sudden chill on his right hand. As he realized what had happened, he cursed happily.

The damn dog had stolen his glove.

Finder Sai Vasilo Aris pulled his feet free one at a time, and fell rather than sat down, his lap immediately filled with writhing canid. Fortunately, its paws stayed away from the more sensitive parts of his anatomy. Vasi hugged the creature to his chest to still it, then looked around himself, trying to understand what he saw.

It was as if the glacier had been stirred by Medya's giant god. The sunlight struck at chunks of blistered ice and shattered rock protruding through the snow, sank into lines and drifts of blood-red dust. Nothing remained of their equipment or the trail. Nothing of Ebbet or Medya.

There was something else. Almost absently, Vasi noted the gleaming bronze of what could be the tip of a pillar or corner of a wall, close enough to touch. The Hoveny site Ebbet had so feared losing beneath the avalanche had, with the perversity of the mountain, been revealed instead.

He paid it no further attention, pushing the weight of the canid from his lap in order to stagger to his feet. A hand signal. "Find them," Vasi ordered desperately. "Find them." He did his best to picture the other two members of their Triad for the beast, unsure if that type of information could pass across their link.

The beast stared up at him, head tilted to one side in apparent confusion. It was panting heavily, the warming rings intact, but blood streaked its white flanks. There was more wherever its worn front paws stepped; blood also stained the snow it had dug away to save him. *He asked the impossible again,* Vasi thought with despair, and didn't even know how to phrase the question.

His neck flaps opened with stress, pumping useless pheromones of hunt, need, anxiety into the frigid air. "I can't find them myself," he pleaded nonsensically, as if the beast could understand the colorless words.

Its nostrils worked at something. Vasi stared, then relaxed his flaps further, the way he would to communicate his urgency to one of his own. "Find them," he whispered, repeating the hand signal.

With a hoarse yip, the canid turned and ran, its tail up and wagging, a limping run leaving a trail of dappled red. It couldn't run quickly—a mercy, since neither could Vasi. Not only was each step a study in either too-soft snow or upturned ice, but every part of his body hurt when he moved. Nothing broken, he told himself bitterly, but several things definitely bent.

The canid stopped by a rock larger than its body and made the same howling sounds it had on the transport. Forewarned by this and the unsettled feel of the bio'face, Vasi expected what he found as he brushed snow from the figure barely visible beneath the boulder. Professor Emeritus Y Ebbet, of the 114th Siring by Raken, would never analyze the secrets of this Hoveny site, or any other.

Vasi hesitated, wanting to pay proper respect, but minutes counted if Medya was injured. "Find her," he ordered the canid, standing up and giving the signal.

The canid looked from the snow-covered corpse to

Vasi, then back again. The Tidik repeated the signal, frantically. He waved in the direction he thought Medya might have been swept.

Abruptly, the beast seemed to understand. It began to push and jump its way through the loose snow in the direction he'd indicated. Vasi followed, worried by the feel of exhaustion through the bio'face. He had no idea how to tell it to slow down, to conserve energy. He couldn't stop his own urgency from passing to the beast.

He should have tried harder. He should have re-attached the leash. He should have remembered even half of what his father had tried to tell him about mountains and their appetites.

Because the dog ran straight over the crevasse before either of them could suspect this latest treachery, the snow dropping from beneath its wounded feet. There was time for Vasi to throw himself forward and flat, his fingers unable to reach even that stupid rope of a tail; there was time for the creature to yelp in terror, the emotion pouring through the bio'face until Vasi shouted as well.

Then, a searing flash as if a light had lanced through his brain. And nothing.

Not nothing. A weak, terrified sound echoed upward. "Is—Is someone there?" More strongly. "Watch out! Don't come closer! Who fell?" this in a hoarse whisper, as if the speaker feared having lost her rescuer. "Is anyone there?"

"I'm here, Medya. Vasi."

"Who fell?" the voice asked, confused and querulous. "Was it—Ebbet?"

"Just the damn dog," Vasi told her in his calm, emotion-free voice, licking tears from his lips, hands gripping the snow.

Waiting rooms seem unsettled, like weather over a mountain's peak: welcoming, but never comfortable, friendly, but never personal. Vasi didn't care for them, especially when he was surrounded by aliens.

He didn't like the room and the aliens, two male and three female Humans, probably didn't like him. At best, they likely suspected he was spying on them. At worst?

Could they tell he was here without permission? Without authorization from the First? Vasi kept his back straight and flaps courteously closed—as if a Human might notice—and tried to remain as inconspicuous as the only non-Human on this world could be.

The door opened. A pair walked out, a Human female and a dog. Vasi was startled to see such a different beast. This one was heavyset, and darkly furred with a coat that rippled like issa-silk. Its head was larger than the entire body of that damn dog at the bottom of the crevasse. But the soft brown eyes surveying him curiously, the wet moving nose, were the same. Vasi opened his mouth, wanting to ask—

"Sai Vasilo Aris, please."

He closed his lips and answered the summons, stepping past the pair.

The Human behind the desk—there was always a desk after a waiting room—stood when Vasi entered the room. Another Human remained seated, a frown on her face. "Welcome, Finder Aris," the standing Human said in a pleasant voice. Comspeak, of course. "I'm Samuel Edwards, Assistant Director of the Biointerface Project. This is our Liaison with the Research Council of the First, Atima Seung. Please. Have a seat. What can we do for you?"

Vasi sat; the Human matched his movement. "I want one of your dogs," he informed them.

"Our dogs work with Human partners, Finder Aris," Seung said in a soft voice, with a hint of steel beneath.

"So your species can be of value within a Triad," Vasi countered. "I am aware of the political rhetoric. It means nothing to me. I want a dog. I'm willing to pay what you require." The words came out flat. Perhaps they were harsh. He saw their reaction, the tightening of their mouths, the way they looked at each other as if summoning support. But Vasi didn't know what else to do. His flaps opened despite his best efforts to restrain them, surely another feature of his alienness that would offend these beings.

Edwards tapped a datacube with one blunt-nailed finger. "We're aware you had a bio'face installed—without

our approval—to allow your Triad to continue working
with Finder Durgin's dog. That wasn't meant to be a
permanent arrangement, Finder Aris. You've already
had the implant removed. I really don't see that we can
accommodate you. Surely a Finder of your abilities
would prefer to use technological means—and you already have a fabulous new site to explore."

Vasi's flaps began to tremble, and a tear trickled mad-
deningly along one lip. "I want another dog," he said
evenly, dreadfully sure they were going to refuse. Why
wouldn't they? They couldn't understand.

He didn't.

Seung held up her hand when Edwards would have
answered. She leaned forward, her strange pale eyes intent on Vasi. "I feel for your loss, Finder Aris."

"The Professor Emeritus—"

"Mesky," she corrected. "Your dog."

He hadn't known the damn dog had a name—or that
Humans named their animals. "Mesky," he repeated. "I
want another."

"Why? And don't tell me it's because you couldn't
have found the site without him," the female's voice was
sharper. "I won't accept that."

"Because. Because." Vasi stopped on the word, unable to frame the thought, let alone wrap it in their mutual, pitiful language. *Comspeak. Common speak. Useless
speak.* The way it was on Aeande XII; the way it always
was away from his own kind. He gave up, flaps quivering, dumping unsharable scents of misery and loneli-
ness into the room.

A warm hand touched his arm. The Human female
had come to crouch beside him, her expression now one
he couldn't read. "I didn't mean to upset you," she
told him.

"How do you know I'm upset?" he asked. "I haven't
told you so."

"You are Tidik." A slight wave to his neck. "I may
not be physiologically able to detect your messages
through the air, but I do know they are released during
stress. I also know you can't change the inflection of
your voice, so I must discount that as a measure of your
emotions. But the droplets on your upper lip? I've read

Tidik literature, Finder Aris. Those are what we would call tears, are they not? Released, as ours, during sadness or pain. So I know. You cared for Mesky. That's why you want another dog."

"He could do that, too," he confessed, overwhelmed by such unexpected empathy. "Understand what I felt, without this nonsense of speech. We Tidik—it's not easy for us to work with other species. They call us cold and unfeeling, because we don't wail and shout as they do. But the dog knew—" Vasi stopped, embarrassed, and looked from one Human to the other. "It made me feel less alone," he admitted to them and to himself. "A silly reason, isn't it? I've wasted your time. I apologize." He stood to go.

"I can't promise another dog for you, Finder Aris," Edwards said with what sounded like honest regret. "The bio'face is the only trump card we have right now, the only way we can gain access to the Hoveny sites for our species. Maybe, one day . . ."

Vasi nodded. "I know. I just hoped." He understood the reluctance of the First. Humans were numerous, but possessed unremarkable technology, biology, and culture. Why admit more of the species to the secrets of the First? But Vasi looked at Seung and suddenly wondered what they didn't know. He'd never met another alien so perceptive, so willing to work within his own parameters to understand him.

Perhaps the important thing about that damn dog wasn't about dogs at all, but the kind of beings who valued such partnership enough to bring it with them into space.

"As you know, Liaison Seung, my Triad remains in charge of the most significant Hoveny find ever made on Aeande XII, possibly anywhere," Sai Vasilo Aris said in his even, unemotional voice. "We lost our Analyst in the tragedy. Do you have a qualified Analyst available for the coming field season? One who can climb?"

After a shocked pause, they both spoke at once: "What— What did you say? Pardon? Are you serious?" Then, Seung, almost angrily: "You want a Human Analyst?"

"A Human." Vasi didn't know how to show he shared their astonished pleasure, but opened his flaps a trifle and sent out a scent of pleased anticipation for himself. "I think I'll enjoy the company."

Heartsease

by Fiona Patton

Fiona Patton was born in Calgary, Alberta, Canada, in 1962 and grew up in the United States. In 1975 she returned to Canada, and after several jobs which had nothing to do with each other, including carnival ride operator and electrician, moved to seventy-five acres of scrub land in rural Ontario with her partner, six cats of various sizes, and one tiny little dog. Her first book, *The Stone Prince,* was published by DAW Books in 1997. This was followed by *The Painter Knight* in 1998, *The Granite Shield* in 1999, and *The Golden Sword* in 2001, also by DAW. She is currently working on her next novel.

*H*E HAD *a change-flea. He could feel it. The sparkly place inside him was growing larger, growing stronger, every day and the change-flea that had tickled against his mind ever since he'd been born was growing stronger, too. Soon he would have to decide whether to let it feed or whether to scratch it away and remain as he always had been: young, innocent, and blind. But not now. Now he dreamed.*

He was out on the water, moving up and down. The wind blew across his back, first warm and then cold, roaring with the same cadence as the rhythm of the waves. It was a strange dream. He'd never been near the water before, but he was warm and he was safe, so he drifted along until the wind changed pitch and timber, then he opened his eyes.

Urge was snoring.

For a moment the early morning sun dazzled him, then slowly, the tiny brown dog shook himself free of his nest of blankets and peered down at the man whose heavy breathing had been lifting him up and down through a patch of sunlight. His stomach growled and he absently growled back at it.

He was hungry. He was hungry and he had to relieve himself—so Urge must stop snoring, wake up, and feed him. Now.

Standing, the little dog stretched as high as his four-inch legs would take him, then carefully made his way up the chest of his most recent human companion. Staring down, he focused all his concentration on the man's face.

Wake up, Urge.

The man continued to snore, oblivious.

WAKE UP, URGE.

The rumbling beneath his feet deepened, the snoring ceased, and the man tried to roll over, but the slightest pressure from one paw held him in place.

"Inna minute, boy," he murmured sleepily.

The dog gave a disbelieving snort. Balancing on three legs, he dug reflectively into one large, expressive ear. Urge wasn't easy to wake up, but he needed to wake up. Beneath his feet, the tiny dog could feel the slow pounding of Urge's heart. It was soft and uncertain. He didn't like that. Urge needed to wake up and move about so the soft and uncertain heartbeat could grow stronger. And *he* needed to go out! He peered down at him again. In the past two weeks, he'd spent each morning experimenting with various techniques. He'd found that a combination of two or three usually did the trick. Reaching out, he scratched at Urge's chin and was rewarded with a jerk from the man's head.

"Comin', Lucky, good d . . . og."

The little dog sneezed at the sound of his newest name. He'd had three in his short lifetime. His mother had called him Beloved Four. Roos, the old woman who'd carried him away from his mother, tucked inside a soft and woolly sweater that smelled of roses and lilacs, had named him Heartsease. Urge had named him Lucky Charm, but usually just called him Lucky. It lacked a good growly R, but he supposed a pup could no more be called Heartsease his whole life than Beloved Four.

He scratched at Urge's chin again, and beneath his feet, he felt the man's heart strengthen as he came closer to waking up. Lucky's tail began to wag.

He'd spent a lot of time listening to Roos' soft, uncertain heartbeat. He hadn't been old enough to keep it strong no matter how many times he'd pressed himself against her woolly, perfumed sweater, willing all the sparkly power in his tiny heart to hers. They were together almost a full year until the morning he'd felt her own few sparkles fade, her heart stop beating, and the warmth leave her body.

That wasn't going to happen with Urge.

Taking a step forward, he leaned toward the man's bristly face. Urge spent most of his time poking at a small machine in the big eating room—or at least as much time as Lucky would allow him—and hadn't scraped his bristles off in nearly a week. He'd have to be sure to do that today. They were going to Rand's house today so Lucky could have a "play date" with the rest of the family and Urge needed to look his best so the family would be sure to know that Lucky was taking good care of him. Lucky's tail began to wag faster. He liked Urge's family. They all sparkled so brightly it made him feel like a puppy again.

And he especially liked Rand. Rand had rescued him from Roos' nasty son the day her heart had stopped beating.

Lucky had disliked Roos' son immediately. He'd never been to see Roos once in the whole year Lucky had been with her, but on the day she died he'd taken all her sweetly smelling things, including Lucky himself, away to sell. He hadn't even put on Lucky's nice plaid macintosh when they'd left and he'd dragged him roughly down the sidewalk even after Lucky had very politely pointed out that they'd passed his first *and* second marking spots. Then he'd actually tried to kick him. So when Lucky had sensed the three sparkly men coming along behind them, he'd sent out a call. That was all it took.

Rand had scooped him up immediately and his littermate, Red, had knocked Roos' nasty son into the road. They'd both smelled of cigarette smoke and power and they'd punished Roos' son for trying to kick Lucky with the sight of a huge, smelly truck barreling down on him. He'd screamed in a very satisfying manner, but the truck hadn't really been there.

Pressed smugly against Rand's shirt, Lucky had felt the sparkly power pulse in time with his strongly beating heart. It made the sparkles in his own heart dance. It felt safe and familiar, like a half-forgotten dream from puppyhood, but even so he'd known Rand wasn't meant to be his. Neither was Red, but when they'd taken him into the nice, warm place to feed him lovely bits of meat and bread soaked in milk, he'd poked his tiny head out from Rand's jacket to see Urge watching them from across the table. He'd known right then.

Urge *needed* him.

Urge was a lot older than Rand and Red, big and a little bit fat, and rather than swirl through his eyes where anyone might see them, his sparkles were hidden deep down inside. His heartbeat was soft and uncertain—almost like Roos'—but Lucky was older now and he knew he had the power to keep Urge's heart strong.

As long as Urge woke up.

Tired of waiting, Lucky gave himself a shake. This called for drastic measures. Balancing both front feet across Urge's collarbone, he began to wash the man's face; faster and faster, paying particular attention to the right nostril—there was no sense in having a tongue that fit perfectly up a person's nose if you didn't try to get it up there at least once a day. After just a few moments, Urge finally opened his eyes.

George Prescott had never woken up quickly in his entire sixty-seven years. All his life his mother and then his wife—ex-wife—and daughter had resorted to numerous tricks to get him out of bed and off to either school or work on time. Now retired and living alone he'd thought he was well past all that. And he had been, until he'd taken in a tiny, bossy brown Chihuahua. Dog spit dribbling down his chin, he opened his eyes.

A huge, wide-angle nose swam into his vision followed by an immense pair of mischievous, brown eyes.

"Good morning, Lucky," he said in a resigned tone. "Do you want to go outside?"

The little dog tore down the length of his body, spun about at the bottom of the bed, rear end up, tail wagging, front paws paddling the blankets. He gave George as large a doggie grin as would fit on his tiny face, then ran back up, then back down, then back up again, until George rose with a faint groan.

"All right, all right, come here, then."

At his words, Lucky turned so that George could lift him down with one, large hand and, as soon as his feet touched the floor, he was gone, toenails clicking a fast staccato beat on the hardwood hallway. George quickly fumbled for a sweatshirt and a pair of pants. Lucky would need to go out right away—he seemed to have a bladder the size of a hummingbird's—and no waiting was permitted.

"And yet you can sleep on my chest all night long without so much as a twinge," he muttered. A bark was his only answer and, with a shake of his head, George followed the dog to the front door.

Half an hour later they were back and ready for breakfast. Lucky had managed to sniff, and mark, and sniff again, every weed and rock from here to the next field and then had demanded to be carried home. He'd done the same thing without fail four times a day for the last two weeks. George had tried to get him to turn around halfway, but Lucky was having none of that. He would go to the next field come hell or high water and George wasn't entirely certain either would have stopped him. He was the most determined little dog he'd ever known.

He made a bowl of oatmeal—Lucky hadn't liked the cold cereal he usually made do with—then settled down to try and read the newspaper around the squirming little attention seeker. Half an hour later he heard a car pull up. Lucky rocketed off his lap, barking furiously, and George put down the paper with a sigh and followed him to the front door. He hadn't been able to finish the newspaper in two weeks either.

The old Plymouth station wagon that bounced up the farmhouse driveway had seen better days. About ten years ago. George waited until it shuddered to a halt, dropping a dozen flakes of rust like autumn leaves, before opening the screen door. Lucky was out like a shot, tearing across the lawn, yipping and squeaking, as George's cousins, Brandon and Fred Geoffries, emerged from the car. Brandon lit a cigarette before allowing the little dog to leap into his arms.

"Heya, Menace," he said around the filter. "Hey, George."

"Good morning."

"You ready?"

"Nearly. Come in for a moment, I just have to shave and grab my coat."

The two younger men followed him inside. As George made for the bathroom off the kitchen, they wandered into the dining room. Brandon set Lucky down and the little dog trotted over to set up guard by George's feet while Fred glanced over at the jumbled pile of toys, treats, and blankets next to his cousin's laptop.

"What is all this shit?"

George leaned past the door, then shrugged in embarrassment. "Well, dog supplies," he answered vaguely. "Lucky needed food dishes and shampoo and the like. Didn't you, boy?"

Lucky gave a squeak as Brandon pulled a tiny burgundy sweater from the pile and held it up with a questioning expression.

"It's October," George answered defensively.

"It's a warm October."

"It's going to get colder."

Fred lit a cigarette, blithely ignoring Lucky's protesting bark. "You wouldn't see Jack wearing somethin' like that," he pointed out.

"Jack is a ninety-pound monstrosity, not a Chihuahua," George sniffed. "Chihuahuas feel the cold."

"That why you bought the little green doggie house with all the bows on it?"

"No. I bought that because he liked it when we were at the store."

"*He* liked it?" Brandon asked.

"He ran right inside it. And he looked so cute . . ."

"Has he used it since you got it home?"

"Well, no, he actually prefers his dog bed."

Brandon tipped the brim of his ball cap up to scratch at a thin scar on his forehead. "That be the one on the dining room table?" he asked.

"Well, yes, he likes to be near me when I work, don't you boy?"

Lucky reached up to paw at George's knee and receive a soapy scratch behind the ears.

"You are so whipped," Fred noted in mild disgust. "How much did all this shit cost you?" he asked, holding up a rawhide shoe the size of his fist.

"If you must know, Judy gave me a deal on the dog beds and the sweaters, not that it's any of your business, really," George answered primly. He crossed the room to pluck the shoe from Fred's hand. "Here, Lucky."

Brandon shook his head as he watched the dog try to drag the shoe under the couch. "Beds?"

"Well, he needed more than one, didn't he?"

"You've only got one."

"That's different."

"Uh-huh." His cousin lit a new cigarette with an unconvinced expression and Lucky poked his head out from under the couch to bark at him.

"Exactly," George agreed. "If you have to smoke, can you at least do it outside, Bran? Lucky doesn't like the smell."

Brandon looked from one to the other. "Fred's right," he observed as he made for the front porch.

Glancing down, his brother noted the smug expression on Lucky's face, and shook his head. "You are one spoiled little rat-dog, you know that?" he asked.

Lucky ignored him.

A few minutes later, George eyed Brandon's car with a worried frown. "Perhaps we should take my car," he offered as he watched a few more rust flakes settle to the ground.

Brandon just shrugged. "Suit yourself, if you want your fancy sport ute up to its ass in mud."

"Mud? I thought we were going to your place."

"We're meetin' at my place, then we're goin' to the Island."

George's eyes widened in alarm. "I can't take Lucky Charm to Blind Duck Island. It's full of snakes."

"So?"

"So! He'll get eaten!"

"Keep him close. He'll be fine."

"They're all underground by now, anyway," Fred added with a grin as he blew a smoke ring into the air. "It's October."

"So, why are *we* going in October?"

"All four families are gonna be there."

"Again, why?"

"Because Kevin and Gail are havin' another baby."

"Oh, good Lord."

With a resigned expression, George gingerly undid the bungie cord that was tying the back passenger side door closed.

The change-flea was getting hungry. He could feel it tickle against his mind with an itch he couldn't reach. An itch he didn't want to reach. The change-flea would make everything different; he could sense that already. It would make him see things he didn't want to see, know things he didn't want to know: like how much time his beloved Urge had before the sparkles would fade, leaving his heart as cold and silent as Roos'. But it would also make Lucky himself stronger, more able to push that time farther and farther away. Maybe. But either way the change-flea was getting hungry. There was a big sparkly place of power growing closer by the minute, and when it arrived, he would have to decide what to do about that flea, because, one way or another, its tickling was becoming really annoying.

Tucked in the back of Rand's "go for a drive" machine with four children, two other dogs, a large cooler that smelled of food, and three cardboard cases full of bottles, Lucky began to whine as the now familiar power of the family rose up on the smell of dead fish, rocks, and cool water. One of the girls caught him around the waist and lifted him up so he could see out the window.

*   *   *

"I think, Lucky has to go pee, Uncle George."

George turned an anxious glance on his little dog, then smiled.

"He's all right, Caitlin," he assured her. "He's just excited."

Lucky began to paddle his front paws against the glass and George reached over the seat to pluck him from the eight-year-old's grasp and set him on his lap. Lucky leaned over to snuffle the baby strapped into a car seat next to him, then spun about to peer out Urge's window.

"Maybe he can sense the Island," one of the boys in the back offered and Fred craned his neck past his wife Lisa's ample shoulders to glance at him.

"Can you?"

The boy gave a perfectly timed shrug of indifference. "Sure I can."

"Joe's a Mynaker," George said proudly. "Even I can sense it a little. I think."

"You oughta. You've been here nearly a year," Fred noted absently as he fished through a pile of empty cigarette packages on the floor. As he pulled out a crumpled Players, it flung itself into the overflowing ashtray. He turned an aggrieved look on Brandon's girlfriend, Cheryl, and she glared back at him.

"You're not smoking with Kaley in the car, Fred," she said sternly.

"Aw, can't you just mojo the smoke out the window?"

"No."

"We're almost there anyway," Brandon offered as he eased the overladen station wagon onto a steep and muddy dirt road. A dozen cars were already pulled up on the nearby, rocky beach while, across the water, the family Island shimmered invitingly in the morning sun.

George smiled as he felt the faintest of tingles work up his spine. This was why he'd come to the county in the first place, to learn about his family's history. As it had turned out, he'd learned a lot more than he'd bargained for.

Blind Duck Island was the hereditary home of four separate but very inbred county families, the Geoffries,

Frawsts, Akormans, and Mynakers. Half a mile away, deep in the waters of Lake Ontario, a strange anomaly gave off a powerful energy that, if experienced before birth, gave the members of these four families—all descendants of two very gifted and mysterious immigrants, Samuel and Mary Essen—four very distinctive abilities: Geoffries like Brandon and Fred could create frighteningly real illusions; Brandon's girlfriend Cheryl and the other Frawsts could levitate objects and people; the Akormans such as Lisa and her father, Art, could manipulate any engine or machine no matter how complicated; and the Mynakers had the Sight. Before she'd moved away to be a nurse during the First World War and marry Harvey Prescott, George's grandmother had been a county Mynaker. George had been born three hours away in Toronto, but the Island still called to his Mynaker blood, making his mind twitch in the throes of a half-remembered dream, forever on the far edge of wakefulness.

That was why Kevin and Gail Geoffries were going to spend a cold and inhospitable winter on Blind Duck Island—despite the very real possibility of birth defects—so that their fifth child might share in the Essen legacy. And that was why all four families were congregating on the Island today. Most would come and go throughout Gail's pregnancy, keeping the couple supplied with food and company until the ice grew too thick to row across, then they'd drive. Every one of them except George had been born within sight of the anomaly and every one of them, young and old, could feel the transforming nature of its power.

On George's lap, Lucky began to whine again.

"He sure is one licky dog, Uncle George."

Caitlin watched as Lucky very carefully washed all the barbecue sauce off her cousin Debbie's face.

They had been on the Island most of the day—long enough to polish off the constant stream of steaks, hamburgers, and hot dogs that Brandon and his father had cooked on a wide grill across an ancient, brick-lined fire pit—and Lucky had thoroughly investigated the plates, cups, and willpower of every person foolish enough to let him get his nose close enough to their lunch. Which was most of them.

Beside her, George chuckled.

"Yes, he does give a good bath, doesn't he? But he doesn't provide towels." Reaching over, he wiped Debbie's·face off with a napkin. The small woman grimaced and pulled her head away, nearly upsetting Lucky from his perch on the arm of her wheelchair.

"It's okay, I think she likes being licked," Caitlin observed as Lucky continued with his ministrations, causing Debbie to smile happily.

"Yes, still, I think it's time he had a walk. Your cousin Jesse fed him so much hamburger I'm surprised he didn't burst."

The girl giggled. "That wasn't Jesse," she replied. "That was Uncle Fred."

"What, and after he called my pup a spoiled little rat-dog? We shall have to see about that." Scooping Lucky up, he snapped a small, red collar around his neck. "C'mon, boy, we have to go see a man about a sneaky inconsistency."

Setting him onto the grass, George headed for the knot of men drinking beer by an upturned fishing boat.

Ebbie was ill. Even without the change-flea's interference he'd felt the sickness coursing through her blood, making her pale and weak. Her mind was all wrapped in fog, but when he'd pressed his paws against her jacket he could feel the sparkles weaving through her heart, keeping it, at least, healthy and strong. She didn't need him. Not yet.

The change-flea hovered just on the edge of awakening and he pushed it away. It was too soon. He didn't want to be aware so soon. He was still so young and there was still so much fun to be had. Urge didn't need him yet. Ebbie didn't need him yet. He still had time. Hovering on the edge of the change-flea's infuriating tickle was the most intoxicating odor he'd ever smelled. If he could only get Urge to unsnap his collar, he could investigate it in peace. Then maybe he would think about the change-flea after. After the smell.

* * *

"Lucky? Lucky!"

George looked anxiously from side to side. The little dog had worried at his collar until he'd pulled it over one ear so George had reluctantly removed it, telling him firmly to stay. He'd sat so obediently that George had forgotten to glance down every five seconds to ensure that he hadn't been carried off by a mutated garter snake, but now he was nowhere in sight.

"Lucky!"

Brandon tossed his cigarette butt into the water before nudging the older man with his elbow.

"He's just over there."

George turned to see four tiny, brown feet waving in the air behind a piece of weathered driftwood. The image of a giant sea snake trying to swallow his little dog had him sprinting across the beach. The sight of Lucky rolling joyously in the remains of a dead seagull stopped him cold.

"Ew! Uncle George, why does he smell like that?"

Holding Lucky at arm's-length with the first two fingers of each hand, George grimaced. "Because," he wearily explained to the collection of wide-eyed children who'd gathered around them, "he's a dog, a teeny weenie dog, but still a dog. Anyone want to help me give him a bath?"

The children scattered.

He was mortified. The lovely smell he'd discovered was gone and in its place was the nasty, overpowering odor of soap. The only very small consolation was that afterward Rand's mate, Iryl, had given him a long towel dry and a brush-out—Urge would have done it himself, but he wasn't speaking to Urge right now—or to Rand either for that matter. Rand had tossed his beautiful dead bird far out into the water.

But the worst insult of all was that *Jak* had *laughed* at him. *Jak,* a dog who could barely understand three words Red said to him other than his name, a dog whose sparkles were so deep down inside him he probably didn't even know he had any, a dog who wouldn't know a change-flea if it bit him on the—he struggled to form the word he'd heard Rand use earlier but it eluded him—rear end, *Jak*, had laughed at him.

Lucky's ears pressed down against the side of his wide, apple-domed head. He didn't like being laughed at.

The change-flea tickled his mind, but he snapped at it and it subsided. It was the change-flea that was making him think these thoughts. Without it, he wouldn't have cared if Jak had laughed at him. Well, maybe he would have cared, but he wouldn't have spent all this much time thinking about it. He'd have just bitten him. And hard, too.

Warming to the image of biting Jak, he forgot to resist when Urge lifted him up and tucked him into his jacket. All right, fine, he would snuggle down against Urge's chest because it was getting cold and he didn't like being cold any more than he liked being laughed at—but he wouldn't lick him, just see if he wouldn't. And he wouldn't feel for his soft, uncertain heart anymore. He would be a regular dog. He would scratch the change-flea away and that would be that. He stuffed his nose into Urge's armpit and was rewarded with an involuntary jump. Why did he have to make this choice anyway, he thought resentfully. None of the other family dogs had a change-flea. Jak and Maggie and Tex and Dot; they all played and barked and . . . rolled in lovely smells, and cared for their companions just fine, without the knowledge that one day their companions might . . . leave them. Why did he have to have it?

Grumbling low in his throat until Urge began to gently rub his back, he eventually fell asleep.

Much later, after he'd taken Urge to the wonderful little shack with all the incredible smells, and they'd both relieved themselves—Urge in and Lucky on the shack—and after the sun had gone down, leaving the sparkly Island to the frogs and the crickets and the stars, he'd sat with his head poking out of Urge's jacket, absently chewing on his front toenails. Most of the family was sitting on lawn chairs around the big fire Rand and Red had made, drinking beer and smoking cigarettes, with dogs and children sprawled all around on the grass or on blankets. Half dozing, he pressed against Urge's chest, feeling his heartbeat grow stronger this close to the family power. He could almost hear what he was thinking and he smiled contentedly, knowing that he was mostly thinking about him.

But after a time he grew restless—he had important things to do; after all, a dog couldn't spend his entire life cleaning his feet—and he struggled out of Urge's jacket. After a slight argument about the collar and leash, which Atlin won by promising to look out for him, he made the rounds of each person, begging a bit of marshmallow here or a bit of candy there, scratching at their hand to be picked up and pressed against their chests. Atlin laid her cheek against his and he snuffled into her neck, breathing in the woodsmoke and bubble-gum scents on her hair. Isa tucked him inside Ebbie's jacket for a while and he sent all the strength and sparkles he could to her, knowing it wouldn't really help but doing it anyway. He played tug of war with Jo and Jesy and even a little "steal my bone" with Jak before he felt the need to go off and mark something. Scratching at Urge's arm, he made him leave the fire and take a nice, long walk down by the water. You never knew, his lovely dead bird might have washed ashore by now.

He had a squat, marked a couple of rocks, then sat at the water's edge, staring out at the pulsing power place far away. Urge sat down on an old log beside him and for a long time they just sat and stared out at the dark, distant waves together. It felt so familiar and so peaceful that, when Isa's father, Urt, joined them, smoking his sweetly smelling burning thing, Lucky didn't even bother to woof at him.

Art took a long draw on his pipe, then gestured at the log.

"Ya mind?"

"No, not at all." George moved over and Art perched himself on one end.

"Thanks. They're startin' to argue about hockey up there an' I can't hear a thing without my ears in."

"Your . . . ears?"

"You know, my hearin' aids."

"Oh, yes, of course."

They sat in companionable silence until Art's pipe went out.

"A nice night," he said, fumbling through his breast pocket for his pouch.

"It is that."

"They say it's gonna to be an open winter."

"Well, that will be good news for Kevin and Gail."

"Yup."

The silence lasted through another pinch of tobacco, then Art stirred.

"So, how's the old ticker?"

"Not bad. My doctor's pleased that I've lost weight. I imagine I'll lose more what with having to take his little lordship here out every half an hour or so."

Art chuckled. "It's funny," he said after a moment. "That little dog looks right familiar. The way he looks up at you as if he knows exactly what you're sayin'. Irene Mynaker's girl, Donna, has a dog looks just like that. A little chi-bitch named Pippy. Had a litter of puppies right here on the Island around this time last year before she went to Kingston for nursin' school."

"Oh?" George glanced over at the other man with interest. "What happened to them? The puppies, I mean."

"Oh, they all got sold off. There was one, little brown fella now as I remember it, had a white front paw just like Lucky's there. Got bought by an old lady, what was her name, Rose Cook, I think it was, from Torawna. Seemed right pleased with him she did, gave him some fool name only a little old lady would give an animal with teeth in his head. Heartsease."

Heartsease.

Lucky raised his head, staring up at Urge's cousin Urt as Urge chuckled. The change-flea tickled at his mind, but he ignored it. Urt had known Roos. Urt had known Roos, and his mother, and his name before it was Lucky Charm.

* * *

Heartsease.

The change-flea took up the word, rolling it about on its tongue. The word grew larger as the sparkly power out in the water began to pulse in time with his heart-beat.

Heartsease.

He'd been born on the Island. Like Rand and Red, and Isa and Iryl, like Atlin and little baby Aley.

But not like Urge.

Lucky glanced up, seeing the lines of care and age on the man's face, feeling the strain on his heart as his sparkles fought against the fog that blocked them from making him strong, almost like Ebbie's were blocked, but not quite.

The change-flea bit down and Lucky shivered.

Heartsease.

That had been his name. That had been who he was, that had been what he was.

Suddenly needing to be close to Urge's chest, he scratched at his leg until the man picked him up and tucked him inside his jacket. Pressing his paws against his shirt, he closed his eyes.

Urge's heartbeat pulsed against his toes and slowly, very slowly, he felt the time that Urge had left. He almost whined in relief as it washed over his mind. Time. Lots of time. Time stretching out long past Lucky's own time. Urge's heart would not stop beating, Urge would not leave him like Roos had. With a sigh, he stuffed his nose into Urge's armpit and the man gave a faint yelp.

The change-flea had fed and had changed and he had changed with it. He was no longer young and innocent and blind, he was large and strong and he would keep Urge—keep George—strong, too. He had changed, but not as much as he feared, not so much that he wasn't still a regular dog, or as regular as a Mynaker dog, born on the Island, could ever be. Tucked safely in George's jacket, he twitched in his sleep as an intoxicating odor wafted over to him from the darkened beach. His lovely dead bird had finally washed ashore. He would have a nice, long roll in it tomorrow, after he took George for his morning walk, but for now, he dreamed.

A Spaniel for the King

by India Edghill

India Edghill's interest in fantasy can be blamed on her father, who read her *The Wizard of Oz, Alf's Button,* and *Animal Farm,* and her interest in the romantic aspects of English history on her mother, who gave her *Katherine* and *Young Bess.* When she's not writing fantasy short stories, India is writing historical novels. Her first, *Queenmaker,* is a retelling of the biblical story of David from his queen's point of view; her second, *Wisdom's Daughter,* retells the tale of Solomon and Sheba. India lives in the beautiful pollen-filled mid-Hudson Valley with Harry, the Perfect Cavalier Gentleman.

In Memory of Oliver, a true Cavalier

THE MEASURE of a man's greatness lies not in how he treats the highly-placed, but in how he treats the lowly. That is why, although I am by nature warmhearted and affectionate, I never could bring myself to be fond of the Duke of Monmouth. Monmouth treated me well—fawned over me, in fact, as if I were his dearest love—only when he found me with his father, the king.

When I was not close by King Charles' side, I became invisible to haughty Monmouth. That was not a wholly bad thing; many men would have treated me ill, did they find me unprotected.

But James of Monmouth merely did not see me when the king was not close by. And did I bar his way, the duke would brush me aside as if I did not exist.

How very different from the way the king's brother treated me! Oh, I know what they say of *that* James— that the Duke of York is a cruel Papist. Perhaps he is, but I know only that His Highness of York never stared through me as if I were beneath notice, or shoved me

61

from his path as if I were nothing at all. To me, York was kind, as was his pretty young wife.

"See, my dear," York told her, the first time I passed by them in the corridors of Whitehall, "this pert little miss is Nell—the king's favorite."

And the new Duchess of York smiled upon me and called me a "pretty thing." I knew I was pretty, just as I knew myself the king's favored pet—but the duchess' words still cheered me, and I trotted on down the corridor to the king very well pleased with myself.

On such threads do crowns hang; upon such small gestures rest the fate of nations.

My king and I were completely happy together; in his arms I knew myself his favorite, his best-loved in all the world. Just as all the others knew the same, when he caressed and cuddled them. That was his greatest achievement: he made everyone feel loved. No wonder we all loved him in return!

I had never looked to the future; it is not in my nature to brood over what might come. So when the king lay dying, I was plunged suddenly from delight to despair. My Merrie Monarch, my beloved patron, soon would be gone, leaving me wretched and alone.

Charles was not allowed to die in peace either—that is not the way for kings. His ministers badgered him hourly, demanding he name his heir. Unfortunately—and most oddly, considering how fertile a crop his seed produced in unsanctioned alliances—his Portuguese queen had never borne even a daughter to him, let alone a son. Since King Charles II had no legitimate son, most men looked to the next son of the king's father, martyred Charles.

That meant James, the Duke of York, would reign next.

But York was a Catholic. This meant that the Duke and Duchess of York heard Mass and prayed in Latin and believed there were seven sacraments, rather than two. Our England was now a Protestant country, so the Yorks were called "Papist" and people threw stones at their carriage in the street. The things men find to quarrel over!

But whatever his religion, York was the undoubted legitimate heir to the throne, for there were no others.

Or say, rather, no others with so clear and unchallenged a claim. For as well as the king's brother James, there was the king's son James. The Duke of Monmouth.

Long years ago, when my darling Charlie was a young prince, he had been a wanderer. Through no fault of his own (all blame lay at the feet of That Man Cromwell, that betrayer of his own master!), Prince Charles had embarked upon a roving life, seeking always a way to return to his true home and destiny. And, as young rovers will, Prince Charles had entertained a fondness for many a fair maiden—and for many who, while fair, could not lay claim to maiden state. One of those—the first of them, she always claimed—was a girl named Lucy Walter.

Lucy was pretty, I hear. And she was bright as a new silver button as well, I suspect. For not only did she bed young Charles, the romantic exiled prince, but she wed him as well.

Or so rumor hissed. The story had been whispered in bedchambers and murmured in doorways so long that the tale had grown a strange life of its own, dwelling halfway between truth and treason.

I know that James of Monmouth believed the story— well, he would, would he not? It redeemed his mother's character, after all, were she the king's secret wife, rather than his public whore. (Not that my most loved and most loving Charles cared a dead flea whether a woman were whore or holy nun; from orange-girl to queen, he treated all alike. It was the true secret of his endless victories over virtue.)

And in addition to polishing his mother's tarnished reputation, a secret marriage transformed the bastard Duke of Monmouth into the legitimate Prince of Wales. From James, Duke of Monmouth at the king's pleasure to—James, King of England at the king's death.

So Monmouth had everything to gain by vowing the rumored wedding's truth, and nothing to lose.

James of York, on the other hand, would lose the crown shimmering in his future.

King Charles had never confirmed the tale of his wedding to Lucy Walter. But unfortunately for my darling Charles, he had never firmly denied the story either. And now that it was too late, his conscience pricked him.

As well it might, I suppose; he had just spoken in secret with a priest, making his peace with whatever God kings worship. Charles had not sent me away, and the priest had barely noted my presence, so unnerved was he by being called upon to confess the king. Nothing in the whispered confession had touched upon the succession.

Now confession was over and the priest gone, and for a brief, precious time Charles and I were alone together. I lay beside him, his arm about me, trying to console him as he struggled to decide what best to do, now that he must pass the care of the realm into other hands. For we both sensed a door opening for him that night; a door though which he must pass, leaving me behind. The time grew closer, and the king still could not rest easy.

"What to do, Nell?" he asked, staring into my eyes. "What to do?"

I leaned my head against his hand; I did not know how else to offer him comfort. But apparently my warmth, and my attention, were enough for him.

"James and again, James. Two Jameses, Nell, and each a royal disaster in his own way." Wearily the king stroked me, as he so often had before. "James the brother—too strict and too hard. And too Catholic, Nell; never forget that, for the people of England will not. That James will never do."

Again Charles caressed me, his touch heavy with fatigue. "Then there is James the son—too proud and too easy. Too vain of being the king's son, Nell." For a moment Charles brooded, silent; shadow darkened his face. "But he is my son. My Protestant son." He turned his head and stared straight into my eyes. "My legitimate son, Nell."

And then the king told me the true story, knowing at the last that he must confess it to someone, and knowing, too, that I alone could be trusted to never utter a word of what I heard from him.

*   *   *

I was so young, Nell. That is my only excuse; a poor one, I know. But I was little more than a boy—with all the spirit and urges of a man grown. And Lucy—ah, sweet Lucy. So fair, so giving—they wrong her, you know, who say she trapped me. The trap into which I fell was set for me long ago by Venus and by no one else.

She was younger even than I, and neither of us had yet been tamed by the world and its wisdom. I loved her, Nell, and she loved me—me, and not my rank, and blood, and heritage. It was Charles she saw before her, not a future crown. You don't believe me? Ah, you do, I see it in your loving eyes. Her eyes were brown, too—my Lucy's—

Well, Lucy was a loving creature, and gave me whatever I asked, and much I did not yet know enough to desire. It was a strange time, Nelly; I had been driven out of England and my father prisoned by Cromwell; the crown of England tottered and seemed set to roll into the nearest ditch. Despite my mother's grand claims, my French relations gave me only charity, and that grudging.

So you see, my Nell, how ripe I was to fall into a pair of soft young arms, how primed to act the fool. What? I, a fool? Oh, yes, my pretty one, I, clever Charles, fell into the worst folly a king can commit. Marriage.

Mind you, poppet, it did not seem folly when I knelt with her before the priest, nor when I slid the only ring I possessed onto her finger, nor when she looked up at me in love and in trust—just as you look at me now, Nell. Sometimes you remind me of my Lucy, although she was a farmer's daughter and you—ah, well, never mind.

No, the vow did not seem folly then. My father's head had rolled in the dirt before the eyes of curious cowards; Cromwell held all England and I was naught but a poor vagabond, a less desirable guest than a Gypsy rover. For a Gypsy might steal food and silver—baubles. But a landless prince might steal peace, demanding alliances be honored, armies sent to restore his purloined throne. I thought I would never be more than a poor exile. I had no land, no crown. My very title seemed written in water. I was only Charles Stuart now. Why should Charles Stuart deny himself the comfort of a loving little wife?

And the marriage pleased my Lucy, who was already

quick with my child. My first—but not my last—ah, yes, laugh at me, Nell; I know that sidelong smile of yours, you clever little creature. I have fathered many children, but young James was my firstborn and my first son—and my only legitimate child.

Yes, and by rights should have been raised as Prince of Wales. But he was not, because I was a coward, Nelly.

For the tide turned, you see, and I began to fight to regain my father's lost kingdom. And I knew that I had only one treasure to bargain with: the crown of the Queen of England.

By right and by vow, that crown should be set upon Lucy's head, as my ring had been set upon her hand. But Queen Lucy would do my cause no good, and much harm. Kings do not marry lowborn girls, save in fairy tales.

I should have brazened it out, Nell—should have acted like a man. I should have told the truth and shamed the devil; proclaimed Lucy my wife and my queen, no matter what the cost. I know that now. But I did not. Instead, I told my Lucy our marriage must wait in secret until the day I could claim her as my own. I asked her for our marriage lines and she, trusting, gave them into my faithless hand. So when our son was born, I claimed him as my bastard. And I hid that fatal paper Lucy had given me safe away.

Now Lucy is gone, and soon I, too, shall depart. I dare not give the proof of my marriage into anyone's hands and I cannot bear to destroy it. But you, dearest Nell—you I can trust. . . .

As I lay beside him, my beloved king slipped his hand beneath his lace-trimmed pillow and withdrew a slim roll of paper. "My marriage lines, Nelly. Now you shall keep them safe."

I watched with alert interest as King Charles pulled out a wide blue riband and smoothed it flat upon the coverlet. With steady hands, he laid his marriage lines upon the riband and folded the blue satin over until the paper was hidden. Then, to my surprise, the king pulled a small embroidered pocket from beneath the pillow; he opened it to reveal a needle threaded with deep blue silk.

"Surprised, little one?" Charles said, and the smile I so loved to see lit his face once more. "A wandering prince learns many skills, Nelly. Once I darned my own stockings."

I watched his long fingers push the needle through the riband, pull the silk thread through the strip of bright satin. Steadily he worked, stitching until the riband was half its original width, the king's marriage lines hidden securely within the blue riband.

Charles knotted the thread, bit it off, and regarded his royal handiwork with satisfaction. Then he patted the bed beside him and I moved closer. He stroked my forehead and caressed my neck; his fingers knew just how to please me and I leaned into his hand. "Enough," he said. I sat back and Charles took up the satin length of riband and slipped it about my throat.

He tied the riband into a pretty bow. "There now. A true test for a true prince. Ah, I must be farther gone than I thought, Nell, for I grow romantic and think fondly of chivalry and of honor. . . ."

His hand fell away from the blue riband I now wore about my neck; I sensed he tired, and settled myself beside him to guard his rest.

Uselessly, for soon after the king's physician barged into the room, followed by the king's brother and the king's wife and the king's ministers. I whimpered in protest, but as I said, kings are not allowed to die in peace.

Charles spoke sharply to his physician, and gently to his brother. And his last words were of me.

"James," he said, "let not poor Nelly starve." That was all; his hand grew heavy and his flesh cold, and I knew my king was gone where I could not yet follow.

After that, all was noise and confusion and grief. Someone noticed I was still there and ordered me sharply out of the king's bedchamber. Stunned and miserable, I slunk out, seeking my own place to mourn for my beloved.

Finding a quiet place in Whitehall was no easy task; the king's death released havoc in its wake. The corridors of Whitehall were full of people, all of them chattering about King Charles and his death, repeating words

he had not spoken, telling of bequests he had not
made—I knew them false, for I alone had been with
him, constant to the end.

Finally I ran out-of-doors into the pleasaunce, hoping
for a private place in which to huddle until someone told
me what I must do now.

Outside, the day was gray and pale, February's chill
enough to cut sharp. But at least I was alone—or nearly
so. For the Duke of Monmouth walked slowly along one
of the red brick pathways through the wild garden, deep
in talk with a stout man already somberly dressed in
mourning black. When I saw Monmouth, I remembered
the king's last words to me, and how he had tied the
blue riband containing the royal marriage lines about my
neck, his fingers moving with slow, dying grace.

Surely King Charles had meant his son to be king
after him. Why else had he given Lucy Walter's marriage
lines into my keeping? He knew I could move unhin-
dered among the courtiers, could approach any man
freely.

Yes, that must be what my king had meant. So I ran
down the path to the Duke of Monmouth, catching frantically at his coat. He stopped and looked at me, and
frowned. "Get away from me, creature," he said, and
shoved me aside with a sweep of his leg.

Startled—for never before had Monmouth proved
cruel—I tried again to claim his attention, only to have
Monmouth slap at me with his scarlet leather gloves.
"Begone," he commanded. He did not have to tell me
three times. Dodging his blood-bright gloves, I turned
and hurried off. Behind me, I heard Monmouth say
crossly to his companion, "My father harbored far too
many of those creatures. When I am king, I shall cleanse
the palace of them."

At the end of the red brick path I stopped, uncertain
which way to go. Monmouth would not heed me. Should
I now seek out the Duke of York? Was that what I was
meant to do?

Grief filled my heart; my body trembled with misery.
With no one to command me, I feared to set my feet
wrongly. I could not decide which way to go.

At last I sat down upon the cold brick pathway, and did not move at all.

"Here now, what's this?" A man's voice, deep and velvety; for a sublime instant I thought I heard my king's voice once more. But the scent he wore was strange; I did not know it. Then strong hands caught me and swept me up; I struggled and found myself staring into an oddly familiar face.

Black unruly hair, black eyes; a laughing curl of mouth. Not handsome, not as people reckon a man's looks. But he had something better than a handsome face. Like King Charles, this man drew one to him, unable to resist his Stuart charm.

Oh, yes, I knew he was a Stuart—that was clear enough. I did not know him, but that meant nothing, for King Charles had sired children upon women the length and breadth of England. James of Monmouth had almost as many relatives as I did myself.

"What's the matter, poppet?" he asked, stroking my back. "What's a pretty thing like you doing out here all alone?"

A whimper escaped me; I could not help it, for I was so unhappy I wished only to hide away from the world. The man seemed to sense my misery, for he held me close and patted me consolingly. "What shall we do with you, pet?"

I could not answer; I stared at him, beseeching understanding. Ruefully, he shook his head. "Well, come along with me and I shall introduce you to a fair lady. I'm sure she will be kind to you."

Yes, Mistress Comfort was kind, although she had never before laid eyes upon me. The man presented me to her, and she smiled and called me a sweet, pretty thing. "But what are we to do with her? We cannot bring her before the king!"

"Certainly we can, my dear; I've heard it said he's a great fondness for these creatures. They run tame all over Whitehall, although their manners distress some of the more nice-minded sycophants that dwell within these royal walls."

Hearing this, I realized they did not yet know the king was dead. I whimpered again, and the lady touched my nose and bade me hush. So I settled down to listen, and to wait.

Those who do often learn much. As I patiently sat, the pair who had come to my aid spoke freely, and so I learned that Amory Fitzroy and his lady Comfort had come to court hoping, as so many did, to find favor with the king. Amory had more reason than most to believe he would be kindly treated—

"For the king is your father, after all, Amory."

"So my mother said, and she might be supposed to know," he agreed.

"Well, then, he must do something for you."

Amory smiled in a way that made my heart ache; just so had my Charles smiled. " 'Must' is not a word to use to princes, my dear. But our monarch is not only merrie, but prodigious generous as well."

"He's generous enough with his seed, if that's what you mean." Golden curls long and soft as a spaniel's ears swung as Comfort tossed her head. "How many children does he claim?"

"My dear, no one knows. I vow the man himself's lost count." Here Amory frowned, staring at me absently, and the lady Comfort smiled; I sensed she smiled often.

"So long as you do not lose count, I shall not complain. It's not every fine gentleman who'll give his hand to a whore's daughter." She held up her hand as Amory began to speak. "No, it's truth, and we both know it."

"Neither of our dams were what they should be, I suppose." Amory sighed. "I could wish mine had been more clever, if she had to be so accommodating. All she got from her tumble with our royal Charlie was me. Others did better."

"No," said Comfort, after considering his words for a moment, "I do not think they did."

He laughed, sounding again hauntingly like King Charles. "Very well, then; I'm worth a title and estate; 'tis what others received from our Cavalier king, after all."

"Your title is that of an honest gentleman, and that's

more than many can claim. As for estates—you have
Sweetbriar."

"A sweet briar indeed; I vow he who held its deed
cheated to lose and so rid himself of the place!"

As they jested, I gathered that Amory Fitzroy had the
King's own luck; fortune favored him at the gaming
table. Nameless and landless, he had won himself an
estate to live on and a fair lady to wife. He seemed
happy enough with the lady—as well he might, as she
was kind and pretty, too—but the estate whose deed he
had won had been sadly neglected.

Neglected land eats money as a cat eats mice, swiftly
and constantly. And a man with a wife must put her
needs before his own pride. That was why Amory Fitzroy had, at last, come to the king's court, to claim his
father and ask his aid. Being no fool, Amory Fitzroy had
brought his pretty Comfort along; a father's generosity
to a newfound son was not nearly so sure a thing as
King Charles' liberality to pretty women.

But they had chosen their time poorly; arrived at
Whitehall to find the king lying deathly ill. Amory Fitzroy doubted now that they would ever see the king.

Nor did they. As my rescuers plotted strategy, it began
to rain; an icy, bitter drizzle that drove us to seek shelter.
I followed after Amory Fitzroy and Mistress Comfort as
the two of them found their way from the garden into
the great corridor where men and women waited, whis-
pering, as the news of King Charles' death swept through
Whitehall like plague. And like plague, the king's death
killed hopes and dreams, Amory Fitzroy's among them.
I huddled by Amory and Comfort Fitzroy, and waited,
too bemused by grief to do otherwise than cling to their
kindness. For the moment confusion reigned as king; no
one knew which way to bow—toward Monmouth or
toward York.

Amory Fitzroy knew no doubts. "The people of England will put up with a great deal—but they will not
endure a conceited, puffed-up boy grasping what is not
rightfully his. My half brother Monmouth should take
care. The sun of York rises."

He sighed. "And we, my dear Comfort, depart. No
good will come of this—not for us, at any rate."

"Never mind." Comfort laid her hand upon his. "Others manage without gifts from the king, and so shall we. We do have a roof over our heads, after all."

"Almost, my dear, you give me hope." Amory smiled at her, and took her hand. "Come, then, lady; let's away. The player king is dead, long live the prig of York. Whitehall is no place for the likes of us."

They turned and walked away, down the long corridor I knew so well. I stared and then ran after them, catching them just as they reached the door. They stopped; I flung myself upon Amory.

He bent and lifted me into his arms. "What's this, sweeting? Do you want to come away with us?"

I uttered an imploring whine; Mistress Comfort reached to fondle me. "You must stay here, poppet. We can't steal you away."

As I stared into their faces, silently petitioning, a man shoved past, pushing us all aside. "The Duke of Monmouth," he announced. Behind him stood James of Monmouth, an expression of haughty pride upon his face. Giving himself a king's airs and graces already, he was.

I had been granted another chance to do my master's last bidding; I turned from Mistress Comfort and danced over to Monmouth, uttering a sharp little noise to catch his attention. Frowning, Monmouth glanced down at me and then kicked out, his booted foot dealing me a cruel blow that made me cry out in sudden pain.

"Beast!" Mistress Comfort hissed at Monmouth, and knelt to console me. Ignoring her, Monmouth brushed past, shoving us both hard out of his path. Mistress Comfort lost her balance and sat down hard beside me on the tiled floor.

Monmouth began to stride off into the crowd, but Amory Fitzroy caught his arm. "Perhaps it has escaped your notice, sir, but you have tumbled the lady to the floor. Do you not think it behooves you to aid her to her feet?"

Unaccustomed to being hindered—for I must admit King Charles had spoiled him with indulgence—Monmouth glared at Amory in outrage. He shook off Amory's restraining hand.

"Mind your manners and your tongue, sir, when you address the king's son!"

"Why, as to that, I'm a king's son, too, and as such was taught better manners than to knock a lady down." Amory glanced to his wife, but Mistress Comfort had already scrambled to her feet and was shaking her skirts back into their proper draping. She looked at Monmouth with cool, measuring eyes; I pressed against the protection of her skirts.

"I see the lady does not require your aid," Amory went on, "but I'm sure you will wish to beg her pardon, sir."

Monmouth stared into Amory's face, and his own paled. Perhaps he did not like being reminded of King Charles' many bastard sons, since he himself was accounted one. Perhaps he did not like seeing a face so like King Charles when young; Amory Fitzroy resembled their royal father far more closely than did Monmouth.

Or perhaps he simply did not like what he saw in Amory Fitzroy's eyes. "I suppose you came to see what you could get out of the old—out of our father," Monmouth said, sullen as if King Charles had been miserly and strict with him, rather than all too indulgent. "Well, you've come too late to Whitehall. The king will give you nothing now—but I will."

Unable to meet Amory Fitzroy's steady gaze, Monmouth's eyes slid away—and came to rest upon me. "A king's fancy," Monmouth said. "Now she's yours. And I vow to you, the little bitch is all you'll ever get from a king."

I was not his to give, but I made no protest. Nor were his words the apology Amory Fitzroy had demanded of him—but Mistress Comfort decided to accept them as such. All sweet smiles, Mistress Comfort curtsied to Monmouth.

"Thank you, Your Grace. You are as kind and generous as I expected you to be. We shall be most glad to offer her a home. What is her name?"

Monmouth assumed an expression of aristocratic boredom. "Lord, madam, how should I know? Nell, or Moll, or Babs, or Doll—my father named them all after his mistresses. Filthy things."

Saying nothing, Amory Fitzroy scooped me up into his arms; he was as tall as King Charles had been, so that when he lifted me to his shoulder, I looked down into Monmouth's eyes. There I saw only impatience, and greed.

Amory stroked my back and asked quietly, "If she was the king's favorite, are you quite sure you do not wish to keep her for yourself?"

"What would I do with a mangy old spaniel?" Monmouth jeered, and stalked off. Amory and Comfort exchanged glances above my head.

"And that, my dear, would seem to be that," Amory said.

"Yes. Let us go home now." Comfort fondled my ears; I leaned into her caressing fingers. "Dear little Nell—mangy indeed! What a fool that man is!"

That is how I, who once had the free run of the king's palace, came to live at Sweetbriar with a king's son and a harlot's daughter. The estate was a pleasant enough property, although it was not large, and sorely needed repair. As we rode up the overgrown drive to the manor house, I peered past the horse's neck and saw promising signs of rabbits in the meadow and squirrels in the orchard. I wriggled and Amory let me down to run about and learn the bounds of my new domain.

I heard laughter behind me and paused, looking back. Amory had dismounted and was swinging Comfort down from her horse. "See, she feels already that this is home." Comfort looked up into Amory's eyes. "And so do I."

Satisfied, I ran on. Men and women need privacy, at times, and I—I needed to stretch my legs after being carried on Amory's saddlebow all the way from London.

That night I waited until sleep lay heavy over the house. When I was sure neither of my people would wake, I slid down off the wide bed, landing lightly on the night-cool floor. After listening to their soft steady breathing, I trotted across the room and nosed the door open. Then I headed for the kitchen, and its constant hearth.

The kitchen fire had been banked for the night; beneath the ash burned a steady heart of red-hot coal. I sat upon the stones before the fire and began ridding myself of King Charles' last gift.

I scratched and pawed and rolled, but King Charles had tied the knot tight and true, and I could not work the bow loose. I grew more and more frantic, whining and whimpering in frustration, trying vainly to catch the trailing ends of the riband in my teeth.

Just as I had flung myself flat upon the hearthrug in dejection, I heard soft footsteps.

"Good heavens, what a commotion! What's the matter, Nelly dear?" Mistress Comfort set her night-candle upon the kitchen table and came to kneel beside me on the hearthrug. "Poor girl, are you homesick?"

She stroked me; I lifted my head and gazed at her, beseeching understanding. Then I sat up and pawed at the riband around my neck. Mistress Comfort smiled.

"Ah, poor girl—let's have that off, then.'Tis rather grubby by now—and tattered, too."

What I had not been able to achieve, Mistress Comfort accomplished within minutes with her clever fingers. Once the knot was untied and she pulled the riband from my neck, I tried to snatch the length of satin from her fingers. Thinking it a game, Mistress Comfort trailed the riband before me as if I were a kitten.

"Do you wish to play, Nelly?" The blue riband slid back and forth before me on the rug; with a swift pounce, I trapped it under my paws. She laughed softly, and pulled her end of the riband, and then frowned, her fingers pressing along the riband's length.

"What's this?" she asked, and I tried again to snatch the riband from her grasp. But now she had the whole length of the riband in her hands, feeling its odd thickness. Then she rose and went over to the kitchen table, and came back with a small sharp knife.

And as I stared, my eyes intent with worry, Mistress Comfort began to pick apart the stitches King Charles' hands had set in the blue satin.

As soon as she had half the stitches undone, she tugged gently, pulling the folded paper from its hiding place. She set knife and riband aside and spread the paper before us on the hearth. I watched her face anxiously as she read.

"Well," she said at last, and sat back on her heels. Then she looked at me. "Do you know what this is, Nelly?"

I wagged my tail and set one paw upon her knee.

"Of course you don't," she continued, caressing me absently. "Well, Mistress Nell, this paper could set James of Monmouth upon the throne of England. What do you think of that?"

Mistress Comfort stared at the king's marriage lines, the words that proved Charles Stuart had lawfully wed Lucy Walter all those years ago. "What shall we do with this, Nell?" she asked, and looked into my eyes.

"So—this midnight hour we two hold the crown of England in our gift. Well, the preachers do say your sins will find you out." Mistress Comfort laughed softly. She glanced at the king's marriage lines again, and then at the blue riband lying beside the creased paper. "I know what I would say—but I leave it to you, Nell. Do you think a man who kicks dogs is fit to be King of England?"

I knew the answer to that. Had my beloved Charles known how Monmouth treated me the instant his father lay dead, King Charles would have done himself what Mistress Comfort and I now would do for him.

Delicately I caught up the paper in my teeth. Bracing myself for the heat, I edged close to the slow-burning hearth fire. There I hesitated, unwilling to go closer to the red coals. I looked over my shoulder pleadingly at Mistress Comfort. Taking my hint, she took the paper from me.

"All right, Nelly," she said, and took up the poker from its place beside the hearth. While I sat back and watched, Comfort leaned forward and set the king's marriage lines upon the bed of coals. She used the poker to shove the paper down into the fire's smoldering heart. The blue satin riband followed the vital paper.

Thin smoke puffed; small flames danced. Fire danced over the crumpled paper, snaked up the riband's sleek length, consumed Monmouth's future with its hot red teeth. . . .

"What the devil are the two of you about down here?"

Both Mistress Comfort and I jumped, for we had been so absorbed in our task that even I had heard no sound. Amory Fitzroy stood in the kitchen doorway, a candle in his hand. "Pray, madam, why have you taken a fancy to huddle by the cinders?"

Mistress Comfort merely smiled and rose to her feet. "I do think Nell is quite a clever little thing, don't you?" she said, rather than answering. "Come, let's to bed. 'Tis bitter cold down here."

"Why did you come down here, then?" Amory came over and swooped me up, just as King Charles always had. "Women!" he added, but he sounded more cheerful than cross. As he carried me off, I glanced back over his shoulder, past Mistress Comfort to the kitchen hearth.

The king's blue riband and the paper it had guarded were gone now. Gone to ash. My eyes met my mistress Comfort's.

"Pretty, witty Nelly," she said, and closed the kitchen door behind her. With a contented sigh, I snuggled into Amory's arms and let my head rest heavy upon his shoulder.

Mistress Comfort was the first of us back into the high warm bed; she held out her arms to claim me from Amory. "You still haven't said what you were doing down in the kitchen at the midnight hour, poppet," Amory said as he climbed back into bed.

"Nell was moping in front of the kitchen fire," Comfort told him, and kissed my nose.

"Poor little grommet," Amory said, stroking me consolingly. "She misses the king, perhaps."

"Well, of course she does. I think we all shall. Never mind, sweeting, we'll take good care of you." Then Comfort added, "So this is your kingly legacy, Amory—one spaniel."

"Not just a spaniel—a *royal* spaniel. A king's favorite, no less." Amory Fitzroy put a hand under my chin and turned me to face him. "And what does your royal legacy think? Will we do?"

I looked into his eyes and the warmth of new love

filled my sore heart. I kissed him upon the chin, and wriggled around to kiss Mistress Comfort, too, with a lick of her cheek for good measure, just to reassure her that I loved her quite as well as I did him.

"Well, that seems definitive enough," Amory Fitzroy said. And then we all three nestled down under the covers and slept.

The Duke of York became king—an unloved king. The Duke of Monmouth tried to be rid of him, and failed, and lost his own life, a condemned traitor. In the end, he paid a high price for kicking a dog.

Not long afterward, King James lost his throne to his own daughter and her Dutch husband. Now King James is king in exile, over the water. I think, from what I have overheard in our household, that he is likely to stay there.

It does not matter to me, for my home is here at Sweetbriar now. I, too, am faithful, in my fashion—but that does not mean I can love only one, and only once. Now I love Amory and his lady Comfort, and they love me. For now, that is enough. I can wait.

For someday that door into forever that opens for us all will open for me. And then I shall rise and shake off pain and age and time and run through the doorway into the golden fields on the other side—

—and there my Charles will be waiting for me.

Author's Note: Charles II (born 1630; reigned 1660 to 1685), fondly and cheerfully known as "the Merrie Monarch," had two passions: women and spaniels. Both had free run of Whitehall Palace, much to the dismay of many of the king's courtiers. Charles did indeed sire many children, although none with his wife, Catherine of Braganza. When Charles died, his brother, the straitlaced, Catholic, and unpopular James, Duke of York, became king—over the protests of Protestant James, the Duke of Monmouth, who claimed to be the king's legitimate heir, rather than the king's bastard. But although there had long been rumors that a wedding had taken place between young Charles and his first acknowledged mistress, pretty Lucy

Walter (or Walters, or Water, or Waters), no proof of such a union was ever found.

There is, of course, no proof that a spaniel altered the succession of the crown of England. Then again, there's no proof that one didn't.

We do know that Charles II was exceeding fond of the little dogs—and in his honor the breed he loved so well now bears his name: the Cavalier King Charles Spaniel.

* * *

Profits from this story will be donated to Cavalier King Charles Spaniel Club, USA Rescue; and to Lucky Star Cavalier Rescue.

Among the Pack Alone

by Stephen Leigh

Stephen Leigh is the author of sixteen science fiction and
fantasy novels, including the award-winning *Dark Water's
Embrace* and its sequel, *Speaking Stones.* Stephen has also
published novels under two pseudonyms. Along with the
novel-length work, he has several short fiction credits and
was a frequent contributor to the *Wild Cards* shared world
series, edited by George R.R. Martin. Stephen lives in Cin-
cinnati with his wife Denise and two children; in addition
to his own writing, he teaches creative writing at a local
university.

HE WATCHED her from the moment she entered
his territory.

He could smell her in the breeze: a human, no more
than three days past her menses, with the overlying scent
of perfume as if she wanted to hide her own musk,
something he could never understand. Why would you
want to hide the truths the nose could understand?

He sniffed again. There was apprehension bordering
on fear underneath it all, like the scratch of fleas at the
base of your ear just where you can't easily reach. He
could hear her shuffling in the dry leaves and pine nee-
dles, hesitant, then a long inhalation as she tried to calm
herself. Another sniff: she was alone. He'd known that
from watching her this morning, but with humans he'd
learned to be very careful. She was waiting for him:
Karen.

Carefully, he stepped two-legged from the cover of
the blackberry thicket, deliberately letting himself make
enough noise that her head suddenly snapped up and
she rose from the log on which she'd sat, unmoving,
since the sun had risen behind banked, dark clouds. In
the clearing, the faint light glinted from a chain around

her neck; a rectangle of plastic hung in the valley of her denim shirt with her image on it under the EGC logo.

"Madra?" Karen asked huskily, her voice cracking mid-syllable. The smell of apprehension intensified, yet underneath it there was something else, something he didn't want to trust. "Is that you?"

He didn't answer. She was turning around, looking all around her in the thick forest without seeing him. The wind shifted abruptly, leaving him with only the odor of impending rain and the moldy sharpness of the forest; he knew that the air carried his scent down to her, yet she didn't react, unable to read the subtle, telling odors in the air. "Madra," she called again. "Please come out. You know I won't hurt you. I just . . . I just want to talk with you. Please. As a friend."

He didn't move, didn't respond. He hated speaking the human language anyway; it hurt his throat to form their words and he'd heard the others laugh at his slurred attempts. He'd begun to make his own language, one that felt more natural and easy—but there was no one else to teach it to. Not now.

"I know you're there," she continued. "At least I hope so. I hope you can hear me. I need to talk with you, Madra. You know me. You know you can trust me. Please . . . let me see you."

He remained still and silent. Karen sighed. She placed a packet on the log next to her. "I have to go now," she said, "But I'll be back here tomorrow. Alone. Madra, let me talk with you." She waited a few minutes longer. As she started to turn away, Madra dropped down to all fours hard enough that twigs snapped under his stubby front hands. He padded out into the fringe of the small clearing up the steep hill from her; she stopped. He rose up two-legged and urinated on the ground in front of him, trusting that she would understand what he said with the gesture.

She didn't try to go to him. She knew better. Instead, she nodded. "Tomorrow," she called up to him, then started walking away down the hill. When he could smell that she was far enough away, he dropped back to all fours and made his way down the slope to the package she'd left.

He caught the scent even before he sat on his haunches and reached for the folded, heavy paper: *her* scent. Soith's scent, rich and powerful. His fingers, short and thick-nailed, ripped clumsily at the paper. Inside was a leather collar, one he recognized all too well.

Madra lifted his muzzle, releasing a howling wail of pain and grief that rose from ancient, ancestral genes and threatened to tear the rain from the sky.

Karen was there the next day, as she'd promised. Madra prowled around the clearing first, sniffing to make certain that she was alone and none of the others had followed her. He listened for the air-ripping sound of the aircraft that had passed over the mountainous forest many times since his escape; there was only the wind hissing through the pines. When he'd returned full circle while Karen sat patiently on the log, he slipped two-legged from the trees into the clearing in front of her.

Part of him wanted to go to her as he had in the past, wanted to crouch in front of her, tail wagging, so she could scratch his head and ears. He wanted to be part of the pack again—to submit to her will in the natural order of dominance. He wondered, if Karen gestured to him, if he would do exactly that. He forced that inclination deep inside, buried it in the hatred where he couldn't smell it at all.

"Hello, Madra," she said softly, revealing teeth in that strangely-threatening gesture that they called a smile. He didn't respond. On all fours now, he padded around her, sniffing. Unlike most humans, she didn't try to turn with him, but let him complete this smaller circuit until he lifted himself up to two legs in front of her. Her eyes went immediately to the collar he'd wrapped around his wrist.

"She's dead," he said, hearing his own tongue and mouth slur the words almost beyond recognition.

Karen nodded, her gaze moving from the leather on his wrist to his eyes, her face twisted with an empathy he could also smell. The water that humans leaked from their eyes when they were upset trickled down her cheek, a salt presence in the air. "Yes. She is. Tomas put her down two days ago. I couldn't stop it. I tried to get the board to stop him, but they wouldn't get back to me. Tomas was her pack supervisor; the standard protocol didn't allow me to stop him from making the decision. He said she attacked him when she came out of the anesthetic, that she was dangerous."

Madra whimpered, feeling the grief and emptiness hammer at him again. Karen started to reach out a hand as if to stroke his fur, and that made him growl deep in his throat and take a step back. Karen's eyes widened and she pulled her hand back. "I'm sorry, Madra," she said. "I truly am. I know what Soith meant to you."

He snorted. He shook his head fiercely, his brows knotting around his eyes. "No," he answered her simply, leaving all the rest unsaid. *You don't know. You couldn't know. You see others just like you every day. You've never been as alone as I am now.* "No." He dropped his head, sniffed at the leather again as he had all the night before, catching the faint traces of her scent still there, and wanting to drop to all fours and run, to succumb to the primal animal within him and mourn with blood and anguished howls.

He knew whose blood he wanted.

"I want you to come back with me," Karen was saying, her voice almost unheard against the roaring fury inside him. "I know, Madra. I know you don't want that, that you don't think you can trust me or management. I know you're afraid of what will happen if you go back and I understand, I do. But I'll be there with you. I promise. Corporate will have to listen to me because they'll be afraid that I might go public, and there are more people than you think who were sympathetic toward Easies even before you came along. I *will* go public if I have to. This isn't hopeless."

He was shaking his head again, already backing away from her and dropping down on all fours, the fur rising along his spine, and she hurried to speak, dropping down onto the ground in front of him. "Madra, don't. You can't hide here forever. Tomas will bring in your own kind to hunt you down next. Is that what you want? If they drag you in, it won't look as good. Give me a chance to help you."

"What you have," he answered, forming the words so she could understand, "I don't want." *So much to say, but the words come too slow. With Soith it had been different. With Soith there'd been no clumsiness, no impatient glances, no grimaces of misunderstanding. With Soith . . .* But it could never be "with Soith" again. "Go!" he grunted at her. He gave a primitive, wordless bark. "Go!"

"Madra," she persisted. "Listen to me—"

He bared his teeth. He growled. He raised the fur on his back. "Go!" he shouted again. He could smell the fear rising in her, the uncertainty. She rose slowly, not daring to look away from him, her hands open at her sides as if she were ready to fend him off if he sprang at her. She backed away, stepping carefully over the log.

"Madra, I'm so sorry for your loss," she said, still retreating. "I truly am. It's not what I wanted."

The sympathy in her voice smoothed the fur of his ruff. He covered his teeth. "I know," he said, giving her that much, at least. "Not going back. Not alive."

"But it doesn't have to be this way, Madra," she pleaded with him. "Things can change. *We* can make them change."

"You believe that," he told her, forcing the words out though he wanted only to snarl. "I don't. Not anymore."

Madra slept restlessly in the forest, hearing every sound and smelling every scent that the faint breeze below the pines brought to him. The sounds and smells mingled with dreams and memories. . . .

Madra had still been a pup when he realized that he was different. His mother, his litter-sibs, the other Easies—"E.C.s" or Enhanced Canines—who lived with them in the kennel, they were all . . . slow. They could barely speak more than a few words of Master speech and understood it far less well than he did. It quickly became obvious that he was different—smarter—than the others: he didn't have to be given instructions more than once; he could understand complex instructions without having to have them repeated; he could perform his tasks without needing much supervision at all. What

was difficult for him was to pretend, to slip into the
anonymity of the pack and act as they did.

The pack could smell his difference, and they didn't
like it. From as early as he could remember, he was
involved in dominance struggles. Moving him from his
birth pack to another didn't help. The Easies didn't like
him, even if the pack supervisors did.

It was enough to bring him to the attention of Karen.

Enhanced Genetics Corp had won the contract for for-
estation and wildlife stocking of the Schroeter Crater
Highlands near the Martian equator, and Karen was
EGC's District Supervisor, responsible for the thousand
or so humans and the packs of Easies who did most of
the grunt labor for the terraforming project. Easies were
vital to the labor-intensive project: accustomed to working together, loyal to their Pack Supervisors, short-lived
but quick to grow. More importantly, they were cheap:
the females, like their ancestral relations, bore offspring
in bunches. Best of all, they were legally nonsentient and
the property of EGC, who had developed the enhance-
ment program as part of their genetic research. As long
as EGC treated them no worse than one treated any
other working animal, there were no issues.

Madra, though, was a potential issue. Madra, by his very
existence, threatened to change the rules. He still remembered the conversation between Andrijana, his current
Pack Supervisor, and Karen; they spoke to each other as
if he weren't there, not worrying about whether he heard
or not, despite what Andrijana was telling Karen.

Habits, as Madra knew already, were hard even for
humans to break.

"I'm telling you, Karen, he's no normal Easy. Maybe
one of the techies back at corporate can tell you why,
whether it's some freak mutation or chance mix of genes.
I'm just a field supervisor. But I *do* know that this Easy
is making everyone uncomfortable, even in his own
pack. I sent Tomas a memo suggesting we neuter him
now just in case; Tomas wanted to put him down instead
rather than risk some newsie out of Bradbury getting
wind of this and deciding that Madra's a ticket back to
some Earthside assignment. I couldn't do that."

"Why not?" Madra felt Karen's gaze flick over him, though he was standing on all fours with his head and tail down, ears flattened against his furred skull, as any Easy did when being scolded by a PS.

"He's *smart*," Andrijana answered. "Not smart like an Easy. Smart like my little brother." Madra could smell the strange almost-fear scent from her as she gestured toward him and shivered. "*I* can't put him down. And I'll bet you can't either, once you talk to him."

. . . He didn't quite manage to sleep. To sleep deeply was to be vulnerable. Like all Easies and canines, he could keep some part of his consciousness alert even when his eyes were closed and his mind slumbering lightly. That first night after his escape, if he'd not been able to smell the approach of the search party or catch the faint, frantic thrumming of the helicopters in the thin air, they'd have caught him in the barren prairie grass meadows at the feet of Schroeter Crater. . . .

Karen *had* talked to him, many times over the next days, and he'd been neither neutered nor put down. He knew by her scent that she was, at least partially, afraid to make such a move, despite what she said. It was another thing he'd learned: humans might lie with their words, but they couldn't change their odors.

She was not his pack leader, like Andrijana. He could defy her, fight for dominance until it was clear that one of them had the stronger will. "I frighten you," he told her bluntly, and she'd nodded. "Why?"

"You're not supposed to exist," she answered. "That's why we didn't choose chimps or gorillas to enhance, even though on the physical level that would have been much easier; we wouldn't have had to reengineer the hands or do much neural grafting at all. But chimps . . . they're too close to us. They'd awaken too many guilt reflexes, too many echoes. And the legalities, the protests from Animal Rights organizations . . ." Her shoulders lifted in that strange human gesture he'd never entirely understood. "We're comfortable with dogs and our relationship to them. A dog with hands instead of front paws, that can stand and move on its hind legs at need and carry out complex commands, even say a few recognizable words—that's a special kind of dog, but it's still a dog. Loyal, helpful, easy to train, and comfortable working in a group . . . every desirable quality you could want in a worker. But still just a dog."

"Not me?"

She shook her head. The fear-scent increased. "Not you, Madra. You blur the boundaries. And you make us worry how many more like you we've inadvertently made."

. . .He'd managed to elude them for a week now. The last two days, he hadn't smelled or heard them at all, except for Karen—evidently corporate was waiting to see if she could bring him out herself. But they wouldn't give her much more time to do that, and he was certain it was a ploy. Where could he go? And even if he managed to stay free of them, for what purpose? What did it accomplish now that Soith was dead? In the end, it was all futile, and yet he couldn't stop struggling. . . .

Karen put him back in Andrijana's pack with the admonition that he should act as much as possible like the rest of the Easies. She told him—though he didn't really understand—about the uproar he'd caused within EGC, how the officers of the company and the board were divided about how to handle the crisis: afraid that if they disposed of "the problem" the news would still eventually leak out; afraid of the implications if they instead went public.

Paralyzed, they did nothing. Madra understood that. He'd been caught often enough between his instincts and a more dominant pack member's wishes. Back in the pack, he'd behaved, because that was what Andrijana and Karen (who he now realized was dominant over Andrijana as Andrijana was over him) wanted. And he watched the other Easies, wondering.

Within a month, while corporate EGC was still feuding within itself over him, he found the answer to the questions he had. There was at least one other like him, a female in Tomas' pack named Soith.

It wasn't anything overt. She'd masked herself well—

in that, perhaps, she'd been smarter than Madra, who
hadn't realized the implications of his behavior. But he
knew what to look for, the little signs that an Easy understood the humans too well or did things too quickly
or could speak better than anyone else in the pack.

But he knew. Tomas' pack, like Tomas himself, supervised the other packs' work. His Easies were all alphas
who had demonstrated exceptional qualities. Soith tried
to be no more than any of the rest of them, but she
couldn't hide herself from Madra.

"I know what you are," he told her, not caring about
the way the words were slurred and accented, trusting
that she would understand. She stared at him, a challenge that made him want to raise his hackles, but he
forced the impulse down. "You're like me. I know how
lonely you must feel sometimes."

She said nothing, did nothing. But he noticed, later
that day, that she was always there when he looked.
That evening, after the fast-grow saplings had been
planted and the modified prairie grass sown over new-
plowed ruddy soil, she passed close to him as Tomas
called the packs back to the transports that would take
them to ECG's base camp, and the scent of her was
receptive and curious.

"Yes," she said. "It's lonely."

Then she looked cautiously at Tomas, who was staring
at them, and dropped her head. She scuttled past him
into the transport.

. . . *he came alert, awake all at once with his fur bristling and ears up. Something moved in the trees not far
from him, a shadow in shadows. But there was no human
smell and the odor was familiar: one of the long-legged
deer EGC had let loose last year in the area, a doe. There
was another, smaller shadow next to the doe—a fawn.
Madra felt twin impulses warring within him—hunger
that made him want to leap from where he was hidden
in the bramble and bury his teeth in the fawn's neck, and
delight at seeing the new life in this refuge he'd helped to
create. And sorrow, too, knowing that this was something
he might have had himself. . . .*

*   *   *

It was never love, at least not in the sense that the humans used the word, bound and constrained with constant lust and emotions. Soith was a completion, a piece fitting a hole in himself he hadn't even known was there. She was part of him. She was essential.

Perhaps it *was* love. It was certainly something that no other Easy seemed to experience.

It was difficult to find places and times they could be together. Tomas' pack and Andrijana's rarely worked together. When they happened to be in the field during the same day, Tomas watched them; sometimes Karen would come in from the base office as well and Madra would notice her talking with Tomas and Andrijana. Once he heard Tomas tell Karen: "That fucking freak of yours likes my bitch too much . . ." After that, they tried to be more careful when he was around.

At night, the packs were separated into their own kennels—Easies were loyal to their own packs, but other Easies were not so placidly accepted. Still, the kennels weren't locked, and hands could open doors and no one particularly guarded the corridors between.

Those times were wonderful. For a few brief hours, none of the rest of it mattered: not the pack, not the human managers, not the cold thin air of the planet they were slowly changing. It was then that he realized why the humans were so concerned about them: they were something new—not Easies, but something more.

He remembered: the lick of her tongue on his fur; the smell of her musk; the reflection of himself in her eyes; her voice, telling him in tones that whispered in a joy so intense as to almost be pain, "Yes, I feel what you feel, I want what you want . . ."

He also remembered the last time, not far from where he was now . . . Soith had come to stand beside him, touching his side gently as a land-roller roared toward the work site on great, dust-raising tires. Karen stepped down from the cabin. Two men followed her, men he'd never seen before, and they called Tomas and Andrijana over to them.

The wind brought the taste of dust. The wind brought

the scent of revulsion and antipathy. The wind brought the
sound of angry voices as Karen shouted something that
made the faces of the men tighten and scowl.

Soith growled, a low sound deep in her throat; Madra
echoed her, the response coming from some primitive
place within. The fur crawled on his spine, his lips curled
back.

"Soith, *come!*" Tomas called, waving. Karen said
nothing; Madra caught the scent of defeat around her.
"You, too, Madra. Come here! *Come!*"

Soith looked at Madra. There was no need for words.
They ran in the opposite direction, as one. Together.

He remembered also the high cracking sound in the
air as they fled and Soith's yelp of pain. He turned, ready
to stand over her and fight, but she pushed at him even
as she was falling, the dart dangling from her side. "Go!"
she said. That one word, only. Dominance was in her
voice. He obeyed.

*. . . the smell woke him first: a tang of metal and oil
that always spoke of humankind. Even as he came fully
alert, lifting his head as he remained crouched in his
cover, he heard it: the howl of packs. . . .*

. . . the howl of packs . . .

The howling drifted through morning fog, mournful
and muffled. This was what Madra had feared most. It
was one thing to be hunted by the humans with their
machines; it was another to be hunted by his own kind.
His own pack, for he heard familiar voices among the
group.

He wondered if any of the Easies found the task dis-
tasteful or immoral, if it bothered any of them or was
simply another job they'd been ordered to do.

The wind was in his favor still, blowing toward him
from down the slope of the ancient crater's ridge. Judging from the sounds and the smells, there were three
packs in the hunt with his own old pack in the middle.
From farther up the steepening hills of the crater's rim,
near the High Lake that filled the kilometers-wide de-
pression of the actual crater, there was the sound of

helicopters, hovering and waiting for him to be driven from the cover of the trees as he fled from the packs.

That's what they expected him to do. That's what any Easy would do in his situation. So he would do something else. The rocks here were glassy, primarily stone melted by the violent crash of the meteor into the Martian surface and flung away from the impact site. They littered the new soil, the EGC-manufactured dirt. Madra dug out a hand-sized stone, then smashed it against a larger boulder a few feet away. With a few strikes, he had a sufficiently sharp and long edge. Sniffing the air, growling so faintly that the sound was only a rumble in his chest, he moved along the line of the slope.

Yes . . . the deer were still there, nested already for the day, though the doe was awake and nervous from the sounds of the packs. Madra approached, carefully staying upwind of the deer, then at the last moment he sprang forward at full speed. The doe leaped in alarm, scrambling away and crashing through the brush as the fawn tried to follow its mother. But the fawn was slower and clumsier and Madra crashed into it before it took two strides, hands around neck, his teeth ripping into the soft flesh there, tasting the sweet hot blood that pulsed out. The fawn whimpered and went down, thrashing wildly as Madra continued to tear open the wound.

A final twitch. Wide-eyed, scented with terror, the fawn died. Madra stood up, standing two-legged over the creature he'd slain. Regret filled him, and sadness at having destroyed such fragile, new beauty. "I'm sorry," he said. Then he bent down once more, crouching alongside the fawn as he sliced its belly open with the crude blade he'd made. He pulled out the entrails and smeared his body with the blood and gore.

He dropped the rock on the ground near the corpse. He found a pine that had conveniently low branches and pulled himself awkwardly up. His body wasn't well-designed for climbing, but he didn't have to go far to be shaded by the pine boughs. He hugged the trunk with his hand, pressing his befouled body as close to the bark as he could on the upslope side.

He waited.

It was Tomas' pack who finally came into view. They milled around the fawn's torn body for a few moments, excited by the sight and smells, growling and barking madly, but they didn't catch Madra's own scent, masked by the blood of the deer.

"Tell Tomas?" he heard one of them grunt, and another answer: "No." He could hear Tomas struggling through the bracken well behind the pack. The Easies swarmed around the deer once more, sniffing, then hurried off upslope again, howling. He listened to their receding cries, heard Tomas' boots crunch over dead branches as he strode over to the fawn's body, smelled the man's exhaustion and irritation, caught the metallic whiff of the rifle he carried cradled in his right arm. "What the hell?" the man grunted. Madra could glimpse him, scuffing at the bloodied ground and staring at the violated carcass. "Jesus . . ." He shook his head, then started away again in the wake of his pack.

Madra let go of the trunk. He dropped to the ground, crouching down and snatching up the rock all in the same motion.

"Tomas!" he called.

Tomas had already begun to spin around with the noise. Even as Madra uttered the man's name—a curse, a howl—he slashed at the man with the rock, slicing him across the right arm. Blood flowed from the long, ragged cut and Tomas dropped the rifle. Madra kicked it away as Tomas staggered back, clutching his wounded arm.

Fragrant darkness streamed between the man's fingers.

He stared at Madra, eyes wide and radiating fear. Madra knew what he must look like, smeared and sticky with clotted blood, teeth bared. The man's fear pleased him. "You're a dead dog. Easy now, Madra," Tomas hissed, his eyes narrowed with pain. "Mad dogs get shot."

Madra didn't bother to answer. He hefted the rock and took a step toward the man, who stumbled backward and nearly fell. Madra barked, a sound of exultation; he rushed forward and pushed Tomas down hard. He stood over the man and lifted his hand, the edge of the stone glittering like glass.

"Madra, don't!" She'd come from the side, out of the wind, but the voice was familiar and strong enough that he hesitated, glancing toward her. "Please—don't. I know what you're feeling, but there's still a chance. I've talked to corporate. They want to know what happened, how you and Soith came to be; they want to talk with you and study you. They want to understand. That's all. But I can't promise that if you hurt Tomas—they'll think you're too dangerous."

"Soith," Madra raged, her name the only word he could utter in his fury.

"I know," Karen said. "But you have to show them that you're beyond what a renegade Easy might do. Throw the rock away."

He forced away enough of the rage to form words, though they were slurred with froth and his muzzle was furrowed. "What would *you* do?" he barked at her.

He wondered whether she understood the rest, all the words he could think but couldn't say. *What if he'd killed your mate? What if you believed this was your only chance? What if you didn't want to be studied and probed, but only wanted to be free, with her, the one he's taken from you. The* only *one* . . . Karen looked at Tomas, then back to Madra.

"I would do what's human," she said. "That's all."

"I'm not human," he answered.

Madra looked down at Tomas. He felt the satisfying weight of the rock in his hand, the choices it represented.

His hand moved.

After the Fall

by Kristine Kathryn Rusch

Kristine Kathryn Rusch is an award-winning author in three genres. In 2001, she won science fiction's Hugo for best novelette, her second—making her the first person in the history of SF to win the Hugo for both editing and fiction. Under her pen name Kris Nelscott, she won the Best Historic Mystery Award (and was nominated for an Edgar), and as Kristine Grayson, she won the Best Paranormal Romance Award from *Romantic Times*. Even though she's published more than fifty novels, her first love is and always will be short fiction.

TO UNDERSTAND the entire story, we have to start at the beginning—and the story starts, ironically enough, with my very first memory.

I am three, a small three, especially for a boy whose male relatives are all six-two and two hundred and thirty pounds of solid muscle. If you look at pictures from the time (and there's no reason why you should), you'd see a wisp of a child, hair so blond it's almost white, skin so white it's almost pale. Even in photographs taken in full sunlight, I tended to disappear, almost as if I were a ghost instead of an actual living boy.

The memory is mostly sensation: me on my back in the cold spring grass, a weight pressing down on my shoulder, hot drool dripping onto my face as I screamed and screamed and screamed. If I close my eyes, I can still feel the terror—the absolute conviction that this monster on top of me, teeth bared, claws scraping my fragile skin, is going to eat me—that the powerful jaws, so close to my face, are going to open, taking me inside with a single gulp.

If you hear the family tell it, the truth is less dramatic: our new neighbors, Sissy and Arnold Kappel, are holding a barbecue in the backyard. My father has just mixed the drinks—his specialty even now—when Michael Kappel, the six-year-old who resents being told to play with me, chases the family's Great Dane across the yard.

I run, and the dog thinks I'm playing. He chases me, tongue lolling, barking happily, with Michael Kappel—already on his way to being the neighborhood bully—scurrying nimbly behind.

I head for our house, for the safety of the back door, when the dog pounces, knocking me down. His paws are on my shoulder, his tail still wagging, as he licks my face.

The parents don't come over right away because they think my screams are cries of joy, just Peter's delight at his first introduction to a dog.

A dog, mind you, who weighs six times what I weigh; a dog who, when he stands on his hind legs, is nearly as tall as my mother was; a dog who, five years later, is put down for biting a toddler so badly that the poor kid never regains the use of her hand.

The story continues—college, graduate school, assistant professorships, until I finally amass enough experience to be offered tenure. Fortunately, I was offered tenure at a university I love, in Montana, a state I adore.

During those years, I had grown into my heritage, reaching six-two at sixteen, just like my grandfather and father before me. Unlike them, however, I remained whip-thin—"rangy," the women out West called it—and my pale skin had become sun-baked, leathery, and tough. When I put on a cowboy hat, I looked like an icon of the American West.

Such a man needs a dog, or so the locals believed, and everyone tried to foist off their newest puppy or a particularly well-behaved hound on me. I smiled politely but didn't go near the animals, claiming allergies I didn't have so that I wouldn't risk showing the fear that I felt every time a dog got too close to me.

Montanans believed their dogs were their best friends, silent companions who forgave everything. It wasn't unusual to see grown men, hats pulled low over their foreheads and toothpicks in their mouths, driving their four-by-fours, one arm resting on top of the steering wheel and a big dog—generally a collie, a lab, or some kind of hunting dog—sitting in the passenger seat beside them.

I happened to wear cowboy boots and faded denims to class, and I had bought an old farmhouse just outside of Missoula, but I wasn't a cowboy any more than I was a Westerner. The dog attack incident had happened in upstate New York, and my parents, still cosmopolitan socialites, wondered what made their son, with his Ivy League education and all his bright shiny promise, head off for parts unknown the moment Yale sent him his embossed Get-Out-of-Jail-Free card.

No one understood me and I thought that was great. I thought that was the way life should be.

That June—the month everything changed—I attended five weddings, two in the space of a single weekend, was invited on and turned down three separate hiking adventures, and had broken up with six women over the past six months. Spring in that part of Montana lingers damn near into July, and one cool sunny day, I decided to leave my home study, where I was examining two new statistics books, sent to me so that I could see if I wanted to upgrade the text for the fall course.

Reading about numbers was pure joy for me, but that afternoon, with the sun beating into the double-hung windows decorating my corner office, I felt restless. I decided to pull on my boots and walk the property to see what kind of presents the winter storms had left me.

I had twenty acres, much of it sporadically cultivated. I let one of my neighbors use a section as a garden, and rented out another section to the neighbor on the other side for his mother's double-wide.

The rest I wandered when I could. Over the years, I had worn a small hiking path along the property's edge. The path went in and out of a large stand of pine, and one entire area cascaded down to a creek that I shared with yet a third neighbor.

No one could understand why I didn't have a garden, or start a small tree farm, or keep horses so that this beautiful land wouldn't go to waste. But over the years, I'd come to appreciate my solitude, and having twenty acres all around me didn't feel like isolation, it felt like protection.

I put on my hiking boots and thick jacket, and started my hike.

The birds had returned full force, and the sun made them sing. I heard a variety of song as I passed in and out of the trees. The air was fresh, carrying on it a hint of pine, the crisp clearness of the creek, and a faint tang I could only identify as spring. The path was still spring-muddy, with deep pockets of rainwater and mush along the edges. If I wasn't careful, I would find myself up to my ankles in muck.

No tree limbs had fallen, but in several areas, the rains and heavy spring runoff had washed entire sections of the path away. I went around, over, above, whatever got me past, and as I walked, found myself thinking about the texts I'd been reading.

Statistics wasn't my favorite subject. I preferred the classes I taught to my graduate students, classes in theory and equations so pure that contemplating them made me feel more than human.

Statistics and its cousin probability were the workmanlike courses of the advanced math student, classes that attempted to define the world we lived in, not rise above it.

The professors who had written the two texts I was reading seemed to revel in that world, loving the way that numbers defined it, the way that the path defined the boundaries of my land. Unlike the path, though, the numbers didn't wash away. They formed a permanent barrier, a fence or a rock wall, something that outlined the edges of the world and wouldn't let us see past it.

Perhaps that was what I did not like about statistics. I appreciated definition, but I liked my mind to roam free, to explore possibilities that human thought hadn't entirely considered. One of my Ph.D. students once claimed that she believed people who studied mathematics—taking it to its outer edges—learned to think differently than the average human. At some point, she said, the mathematician's mind reformed, becoming something greater than it had been before.

I liked the theory and had never forgotten it. She had taken her mathematics Ph.D., taught for a year or two, and decided that wasn't enough. The last I had heard, she was attending Divinity School, continuing her quest for the great beyond.

When she left, she had given me permission to build on the theory, and I toyed with it, especially on walks like this one, where the air was so fresh, the sunlight so bright, the birds so loud, that part of me assumed this world couldn't be real. Sometimes I felt like it was a fevered dream, conjured by a delusional mind, in search of something better.

I hadn't been looking—and I stepped on a washed-out area, my foot seeking purchase where there was none.

I tumbled forward, my leg still extended. When it finally hit the earth, my ankle buckled beneath me, and I landed with a thud on my side. The breath slammed out of my body, and for a stunned moment, I felt like I had when the Great Dane stood on me, airless, frightened, about to die.

My weight forced the mud to move again, and a tiny avalanche of dirt, water, and rock carried me down to the creek. I grabbed at anything, my fingers finding mud so deep that it felt like a river.

A boulder caught me at the very edge of the creek. My back slammed into it, sending a rocketing pain up my spine.

But my breath came back, knocked into me, apparently, the way it had been knocked out. I gasped like a drowning man who had been dragged into the air.

I sat up, dizzy, drenched, caked in mud. The creek, swollen with spring runoff, passed two feet below the boulder. If I hadn't hung up here, I might have fallen in, got swept away, and drowned for real.

I'd fallen on slides before, and knew the best way out of them was to move horizontally across until I found solid ground. I wedged my hands behind me, pushing myself up, and felt a tug on my left leg.

My boot was caught between two smaller rocks, shoved in at an impossible angle by the force of my fall. I pulled, but couldn't get the boot free.

Then I leaned forward and tried to wedge it out.

That didn't work either.

My teeth were chattering from the cold, my fingers already red beneath their muddy surface. Staying out of the creek was lucky only if I could get back to the house to get warm. If I was trapped here, even on this sunny day, I could die of exposure, thanks to my wet clothes and the icy temperatures deep in the mud.

The thought made my numbing fingers more nimble, and I dug the muck out of my boot laces, struggling to untie them. I parted the eyelet, wiggled the tongue. A cool breeze found my foot and I hadn't realized until then how warm that foot felt, as if it were somewhere different than the rest of me.

I tugged again, planning to slip my foot out of the boot, then grab the boot and head across the slide on my escape back to civilization.

But my boot wasn't the thing that was caught. My ankle bones were wedged between those rocks, shoved in by the force of my fall, or perhaps by some odd movement of water and slime, and nothing I could do, it seemed, would set me free.

No one knew I had gone for a walk. No one even knew the route I normally took. This path was so isolated that the only footprints on it were mine, even though the mud had clearly been part of it since the last storm weeks before.

The neighbor's garden was on the opposite side of the property, and the double-wide was near the road, at least ten acres and a ridgeline away.

I had no appointments, nothing to do until the following week, when summer school started. I rarely answered my phone so my friends—who were probably more accurately termed acquaintances—wouldn't think anything amiss if I failed to talk to them for days.

Not even my parents, who called once a week just like they had done since I'd gone to college, would find my silence unusual. Sometimes I would take trips and forget to tell them I'd be out of town.

It was just me, the mud, and the creek below. And the sun, disappearing behind the Bitterroots quicker than I ever could have imagined.

*   *   *

He appeared on the boulder at twilight. He looked like I always thought Puck should look: tiny, square, dark, his eyebrows slashing his forehead, his lips permanently turned up in mirth.

He had wings, thin as gauze and almost invisible in the dimming light, and as he peered down at me, I felt even colder, as if through his vision alone he could steal my soul.

He wasn't real and that didn't scare me. I accepted it as part of my experience, a delusion brought on by pain, exposure, and trauma.

"Your path brought you here," he said.

"Of course it did," I snapped. I was cold, hungry, and more than a little angry—at myself, at him, at being forced to see imaginary creatures simply because I had not been paying attention.

"Not the path you fell from," he said. "The path you walked every day of your life."

The last thing I needed was for a hallucination to spout New Age crap at me. "You gonna get me out of here?"

"It's not my job to free you."

Because he wasn't real. But there was a slight chance that he was. An ever-so-slight chance, but one I had to take advantage of. "All you have to do is climb down here, help me move the rocks that are holding my ankle."

"Rocks that broke your ankle, and no, I can't."

Because I had made him up, of course. Although he shook his head slightly, as if he'd heard my thoughts. His voice, when he continued, sounded slightly indignant.

"They're rock outcroppings, part of the layer of rock underneath. They will not move."

"Then help me dig my way out."

"They narrow into a V. Removing the mud will not help you."

He was merely confirming what I had learned during my long afternoon, my fingernails broken and bleeding from the force of my lessons. But I didn't want to hear his answers. At least not spoken aloud.

"Then go to the road, flag someone down. Get help."

He leaned back and smiled. A slow small smile. "Even if your people could see me, they wouldn't believe me."

Strange that I did. Perhaps it was part of the experience. Perhaps I was unconscious. I certainly accepted this fantasy creature as if he were part of a dream.

But that didn't stop me from trying to save myself. "If you don't help, I'll die here."

He shrugged, and his wings glistened. They weren't transparent as I had initially thought. They were iridescent.

"It was your choice." His voice rumbled.

"I didn't choose to walk some life path," I said. "Things happen."

"Do they?" He turned his head toward me. The movement was not human. It was insectlike; his entire head swiveled so that he could see me more clearly.

"Yes, of course they do. I didn't plan to fall today. It just happened."

"Because you forgot to watch where you walked, something people have warned you about often." He squatted, his hands dangling between his knees.

"That's an easy prediction to make," I said, not trying to hide my sarcasm. "Everyone gets warned about that."

"And most people heed. You never have. You prefer to analyze, to think of statistics and numbers and equations as if that makes you different. As if that makes you special."

A chill ran through me, making my shivers grow. He was guessing. Of course he was guessing. What else would a mathematician, who had just finished reading statistics texts, be thinking about?

"You haven't heeded anyone's advice," he said. "You have gone along, ignoring everyone. And now you shall be ignored. Forgotten, even in death. They won't find you for nearly a month, you know."

That sounded likely. I supposed, if I had known the average time it took to find someone missing in the woods—someone whose movements were known—and then add to it the number of days it would take before someone realized that I was missing—

"But we can change that," he said.

Had he been speaking? I hadn't noticed. Concentration was becoming difficult. My shivering had grown worse. Wasn't that a sign that hypothermia had set in?

"Change what?"

"Your time of death, if you want."

I squinted at him. The sun had nearly disappeared. All I could see was his outline, dark and foreboding.

I wasn't sure if I believed him, but I wasn't sure if my belief mattered. I had a hunch he would do what he wanted to, whether I liked it or not.

"Why would you change my time of death?"

He shrugged again and I wished I could see his face. "Why not?" he said, and vanished.

Actually, he didn't vanish. Everything vanished. The woods, the creek, the cold. The next thing I knew, I was sitting in an ancient station wagon, the radio blaring ZZ Top. A piece of plastic dug into my back. The seat was ripped, even though I had no idea how I knew that.

The station wagon was parked in front of a church. The building was large and gaudy, with a white cross rising from the center like a malformed spire. The land around me was flat and the streets carved into blocks.

Even, uniform blocks, covered with houses—all decked out in ticky-tacky and lined up in a row.

I shivered again. Or for the first time. I wasn't certain.

I had no idea how I had gotten here, or if this was yet another hallucination. I must have been pretty far gone—and that had happened fast, hadn't it?—in order to be unconscious and dreaming.

A woman came out of the church. She wore a gray knit dress with a flared skirt and a pair of low-slung pumps that matched the cheap purse she carried over her arm. Her brown hair swung in rhythm to the skirt, and my breath caught.

She looked familiar.

She smiled when she saw me, and then she jogged down the last part of the sidewalk. When she got to the car, she pulled the passenger door open.

"Well?" she said as she got in. "Aren't you going to ask me how it went?"

I couldn't remember her name, but I did remember

her voice, telling me that mathematics reshaped the brain, that human thought could reach beyond the mundane—

"Aren't you?" she asked again, her smile now gone.

"How'd it go?" I tried to make myself sound interested.

She reached forward and shut off the radio. "I don't know how you can stand that stuff."

I couldn't. At least, not now. Or then. I knew what was going on. I'd seen it in countless movies and now my brain had chosen to re-create the plot, perhaps as a way to ease my pain in dying.

". . . and are you listening?" she asked.

"Sorry."

"Peter, this is important."

I nodded.

"Are you all right?"

Obviously not. Obviously something had gone wrong here, but I wasn't about to tell her that. "Fine."

"Do you want me to drive? You look funny."

It would be better if she drove. She, at least, knew where we would be going.

I got out of the driver's side and walked around the back. The station wagon was full of junk—toys, folded comic books, theology texts, and a blanket. A child's safety seat had been installed behind the passenger seat. I hadn't noticed before.

She was waiting for me at the passenger door. She kissed me, and I felt nothing. I should have felt something, right? This was my fantasy after all.

"I didn't get it," she said, and I heard the disappointment in her familiar voice. "The committee told me that I would be better off in some ivory tower, that a church had pragmatic concerns, and I was too intellectual for them. I guess they're trying to draw from outside the university neighborhood. They didn't like Pastor Wilkinson, despite his reputation as a scholar. No one warmed to him."

She sighed, squared her shoulders, then walked toward the driver's side. I was supposed to soothe her, I knew, but I was at a disadvantage—I hadn't seen her in nearly a decade, and I couldn't remember her name.

I slipped into the passenger seat, listening to the rhythm of her speech, making an occasional "uh-huh" or "mmm" in the pauses. The irony was that I didn't even like *Twilight Zone* stories. I always thought men who dealt with the devil were dumb, and I certainly had no respect for whiners like Jimmy Stewart in *It's a Wonderful Life* or Nicholas Cage in *The Family Man*.

In fact, it looked like I had walked into a new version of the latter two films. A man, enjoying his single life, discovers he's isolated and finds contentment in domestic mess, a wife, some children (I glanced at the car seat behind me and shivered), and a dog.

Always a dog.

I would have wagered that Jimmy Stewart had a dog, too, although I couldn't remember one. I tended to blank out dogs from movies.

". . . not right," she said, "asking you to go out of state, lose your job so that I can find mine. I could teach or write a few books. And then I could stay home with the kids."

I looked at her. She had crow's-feet around her eyes, and gray dusted her hair. Sorrow and disappointment lined her face, but it still remained pleasant. I could get used to that face—if I could only remember her name.

"It sounds like you're giving up," I said, because I knew that "mmm-mmm" would no longer cut it.

She turned the car onto a side street. I had no idea how she knew where she was. The houses in this subdivision—obviously built thirty years before—looked the same as all the others.

"No one wants a philosopher anymore," she said as she turned the wheel again. She pulled into a driveway, and stopped so suddenly that I jerked against the seat belt. "They either want someone who is positive about who she is and what she knows or they want the same old thing, a warm loving people-person who gives hugs and canned sermons on Christmas Eve."

She opened the car door and stepped out. I stared inside the open garage. An ancient Volkswagen Rabbit hid inside, surrounded by two bright pink bicycles, with ribbons hanging off their handlebars. Matching helmets hung on the seats. Another bicycle, boy's style, built for speed, hung on the wall, next to skis that looked like they hadn't been used. A snowblower, a riding lawn mower, gardening equipment scattered along a tool bench.

It looked like she—we?—had been here a long time.

I unbuckled the seat belt, opened the door, and got out. The air was humid, and instantly I started to sweat. The front door opened and a dog bounded out. A sheepdog, like they use in the movies, only this one had tangled hair (no mats, though) and bows.

Pink bows.

He barked as he came toward me, pink bows sailing in the breeze.

I pressed against the car, wanting to get back inside, but knowing there wasn't enough time.

"No!" I shouted at the creature that sent me here. "I won't do it!"

Behind the dog came two little girls, maybe six, obviously twins. They looked like my cousins had at that age, just as willowy, just as determined.

"I won't!" I shouted, not looking toward the sky because I had to keep my eye on that dog. "I'll be Ward Cleaver, but I won't have a damn dog. *And you can't make me!*"

"Of course I can."

The creature sounded so reasonable, up there on the boulder. The sun had vanished completely, but a thin silver light bathed everything. The creek looked beautiful, the water reflecting the light. The water babbled as it hurried past, as if reminding me that I would have been no better off had I fallen in there.

I was so cold that I had turned numb. My clothes had caked on me, and my ankle ached.

"No sense in making you more miserable than you already are." He turned toward me, this Puck-like creature, and I realized that the silver light was coming off his skin. He was the thing that glowed. I had never seen anything like it and because this was my hallucination, I was all right with that.

I even found it slightly fascinating.

"What are you doing here?" I asked. "Why did you come to me?"

He was still crouched, hands dangling between his legs. He'd clearly been holding that position for hours, and it didn't seem to bother him. His legs seemed longer than they had before—or maybe I had just noticed them—and his arms were short. Like a grasshopper's.

"Her name," he said, answering a question I hadn't asked and ignoring the one I had, "was Annabeth. What I want to know is how could a man as intelligent as you are miss the attraction? She is perhaps the only woman in your sphere who thinks like you do, about the larger issues, stretching her mind, and you refused to take note."

I had noticed how she thought. I hadn't noticed much else, true enough. But she had been a student.

A student with long brown hair and wide, almond-shaped eyes. A student who wore a light perfume that reminded me of summer rainstorms. A student who had clutched her philosophy of mathematics books as if they held the secret to the universe.

It seemed a shame to marry her, force her into the 2.5 children mode, buy her a dog and a station wagon (probably because we had been unable to afford the now-obligatory minivan), and live as if we were just like everyone else.

He hopped to the edge of the boulder, peered at me, and blinked his round eyes. They had slits in the middle of the pupil, like cat's eyes.

"So," he said, "you would have been Ward Cleaver if it weren't for the dog. Do dogs frighten you that much?"

Unbidden, the stench of the Great Dane's breath filled my nostrils and I could almost sense the drool on my face. I shuddered, deep, racking, and it had less to do with the fading chill (fading. That was bad, wasn't it?) than it did with the memory of that monstrous dog.

"I don't want one," I said stubbornly. "I never have."

"Nor have you wanted a wife or a child or any human contact at all. How strange that all is." He leaned closer, extending his neck. Something brushed my face. Feelers. Soft, translucent, even in the silver light from his skin.

"If you have magic," I said, "you can spell me out of here."

His head retracted, the feelers gone. Only the sensation of their touch remained, burning against my benumbed cheeks. "You misunderstand the nature of our encounter. I give you choices. I do not make them."

"Between dying here and living there? What kind of choice is that?"

He scuttled farther from me, hunkered in the center of the boulder, and then grinned, Puck no longer. Now he was the Cheshire Cat—all teeth and attitude.

"It's the usual choice. Most don't want anything else."

"I'm not most," I said.

"I should have known that when I realized you could see me." His smile faded. With his back foot, he reached up and scratched behind his wing. A hum, the cross between a violin and a sustained piano chord, sounded faintly in the evening air.

My cheeks were feeling flushed. In fact, I was growing warm.

"I'll have to be more creative," he said, and for a moment, I thought I was the one who had spoken.

My confusion was not good. Not good at all. I wondered if we both knew it or if there was only one of us. If there was only one, then of course we both knew the entire situation was not good, because he had to be a part of me.

But if he wasn't—

If he wasn't—

Annabeth sat across from me, stirring a large ice coffee topped with whipped cream. She was the girl I remembered, not the woman she would become. Her hair, long and brown, was tucked behind her ears, and her face was narrow—a young face, filled with promise, none of it fulfilled.

The coffee shop smelled of roasting beans—a sign behind her claimed that the place roasted its own—and behind the counter, a coffee grinder roared. Conversation hummed around us—mostly young people, wearing that season's uniform of black leather and pale makeup.

I recognized the shop. Far from campus, near the high school and the bad section of town. The kids here didn't carry books or homework. Instead, they hauled wads of money from their jacket pockets and traded tiny bags for cash.

Annabeth looked uncomfortable. Her backpack hung over her knee, as if she was afraid someone would steal the books. Overhead, Ella Fitzgerald sang Cole Porter— the eerie song about Miss Otis, who regretted missing lunch, but didn't regret murder. I learned to love Fitzgerald in this place; I used to come alone, read a book, and spy on the parts of humanity I would never inhabit.

Even though I wasn't cold, even though I clutched a warm mug of coffee between my hands, I knew I was still sitting in the mud near my house, imagining that a creature which was half-human, half-insect had control of my mind.

"I've never been any place like this before," Annabeth said, and the words echoed in my memory.

We had been here before—I had brought us here, at her request. Not that she wanted exotic coffee, but because she wanted a conversation someplace where we could be alone.

I suspected then that she had been thinking of my house or my office, a place that was both intimate and personal, but I was conscious of the fact of the differences in our status. Even though I didn't want any other faculty member to overhear what she had to say, I didn't want to risk being caught inviting a female student into my home.

She looked over her shoulder. "I can't believe they're all in high school."

The other kids did look too tough to be in school. I had suspected most of them weren't. Or I remembered suspecting it.

I knew this conversation now. I had shoved it into the deepest recesses of my memory, but it was returning, with all of its despair and embarrassment (hers), and slowly dawning understanding (mine).

On that afternoon, in a place filled with Goths, Annabeth—Ph.D. candidate and future theology student— propositioned me.

I had turned her down.

And now the creature on the rock was giving me a second chance to accept.

"No," I said, not willing to go through the banality a second time. The small talk, the flushed moment where she spoke of her attraction, the way she had looked at me when she talked about how much she admired my mind.

Annabeth frowned at me. "What?"

"No." I looked up, like I had wanted to do when that sheepdog was running toward me. "I'm not changing my mind. I lied. No Ward Cleaver. No marriage. Not everyone needs 2.5 kids and a dog."

Annabeth's face turned white. "I wasn't going to talk to you about marriage, I was—"

And then I was back in the cold. A moon had risen overhead, its white light negating some of the silver flowing from my strange companion. An occasional throb from my ankle told me that my body still existed—although it existed in a strange half-world where it was sometimes cold, mostly numb, and no longer feeling like my own.

The creek burbled past, strains of Ella still echoing in my ears. I had made myself forget Annabeth because she had made me uncomfortable. That afternoon was not the best of my life.

"I already made that decision," I said, sounding peevish. I never sounded peevish, but beneath my bravado, I was scared. A night was going by, and I was wet, cold, and exposed. I had no idea how much longer I had before the life leached out of me, one degree at a time. "I don't know why you thought that was creative."

The creature hadn't been looking at me although I hadn't realized it. When his head swiveled, I was startled. The front of his skull was shaped the same as the back of his skull. Only his glowing eyes—red now that complete darkness had fallen—marked the difference.

"No dogs, you said." His voice rasped. I hadn't noticed that before. Or perhaps I was adding details, recreating him as I slipped deeper into delirium. "So I went back to a fork on the path. Allowed you yet another choice. Which, you claim, you would not take."

"Had not taken," I said. "Will never take."

His eyes widened, glowing beacons in the darkness.

"See?" I said, the anger returning. "That's what I don't get. You wish-granters, all of you have such conservative tendencies. You seem to think alternate lifestyles are bad, that people should live one way and one way only. Don't you understand that *It's a Wonderful Life* is a movie about how to live with failure? Its message is to take what's offered and be content. The people who love that movie are people who fail to strive, who need some affirmation of their humdrum life."

"You have a humdrum life," the creature said.

"I have a life I like." Except for this part. The dying part. But I didn't know anyone who was looking forward to that. "I don't want a wife. I don't want to live in a suburb. I like it here."

"In the mud," he said.

I shook my head. "On my land."

"Where you'd rather die than go back and start over."

I crossed my arms, felt the swollen material of my jacket sleeves push against my chest. Some feeling was left, then, but not much.

Actually, dying of exposure wasn't a bad way to go— considering all of the other possibilities. I wasn't going to be hatcheted to death by one of my students or shot by a jealous lover. I wasn't going to suffer through operation after operation trying to stem a wasting disease like cancer, and I wouldn't feel the sudden, sharp, breathless pain of a massive heart attack.

"You're being difficult," he said, and it sounded as if he were angry at me for being content with my life.

"No," I said. "You are. All I did was ask you for help out of this mud."

"I am not here to help you." He said this slowly, patiently, as if he were speaking to a particularly dumb child. "Oddly enough, this is not about you."

Then he blinked. The effect was eerie, like one of those slow motion nature videos of a reptile watching its prey. The redness vanished for just a moment, only to reappear even more powerfully than before.

"If it's not about me," I snapped, "what is it about?"

His eyes closed again, and then his skin stopped sending its luminescent glow across the boulder. Even the moon seemed to have faded.

Blackness grew . . .

. . . and I realized it was rain, so thick and heavy on the windshield that I couldn't see the road. The headlights illuminated drops right in front of them and little else. I slowed, not knowing where I was.

The car was old, familiar, the used BMW I bought as an indulgence in the early 1990s. I had sold it when I got tenure, splurging on a brand-new four-by-four, bright red, which suited my life in the Montana countryside.

An NPR voice—chatty, deep, and knowledgeable—tracked midterm election results, reciting Congressional districts state by state—as a corner loomed ahead of me, suddenly clearer than the rest of the road.

The rain was letting up just enough to let my headlights defeat the darkness. I saw the large white lump ahead in time to swerve around it.

My back wheels skidded, and I spun, crossing lanes, circling madly, the car hydroplaning. I fought the spin, pumped the brake, and eventually, the wheels caught. I eased the car to the side of the road, and sat there, my heart beating so hard that I could barely catch my breath.

Sweat ran down my face, even though I was still unnaturally cold. My fingers looked blue in the light from the dash.

I had been through this before, too. But there had been no woman beside me, no dog or children looming in my future. Just me, the car, and the deserted road—the highway coming off of Lolo Pass. I had been to Idaho for a seminar, and I mistakenly decided to drive home instead of staying the night.

Tired, hungry, horrible weather. I had vowed, after this trip that I would be more cautious with myself and my life in the future.

Obviously that took.

I shivered, then wiped the sweat off my face. What point was the creature making now? I remembered sitting here, remembered putting the car in gear, remembered switching to an oldies station because I needed something to match the rhythm of my pounding heart.

I knew how this night played out. I went home, slept, and woke with pulled muscles in my back. Then I went to my probabilities class to see how well they had done with the election results, not caring one way or another, and never bothering to do that lecture again.

What would one swerving car, one near miss, have to do with a slide in the mud on a spring day?

My brights were off. Sometimes I did that in heavy rains, finding the glare of the brights lessened visibility more than adding it. I flicked them on, and saw the thing in the road again, a white lump that looked like a matted rug.

I hadn't seen that the first time I went through this night—not after the spin. If I remembered correctly, I saved myself from the spin, rested a moment, and drove east to Missoula.

Instead, I felt an obligation. If I didn't move that rug, someone else might not be as lucky as I was. Someone else might slam into a tree, hit a car in the opposite lane, or tumble down the embankment into heaven knew what lay below.

It wasn't until I had gotten out of the car, pulled up the hood on my Gore-Tex, that I realized how cold I was. I shivered again, and felt the wet, even though my clothes beneath the Gore-Tex were dry. The rain had stopped, but the pine trees dripped on me, and the road was slick. I had nearly reached the carpet when I realized it wasn't a carpet at all.

It was a dog. A sheepdog. And its sides went up and down as it took shallow breaths.

No one stood near it. There wasn't a car down the embankment. The dog had been hit, and no one had done anything.

Leaving it to me.

"You son of a bitch," I muttered to the creature. I supposed I could call to him, and he would probably pull me from this past, like he had pulled me from the previous one, like he had pulled me from the alternate time line.

But I was probably dying, just like that damn dog. My

chances were nearly used up, and all of this was a figment of my imagination anyway.

Besides, this wasn't like a wife not getting a job, or failing to take a woman up on her first-ever proposition. This was a situation I hadn't seen, one I had been in and hadn't realized how very dangerous it was.

The first time this happened, if my car had come out of the spin facing west instead of east, I would have seen the dog. I would have gotten out, and I would have gone to move it off the road.

If the dog had been alive then (and what's to say it wouldn't have been?) I would have been furious, but I wouldn't have been able to leave it. Much as I hated the creatures, I couldn't let one die alone and in pain on the side of the road.

But I was terrified, even now. Even when I knew I could go back to my own muddy isolation with a single shout.

I didn't shout. Instead, I went back to the car, and got the blanket I carried for emergencies. Safety first, something you learn on Montana roads in the winter.

Only I'd never planned to use that thick blanket to protect me from a dog bite. I'd planned to use it to stay warm if the car broke down in weather worse than this.

I was shaking violently, my fear making me queasy. I'd never volunteered for a dog bite before. That dog, in pain and dying, would probably lash out blindly, hoping to hurt whatever had hurt it.

I walked close. I made myself take deep breaths, mostly to stop the urge to beg my Puck-like hallucination to get me out of there. If I did survive, even if this were all a dream, I didn't want to know I could be the kind of man who could leave a dying dog in the middle of the road, a dog large enough that, when another car hit it, that car would probably spin out of control worse than I had.

I didn't want to be that man. I didn't want to die knowing I could be.

I swung the blanket over the dog's head and body. The animal whined, but it tried to lick me, a response I hadn't expected. I slipped my hands underneath it, feeling warmth.

The dog whined again.

The air smelled of fresh rain, oil, and blood.

Who left this animal here to die? Who had been cruel enough to feel the double thud of the wheels as they drove over the body, and then just continued onward?

I knew it hadn't been me—not even the previous time I'd lived through this. I always stopped when I hit something—and hitting something wasn't uncommon on a country road. Usually it was mice. Once, I hit a mole and I had to use a shovel to move it off the road. And once, worst of all, it was a rabbit, skull crushed and little feet still moving.

I had used the shovel on the rabbit, too, just to make sure it was dead, since there was no hope of saving it.

I supposed I could have used the shovel on the dog, but I saw no obvious injuries and, much as I feared them, dogs were something more than rabbits.

Dogs were almost human.

I lifted the dog, startled at the weight. The warmth spread along my hands. Blood, then, a serious amount. The wet fur stench nearly gagged me, bringing up memories—the pressure of the Great Dane's paws on my shoulder—and I banished them, sent them away as if they hadn't mattered at all.

Then I carried the sheepdog—who didn't try to bite me—to the car. I realized, as I struggled to open the back passenger door, that I had been crooning to the animal, talking to it as if it were a frightened child.

Ironically, or perhaps not so ironically, I knew what it felt like to be alone in the wet, knowing you're dying, and realizing that nothing you could do would save you.

No matter how much you wanted it.

No matter how much you tried.

A dog was barking in my dreams. A deep rumbling bark with a hint of a rasp. It sounded like Pythagoras, only panicked. Why would Pythagoras panic?

I opened my eyes. Sunlight, filtering through the pines, momentarily blinded me. I raised a hand, and cold water dripped onto my face.

I'd fallen. Mud held me like a lover.

Below, I heard the creek, still filled with snowmelt,
roar by. My ankle hurt. It was caught between two rocks.
I looked up.

Pythagoras was peering at me from the path, his face
caked with mud. His legs and long fur were caked, too.
He would need a bath when I got out of here.

Nothing I hated worse than bathing the dog.

And then the chill that had filled me from the moment
I landed here got worse. I remembered bathing the dog.
Long careful baths to ease his pain after the car accident,
then regular fighting baths after he had healed. Years
had gone by. Years, just the two of us. He even accompanied me to class.

But I remembered the years without him, too. Years
that ended in me sliding off the path, dying of exposure
here, between the rocks and the creature, like something
out of Kafka, watching me from the boulder that had
broken my fall.

There was no creature. Just a raspy voice still echoing
in my ear. And music, a cross between a violin and a
sustained piano chord, humming nearby, even though I
couldn't see the source.

Pythagoras still barked, but he didn't try to come
down. Had he tried before? Had he been trying to rescue me the way that I had rescued him?

It's not about you.

I looked, couldn't see where the voice had come from.
I'd passed out, had a strange dream, and now I was
awake. Pythagoras had awakened me with his barking,
and I had to get out. I had to figure out a way.

I sat up, feeling a sense of déjà vu. I knew, before
I tried, that the rocks would go beneath the surface,
that when I dug in the mud, I'd find a V, narrowing
as it went down, that trying to remove my boot would
make no difference. I'd been through this—and yet
I hadn't.

The barking had stopped. I looked up, but the sun
caught my eyes again. Still, I couldn't see Pythagoras up
there. Maybe he had found a way down the path. Maybe
with his combined strength and mine, we could pull me
out of this mess.

It wasn't right to save him like that so that he'd have to find yet another owner, one he'd have to train all over again.

The dreams had been odd, though. Not just the creature. But the woman—Annabeth? Amazing that I would remember one student out of hundreds, the one I'd found mentally fascinating, who'd been the only one I'd ever allowed to proposition me.

Pythagoras had been in one of those dreams as well. Running toward me, with children following him. Apparently, even in that alternate life, I had saved him.

The creature gave me the chance not to, when he'd sent me back to that coffee shop, allowing me to try all over again.

You have to ask yourself: how many of those stories— those traditional stories you claim to hate—have dogs?

I squinted. Was there a shape on the boulder? I couldn't quite tell. Something iridescent flashed before my eyes—a dragonfly wing? A splash of creek water in the sun?—and then it was gone.

"I don't think Jimmy Stewart got a dog," I said to the voice. "Zuzu's petals, but not a dog."

"Peter?"

I squinted again, but saw nothing. Not even the iridescence from before.

"Peter!"

I looked up. My neighbor stood there, Pythagoras at his side.

"Jesus, Pete, let me get a rope."

"My ankle's wedged," I said, feeling relief. Someone human. Someone real.

"This is going to take more than me, then." My neighbor. So practical. One of the real Montanans, crusty and strong. Not just someone who looked the part. "I'm going to get help. You stay, Pythag."

My dog looked at him, then looked at me, and started barking all over again.

"Christ!" My neighbor said, voice fading. "That dog could wake the dead."

And probably had. No one could ignore Pythagoras for long. The students never had. My friends couldn't.

Hell, half of them became my friends because he led them to me, as if he felt we'd be a good match.

He was rarely wrong.

He sat, and looked down at me, like that Great Dane had so many years ago. Only Pythagoras would never hurt me. Couldn't, really.

The Dane might have, but that wouldn't have been his fault. That would have been caused by Michael Kappel, Neighborhood Bully, or the parents that created him. People who didn't know how to treat an animal, let alone a child.

The fact that that dog had to be destroyed wasn't the Dane's fault. It was theirs, for treating him wrong.

Pythagoras had taught me that, too.

"It's okay," I said to him. "They're going to get me out."

He glanced over his shoulder, as if to say if they didn't, he'd find them, he'd find someone, he'd make sure I was safe.

I leaned against the boulder, conserving my warmth. And, after what seemed like a moment—even though it had to have been much longer—there were voices on the trailhead, followed by my dog's happiest, most welcoming bark.

I still walk with a limp. The ankle had been crushed, the bone only shards. That, the doctors proclaimed, was how I got wedged into such a narrow space.

Even if I had been able to get out, they weren't sure I would have made it up the hill. The land was fragile, slides common. There were two when my neighbor tried to rescue me—fortunately neither of them serious.

But it could have been. Everyone impressed upon me how serious it could have been if Pythagoras had fallen with me, or if he hadn't barked incessantly, drawing all that attention.

As if I didn't already know. The dreams—the creature—all seemed so real, although everyone assured me they couldn't have been. Fever dreams from the pain, from the cold, from the exposure.

It had been spring, yes. June, even. But not warm.

Dangerous, as those of us who live in the mountains know.

Still, I had convinced myself they were right—my friends, the doctors, even Pythagoras, who listened to those conversations and looked at me with a hurt expression, as if he thought I wanted him out of my life.

I didn't. I just could remember a life with him and a life without him. Not only a life before him—I could remember that too—but a life in which my car, after spinning, faced east, and I never realized that the thing in the middle of the road had been a dog, not just some vague, ruglike shape.

Funny how we both would have ended up the same way. Dead from our injuries or exposure or both.

Three weeks ago, I received a new text in the mail. The volume was slim, the binding simple, the pages thick and smooth.

Mathematics and Thought by Annabeth Lillys, recommended for Philosophy of Mathematics courses.

I read her bio first. Now teaching courses on the brain at Harvard, Lillys had gotten her Ph.D. in mathematics at Montana. She had gone on to study theology and biology, settling on sciences which focused on the structure of the mind.

The nature of thought.

Just like she used to talk about.

The book was fascinating, but a bit above the coursework I taught. Annabeth postulated that thought patterns could change the brain itself—how thinkers who focused on theory seemed to have a capacity for seeing things that were beyond the average human ken.

The link between genius and madness, she claimed, wasn't that geniuses were close to being insane. It was that they saw dimensions inaccessible to the rest of us.

Dimensions where creatures who looked like Puck if he had been part grasshopper played music when they scratched behind their wing, and smiled like the Cheshire Cat when they forced recalcitrant humans to live up to their responsibilities toward the animals they had domesticated so long ago.

At least, that's my theory now. My theory as of this afternoon, when I found a box of photographs beneath the eaves of my house, photographs of a four-by-four truck, bright red, one I never bought. One I couldn't afford after all the vet bills from saving Pythagoras' life.

The truck wasn't in just one or two. It was in a lot of those pictures, taken over years. The shiny red paint became dull, mud-splattered, and dented as time went on.

And I was skinnier in those photographs, as if there were times when I got so absorbed in thought that I forgot to eat. I looked like a pale ghost of my current self, a man who existed half in this life and half out of it.

A man who might have found a partially open door to another dimension and tumbled, Alice-like, toward the rabbit hole.

I am still not Ward Cleaver material. In the years since the fall, I have had more opportunities to marry and I have avoided them all. I like being childless. I don't believe in the suburban dream, and I see no point in living in a house that looks like all the others on the block, without a creek or a mountain in sight.

I will never have 2.5 children, but I know now that I will always have a dog.

With the help of friends, I've rebuilt the path. I've walked it maybe a hundred times since my fall. And even though I enjoy the hikes, I've never achieved the fugue state of my memory—my pre-Pythagoras memory—the one others claim is a dream.

It's impossible to get lost in thought with a dog beside you, snuffling the ground, reading messages in the leaves, leaving his own on tree trunks. Impossible to think of equations and higher numbers with a creature who finds joy in a chill wind, who knows—perhaps better than you do—how close he came to death, and how very happy he is to be alive.

I know I am living a different life from the one I started in. I suspect that the man I had been died that afternoon, propped against a boulder, near a dangerously swollen creek.

But I never discuss it anymore. I'm not sure if it matters whether that death was real or metaphorical; the result is the same.

I am solidly here now, a man whose presence will be

missed if he disappears again. A man with contacts, friends, and a dog. A man with a life.

The events of that afternoon may not have been about me, but they changed me—and the change, I like to believe, was my choice.

It still is.

Final Exam

by Rosemary Edghill

Rosemary Edghill's first professional sales were to the black & white comics of the late 1970s, so she can truthfully state on her résumé that she has killed vampires for a living. She is also the author of over thirty novels and several dozen short stories in genres ranging from Regency romance to space opera, making all local stops in between. She has collaborated with authors such as the late Marion Zimmer Bradley and SF Grand Master Andre Norton, worked as an SF editor for a major New York publisher, as a free-lance book designer, and a professional reviewer, as well as a full-time writer. Her hobbies include sleep, research for forthcoming projects, and her Cavalier King Charles spaniels. Her Web site can be found at: http://www.sff.net/people/eluki

SHE WAS BORN to do the most important thing that anyone could do in her world, but for the first twelve weeks of her life she was precisely like her brother and two sisters: a small, squirming ball of fluff who ate and played and slept.

She was born in a house—that was very important— and lived among several dozen others of her kind. Some would go on to do her work. Others would go on to make other, equally valuable contributions to Society. It had always been thus, since the War.

It was an undeclared war, but no less terrible for that. No one now living was really sure when it began, or when it would end, only that they were in the middle of it now, and that it was a war they dared not lose, for the sake of every person who lived and breathed and walked upon the Earth. It was a war that could not be fought with weapons, only with tools, for the enemy was a vast and formless one, difficult to identify until the damage had been done.

For a very long time Humanity had only known there was a war, but not how to fight it. They had suffered and fought and died, until, on the verge of despair, they had turned at last to their oldest allies. . . .

"This one?" The young man—little more than a boy, for all that he wore cadet blues—looked down at the pen full of squirming puppies.

"That's for you to decide," Alphaeus said. The older man gazed down with approval at the spaniel puppies. One of them, chestnut and white—and female, by the pink collar around her neck—had abandoned her play and come to the edge of the pen to gaze up at the strangers fearlessly.

"She's so small."

"She'll grow. They're bred for this, you know. Best breed for the work. Nobody in their right mind'd want to hurt one."

By now the little female was trying to climb the side of the exercise pen to get at the fascinating humans outside. The young man reached down and picked her up. She nestled under his chin—all three pounds of her— and closed her eyes with a sigh.

"I'll take her," he said.

"Thought you would," said Alphaeus.

And so Talitho Thunder and Roses—known soon after as Fancy—went to live at the cadet barracks, along with many other puppies and many other cadets.

Of course, there was a period of adjustment.

"Hey, Baker, I heard you got your dog today."

Alex froze. Of all the people he hadn't wanted to meet on the way to quarters, Carl was at the top of the list. You could explain to Carl all you wanted that based on the evaluation and testing scores, he'd flunked and you hadn't. What Carl knew was that he was going to be training with a Malinois—a Belgian Herding Breed— for security and crowd control—he was going to North

Carolina at the end of the week—and you had a fluffy little lap dog.

Alex pretended not to hear him and walked on.

"Hey, Baker, is that your dog or your purse?"

It would have been better if Carl was big, slow, and dumb. Instead, he was small and fast. Alex felt a tug on the shoulder strap of the carrykennel and felt it slipping off his shoulder. Fancy gave a worried whimper. Alex (who was both big and slow, and not stupid enough to think that Carl couldn't take him apart six ways from Sunday) spun around, clutching it tightly and praying for an officer to show up. If anyone saw Carl interfering with another cadet's dog, Carl could whistle for North Carolina, or ever being allowed near a dog again, in civilian *or* professional life.

"Just think about this, Carl," he said softly, meeting the smaller man's eyes. "You don't want to hurt a puppy."

"Why'n't you put it down and we'll settle this, just the two of us?" Carl said. He didn't let go of the strap.

"I don't think we have anything to settle," Alex said, keeping his voice calm and low. "And I need to get my dog settled in. It's been a long day and she's tired. So why don't you let us be on our way, Carl?"

He isn't going to let go. For one sick moment of terrified certainty Alex knew that Carl wasn't going to let go of the strap, that he was going to try to hurt Fancy, or Alex, or both. But finally visions of North Carolina were strong enough to sway him. Carl let go and turned away.

Alex stayed prudently still and watched him walk out of sight. When Carl had gone, Alex unsealed the top of the carrykennel. Fancy regarded him worriedly, tail wagging hopefully.

"Looks like you and me got started a little early, girl," Alex told her. He lifted her out of the bag and carried her in his arms the rest of the way to the barracks.

Fourth year for Watchmen-trainees focused less on class work and more on the dogs. Most of Fancy's classmates were also so-called "toy" dogs, though there was a golden retriever or two, a few members of the Herding

Group, and even one bloodhound. Together they learned to be good pets and companions and to think well of everyone, as well as to obey (generally) the basic commands that define a dog's life: sit, stay, come, down, heel. Most of all, Fancy learned about people: who they were, how they thought, what they were like. Meanwhile, she got her certifications, and she was now officially known as Talitho Thunder and Roses at West Point, CDX, CGC.

Graduation for Alex and Fancy's first birthday came more or less together. Together they went out into the world: Alex to serve his apprenticeship year, and Fancy to continue her training for her future task. He wore Watchmen's grays now, though he still couldn't perform Judgments. The general public didn't know that—to them, all Watchmen were the same, and the Watchmen preferred to keep it that way.

For Alex, apprenticeship was a series of very boring desk jobs, reading and reviewing files while Fancy slept in a basket at his feet. That was the first three months. The next three months were nerve-racking, because that involved interviewing the people those files were about—which meant they came into his office, where Fancy was.

By now she was full-grown, a chestnut and white Cavalier King Charles spaniel of about fourteen pounds, with big brown eyes, a plumy white tail, and the certainty that the whole world was her friend. No one had ever hurt her, or said an unkind thing to her (that she understood, at least) and it was Alex Baker's ironclad determination that no one ever would. The thought that he was exposing her to the attentions of muggers, hookers, pimps, junkies, burglars, and grifters disturbed him greatly.

But the fact of the matter was none of them was ever in the least cruel to her. The hookers held her on their laps while telling him perfectly hair-raising tales of life on the street; the pimps would tell him about cutting the ear off a "ho" while stroking Fancy's ears gently; and after a while Alex figured out the lesson he guessed he'd been sent down here to learn: that people could be very bad at being citizens, and very bad people, without being bad at *being* people.

And so eventually (and for the rest of the year) he relaxed. But he still kept a sharp eye on them, because while none of them would try to hurt Fancy, many of them would perfectly willingly try to steal her, and that Alex wouldn't put up with.

While Alex was learning about Life, Fancy was learning more things about being an exceptionally friendly dog. She received her Therapy Dog Certification, which meant she could be taken into hospitals and schools to minister to the sick, and Alex took her to a number of those places, because that, too, was a part of Fancy's job. The schools were the most important part, though. When one of the Watchmen came in with a dog, everyone felt happier just to see them, and somehow Alex hoped that if he and Fancy saw them then, they wouldn't have to see them later.

Finally the day Alex had looked forward to and dreaded came. His Apprentice Year was over, which meant he and Fancy could be called to a Judgment at any time. He exchanged his gold class ring for a silver one symbolizing the impermanence of life (he'd get his gold ring back when he retired), and Fancy got a Watchman tag for her collar. It didn't really matter: she'd been computer-chipped when she was a puppy, and she could be located anywhere on the planet, but it was a nice gesture. And Alex went back to his job and waited for the call, hoping it wouldn't come.

But of course it did.

He and Fancy were at home asleep. The special phone rang—he never took it off, except to shower—and Fancy jumped up, barking wildly at the strange noise.

"Baker." He put out a hand, stroking Fancy to silence. She quivered, making faint gurgling growls.

"Watchman Baker, we have a Judgment pending. You are the closest Watchman. Can you respond?"

Alex sat up, waving on the light and looking down at the readout on his wrist. The station house was only a few miles away. "Yes. Send a car, please."

He got up and dressed quickly, knowing he had to look professional for this, or at least kempt and awake. He got Fancy's collar and lead—she regarded him curi-

ously, knowing that this middle-of-the-night outing was
not a part of their usual routine. Needing to receive
comfort more than to give it, he picked her up and held
her in his arms. What was going to happen? He'd heard
of Judgments that went horribly wrong. How could he
have been such an idiot as to volunteer for this service?
How could he risk Fancy this way? This wasn't about
him, this was about *her*.

She licked his face, greedy as always for the taste of
his depilatory. Automatically, he pushed her head down.
For the people. Wasn't that what the oath he'd sworn
had said? For the people, and because there was no
other way.

Oh, God, but what if something went *wrong . . . ?*

There was no more time to waste. He went down-
stairs, his partner in his arms.

The car was already waiting for him. He tucked Fancy
under one arm with the ease of long practice and let
himself into the passenger's seat. The driver, a uniform
ranker, stared at him curiously.

"First time I ever seen a Dog So— I mean a Watchman. Sir."

*Dog soldiers. That's what they call us. And soldiers die
in war.*

"That's all right. I'm Alex Baker. This is Fancy."

Fancy squirmed around on Alex's lap to investigate
the interesting new person. The officer reached out his
fingers for her to sniff, and Fancy licked them enthusiastically.

"Hey," the officer said. "He like that with everybody?"

"She. And yes she is. Everybody."

"I thought a, you know, Watch-Dog would be . . .
bigger," the driver said, pulling away from the curb.

"Well, that's the whole point," Alex said. There
wasn't any point to explaining, and he knew he was babbling, but at least if he was talking he didn't have to
think. "The point is for the dogs to be small and harmless looking. You don't want a dog that looks big or
threatening or aggressive, a dog that would fall within
the normal range of triggered threat response. That
would defeat the whole point of the exercise. You need

something that's going to evoke a protective or nurturing response from 99 percent of normally-socialized human beings. Who'd want to hurt something that looks like Fancy here? Nobody nice. Nobody normal. Nobody sane."

"Yes, sir," his driver said doubtfully.

They reached the station in silence.

Fancy trotted cheerfully beside Alex through the station house halls, her tail waving happily the way it always did. Alex got occasional curious looks from passersby, but very few people didn't know what the gray uniform and the dog meant. Someone here tonight faced Judgment.

"This way, Watchman," a uniformed officer said.

Alex and Fancy followed him into an interrogation room. To his surprise, his mentor from his Academy days was sitting there.

"Sir?" he said, surprised.

Fancy had sat when he stopped. He could feel her looking up at him inquiringly.

"This is your first Judgment," Alphaeus said. "I've come to make sure you can do what needs to be done."

Alex looked down at Fancy. She stared up at him out of wide, trusting brown eyes. Receiving no response, she popped up and put her front paws on his leg. Alex picked her up automatically. He couldn't say anything.

"You don't want to hurt a puppy, do you, Carl?"

People could be very bad people, without being bad at BEING people.

"We have to find them, Alex. You know we do. This is the only way."

The War had begun a long time ago, and for many years they hadn't realized they were fighting it. It wasn't a war you could fight and win with guns, because guns only created more of the enemy, the soulless predators that saw their fellow humans as nothing more than prey. It was a war against itself that the human race could only win with tools—tools to find the enemy, destroy the irredeemable, and create allies instead of enemies whenever possible.

To do that, humanity needed to be able to judge itself

without mercy, without malice, without pity, without hate, and eternally without regret. To judge, and to be always right.

No human could do it. . . .

"I can do it," Alex said, sighing. "Where do we go?"

The Evaluation Cell was at the end of a long corridor of holding cells. A number of Alex's clients were there, and some of them were awake. Normally they would have greeted him rowdily, but they all knew what it meant when a Watchman and his dog came to the station house. They watched in silence as he walked by, Fancy trotting at his side.

The Evaluation Cell was double-chambered and opaque. Alex let himself, Fancy, and Alphaeus into the Watchman side. He could see through the one-way glass on the connecting door into the other half of the cell, to where a man in an orange coverall sat on a bench. The nametape over his right breast pocket said "Donohue."

"What's he done?" Alex asked idly, unclipping Fancy's leash.

"You don't need to know," Alphaeus said. "Maybe next time. Not this time. It doesn't matter, does it? Only Fancy's opinion matters, and yours, and his."

"Yes. That's the law," Alex said slowly. He unsealed the dog-door at the bottom of the connecting door—the pass-light glowed green—and unsealed the whole door just to be sure. If something happened, he could be in there in seconds. That was his job.

Now it was time for Fancy to do hers.

"Go get it, Fancy! Door! Find him!" These were all commands Fancy knew, and she'd trained with this sort of door frequently. She pushed it open with her nose and paws and wiggled through.

Alex waited, staring through the glass as Fancy made a beeline for the man and began making overtures toward him. There were so many ways this could go, and all of Alex's training was in two things: interpreting the signs he saw in order to make a true and accurate report . . . and protecting the life of his dog.

As he watched, part of him wondered how this man before him had come up for Judgment. Judgment wasn't for simple crimes. It was only exercised in those cases where neither punishment nor rehabilitation might be effective.

He was ignoring her. That was bad, but not conclusive. It was also not what Fancy was used to. She barked once, sharply, and sat back, looking pleased with herself.

The man on the bench seemed to notice her at last. He reached for Fancy, and Alex tensed. But Fancy simply jumped up into his arms as if they were old friends and she hadn't seen him in ages. She put her paws on his shoulders and began licking his face comprehensively. Slowly he cradled her in his arms, holding her as he might a baby, weeping and rocking her.

"Does he pass?" Alphaeus said quietly.

"There will be no execution," Alex said, not taking his eyes away from his dog. "This one can be saved. Fancy says so." It was as simple as that—and as hard. He and Fancy would do this, and would keep on doing this, as many times as they were called to it. Not for the power to send men and women down into death. But for the power to recall them to life, to save them for the future.

He opened the door.

"I'm afraid I need my dog back now," he said gently, holding the door open.

"Can I just keep her until they come for me? It won't be long. They do it first thing in the morning," Donohue said listlessly.

"You're going to be evaluated and sentenced, and I'm going to need my dog back before that. But don't worry, there will be plenty of dogs where you're going."

The man looked blank. "You're the Watchman. I'm going to be shot."

"I'm the Watchman," Alex agreed. "You're going to be evaluated and sentenced, not shot."

"But I killed a lot of people," Donohue protested, animation beginning to enter his voice for the first time.

Alex raised his hand. "That isn't my concern. All

Fancy and I do is determine if you *can* rejoin the human race. Whether you do or not, or want to or not, is up to you and your Sentence Counselor."

Fancy had started to wriggle as soon as she heard Alex's voice, and when she did, Donohue let go of her. She trotted over to Alex, happy with her evening's work. He pointed, and she went through the door behind him.

"Good night," Alex said. "Good luck." He was surprised to find he meant it.

"Now what?" he asked, turning to Alphaeus.

"Paperwork, I'm afraid," the older man said with a smile. "You'll need to let the sergeant know to put the prisoner on the docket for the morning. They'll give you a desk and a corner to work on your report. Once you've turned it in, you can go home. You'll need to file an expanded version with us, but that can wait a few days."

Alex groaned, but only for the look of the thing. A vast unspoken burden of worry, carried with him from the very beginning, was gone now.

"You won't be here next time, will you?" Alex asked.

"No. It was essentially luck that it was me this time, though someone would have been here to see you through it. Something came up, and I had to come down here from the Point."

By now they were walking back up the row of cells. Though there was no possible way for communication to have occurred between the sealed cell and the long double row of open ones, somehow everyone seemed to know that Donohue had been spared. The atmosphere was festive.

In all cells save one.

At the top of the row, a new prisoner had come in, wearing the orange jumpsuit indicating he was a dangerous man, bound over for trial or Judgment.

Alex slowed, then stopped before the cell.

"Carl?" he said in confusion.

There was no response from the man inside.

Alphaeus took his arm and hurried him along.

"I don't understand," Alex said, once they'd reached the corridor. "Why is he here? Will he be Judged? Do I—"

"He is here because he has committed a crime. Several of them, in fact, though it was the last one that betrayed him to us. He is to be executed in the morning, but no Judgment was required, nor will be. You see . . ." There was a long pause. "He killed his dog."

Precious Cargo

by Bernie Arntzen

Bernie Arntzen lives and writes in New England. He has published a variety of short fiction and is always at work on the elusive novel. Unfortunately, the only dog he can host in his apartment is a Beanie Baby, who carefully supervised the writing of this story. He keeps hoping one of his adored nieces and nephews will get a dog and share with him, but no luck yet. For now he makes do at the local Humane Society shelter.

"DOGS?" Gilly stared at the crates in disbelief. "Not just any dogs—"

"DOGS?" She transferred her blistering glare to the man towering over her. "I *hate* dogs."

"Oh, but hate is such a strong word—"

"Not strong enough, obviously! Scott, what were you *thinking?*" Hearing her voice spiral toward shrill didn't improve her mood. "How could you accept a consignment of *dogs* without checking with me? You know transporting live cargo is always questionable." As in, he questioned, she said no. Her partner's tendency to buy anyone's sob story grew exponentially in proportion to the number of big, wet eyes staring up at him. Add fur and he was anyone's bitch.

"They're important—"

"*Who* exactly gave you this *important* cargo?" Eyes narrowing, she didn't miss his hesitation or the way his cheeks flushed. "If this lot came through Teddy, I'll kill her."

"No, not Teddy. Not exactly."

"Not exactly?"

"Actually, I'm . . . doing a favor for my mother."

"YOUR MOTHER?" The gentle patience in her next

words didn't fool Scott for a minute. "But you don't even *like* your mother."

"That's sort of why I'm doing her the favor."

She couldn't even find it within herself to argue. It was perfect Scott-logic, the sort that never got any easier to understand. She transferred her gaze from his honestly angelic face to the faraway ceiling of the docking bay and tried to control her breathing.

When the silence held for a little too long, Scott broke first. "They're *special* dogs, so they're pay—"

Gilly looked down at the expensive crates that shifted with the muffled thumps of moving bodies. "Special dogs. Right."

"—they're paying us L60,000."

That got her attention. "L60,000?"

"That's why I thought you'd understand."

Fair assumption. Sixty thousand leetas could go a long way, and the *Penguin* could use a few modifications. But the high payday only made her more suspicious. Offers like that were usually reserved for running arms. Or worse. "L60,000 for ferrying a bunch of mutts off-planet?"

"The destination—"

"With resources like that, why aren't they using a standard shipper? One that *specializes* in animals?"

Scott riffled a hand back through his dark hair, making it stand up on end, the only sign of his increasing frustration. "They like our speed. The standards can't match it. But the real deal kicker is the destination. Maddox II. You know the routine—the minute Maddox went into potential civil unrest over Earth colony status, the standard transport services embargoed. Nobody on the legit side is going near there for the foreseeable future. Mother met the seller at a social event, and mentioned that she has a son in the . . . import/export business, that we're independents, willing to breach embargoes—"

Gilly raised her eyebrows. "Your mother mentioned us at a social gathering?" She'd never had the questionable pleasure of meeting Mother Ashford, but she'd heard plenty from Scott. More than enough to know she wasn't in the habit of discussing socially what her son and his business partner did for work.

Scott gave her a hard look that told her he knew what she was thinking. "However we came up, he was looking for immediate transport to a tough location, and she gave him my information. His broker here looked me up the day after we docked. He must have had a watch on for us on the docking records. Mother called me, 'asking' me to *please* take the job." He rolled his eyes. "I tried to raise you, but you weren't answering."

She ignored the reproach couched in the words. True, she'd been avoiding her messages, but he hadn't tried to raise her on an emergency channel. She wouldn't have ignored a flag. Accepting *dogs* as cargo warranted a flag. And it wasn't like disappearing for a snap when they docked was unexpected. After any of their longer runs they could both use a few days out of each other's faces.

She wondered for a split second if he'd taken on the canine cargo specifically to piss her off after her disappearance and inaccessibility, but she shrugged off the thought. Scott wasn't usually the passive-aggressive type.

One of the dogs yipped loudly and Gilly winced.

"Usually" perhaps being the operative phrase.

"Are we locked into this?"

"You'd turn down L60,000?"

"I'd give it serious thought, yes."

His jaw firmed. "The dogs are checked in, signed for, and half-loaded. I've given departure and arrival commitments. And the deposit cleared our account. Yes, it's safe to say we're locked in."

"It didn't occur to you I *might* have a problem with this?"

"Well *duh,* but I thought you'd see I was in an awkward position, and appreciate the L60!"

"Awkward position? Telling Mommy no?"

"You know it's slightly more complicated than that."

"Mama's boy," she muttered under her breath. She didn't bother trying to decipher his equally low retort. She could guess. She tilted her head to one side until her neck cracked, then sighed. "Okay, so we're locked in, and we make the best of a fuck-rotten situation. Did you at least do a background check?"

"He's a friend of my mother's."

"And your point would be?"

"That I've already got Teddy's information on him · downloaded to your station."

Sometimes the boy wasn't as dumb as he looked, she thought fondly. "I assume since the critters are here he checked out."

"Teddy doesn't find anything out of the ordinary. Grayson Frankes, Earthbound dog breeder, specializing in rare and show breeds. Hasn't traveled much himself, but has a good network and a branch of his business here on Regal. His handler who delivered Felt fine to me. Decent, solid guy . . . obviously cares about his dogs."

"Because that *is* the most important thing," Gilly muttered sarcastically. At Scott's exasperated look, she held up her hands. "Okay, okay. I'm off your back . . . you're the one with the genetic Ph.D. in reading people, not me."

"And, Gilly, look." Scott knelt by the closest crate, opened the door, and drew out a puppy. Cradling it, he grinned. "Look at them."

The little head cocked and the requisite big, wet eyes blinked at her. Cuddled to Scott's chest, the puppy was right on eye-level with her. Big paws on short legs, floppy ears, a blunt, fuzzy muzzle . . . spiky, plentiful fur in a soft spring green. She reached out and touched a silky ear. "Genetically modified." It wasn't a question.

"Well, yes."

Staring dispassionately at the warm ball of adorability, she sighed. "You're cleaning up after them."

Try as she might, Gilly couldn't find any good reason to turn down the job. She sat, feet up on her desk, rereading Teddy's notes on Grayson Frankes, breeder extraordinaire. Poring over the manifests describing the dogs. Confirming the veterinary process each went through to be approved for space shipment. Rechecking the contract Scott initiated with one George McDougal, senior handler employed at the Regal branch of Frankes' breeding business. Checking the destination, the embargo conditions, the docking arrangements. Reading up on the buyer, one Zac Russell of Maddox II.

That identification at least helped explain the amount

of money changing hands. She knew Zac. Big name on
Maddox II, and one of the leading proponents of separation and self-governance. No one ever asked too pointedly where all his money came from. Apparently, he had
a weakness for dogs.

Occasionally, her eyes strayed over to the screen
blinking the confirmation of deposit in their business account. Happy little zeroes stared back at her.

Nothing aside from the destination rang out of the
ordinary. And even delivering to an embargoed planet
didn't constitute unusual. Civil wars, planetary conflicts,
political posturing . . . they all occurred regularly and
embargoes were common, especially when the great
prima donna Earth was involved. But she and Scott had
practically created the *Serendipity*'s less-than-legal reputation on jumping embargoes and safely traveling where
other fliers avoided. Embargoed planets made for big
business.

She didn't even find it odd that some Earthbound
businessman wanted to ship dogs to Maddox II. Any
number of businesses tried playing both sides against the
middle and maintaining cordial relations with colonies
as well as colonizers. Why should a high-end dog breeder
be any different? Make Zac happy, and gain an in should
Maddox end up independent.

She drummed her nails on the desk and considered
the possibility that the job had come about as Scott described. Two wealthier-than-could-possibly-be-healthy social climbers meet at a party and family business gets a
leg up. Except the senior Ashfords had never displayed
an interest in helping their son's business in the past.
Not since he'd been chased out of the diplo-corps with
her, scandal hovering over their heads like a particularly
gaudy vulture. It could be as simple as Mother Ashford
seeing a way her embarrassment of a son could be of
use, but still . . . Her fingers stopped moving and curled
into a fist. It rang the weird bells for Gilly.

And not just because she hated dogs. She hoped.

Finally admitting defeat, she closed out the Frankes
file. With no legitimate way to kick Scott's dogs off the
ship, she swiveled her chair away from her desk and rose
to search out the man himself and make his life misera-

ble. She tracked him down in the rec room, sprawled on the floor with two tussling puppies and three cooing humans.

Two purple puppies. According to the manifests they changed colors. Gilly's arms crossed over her chest reflexively, in preparation for the onslaught of "Aren't they *cuuuute?*" and the inevitable dirty looks when she didn't concur and refused to gush over an immature canis familiaris.

Spense grinned, reaching out to tumble one of the pups onto its back. "Hey, Gil, I'm sure this just thrills you."

"We thought Ash was nuts agreeing to live cargo without your say-so," Emily chimed in, her eyes never leaving the capering fluffballs. "But he did try to get hold of you. And the price sure was right." She scooped up the puppy from Spense, hugging it close to her face and laughing in delight as it investigated her hair. The purple fur contrasted nicely with the loose, dark brown waves. When Emily peered over the puppy, her ice-blue eyes sparkling, Gilly had to admit, internally at least, that it made an adorable fashion accessory for the young woman. *But Em's such a cutie, what wouldn't,* her snarky side countered.

"And they're *so* adorable, how could you object?" Emily continued as she nuzzled the puppy.

Gilly bit her tongue. "That color changing may be cute while they're little, but it'll look pretty stupid when they're full grown."

"They are full grown."

She blinked at Scott. The manifests didn't mention that. "Say what?"

"They're as big as they're getting."

"They're permanent puppies?"

"More or less."

"That is so wrong," she muttered.

Alistair snorted from his position on the floor, letting the other puppy worry at his bootlaces. He shot her an amused look but said nothing. She knew what he was thinking—that with her genetically-enhanced reflexes she should be the last person criticizing genetic alterations—and she ignored him.

"Ready for departure?" Scott asked.

"Ready for departure," she confirmed, silently acknowledging she'd found no way out. "You guys sure you should be manhandling this *special* cargo?"

"It's good for the dogs," Scott answered without thinking. "I talked at length to George, and he encouraged us to have them out around the ship. Exercise, interaction—" Catching sight of her expression, he tripped over his tongue and changed tack mid-sentence. "But we'll keep them out of your way. Em and Spense have agreed to help me walk them, and we'll break them out in twos and threes for playtime."

Her eyes skated from the anxious man to the oblivious pups. Her jaw clenched and she forced herself to relax the tension and count to ten. Addressing the suspiciously grinning crew, she hardened her voice. "Somebody take charge of them now, and the rest of you get on your preflight stations. I filed for clearance before I came down here. Mr. Frankes is paying for speed; let's give it to him." She spun on her heel and walked out, but not before noticing two sets of alert eyes focus on her from fuzzy lilac faces. She couldn't escape the creeping sensation of the adoring gazes following her as she left, but she chalked it up to imagination born of irritation and ignored it.

Piloting the *Serendipity* kept her out of contact with her cargo, and offered the bonus of relaxing her. Gilly lost herself in her favorite activity and concentrated on maneuvering the heavy congestion surrounding the *Angel One* space station, then held the controls even when the automated flight plan could easily take over. But after hours at the helm, and guiding the ship manually through the Luca asteroid field, she had no excuses for not taking a break. Luca was the last hazard for a while and she needed to pace herself. Switching to AFP, she handed the ship off to Spense and stretched out her back and shoulders.

"Ash really did work hard to raise you, Gil," he said as he slid into the seat. "He wasn't trying to purposely piss you off."

One red eyebrow arched. "He didn't try an emergency channel."

Spense laughed. "He had a job offer for L60 being handed to him on the proverbial silver platter, and you expect him to raise the boss lady on an *emergency flag* on her days off? I don't think so! He's in charge when you're not here, and he did good by Serendipity Enterprises. It's not like he took on a shipment of *cows*." He leaned over his screen and studied the star map. "And you disappeared so completely and so fast we assumed you might not want to be disturbed." He pushed chestnut hair off his forehead and glanced at her, dark eyes asking what his words didn't.

Leaning back against Scott's conspicuously empty seat, blue eyes stared down brown. "Yes, I had a date."

He grinned. "We wondered. See, Ash was better off not raising you. They're just puppies. Trust me, this'll be an easy job."

Gilly snorted. "Famous last words. Alistair's been on me for three hours to get something to eat. That's where I'm at." She left the bridge, ignoring his shouted, "What do you have against dogs anyway?"

Talk about no-win conversations.

She descended to the small mess, finding Alistair hunched over a steaming mug, making notes on a handheld. As she entered, he looked up and smiled, severe face softening. She slipped into the seat across from him. "Don't start with me about how Ash didn't mean any harm. What I'd like to know is when you guys all decided you needed to defend poor little Scott against big bad me."

"Probably when we all noticed what a piss poor job he does of defending himself. The boy's too nice by a damn sight."

Gilly rolled her eyes. "I'm hardly an ogre."

"You have a temper," Alistair shrugged, still smiling. "But what *I* want to know is what you have against dogs. What's not to like?"

Gilly leaned forward, banging her forehead gently against the smooth table surface. "And I'm going to be chased around by this conversation until we finish this trip. You all wonder why I'm so annoyed." She lifted her head, propping her elbows on the table and resting her chin in her hands. "Trying to explain why you don't like dogs is next to impossible. People look at you like you're an ax murderer."

Sitting back, Alistair sipped from his mug to hide his grin. "Try me?"

She wrinkled her nose. "They're sloppy. They stink. They jump all over you and don't respect personal space. They're loud and obnoxious. They pant and slobber and . . . just *yuck*."

Alistair nodded. "Some of that can be addressed—"

"CAN be, but rarely is, and some of it just comes with the canine territory, admit it."

"Still—"

"And that's not all. People say they're smart, but I seriously doubt it. They're just so . . . *subservient*. Which makes me wonder about their vaunted 'intelligence.' "

Alistair blinked at her vehemence. "Eh?"

"It's that *fawning* thing I can't stand. They're so bloody obsequious."

"Obsequious? Gillian! That's going a little far. It's called unconditional love . . . it's one of the reasons people adore dogs."

"Not this people."

"They're pack animals, it's—"

"I *know* they're pack animals. I understand the whole dynamic, I get *why* they're so devoted and obedient. I just don't *respect* the whole pack thing, okay? You asked, I'm telling you. Personally, I think it's a guy thing," she grumbled.

"What?"

"I said I think it's a guy thing. Men and dogs. The male ego likes that unquestioned adoration, that whole alpha/beta pack nonsense. Women are secure enough to appreciate a pet with a mind of its own . . . a cat."

"Oh, please!"

"I'm serious. Admit it, you guys like to be fawned over, looked up to like small gods."

"Plenty of women like dogs!" Alistair's mug hit the table.

Gilly sighed. "I know. I can't explain that as easily. Except to point to the human ego in general."

"You are nuts. Have you ever spent time with dogs?"

Her lip curled. "As if."

He pointed a finger at her. "You don't know what you're talking about. Spend some time with one and tell me at the end of the trip you don't warm up to it. There's a reason the human/dog relationship goes back so far."

Gilly snorted. "And see? Everyone just assumes if you spend a little time with a dog, you'll get over your dislike. HA! I say."

"You could try it."

"I could."

"You could start right now," Alistair nodded over her shoulder, gathered up his handheld and stood. "Ash, bring that little darling over here."

"Ooooh-ho-no," she moaned as Scott came to the table, a squirming bundle of bright orange under one arm. "I think I need to go back to the bridge."

Scott settled across from her as Alistair leaned in and scratched the puppy's head, making exaggerated kissing noises. "Aren't you a little beauty? Yes, you are!" He jerked his head in Gilly's direction. "Wait until she tells you her theory on why men like dogs. She just finished telling me about how stupid, smelly, slobbering, obnoxious, loud, space-invasive, and *subservient* dogs are."

Scott looked shocked and covered the puppy's ears. "Gilly!"

She gave Alistair a killing look. "Thanks." To Scott, she added, "I didn't exactly say it like that. I just . . . well, he asked!"

Alistair walked away, chuckling. "Don't forget to eat, Gillian."

"I've lost my appetite," she retorted, watching the puppy stretch up to lick Scott's chin. Her lip curled again as the slobbering habit made its appearance. She etched a little check on the list in her head. "I find it difficult to believe people voluntarily put themselves in the way of that."

The orange pup left off its wet attentions and turned its head. Studying her, it suddenly yipped and started squirming in earnest, trying to wriggle out of Scott's hold and cross the table. "He wants to say hi," Scott explained. "You want to hold him?"

Gilly shook her head. "You know redheads can't do

orange. You keep him." Staring at the anomalous animal, she had to admit . . . down deep in her cantankerous brain . . . that she could see the appeal. Unlike full-grown dogs, which seldom failed to inspire anything but apathy or outright antipathy in her, the puppy pushed all the "cute" buttons. The snub muzzle, oversize ears, touchable fur. The cuddly, clumsy, endearing quality. Made her believe humans were still genetically predisposed to respond to small fuzzy creatures, or just "the young" of any species.

As she mused, she became aware of the big eyes still focused on her. The puppy stared back with . . . expression. Gilly narrowed her eyes and met the look head on. The puppy tilted its unnaturally hued head, gave another small yip, then resumed the struggle to go to her.

"Come on, Gil," Scott laughed. "He really wants to say hi. No one's around to complain that he clashes with your hair. Hold him for a minute while I get us something to eat?" At her silent look, he lifted the puppy carefully and held him out to her. "I won't tell anyone you held him. Your ornery reputation will be safe. I promise." The light green of his eyes sparkled and he lowered his lashes in a quick wink.

With a groan she gave in and accepted the warm body, holding it awkwardly at arm's length. She watched the dog in suspicion, but to her surprise, the puppy held quite still from the moment he came into her hands, in direct contrast to his behavior with Scott. When he continued to hang motionless in her grip, she brought him in closer, until he rested on her lap. The little head tilted all the way back, so he could continue to meet her gaze. She cocked her own head out of reach, having no interest in any wet kisses. But even in her lap, the puppy made no move to jump or lick, or even do any offensive sniffing. He sat perfectly still, just watching her.

Slowly relaxing, Gilly lifted one hand and reached for the tag hanging around his neck. "What do they call you?" she muttered. The puppy continued to sit motionless, lifting his head out of the way so she could read the tag. A line of tiny numbers and letters came first, then below that in larger print "Marlow." "Marlow, eh?" She released the tag and let her fingers comb through the fur, stroking over his head. He tilted into the caress but made no other move, just watching her almost . . . intelligently. She resettled Marlow so he looked more comfortable, and once again his only movement was to keep her in his line of sight. "Hunh. Apparently you have a self-preservation streak, eh?" she murmured.

Marlow's jaw gaped for a moment in what she would swear was a toothy grin.

Puzzlement segued to a return of tension to her shoulders while, even as she watched, the bright orange fur began to shift to a soft peach. The red pigment continued to leech until Marlow sat proudly on her lap, a soft, fluffy lemon yellow.

A color much more complimentary to redheads. Not to mention her favorite.

A frisson of unease crawled up her spine. Impossible. She leaned in closer, purposely tempting him to lick her. Nothing. He just sat looking cute and smart. Something about his expression differed from the blank, playful look she'd seen on the puppies earlier. "I am not thinking what I think I'm thinking," she whispered. Still, the suspicion grew. "I prefer blue," she lied in a louder voice.

In seconds the fur took on a greenish tinge. Slowly Marlow cycled through green as blue chased out the yellow, until he sat in puffy cobalt splendor.

Gilly felt faintly sick.

Scott reappeared, setting down two plates. "You two look like you're getting along fine. Wow, that's the first time I've seen one go blue. Beautiful." Marlow glanced over at Scott, then turned back to Gilly as if the tall man he'd been worshiping earlier was of absolutely no significance. Settling down, he curled against Gilly's stomach and leaned his head against her.

She looked up at Scott. "I think—" She stopped. Started again. "Ash, have you noticed anything . . . odd about these puppies?"

"Odd?" Brow furrowing, he shook his head. "No, not once you get used to the colors."

"Marlow here . . . he's really . . . *responsive*."

Scott laughed. "You haven't been around dogs much, have you? That's what people like about dogs. They're smart and responsive. They look at you and listen and they *hear* you. Their level of understanding is amazing."

Gilly shook her head. "No, it's like he *really* understands."

Scott grinned triumphantly. "You're getting sucked in! Ha! I knew if you just—"

Exhaling an exasperated breath, she interrupted him. "No! No, dammit, I mean this dog heard me say I liked blue better than yellow and he turned color. To blue."

Scott blinked. "But yellow's your favorite color."

She closed her eyes and counted to ten. "So not the point. I said I liked blue and he turned blue. That's not odd?"

"Maybe coincidence? It was time for him to cycle to blue?"

"I'm not a big believer in coincidence," Gilly growled. Marlow looked up at her change in tone, but didn't otherwise react.

Scott thought for a moment, then his face lightened. "I know, I bet they've been trained."

"What?"

"Trained. To respond based on the color being spoken aloud as a verbal command like 'sit' or 'stay.' Watch . . . PURPLE."

Marlow lifted his head and stared across the table at Scott. Then he looked up at Gilly expectantly. "Purple?" she said dubiously. Almost immediately the blue fur shifted to indigo, then a deep royal purple. "I'll be damned," she breathed.

Scott nodded in satisfaction. "There. See? Dogs are smart, but they're not that smart. And I think he likes you."

Something tugged at the back of Gilly's brain. "Still . . . that's just weird. It means the dogs have conscious control over the color."

He shrugged. "Or it's just a trained reaction."

"How do you train a dog like that?"

"I don't know, I'm not a dog trainer. If dogs can be trained on verbal commands, doesn't it make sense that a genetically-modified color-cycling dog could be trained to cycle based on verbal command?"

"I suppose. Although can I go on record as saying I

find this whole thing sick?" At Scott's questioning eyebrow, she pointed at Marlow. "Genetically altering them for entertainment purposes."

Scott sighed. "I know. Believe me, it occurred to me, too. But, Gil, the two of us are hardly in any position to be throwing stones at genetic modifications." He arched his brows meaningfully.

"I know," she grumbled. "Although it's hardly our fault our parents decided to ignore the laws and play gods."

"No argument from me. Just the same as it's not their fault Frankes decided to alter a few of their genes to make a little extra profit from particolored permapuppies."

"At least our modifications have practical applications. Not just decorative."

Scott snorted and pointed at the puppy. "At least *his* modifications are legal, therefore very likely not bought on the black market, and he doesn't have to keep them a secret."

"Point," Gilly conceded. "So you really think it's trained behavior? Cycling on command? Didn't mention that on the manifests."

He shrugged again, speaking around a mouthful of food. "I doubt they listed every little thing the dogs do."

You're being paranoid, her mind scoffed. "Whatever. You take him back." She picked Marlow up and shoved him across the table at Scott. Dropping his sandwich, he caught the dog as she released him.

"Okay! You really don't like animals, do you?"

"I like cats just fine," Gilly responded absently, watching as Marlow responded to his relocation. He immediately started squirming and wagging his tail, climbing all over Scott, panting and yipping, trying to get to Scott's face with a swiping tongue. The niggling sense of unease made Gilly's spine tingle again. She stood up abruptly, wanting to be anywhere the puppy wasn't. "I'm going back to the bridge."

"Hey! Alistair will give me hell for not making sure you ate. Come on, doctor's orders."

"He's not a real doctor," she snapped, but reached back and snagged her sandwich off the plate. "I'll take

it with me, satisfied?" Stalking off before he could respond, she'd almost reached the bridge before she finally
remembered what was wrong with Scott's "verbal command" theory.

Marlow turned yellow all on his own, with no verbal
command from her.

Gilly cut more time off their flight by taking a straight-
line course through another asteroid field most pilots
plotted around. Amusing herself dodging high-speed
projectiles, she whizzed the *Serendipity* through in record
time, without a ding. Resetting the AFP, she let her
chair tilt back and ran through an old set of finger-
limbering exercises her father taught her. She stared at
the star field for uncounted minutes until the feeling of
being watched crept up on her.

Swiveling her chair around in a move faster than a
human should rightly be able to perform, her eyes went
immediately to the bright spot of blue fur on the floor.
The little blue puppy stared up at her. "How the hell
long have *you* been there?" she demanded, trying to
calm her racing heart. No answer forthcoming, the puppy
cocked its head and continued to stare.

The unease came back, slinking around the base of
her spine and lurking up to tickle the hair on her neck
into a standing position. She watched the dog and the
dog watched her. Finally, she couldn't stand it any
longer. "Marlow?"

The puppy stood and yipped once, then trundled
toward her. When it got to her feet, she reached down
and pulled the tag out where she could read it. Sure
enough. Marlow.

"Okay, so. I'm right and you're . . . weird." Catching
the puppy up in her arms, she settled him on her lap
and swiveled back to the instrument panel. Hitting the
com button with more force than necessary, she rapped
out, "Spense, on the bridge, *on the double.*" The muffled
affirmative sounded half asleep, but she switched off the
link before he even finished. Marlow listened to the ex-
change with perked ears, then turned his attention to
the multiple buttons, switches, and readouts on the

panel. One paw lifted and settled on the contoured surface.

"Get your fuzzy fingers off my ship."

Marlow looked up at her and withdrew his paw. If she didn't know better, she'd have said he was being careful not to let his toenails come into contact with any surface. Of course, that was essentially the conundrum . . . did she know better? He curled closer to her and she felt her hand drawn inexorably to the velvet of his ears. He butted into her hand and she found herself rubbing his head without thinking. She stopped immediately, and he looked up at her with hopeful eyes. She glared down at him, but he just sat, tail wagging, looking adorable.

The thumping footsteps of Spense arriving on deck brought Marlow's attention around, and he twisted and leaped to the floor in one quick move. Scampering a few steps away, he braced himself like a little blue bodyguard and barked at the intruder.

Spense slid to a stunned halt, then lifted a bemused gaze to Gilly. "Got a friend, I see. Get lonely up here all alone?"

"Yeah, right," she snorted. Running a practiced eye over the *Serendipity*'s settings, she stood and gestured Spense to the pilot seat. "Take over. I need to go deliver a little cargo to the gentleman who said they wouldn't be in my way." She swept a glance over his rumpled clothes. "I take it you weren't on puppy-duty?"

He shook his head. "I was off-rotation. Hell, I was asleep. How'd he even get out here?"

"Damned if I know, but I know how he's getting back. Marlow," she commanded, snapping her fingers and pointing to the floor directly in front of her feet. Her mouth fell open as the dog trotted over and sat down in the indicated spot, just before her toes. He looked up expectantly. "Spense, is that *normal?* I mean, you know . . . for dogs?"

Spense appeared to be biting his lip to keep from laughing. "Yeah, actually."

"They respond like that when you call them?"

"Standard behavior. Granted, he's a little young to be

so well-trained, but that is one of the beauties of dogs. The whole intelligent trainability thing."

Gilly's lip curled back off her teeth. "Right. Obedience." Still, her curiosity rose. Instead of picking him up, she headed for the door. Marlow trotted after her, keeping pace just behind her feet. Leaving the bridge, she let the door slide shut behind her. "I don't care what he says, I still say you're weird. And not just because you look like a giant moldy blueberry on legs."

Gilly flipped from her side onto her back, then to her side again. Then her back. Then straightened the sheets with sharp tugs. She stared up at the ceiling, then resolutely shut her eyes. Slow, steady breathing. Relax.

Insomnia.

Counting sheep didn't work when all the little woolies turned blue and barked. Her eyes popped open. She didn't know exactly what she suspected, she just knew she suspected something. Every intuition antenna, quivered. Of course, the fear lingered that she was just being irrational based on her annoyance at getting boxed into shipping dogs.

Scott had been appropriately chagrined when she confronted him with Marlow's visit to the bridge. The problem arose when neither he nor Emily could account for how Marlow could have gotten to the bridge. Scratch that . . . how he could have gotten out of his crate, out of the cargo bay, and up to the bridge.

She didn't put it past one of the crew to play a practical joke on her, especially given her distaste for dogs, and their lack of sympathy. But their reactions had been all wrong. No smothered snickers or too-innocent faces. Of course, the alternative was Marlow letting himself out and going on a scouting mission for her. Not exactly preferable.

Forcing the thoughts out of her head, she shut her eyes, deepened her breathing and resisted the urge to get up, go back to the bridge and take over the *Serendipity* again. She needed to be fresh for the embargo zone and the crossover into Maddox space, and besides, Alistair would have her forcibly removed if she went any longer without sleep. Times like this she regretted ever

bringing him onto her crew. Used to be she could abuse
her genetically-enhanced body however she wanted. Of
course, she had to admit he came in handy in emergencies. Actually, came in handy most of the time. She
switched over to counting the number of times Alistair
had saved their asses, and drifted off without even realizing it.

Only to jerk awake. Blinking wide-eyed in the dark,
she tried to place what had yanked her out of sleep. Her
heart raced. She had no idea how long she'd been out,
couldn't remember any dream. Something . . . she sat
bolt upright and almost screamed.

On the foot of the bed sat a semicircle of three puppies. Silent. Still. Staring at her.

"Bloody HELL! What are you DOING here?" she
hollered, instinct pulling her back against the head of
the bed, yanking the blanket up as she went. "Full
lights!" Light flared in the room at her command. As
her eyes adjusted, all three puppies cocked their heads
to the left. The middle puppy yipped, and by now she
recognized Marlow on sight. The two to either side of
him suddenly began to darken from light green, through
aqua, to the same bright blue as Marlow.

Huffing out an exasperated breath, she flung back the
blanket and shot out of bed. "Blue really isn't my favorite color," she snapped. Whirling to her bedside com,
she slammed the ship-wide button and hollered, "Everyone get to the bridge *yesterday*." She grabbed Marlow,
tucked him under her arm and stormed out of her room.
The two puppies left behind woofed, jumped off the bed,
and followed her at a trot. Ignoring them, she stalked
onto the bridge. When she saw Scott, she practically
flung Marlow into his arms.

"What the hell *are* these things?"

He caught the puppy and stammered. "Labrador
retrievers?"

Spense shook his head and glanced away from the star
field. "I think they look more like goldens, with that
coat texture."

"Which might make sense, if they were golden,"
pointed out Emily.

"That's NOT what I mean," Gilly erupted, silencing

the deck. "If any one of you is pulling some cute little joke, out with it, NOW." She rounded on each person in turn, eyes flashing. Once again, the puzzled expressions and dubious silence didn't indicate a crew stunt. "I assume all the darlings were locked up tight?" she ground out.

Exchanging glances, Scott, Emily, and Spense all nodded. Understanding finally dawned on Scott's face. "Gilly, you don't mean . . . not again!" He looked to the puppy in his arms and checked the tag. His face paled.

"Exactly. I woke up with three of them sitting on my damn *bed*. Just *looking* at me. I don't care what you all say, this cannot be normal dog behavior."

"I don't get it," Emily protested. "They're just puppies! They've been perfectly normal with the rest of—"

"Well they haven't been normal with *me*," Gilly interrupted. Reaching out, she plucked Marlow from Scott and thrust him at Alistair. "Examine this . . . thing. Find out if there's anything biologically or chemically weird about it."

"But, Gillian, I'm a doctor, not a veterinarian," he objected, trying to push the puppy back at her.

"No, you're not a doctor *or* a veterinarian, but you're the best we've got," she snapped, refusing the puppy. "Run some scans on him. Do a blood test. Do *something*. And, Em, take the other two back to the cargo bay. And stay on watch with them, will you? All I need is more of them running around the ship. In fact, check every crate. You," she pointed to Scott, "help me go through the Frankes file again."

As she left, she knew this time she wasn't imagining the three pairs of puppy eyes burning into her back.

"It is, in my studied opinion, a dog."

"Alistair—"

"What do you want me to say? As you know, I'm *not* a veterinarian, but I called up some files on dog biology for comparison, and ran some basic tests. There's nothing out of the ordinary. Marlow here is biologically a *dog*."

Gilly glared at the little blue dog in vexation. "Nothing cyber, eh? No chips or implants or . . . anything?"

Alistair shook his head. "Not that I can find. And I've scanned him nose to tail and back again. Just pure doggy. You didn't find anything in the Frankes files?"

"No," she sighed. "I didn't think we would. We'd already combed them." She reached out and tilted the little dog's face up to hers. "What are you? Why do you seem so damn . . . smart?"

And in that instant, it hit her. Smart. Her head snapped up and she looked at Alistair in shock.

"Gillian? What?"

"If it's nothing cyber, and the dog is biologically a dog, and yet it's genetically altered . . . what does that say?"

"Say?"

"It's at the cellular level. It's the brain. The *mind*. His mind is what's not normal dog." She looked back down to the puppy and grinned. "And if your mind is as advanced as it seems, why wouldn't a mind reader be able to take a peek?" she asked him rhetorically. A small yip was the only answer she got from Marlow, but Alistair snapped his fingers.

"Ash!"

"Yes, indeed. Ash." Strolling over to Alistair's com link, she accessed it and buzzed Scott. "Scott, get your ass down to medical. I've got a mind for you to probe around in." She turned in time to see Marlow backing away, looking for all the world like he was about to slip off the table and run for the hills. "Oh, no, you don't!" She dove and caught him. "Where exactly do you think you could go?" she asked.

Instantly, he looked like the blank, carefree puppy the rest of the crew had been encountering. He panted and squirmed and tried to lick her . . . even threw in a woof for good measure. She laughed in his face. "Too late, little boy blue. You've tipped your hand." He went limp in her grip and just hung there. His nose twitched, and she could swear he sighed. Now the vexed look was on his face. She was stunned at how much expression he could get on his fuzzy little muzzle.

Scott burst in. "You want me to what?" He saw the puppy hanging from her hands and stopped. "You've got to be kidding."

"It makes sense," Alistair insisted. "They do seem too intelligent, and you should have seen this little bugger when Gillian said 'read his mind.' "

Walking to the med table, Scott reached for Marlow. Once in his hands, Marlow put on the full dumb-puppy show.

"Nobody's falling for it, Marlow," Gilly deadpanned.

Scott looked at the dog helplessly. "I've tried animals before. I never get much of anything. Too alien a thought process."

Gilly leaned on the table and gave him a sunny smile. "But these are *special* dogs, Ash."

"But how—"

"However you do it with people. Go for it."

"This is too weird."

"That's what I've been saying ever since we started this job. Just give it a try, okay? If you don't get anywhere, that's that. But take a shot." She grabbed Alistair's arm. "We'll leave you to your interspecies communing."

Scott watched them make for the door. "Thanks a lot." Looking back at the puppy as the door shut, he sighed. "I knew taking this job would come back to bite me in the ass." Marlow yipped enthusiastically and Scott tapped him on the nose. "No, that was not intended to give you any ideas."

"They're *what?*" Gilly demanded.

"I know it sounds strange but my best guess is they're . . . semi-intelligence agents."

"Spies? They're *dog spies?*"

"I think so. Once I got over the concept of him being . . . well, a dog, I just treated it like any mental exercise, like when I'm reading our clients. His thought processes are amazingly human. With the expected variance of species-related perception."

Gilly rolled her eyes. "Of course. Why did I know you'd be good for mind reading a dog?"

"Thanks. I think."

"Anyway," she prodded.

"Anyway . . . you're right about the intelligence. His

thoughts were too clear, too much like language. Like *our* language. He understands us, and in more than just the 'sit, stay, purple' variety."

"Purple?" Alistair interjected.

"Long story," Gilly waved him silent. "Go on."

"They're the ideal observers." Scott shrugged. "They're harmless, they're adorable . . . who wouldn't want one? They'll always be adorable, they're unique, everybody loves puppies, nobody's going to watch what's said around them, and they can subtly adapt to whatever their people want of them . . . turn into the perfect pet. The only reason they didn't know how to deal with you, Gilly, is because apparently they weren't tested on anyone who doesn't like dogs. They zeroed in on you because you're in charge, but they didn't expect or know exactly how to handle your distaste. So Marlow started studying you to adapt, but the problem cropped up when the behaviors you wanted were undoglike. Ordinarily, and particularly in the case of a dog fancier like Zac, they'd be living, breathing, listening devices. They take it all in, but no one expects them to understand, or to be able to transmit it back."

"That's the question," Alistair mused. "Can they transmit it back?"

"They must be able to," Gilly answered. "Why make a dog that understands and retains language if you can't get the information back out?"

"Maybe they're just supposed to be really intelligent pets?"

"No," Scott shook his head. "You know my specialty is the feelings that come with the thoughts. Trustworthiness, truthfulness. These puppies definitely have something to hide. Marlow has a . . . sneaky feel. From what I got from him, I guarantee they're being used for information gathering. The latest technologically advanced bugs. Bugs people willingly take everywhere with them."

"Which means they must have a way to communicate," Gilly stated. "They can't . . . talk?"

"No," Alistair shook his head. "I can tell you that. They're not physically set up for it." He tapped his throat. "Frankes' geneticists may have boosted the sentience, but they didn't toy with any of the basic biological structures. They've got to be communicating in other ways."

Scott nodded. "Stands to reason. If the dogs have a concept of language, if they *think* in language, they can find a way to communicate."

"Although without knowing that trick, they've got no resale value for us," Gilly muttered thoughtfully.

"Gilly! We can't resell them! They're still puppies. Just because they were designed to be intelligence agents doesn't change that. You and I were 'designed,' but we're still people."

She gave Scott a noncommittal look. "It just occurred to me I know a few people who'd be interested, that's all. I'm more interested in knowing what Frankes is up to."

"Offhand, I'd say he's got government contracts," Scott tapped the side of his nose and raised an eyebrow. "His man George was definitely clean, so I'd guess it's pretty hush-hush even inside the business. I don't believe George even knew what he had."

"Definitely government contracts," Gilly murmured, eyes lighting up, a slow smile curling her lips. "Earth government contracts."

Alistair and Scott exchanged a glance. Both knew she had no overwhelming love for Earth, having grown up on a colony planet herself, but she also steered clear of even appearing to choose a side in political tiffs. "I don't like that look, Gillian," Alistair finally voiced.

"I was just thinking," she said innocently. At the dual wary looks she smiled wider. "Thinking that I don't care to be used for delivering intelligence agents when I think I'm delivering dogs, no matter how well I'm being paid. And that I'm not about to just drop off a boatload of furry little information sponges to Zac with him none the wiser."

"Think he'll believe us?"

"Who said anything about telling him? I need to think about this." Gilly stood up. "I don't think this shipment is going to reach its destination. In fact, I feel a course change coming on as we speak." She tugged her handheld out of her pocket and keyed in on it, then handed it off to Alistair. "Take this to Spense, tell him to lay in the changes."

"Where are you going?"

"To chat with our cargo."

She stood in the middle of the rec room, the entire shipment of puppies surrounding her. They sat unnaturally still, glancing from her to Scott and Emily, who stood guarding the door.

"We know what you are. There's no point in you pretending otherwise." She dropped down to her knees and swept the lot with a no-nonsense look. "Scott figures even super-smart, you're still dogs at heart." She looked at all of the little faces focused on her. "Puppies at heart. We're not about to hand you off to an unsuspecting Zac. We thought maybe we'd give you a choice in the matter." She could swear she saw suspicion fall over the puppies, and felt a surge of appreciation that she had backup at the door who knew how to aim. Well, at least Emily could aim.

"We can turn you over to the Intergalactic Assembly authorities." She hoped her voice sounded convincing, and the pups hadn't picked up enough on her personality to know that wasn't even close to being an option. Not only was it not in her nature, Serendipity Enterprises would be finished if it got out that she'd turned an illegal cargo over to the authorities. "We doubt very much Frankes has cleared his breeding program with them and we think they'd be rather interested. Or we could try to resell you to other interested parties, with full disclosure of what you are. I know a number of people who would snap you up." Again, more bluff than truth. She doubted Frankes would take that lying down, even with the threat of turning him in to the IA looming. Given the assumption he was working for Earth government, it stood to reason he had more resources than he made public. And his public resources were nothing to sneeze at. "Or we can deliver you to a state school on my home planet, Sarrecen 3. Lots of kids, not many parents. My old school actually. A bunch of students who could use some smart pets. They'll be extremely happy to have you, and you can . . . be dogs. No reporting to anyone, and no loyalty conflicts, which Scott thinks is something that's definitely down the road for you lot, something your makers didn't think through." She watched as the puppies turned and looked at each other, soft whuffs rising from the collective. "Any preferences? The bureaucrats? Take your chances with new individual owners? The kids?"

One puppy stood up, and to her surprise she recognized Marlow. All the puppies were currently various shades of pink, from soft rose to bright magenta. Marlow barked once, and the puppies moved as one and clustered around each other. Gilly stared in amazement as they obviously communicated with each other. Even knowing it for fact, it still made for an unbelievable, and creepy, sight. As the puppies parted, they fell into evenly spaced rows, almost military in formation. Marlow walked forward and sat, giving a soft woof.

"Decision reached?" She stroked his head. "One bark, the IA. Two barks, resold to interested, and *informed,* owners. Three barks, Sarrecen 3 State School Number Six."

Marlow didn't even pause, but woofed three times in quick succession. One by one, the formation behind him sounded off in rows, from right to left. Three barks each.

"Good choice," she nodded. "We'll let you know when we get there." Marlow stood and bounded forward, paws on her knees, and gave four short woofs. "What, you want a fourth option?" He bounced into her lap, stretching up, licking enthusiastically and pawing at her. She caught him and craned her face back out of reach. "You want to stay here? Sorry, I don't think so."

She stood to leave, wondering how such little dogs managed to make their gazes mean so much.

"How does this sound?" She handed Scott the letter she'd drafted for Grayson Frankes to sign, authorizing the donation of twenty Perma-Puppies to State School Number Six on Sarrecen 3.

Scott read it over. "You think he's going to be satisfied with the tax write-off?"

"He'd better be if he doesn't want to end up in an Assembly court on intergalactic espionage charges. I'm sure he and Zac will come to an . . . agreement. And we're being very understanding by taking just the deposit, not requesting full payment."

Scott gave her a look. "Gil. We hijacked his puppies. His special super-spy puppies. We gave them to a bunch of kids on a completely separate colony. You think he's going to think we're being *understanding?*"

"Hey, he's not in trouble with the IA, he can keep his legit breeding business, and he gets a big tax credit for the 'donation.' Just because we know we'd never go to the Assembly doesn't mean he knows. He's met your mother. He must know all about your inconvenient morality and how you're such an honest guy. He'll probably count himself lucky we didn't turn him in on the spot."

"And probably wonder why such an honest guy is working with you."

She slugged him in the arm. "I gave you a choice, angel-eyes. You could have hung out in diplo-corps."

"Yeah. Wouldn't have had near as much fun, though." Scott sighed. "My mother is not going to be pleased."

"Won't be the first time."

"True. Hey, about Marlow . . . can't we keep just one?"

"No. No, no, absolutely not."

"Gilly—"

"No."

"But he likes you!"

"No."

"I can see it in your eyes. You *want* to keep him."

"No!"

"You just can't admit it."

"No no nononono—"

"I'll wear you down before we reach Sarrecen."

"Ha."

"Or he will."

"HA!"

"Never underestimate a puppy . . ."

Hair of the Dog

by Doranna Durgin

After obtaining a degree in wildlife illustration and environmental education, Doranna Durgin spent a number of years deep in the Appalachian Mountains, riding the trails and writing science fiction and fantasy books *(Dun Lady's Jess, Wolverine's Daughter, Seer's Blood, A Feral Darkness . . .)*, ten of which have hit the shelves so far. She's moved on to the northern Arizona mountains, where she still writes and rides. There's a Lipizzan in her backyard, a mountain looming outside her office window, a pack of dogs romping in the house, and a laptop sitting on her desk—and that's just the way she likes it. You can find a complete list of her books at www.doranna.net, along with scoops on new projects (and of course, tidbits about the four-legged kids).

THAT was no accident.

Brenna whirled to watch the pet store's assistant manager retreat down the aisle, paperwork in hand. To judge by his casual stroll, he didn't have the slightest idea that he'd just brushed against her backside firmly enough to create a susurrus of sound, denim hissing across denim.

As if.

Brenna exchanged a glance with Druid, her companion at work and home. Druid, a Cardigan Welsh corgi at just the right height to covet the low shelf of rawhide bones beside them, had nothing more significant in his expression than a strong desire to make off with one. He licked his lips.

"That just about sums it up," Brenna muttered darkly.

When she'd offered to sub for her honeymooning pet groomer friend, she'd sensed something had been left unspoken. A hesitation in Elayna's expression, the almost invisible decision to *not go there*.

But Elayna surely would have warned Brenna had she known Aron Miller would find so many occasions to bump Brenna in so many personal ways. Maybe she thought Brenna would be safe; she was there as a favor to the small store's owner as much as to Elayna, providing experienced coverage for their customers. No grooming business could afford to disappoint customers at the beginning of the busy season. Word got around.

In truth, Brenna considered herself safe enough. After last year's supernatural encounters with the ancient god Nuadha on her old western New York farm, the behavior of mere mortals rarely bothered her anymore, not even those who thought of themselves as gods. After all, Nuadha wasn't the only force she'd encountered last spring. *An ancient source of angry power* . . . and one about which no one but her very significant other knew the truth.

No, Brenna wasn't worried about handling Aron Miller. No matter that he was a big man, and given to lifting weights. Or that he was actually as good-looking as he thought he was.

The worst kind.

Druid whined gently and cocked his head at the rawhides, huge ears perked to their utmost. "As soon as we finish here, we'll go back to the grooming room," she told him. "You've got a fresh chewie waiting there."

But Druid's attention shifted, his ears lowered . . . warning her. A glance confirmed it. The man was coming back.

If it weren't for Elayna, she would have quit the first time Miller ran a familiar hand down the long, thick length of her dark hair . . . and all the way to the back jeans pocket in which she tucked the doubled braid. *Only ten more days.* Then she'd go back to supervising her own groomers in her own converted barn shop with her own Iban Masera running his dog training business beside her.

Brenna thought of what Masera would do to Aron Miller if he caught the man touching her and it put a smile on her face. Aron Miller took it as a welcome and hesitated as he reached her, his ever-present paperwork in hand. "Don't normally let employee dogs come in,"

he said, in case she hadn't previously caught his munifi-
cence in the matter.

"Part of the agreement to get me here," Brenna said
calmly, ruing these rare moments of spare time during
which she was required to sort merchandise within Miller's reach. "Do you want me to pull the bones that don't
seem to fit any of the shelf labels?"

"Leave 'em," he said. "Put 'em in the front. With
luck, someone will buy them before we have to explain
them in inventory. Funny-looking thing, isn't he?"

He was still eyeing Druid. Druid, everything a Cardigan
could be. Crisp black and white markings with rich
brown points and a smattering of freckles over his white
muzzle and forelegs, thicker freckles charmingly
crowded onto the backs of his ears. In body, much like
a dwarf-legged border collie or German shepherd, perfectly built for droving cattle over the breed's native
Welsh hills and ducking the kicks that might come his
way. Funny looking? Champion Nuadha's Silver Druid?
Dryly, she said, "Luckily for me the judges didn't
think so."

"Ah?" he said, meaning, *no kidding, it's a show dog?*

"Ah," she confirmed.

She shouldn't have turned her back on him.

His touch was too personal, too definite. Brenna gave
an exaggerated squeak of surprise and jerked around,
making certain her elbow encountered the pit of his
stomach on the way.

Impact. He doubled over, emitting noises like a dog
with food on the way back up.

"Oh!" she said loudly. "Oh, I'm so sorry! You startled
me!" Druid leaped to his feet, most interested in Aron's
noises, white-tipped tail waving—but Brenna found herself suddenly facing a surge of anger so dark as to be
startling. Made uncertain by her own feelings, she was
entirely convincing when she asked, "Really, are you all
right, Aron? Do you need to sit down?"

He straightened with effort, speaking through gritted
teeth. "No, no, I'm fine. Just an accident. You barely
touched me."

She knew otherwise, but she also knew her point had

been made. "I really am sorry." *Sorry you're such a jerk.*
"Sometimes I startle so easily—you just never know."

He smiled grimly at her. "Think nothing of it, Brenna.
My mistake."

You better believe it.

But she should have known someone else would pay
for it.

She found out soon enough.

Druid trotted by her side as she returned from lunch,
striding the length of the long, narrow pet store to the
grooming room off the back. Ordinary Druid, a maturing
companion who showed none of his once unavoidable supernatural quirks—aside from his uncanny ability to read
people. No more uncanny than Brenna's ability to read
dogs, a reputation that had made the Pet Corral management jump at her offer to sub for Elayna. Otherwise
Miller might have offered her more than a tight smile and
silence as he passed her, finally keeping his hands to himself. He might have muttered imprecations, or dismissed
her on the spot. His face had that look to it, the look of
a man who's been dwelling on his humiliation, the look
of resentment swelled to the bursting point.

But there was satisfaction around the edges. And
Druid, rather than brush Miller's legs as they passed in
the limited space, dodged behind Brenna and took up
the heel position on the wrong side.

When she entered the grooming area, Brenna found
the teenaged cashier/floor help/cage cleaner very busy.
Stacking towels, straightening shampoo, the crates pulled
aside so she could sweep up the inevitable piles of pet
hair behind them . . .

"Aron asked me to help clean up before your afternoon appointments," she said quickly, meeting Brenna's
questioning gaze for the merest second before staring
fixedly at the shampoo bottles she'd nervously shuffled
into confusion, a Rubik's cube of clear plastic containers
full of distinctly colored, diluted shampoo. Realizing
what she'd done, she fumbled to put it right again.

"That's funny," Brenna said. "I've got a light schedule today."

Coretta's pale skin turned pink with a blush, and her averted glance couldn't hide the extra shine in her faded blue eyes. Brenna's mind went to the look on Aron's face as they'd passed in the aisle. "Coretta," she said, eyes narrowing, "Aron hasn't bothered you, has he?"

"Of course not," Coretta said quickly. "And anyway," she added, not seeming to notice the contradiction of her own words, "I need this job. I need this job *bad*."

"Coretta—"

"I need this job," Coretta said, and this time desperation drove her words. She knocked over a bottle and snatched it back upright before it could spill, movements jerky.

Brenna knew it to be true. Small town jobs that a teenage mother could reach on foot from the home where her own single mother struggled to keep the family together . . . those were rare enough. But Mr. Lowry, the Pet Corral owner, also supported Coretta's efforts to earn her GED, and even offered incentives for Coretta to attend the community college on the other side of the nearby city.

She *did* need this job.

Maybe Aron Miller didn't need his.

The thought crossed Brenna's mind as if someone else had thought it, full of intensity . . . and bearing just a hint of a dark skitter down her spine.

Just like the previous spring . . . except then, the sensation had been driven by the evil that stalked her, and this time it came from . . .

Within.

I'm not like that.

Surely not.

We cleansed the evil. A year *ago we cleansed the evil. If anyone here still has a connection to otherworldly power, it's Druid.*

But Druid, snuffling with great interest at the gap between the stacked crates and the wall, was having a distinctly ordinary—if obsessed—moment. Not so much as a flicker of the wary sensitivity he'd once displayed to the threatening feral darkness.

Out loud she said, "I understand," to Coretta. And she did.

But she didn't think this would be the end of it.

The atmosphere changed overnight within the store, making the other employees wary and tentative and not knowing just why. Mr. Lowry, a kind older man, supervised the weekly merchandise sorting by cracking jokes that were too hearty as he tried to hide a puzzled frown. Even Coretta seemed uncertain, not understanding exactly what had happened.

But Brenna knew. She'd seen it the summer before—seen a man touched by power and liking it. A different kind of power, but power nonetheless.

The question was how to stop Miller's power trip. She could not ask advice of Masera, the man she normally told everything. She could not bear to admit to him the dark intensity rising with her anger; she feared to hear from him—he who knew so much of the old ways from his Basque mother—what malicious thing it might be. Malicious, like that which they'd destroyed only the summer before. And she could not ask advice of her best friend Emily, who had never known of the supernatural battle waged on Brenna's land and would never understand her reactions now.

She was on her own, except for Druid. And Druid remained more interested in snuffling behind the grooming crates than in cocking his beguiling ears at her frustration and fears.

Just over a week to go and she was out of here.

But she didn't think she'd be able to leave it behind. Not Coretta's plight, not Aron Miller's behavior.

Not the darkness she felt within herself.

Brenna had a Lhasa apso on the grooming table when Coretta burst in; she jumped in surprise, barely jerking the clippers away from the dog before she shaved an unintended path down the side of its abbreviated face. "What—"

"He just came in," Coretta said, panic in her voice and panic on her face. She didn't have to identify *who*. "He's not supposed to be here today! I'm *closing*."

The grim darkness surged inside Brenna's mind; she clamped down on it, deliberately switching off the clippers and taking an unnecessary comb to the Lhasa's long grizzled coat. "Tell Mr. Lowry, Coretta. I'll call him for you, I'll stand right with you while you talk to him—"

"It'll only make things worse," Coretta said bitterly, the words hard and certain. Words of experience. "Aron is management, and he's a man, and he's older. Mr. Lowry won't believe me against him."

"Then what—"

"Come back for closing," the teen said, going from bitter to pleading, with such desperate hope on her face that Brenna, flooded by all the reasons she couldn't or shouldn't, stopped herself in mid-shake of her head. Closed her eyes on the frightening power she felt break loose within her and opened her mouth to say—

Druid barked, startling them both. "Hush!" Brenna told him, unnecessarily sharp. Druid only wagged his tail, pawing at the space between two crates and looking expectantly at her. "Not *now*," she said, trying to change her scolding tone to merely firm and not quite succeeding. Normally sensitive Druid only went down on his elbows, sturdy corgi butt stuck in the air as he peered—silently but no less interested—between the crates.

"Come back for closing," Brenna said, trying the words out for size. "It won't solve anything, Coretta. I can't *always* come back for closing."

"It doesn't have to *solve* anything," Coretta said; she clutched the side of the grooming table—young, so young, and so much smaller than Aron Miller—and said, "*Please*. This once, until I can figure out what to do. I don't want to be alone with him at closing!"

And Brenna didn't blame her. She shoved away her own fears about that which lurked inside her, fears that Aron Miller so easily drew from her. "I suppose," she said, "I could leave the dog room without cleaning up." The waist-high tub uncleaned, the towels tossed over crates and cranelike stand dryers, and worst of all the day's accumulation of pet hair still strewn into every nook and cranny. "I'll leave a note saying I had to run an errand and I'll be back. That way he'll even know I'm coming—he should leave you alone."

Relief washed over the teen's face. "Oh, please!" she said. "Just this time. I'll figure something out before the next time, I swear I will!"

Brenna wanted to admonish her not to swear to anything. She knew from experience that you never knew who—or *what*—might be listening. Instead, she let out a deep breath and said, "You'd better. This can't go on; the man's out of control." Out of control the moment he started touching people he had no right to touch, but now . . . worse. Over the edge somehow.

Thanks to me. Me and my well-placed elbow.

"This can't go on," she repeated, and softened it. "If you don't say something soon, I will."

"No!" Coretta said. "I'll deal with it, really I will. I just need to do it so people believe what I say about him . . . and not what he'll say about *me*. It's not like people don't already talk about me."

Brenna shook her head. "That doesn't make any of this right. I'll go with you to talk to Mr. Lowry. I'll go with you to the *police*, for that matter. I'll go with you to a support center. I'll do what I can to make it easier— but you've got to do something."

But she didn't know if she could control the forces within herself until then. If in the end, she would be no better than Miller himself, carried away by dark power.

Closing. Seven o'clock with a spring dusk dropping into cold evening and a small town closing its doors for the night.

Brenna was late.

Stuck behind Parma Hill's single major intersection and the three-car accident that blocked it, watching her truck's dashboard clock while her knuckles whitened around the steering wheel. Late. Druid shifted uneasily behind her, ensconced in the truck's half-cab in his usual spot but ignoring his flavored Nylabone, not usual at all. His soft whine made her stiffen in anticipation. *That* whine. The one she hadn't heard since last spring.

She looked back at him, wondering if the warning was *for* her or *about* her. His eyes, glittering black in this

light, gave her no clue. He nudged her arm, cold wet
nose buffered by her jacket.

Abruptly, she'd had enough of the waiting. She jerked
the truck to the side of the street, parking in a customer-
only tow zone for a business just as closed as the Pet
Corral and earning an emphatic gesture of annoyance
from the man in the car behind her.

"Yeah, yeah," she muttered at him, clipping Druid's
leash to his collar and hopping out of the truck to take
off at a jog, cutting cross-lots and picking up speed when
she hit the sidewalk again. The dimmed light of the Pet
Corral sales floor first beckoned her—and then, when
she reached the entrance and bounced off the locked
doors, mocked her. *"Dammit,"* she hissed, breaking a
year-old resolution to avoid functional curses.

Druid barked sharply at the door.

"I know, I *know*." She gave the door a halfhearted
and futile kick with her sneakered foot, and then they
both stared at it with frustrated defeat.

From inside the store came a cry of protest, protest
turned to fear.

From inside Brenna came the darkness, a swell of
strength, a touch of something not of herself. One kick,
two—flying strikes with the potent precision of a trained
warrior—*I'm not*—and enough force to break thick glass.
She landed inside the store as Druid leaped through to
join her, touching down on the old industrial carpet only
long enough to bound toward the back, leash trailing.

She raced up behind him, her head full of pounding
anger, and found the door to the grooming room closed.
Locked. Druid danced before it, impatient, demanding.
Inside, Coretta's protests earned a laugh from Aron
Miller. "You wouldn't have stayed here alone if you
didn't want this—"

"I'm not alone!" Coretta cried. "Brenna's coming
back—" Her voice cut off with a shriek, the sound of
ripping material.

And Brenna kicked that door open, too, throwing herself through it and onto Aron Miller, yanking him away
from Coretta. Bent backward over the grooming table,
the teenager grabbed the opportunity to slither away,
knocking over the little rolling stand that held the groom-

ing tools and groping among scissors and clipper blades. Miller turned on Brenna, flinging her into the stacked crates with the ease of his own fury. The crates toppled beneath her and she sprawled awkwardly among them, unable to gain any purchase—unable to do so much as roll out of his way as he descended on her.

Druid darted in at Miller's legs, barking with fierce purpose—and darted out again. Herding dog heritage coming to the fore, darted in and this time as Miller aimed a kick at him, ducked and dropped to roll, ancestral memory being used. Giving Brenna time to land a solid kick below Miller's knee even as she sprawled among the crates.

It was enough to make him hesitate.

Druid fell instantly silent, leaving room for Coretta's quiet crying, for Brenna to hear her own panting, for Miller to rip off a startling curse.

The darkness hovered within Brenna, waiting. Ready. She struggled with it, afraid it might get out of hand, out of control . . . beyond what she could explain. Her hand landed in a soft pile of dog hair from between the crates, that which she had not swept up before leaving. It poofed out across the floor, dust bunnies on the run. Druid dashed toward it, froze, and silently backed a step.

Miller still towered over Brenna. "If you know what's good for you—"

"I'll what?" Brenna said, finally able to find the floor with her feet. She stood, glanced at Coretta long enough to see the young woman had scooted up against the opposite wall, a pair of scissors clutched in a death grip. "Do you really think you can stop us from leaving and explain it away?"

He looked at Coretta, then back at Brenna—even at Druid, who scented the air around the crates, wary and concerned but keeping an ear cocked at Miller as well. Miller released a gusty breath and shrugged, most casually. "Go, then. It doesn't matter. She's only a slut who had a kid at thirteen years old and you're just a strange chick who talks to dogs. No one will believe anything you say about me."

"You think not?" Brenna raised an eyebrow, reached for the phone on the wall. The dial tone was loud in the sudden silence of the room; even Coretta seemed to be holding her breath. Druid, glancing into a shadowed corner, whined. Brenna said, "I think you're wrong, but that doesn't matter." She hit the number *nine*. "Because Iban Masera will believe me, and Iban has friends on the force. Or didn't you read the headlines last summer?"

She saw from his face that he had. She hit the number *one*. "You'd better get your story together." And touched the *one* again.

"Wait!" Miller shouted, startling her enough so she jerked her hand away, scowling at him. She eyed Coretta, who shifted her grip on the scissors but otherwise seemed frozen—although her expression was clear. *Be ready to run.*

They didn't have to. Miller's voice softened, became what he probably considered soothing. "Look. You're right. Things got carried away here. It was a mistake. A misunderstanding. It won't happen again."

"No kidding," Brenna said flatly. She snapped her fingers, calling Druid away from the precariously jumbled crates; he responded only with a muffled whine. The kind of whine that would have bothered her, had she a moment to think about it. *Did* bother her, without that moment to do anything about it. She turned back to the wall phone.

"Look," he said again, more desperately this time and more smoothly all at once, a tone that made her want to take a shower right that very minute. "At least let me turn myself in. Tomorrow. It'll go better for me. And if I don't do it, you can call them then." He nodded back at Coretta. "When she's not so upset. It'll be easier on her that way."

She gave him a narrow-eyed look.

Exasperated, he said, "What have you got to lose? Take the girl home. Turn me in if I go back on my word. At least give me a chance to talk to my family!"

Coretta whispered, "I'm not a slut. I loved him." And then, with a sob, "I want to go home." She looked small and frail and ready to break.

Brenna slammed the phone down, knowing herself for a fool . . . and unable to put the girl through hours of waiting and questioning and filling out forms and seeing

Miller's words echoed in the faces of those who heard his story. *Slut at thirteen.* Not this young woman who was trying so hard to get her life together. *Darkness . . . power skittering down her spine . . . a weird whisper of sound bouncing around the corners of the room . . .* But only Brenna heard it. Brenna and Druid, who'd come to her side suddenly wary, suddenly ready to leave. Oddly, Brenna thought she heard the faint patter of blunt claws clicking on linoleum.

"Tomorrow," Brenna said, hearing her words as those of a stranger; she fought not to react at the smirk on Miller's face. She held out her hand, and Coretta slipped around the edge of the room to take it. Brenna nodded at the mess. "Get ready to explain why I'm not working here anymore along with the rest of the excuses you'll need to make."

It seemed like he might protest . . . but he didn't. His face took on a secretive air, with nothing of resignation or shame whatsoever. Looking at that expression, Brenna gave an inward sigh. She had no expectation that he'd turn himself in . . . but it didn't matter. She and Coretta would file a complaint in the morning, once she had the names of Masera's friends.

Druid made a noise deep in his throat, looking at Brenna as if he had something to tell her and not enough of Lassie in him to do it. Not fretful, not worried . . . but full of significance he couldn't share. Brenna gave him a quick rub behind the ear as she recaptured his leash, and then she led Coretta through the store, leaving the broken grooming room door askew behind her. At the scattered glass of the front door she hesitated—should she call Mr. Lowry?—and then decided to let Miller deal with it.

Coretta said softly, "He doesn't have a family. He doesn't have anyone to tell. I bet he's not even here in the morning."

And a dark, acerbic voice within Brenna told her that even if he stayed, even if he was arrested, it was still a case of *she said/he said.* The anger welled up and spilled out, coming from the very center of her being and briefly claiming her ability to think.

"Brenna?" Coretta asked, glancing toward the back of the store, then at the broken glass before them.

Brenna shook herself out of it and bent to scoop up Druid lest he cut his feet on that glass. "Hefty," she grunted at him, staggering slightly until she shifted his weight into a more balanced position. Glass crunched under her sneakers as she headed out the store, making arrangements with Coretta to meet here in the morning and head for the little Parma Hills police station together.

In her arms, Druid twisted, uncharacteristically restless, until he could stare at the back of the store. Even as they walked away he watched the store, ears back . . . whining deep in his throat.

Nuadha's Silver Druid.

Knowing something she didn't.

Brenna thought she might be sore and bruised when she woke, but she wasn't. She felt oddly relieved considering the day that lay before her, a day that garnered her an early back rub from Masera and a lingering kiss good-bye. Typically unspoken of him.

Druid, too, seemed fine, and Coretta, when they met her, looked tired but determined. They stared at the cardboard-covered Pet Corral door and exchanged a long look. Finally Brenna said, "I have to check."

To see how Miller had left the grooming room, or if there was any indication that he'd followed through on his word to turn himself in. Inside, Mr. Lowry was talking to their handyman, gesturing at the front door; he gave Brenna a nod and waved that she should come speak to him. "Be right there," she told him, wondering if she should admit it was she who had—somehow—broken the door, and why.

"Let's go out the back," Coretta murmured, nudging her, not wanting to get caught up in talk . . . to answer questions. Druid trotted along behind, unconcerned, and halting smartly at Brenna's heel when she and Coretta stopped short, realizing that the grooming room door no longer hung open; it was simply gone.

Repairs. Mr. Lowry hadn't wasted any time.

But the grooming room . . .

Spotless, compared to the evening before. The equipment stand had been righted, the tools put away. The crates, sparkling clean, were again stacked against the wall. The tub area looked scrubbed.

Miller?

And Brenna frowned. For the first time in over a week, the thought of the man didn't evoke the dark and frightening swirl within her. No skitters down her spine, no fear of who she was or what she was becoming.

Druid sat in the doorway and looked up at her, expectant in some way. As with the night before, knowing something he had no real way to tell her.

Except . . .

Brenna stopped Coretta when the girl would have wandered into the room. She took a few cautious steps forward herself, watching where she put her feet. Disturbing nothing. Trying to understand what was so different about the room, what made it unlike she'd ever seen it before.

Not a single stray hair. No clipped clumps, no brushed-out undercoat, no chunky remains of matted coats. Not even assiduous application of the shop vac had ever left this room—or *any* grooming room of Brenna's acquaintance—so utterly devoid of hair.

Mr. Lowry came up behind Coretta, pausing barely long enough to ask, "Have you seen Aron Miller this morning, Brenna? Coretta?"

Brenna demurred with a distracted murmur, and Mr. Lowry left in frustration, calling up to the cashier to try Miller's number one more time.

"See?" Coretta said, conspiratorial in her whisper even though they were now alone. "No family. He just ran. He'll only do this to other women, in other places."

This time, the skitter did run down Brenna's back. "I'm not so sure," she said. Closer inspection of the floor hadn't revealed hair . . . but she suddenly discovered a few faint patches of a rusty stain. Paw prints. And once she knew what to look for, she saw them everywhere. Faint and secretive and fuzzy around the edges, as if made by a Samoyed or Great Pyrenees or even a cocker spaniel—any breed with hairy feet.

She tried again to call up the anger within her, and found nothing.

Footprints everywhere, fuzzy-edged, faint . . . disappearing if she looked directly, but otherwise filling the edges of her vision.

She fought a sudden impulse to pull the crates out and check behind them for the inevitably lurking dog hair . . . and then didn't. She knew what she'd find.

Or rather, what she wouldn't.

She backed up a step, Druid happy and relaxed beside her, panting slightly with a doggy smile pulling back the black-edged corners of his mouth.

It wasn't my anger. None of it.

Some of it. But not the part that had held the power. Not the part that had so frightened her.

That had belonged to someone—*something*—else. Something that had once come forth at her distress, had once again used her and used Druid . . . and used that which awaited it here in this room. And then subsided again.

Until the next time.

Coretta's words came laced with uncertainty. "I don't understand. He cleaned up and *then* he ran?"

Druid leaned against Brenna's leg. Nuadha's Silver Druid. Knowing better than she the forces that had been at work in this place.

"If he ran . . ." Brenna started, but hesitated, looking at the paw prints she suddenly felt certain Coretta couldn't see at all.

If he ran . . . he hadn't gone far.

All the Virtues

by Mickey Zucker Reichert

Mickey Zucker Reichert is a pediatrician whose fantasy and science fiction novels include her soon to be released DAW hardcover *The Return of Nightfall*, as well as *The Legend of Nightfall*, *The Bifrost Guardians* series, *The Last of the Renshai* trilogy, *The Renshai Chronicles* trilogy, *Flightless Falcon*, *The Beasts of Barakhai*, *The Lost Dragons of Barakhai*, and *The Unknown Soldier*, all available from DAW Books. Her short fiction has appeared in numerous anthologies, including *Assassin Fantastic*, *Knight Fantastic*, and *Vengeance Fantastic*. Her claims to fame: she *has* performed brain surgery, and her parents *really are* rocket scientists.

> ***Near this spot***
> *are deposited the Remains of one*
> *who possessed Beauty without Vanity,*
> *Strength without Insolence*
> *Courage without Ferocity,*
> *and all the Virtues of Man without his Vices*
> ** * **
> ***This Praise, which would be unmeaning Flattery***
> *if inscribed over human Ashes,*
> *is but a just tribute to the Memory of*
> *BOATSWAIN, a DOG,*
> *who was born in Newfoundland May 1803*
> *and died at Newstead Nov. 18th 1808.*
> -George Noel Gordon, Lord Byron
> Inscription on the monument to his Newfoundland dog

RAIN FELL in icy sheets that pummeled the windshield of Sarah Parker's Civic until she could barely see the road lines. She looked for a safe place to pull

over, only to find the shoulder crammed with the cars
of like-minded drivers. She craned her neck, nose nearly
touching the window, eyes slitted, trying to discern out-
lines and bits of paint through the downpour. A flash of
lightning glazed the window, and thunder slammed against
her hearing. Then, steady light poured through the windshield. Her mind scrambled to place it, just as a deep,
continuous horn blast answered the confusion. An image
of an enormous semi truck grille rushing toward her at
a speed too fast to dodge carved itself into her vision.
She screamed, jerking the wheel instinctively. Impact
shocked through her, then she knew nothing more.

Sarah Parker awakened, surprised to find herself clear-
headed. Braced for pain, she opened her eyes to soft,
fair faces staring down at her. Nothing hurt. She lay on
a surface soft as a cloud; and, when she looked around,
found herself surrounded by airy, white-robed people.
The group offered well-formed hands without a hint of
callus.

A blue-eyed woman with waves of golden hair answered the question she had not yet formed. "You're in
heaven, Sarah."

"Heaven?" Sarah sat up, surprised. Though agnostic,
she had always considered herself a good person and
now took solace in the realization that God judged by
deeds rather than by the volume of preaching and
praises. Clouds floated dreamily around a vast vista of
emerald "ground," lit by a softly shimmering light. Humans moved through it with leisurely grace, every one
of them beautiful from the set of their features to the
muscular curves of their figures. She wondered how her
plump, middle-aged person had come to such a perfect
place. "There must be some mistake." She glanced
around at her would-be benefactors. "You're all so . . .
so gorgeous."

A woman smiled graciously, taking Sarah's wrist.
"This is heaven," she reminded. "Goodness of heart, not
appearance, brings us here. Once here, we can shape
ourselves to our liking and eat as we please." She smiled.
"Look at yourself."

Sarah allowed the woman to haul her to her feet, now

more like a size six than the twelve she had lamented most of her adult life. She wore the same gauzy white as the men and women around her, swaddled around a figure that had shed about twenty-five pounds. The belly bulge to which she had lost the battle a decade earlier had disappeared, leaving her with the flat stomach she desired, and the cellulite at her thighs and hips had gone with it. She laughed. "I'm going to like it here."

"It's perfect," the woman said with a subtle curtsy, and the others glided away, leaving the two to chat alone. "But even were it not, it would beat the alternative, no?"

"Yes," Sarah agreed. "My name is Sarah, by the way."

"Yvonne," the other said. "I'm to be your guide."

Sarah felt like the luckiest woman in the universe. "I'd like that, Yvonne." Questions filled her thoughts, but they did not plague her. She had a feeling nothing here ever would. She had all the time in the world to discover the details of a place whose existence she had mostly denied. She could hardly wait to see her mother and Aunt Trisha again, to discover some of the ancient roots of her family. She wondered what they ate in heaven, if its perfection grew boring, if she could have any contact with those she had left behind, if only to reassure them of her happiness.

Yvonne seemed to read Sarah's mind; though, more likely, she simply remembered how she had felt upon her own arrival. "The tour should answer about a thousand of your questions and leave you with a million more to discover on your own."

Sarah believed it.

"Of course, you many feel free to ask me anything along the way, though I may or may not know the answer. Especially if it has anything to do with your personal history."

"Thank you." Sarah followed Yvonne, surprised to find her own gown flowing behind her with every step. She barely had to shuffle her feet, and it felt more like flying than walking. At first, she wondered if the simulation of an even-temperatured, sunny spring day would make it impossible to distinguish one place from another, but she soon found that sprinklings of sweet-scented, multicolored flowers made the pathways easy to discern. People milled around her in small groups, laughing and talking in a happy banter. A massive, long-haired dog walked between two women, its gleaming black fur shot through with rainbow highlights and an enormous blue bow wrapped around its neck. A rope of crystalline drool hung from one jowl. It had a squarish muzzle, deeply set wide-spaced eyes, and a soft face that spoke of a sweet and dignified disposition.

"Ooooh," Sarah squealed, an animal lover practically since birth. "Of course heaven would have dogs."

"Dog," Yvonne corrected. "Just the one."

Sarah froze, shocked by the revelation. "Heaven only has one dog? We all share one dog? But I thought—" She caught herself about to say something ludicrous. Just moments ago, she had not believed in heaven at all. Nevertheless, she spoke her mind, "I would have thought *all* dogs go to heaven."

Yvonne gave Sarah's arm a reassuring touch. "They pretty much do. To *dog* heaven, and you should feel free to visit there as you please."

"Oh." It relieved Sarah to discover that she would not have to spend the eternal afterlife animal-free. "But what about . . . ?"

"Bear is different." Yvonne looked after the retreating animal and his escort, the dog rolling slightly with every step.

"Why?" Sarah had to know. "Why is there a dog, and only one dog, in people heaven?"

Yvonne sat, and Sarah joined her on a patch of grass softer than any recliner. The ground seemed to mold around her, forming itself into a comfortable seat. "I asked the exact same question, and now I will give you the answer I was given." She smiled. "This is the story of heaven's dog, a Newfoundland named Bear."

"The year was 1778 when a dock laborer named Hezekiah Arbon discovered the scraggly, shivering ball of black fur washed onto the shore. Cold, nearly lifeless, the puppy snuggled against the man who found him, whimpering a heart-wrenching sound of thanks and welcome. Hezekiah placed the little animal, then about forty pounds, inside his shirt until it stopped shivering. Then he wrapped it in some old rags and placed it in a broken crate.

"The pup came home with Hezekiah that night, much to the delight of his three-year-old daughter, Martha, and the chagrin of his wife, Gert. Martha fell in love with the fuzzy black furball, its ears like small triangular scraps of velvet, its nose a quivering button of cold dampness. Gert was less certain about having the creature underfoot, the additional work it would require, the extra food it would consume. Then, Martha wrapped her skinny arms around the puppy, her blonde pigtails swinging on either side of the ebony fur, her dark eyes starry with delight, and her laughing mouth wet with doggy kisses; and Gert, too, was caught in the dog's allure."

Sarah could not help picturing a glowing three-year-old, sticky fists wrapped around a thick-bodied, soft-furred puppy with feet the size of dinner plates.

"The quiet, docile nature of the Newfoundland, even as a young pup, fooled Hezekiah and Gert into believing he had found a full-grown dog. By the time they discovered otherwise, it was far too late. Bear had become a staid and enormous part of the family, assigning himself to the task of nursemaid without any training. By the time Martha became old enough to attend the one-room schoolhouse, Bear had grown into a 150-pound giant.

"Martha had no siblings; every one of Gert's subsequent pregnancies miscarried. But Bear served as an overprotective brother. Martha never learned to swim, for the moment she ventured into water deep enough to learn, Bear would 'rescue' her and lug her safely back to land. It was born-and-bred instinct. Seafarers then, and even now I believe, used the breed to rescue men overboard, to help haul nets, or to carry lines to stricken vessels. Size and strength went along with that training, enough to drag a drowning man ashore. Martha could throw herself on Bear's back, tug and jerk at any part of him; even a poke in the eye never raised a hackle. Yet, when a stranger approached, he invariably found the animal between himself and the child. Despite his tremendous size, Bear's calm and quiet demeanor kept his caloric needs low, and he ate no more than a more active dog half his size.

"Gert often found herself thanking God for her earlier mistake. Had she known how large Bear would become, she would never have allowed him in her home. Within a year, however, she could not have imagined her life without him. Martha adored the animal who dogged her every step, and Bear's devotion went at least as far. Gert trusted him wholly with her daughter's safety and never feared for robbers herself. But, one day, there came a worse threat, one from which even loyal and massive Bear could not protect them."

Sarah swallowed hard, debating whether to end the story here, with her images of the sweet, towheaded girl romping with a handsome black dog the size of a pony. She had known from the outset she would get a bitter-sweet story. Any tale that incorporated heaven had to star death as a central character.

Yvonne continued, seeming not to notice Sarah's discomfort.

"One day, Hezekiah returned from the docks with chills and rising fever, pain in his back, and a splitting headache. He vomited twice that night. By morning, he seemed better to Gert, though he acted more anxious and he claimed to feel sicker than he appeared. The following day, Hezekiah lost his fever and returned to work; but his improvement was short-lived. His tempera-ture soared the day after. His mouth and throat became painful, and he found comfort only from the hugs of his young daughter. She and Bear did everything to comfort him: wiping his fevered brow, bringing him food and drink he barely touched, and concocting silly skits that forced him to smile. All these things, however, proved temporary comfort. Hemorrhages formed puddled bruises beneath his skin. He developed an unstoppable nose-bleed, and his eyes wept red.

"While Martha attended school the next day, and Bear waited for her by the schoolhouse door, Hezekiah's bleeding worsened. Bear seemed to sense the end. At exactly 2:00 PM on a Wednesday, he let out a wolfishly mournful howl that interrupted Martha's class. By the time the girl returned to her home, she found her mother weeping and her father dead."

Sarah could not help asking, "Hezekiah Arbon. Did he come here?"

Yvonne grinned through her mane of yellow hair. "Indeed. He's here. You're welcome to meet him later. In fact, I'm certain you will. He's become a bit of a celebrity here." She leaned in closer, as if afraid someone might overhear. "It's much different than celebrity on Earth, of course." She lowered her voice to a whisper. "Not many of them make it here."

Though surprised, Sarah nodded. She recalled the biblical quotation about it being easier to fit a camel through the eye of a needle than for a rich man earn the right to go to heaven. With fame usually came fortune, of course; but most of the movie stars she'd heard of embraced liberal causes. *Liberal does not necessarily equal good.* She reminded herself of the crazies on both sides of the political spectrum who became so enamored of a cause they could not see the harm they did in its name: over-the-top environmentalists who set fires, animal-rightists who killed humans to free creatures into foreign environments where they starved, people enmeshed in their own religions who convinced themselves that killing nonbelievers helped their victims find God or spared them a life of sin, people who slaughtered doctors, then dared to call themselves "pro-life." She knew public figures had a knack for preaching the very values they violated, such as gun-control advocates who carried concealed weapons, preachers who sired children with mistresses, politicians begging money for the poor siphoning off their share for luxury "expenses." Fame, like extreme wealth, seemed to bring out the worst in people.

Once again, Yvonne appeared not to notice Sarah's inner turmoil as she went on with the story.

"Martha's relationship with Bear became even closer, if possible, in those turbulent days following her father's sudden death. She spent hours holding the dog, reveling in his presence even as she mourned the loss of the other big strong man in her life. Gert fought a despair that threatened to overwhelm her, forcing herself to move onward for the sake of their beloved daughter. She and Hezekiah had a warm, tight relationship that had already weathered the scourge of miscarriages and stillbirths. Now, the love and light of her life had died, and Gert found herself forcing a brave front to hold onto the one remaining symbol of their love, their living daughter."

Mind's eye still full of that wide-eyed little girl and her dog, Sarah wrestled against tears.

"For two weeks, Hezekiah's women struggled to put the pieces of their shattered lives together and finally they managed to go through the motions of living. Gert resumed cooking and cleaning, hoping the generous gifts of Hezekiah's coworkers and their neighbors would hold out long enough for her to find a comfortable job. Martha went back to school and concentrated on her studies. Then, tragedy struck once again."

Sarah cringed, no longer fighting the tears that coursed down her face like sparkling pearls. "I'm not sure I can take much more."

Yvonne lowered her head. "It's not a happy story, 'tis true. But now that you know what becomes of the good dead, can you not see the positive side to all that misery?"

Sarah wiped away the tears. Despite the harshness of the story, she did want to know what happened. "Please, go on."

Yvonne obliged.

"Martha developed the signs of flu: aches, fever, and a general feeling of unwellness. Gert put her daughter to bed with a spoonful of castor oil and reassurances that the illness would pass. Bear remained stalwartly at her side.

"But, secretly, Gert worried. She saw the same symptoms that had begun Hezekiah's mysterious slide, and she hated to think Martha might have inherited something horrible from her father."

Yvonne added as an aside, "In those days, people tended to blame 'blood' for things we now know have a viral origin.

"But things looked good. The fever subsided after two days, and Martha did seem to make an appropriate recovery. Bear romped like a puppy when Martha dizzily left her bed on the third day, announcing that she felt well enough to return to school the following morning. Even Gert let out a sigh of relief. Her daughter, it seemed, would be spared the suffering of her father.

"That night, Gert was awakened by Bear's nose shoving against her hand. She awakened to a dark quiet broken only by Bear's whimpers and a moan from Martha's room. Gripped with anxiety, Gert leaped from her bed and ran to her daughter. Wrapped in sweat-soaked sheets, Martha burned with fever. Her skin felt dry, almost brittle. She opened her eyes at her mother's touch, smacked her lips, and declared hoarsely, 'Mama, my mouth hurts.' Tears filled the girl's eyes. 'It hurts a lot.'

"Gert took Martha's hand and bravely fought tears. It reminded her too much of what had happened to Hezekiah: an apparent bout of flu that seemed to be resolving, then the sudden onset of mouth sores and ulcers. By the following day, her husband had been dead. She rolled her eyes heavenward, *Please, God, not Martha, not my only daughter. My only child.* She did not believe she could bear the image of her little girl bleeding from every part while she looked on in helpless horror. 'Sleep, little one. I'm going to fetch the doctor.'

"Back then, people didn't run to the doctor for every itch or ache. Disturbing the learned man of healing required a problem of appropriate complexity. Gert had not bothered him for Martha's birth, instead relying upon the competent services of the midwife. She had not called him for Hezekiah's illness, which had seemed like a simple malady until his sudden and unexpected demise. Now, she knew how swiftly this disease could take the life of a healthy, full-grown man, and she could not bear the thought of losing Martha, too, without exhausting every hope.

"Bear jumped onto Martha's little bed, curling against her like some enormous stuffed animal. Gert raised her hand to shoo him away, then noticed her daughter snuggling against the huge, furry figure. She hugged him tightly, her hot face buried into his neck, her arms encircling one shoulder. She closed her eyes, and her chest rose and fell in a comfortable rhythm. Gert slowly lowered her hand and let him stay, though she could not force a smile. For once, she let the animal disobey the rules of the house regarding dogs and furniture."

Sarah smiled through her tears. She pictured the frail girl embracing a massive animal that took up most of her tiny bed. She could imagine Bear holding statue-still, afraid to move for fear of disturbing his precious mistress.

Yvonne watched Sarah closely, as if gauging whether or not she could handle the rest of the story. Apparently, she decided in favor of Sarah's courage, because she continued after only a short pause.

"By the time the doctor arrived, pustules had broken out over her skin, especially on her face and neck, her soles and palms. He took one look at these and pulled Gert from the room without touching the girl or unloading any of his equipment. 'I'm going to do the full exam,' he promised. 'But I already know what she has.'

"Gert looked up with tears in her eyes. Now that the rash had developed, she believed she also knew. 'It's not the pox, is it, Doctor?'

"He lowered his head, 'I'm afraid it is, Gertie.'

"It seemed impossible to Gert that her family could contract two different lethal diseases in the space of a single month. 'But where did she get it, Doctor? Where did it come from?'

"The doctor sighed, staring at the door leading to Martha's room. 'Your husband died just a couple weeks ago.'

" 'Ay. Do you think those things could be related?'

"The doctor pulled at his lower lip. 'Well, Gert. Two weeks is about the right amount of time for one exposed to the smallpox to get them.'

"Gert slid to the floor, stunned. She remembered how she had allowed Martha to comfort her papa, and guilt nearly flattened her. 'But Hezekiah never had a mark upon him, not a single blister. How could he . . . ?' Tears stung her eyes. She could not believe her dear husband had infected their daughter. That she, Gert, had allowed this to happen.

"The doctor lowered himself to the floor beside Gert. 'Tell me,' he said softly. 'Tell me how he died.'

"Curled into a ball of misery, Gert recounted Hezekiah's symptoms, how it had at first seemed a simple flu, how the fever had gone and returned, the mouth and throat sores followed by the deadly bleeding. The doctor said nothing as she talked, her hand firmly clasped in his, his head bobbing and his eyes gentle with understanding. Only after she finished did he explain.

" 'Gert, in some people, the smallpox goes as you described. When it does, it is always fatal.'

"Terror gripped Gert's heart. 'Martha?' she breathed.

"The doctor gave her an encouraging grin. 'It's the person, not the pox that determines the course. She has the lesions, so it's highly unlikely she'll have the hemorrhagic reaction her father had.

"Gert released a pent up breath. The doctor's words raised a hope that had not existed moments earlier.

" 'But it's still an extremely serious disease.'

"Gert nodded wearily. 'What happens next?' The question had an underlying seriousness that belied its apparent simplicity.

"The doctor answered as well as he could. 'We keep Martha as comfortable as possible while the disease runs its course. You have to understand this: the mortality level is high, and the survivors suffer.'

"Gert nodded again, bravely, though tears dribbled down her cheeks. 'Tell me what I can do.'

"The doctor's news was bad. He said, 'Not much, I'm afraid. We can't risk you catching it as well, nor the neighbors, so we'll have to quarantine the house. Once the disease runs its course . . .' He deliberately avoided projecting the outcome. ' . . . everything she touched will have to be burned: her clothes, her toys, her bed. Everything.'

"Gert ran a list of things through her head. At a time of monetary tightness, it hurt to know she would have to destroy perfectly good possessions, but that seemed far preferable to spreading the pox to others. 'What about her schoolmates?'

"The doctor spoke with reassurance, 'I'll warn their parents, but they should be fine. You said you kept her home the last several days, and the contagion doesn't start until the mouth sores appear.'

"That relieved Gert somewhat. She was a good woman and hated to think her family might inflict suffering on others. 'What about . . . the dog?'

"The doctor raised his brows. 'Dogs don't get smallpox, Mrs. Arbon.' Then, apparently understanding her question, he added, 'But he might hold the virus on his fur, the way a blanket or an article of clothing might.' He considered a moment longer. 'I'll give you a solution to bathe him in. Then you'd best keep him away from her.' He offered Gert a hand.

"Gert accepted it, allowing the doctor to help her to her feet. Martha was going to need her over the coming days, especially without Bear.

"Within a few hours of Bear leaving her presence, Martha took a turn for the worse. Her fever spiked, and the pustules became so numerous that they merged into confluent masses that buried her palms and soles, her face, her forearms, neck, and back. Gert barely recognized her daughter, practically force-feeding water around the ulcerations that filled her mouth and throat. Bear lunged for the door each and every time it opened, whimpering and scratching furiously at the battered panel between times. When Martha managed to croak out anything, it always contained the name Bear.

"The doctor took off the gown he swathed himself in whenever he entered Martha's room and washed his hands at the pump until his fingers turned blue with cold. 'I'm afraid it's not good, Gertie. When the pox join together like that, the chances for survival go way down.'

"Gert wrung her hands. Though she had asked the question a hundred times and always gotten the same answer, she could not help raising it again. 'What can I do?'

"The doctor had no new suggestions. 'It's all a matter of time. It takes about two weeks for the scabs to form. If she hangs on till then, she has a good chance of surviving.' He sighed heavily. 'But it still won't be easy. When the pox covers this much of the body, the scabs do, too. Moving becomes very . . .' "

Sarah inserted the word "painful," though "difficult" would have worked as well. She imagined herself encased in a crust of scabs, the cracking and discomfort of every motion. She appreciated the efforts of scientists to wipe out the disease in her lifetime, scarcely daring to believe some coldhearted terrorist might dare to release it upon innocents. "It was a horrible affliction."

Yvonne nodded her agreement. "Death usually came only after weeks of suffering."

Not wishing to consider such a horrible thing happening to the child Yvonne's story had brought to life, Sarah sought loopholes. "The 1770s and '80s, you say? Your doctor and mother talk awfully twentieth century."

Yvonne laughed. "If heaven could be said to have a curse, that's it. We keep up with events on Earth, assimilating the languages, innovations, and slang. That way, when each newcomer arrives, they have no trouble with communication and don't have to explain every technology." She continued, smiling. "Of course, that means we tend to forget the old ways, the same way the living lose track of what life was like before, say, e-mail and microwaves. The living often wonder what some famous scientist or politician would think of modern life. Assuming that particular historical presence came here, we know."

Sarah considered, reassured by the realization that she would still have at least a passive role in the events on Earth. That had always scared her the most about dying, that the world would go on while, for her, the future held nothing but empty darkness. She had heard people complain that characters in fantasy novels talked like modern day Americans instead of using some unknown language or Shakespearean dialect, never taking into account that such "realism" would make the novels unreadable or an untenable chore. Sarah had always just assumed that the same narrator who translated the stories into contemporary English did the same for character speech. The tale Yvonne was currently relaying had surely survived millions of tellings, each a bit different than the one before.

Yvonne ran her hands through the silken grass. "Would you like me to continue?"

Sarah considered. "Does Martha die?"

Yvonne dodged the question. "Everyone dies."

"Does she die of the pox?"

Yvonne met Sarah's gaze levelly, her features sculpted perfection. "Do you really want to know that now?"

Sarah did. "Yes."

Yvonne's lips bowed into a soft smile. "You're the type who peeks at the last page of a book, aren't you?"

Sarah felt her cheeks warm. "Only to see the name of a character I'm worried about. To make certain she lives to the end." She returned the conversation to the pertinent. "If Martha dies of the disease, I don't want to suffer through the agony with her. Or with her poor mother."

Yvonne sighed, clearly loath to abandon the most emotional parts of her story. "After two weeks, she did. With Bear enwrapped in her scabby arms."

Sarah cringed. "So, he got in the room after all."

"Her mother let him in the same day I left the story. In the desperate hope that his loving presence would help her heal." Yvonne's tone rose. "And it did, by the way. Her fever abated for nearly a whole day, and she became lucid for several more." She lowered her head, shaking it. "But the disease proved even stronger than love and hope and desperation. Ultimately, Martha died."

Sarah nodded, sad despite having prepared for the news. "And Bear's devotion gained him a place in heaven with her?" she guessed.

Yvonne shook her head. "If that were all it took, heaven would be crawling with canines. Few are the families who never know the love, the nobility, the loyalty of a dog. There are dogs, and there are Dogs. Few people have the great fortune to find more than one of the latter, a true hero sweet of temperament and innocent in his faithful service. No dog understands deceit; but more than a few possess the depthless devotion that earns them a place as a family member."

Sarah conjured thoughts of her childhood rat terrier, Jolly. He had never rescued anyone from a fire, cornered a burglar, or warded off some rabid bear; but he had consoled her through many a nasty cold, bathed her skinned knees and teary faces with doggy kisses. No pet she had had since ever compared with him. "So, how did Bear come to heaven?"

Yvonne made a throwaway gesture. "Shall I go on?"

"Please."

"For two days, Bear moped on Martha's grave, taking no sustenance. Like a giant rug, he lay still, his head drooped across his paws, his soft eyes enormous with grief. On the third day, when it seemed certain he would die as well, Gert came up beside him. She placed a hand on his furry head and stared at the same distant nothingness that he did. Finally, she began to talk. 'I miss her, too, old boy. I know how you feel.' No tears drifted from puffy, scarlet eyes too sore and empty to summon them. 'Why go on without her?'

"Bear loosed a commiserating whine, followed by a howl. Gert knew that sound, had heard it haunt the air throughout the first day and night of her grief. Now, it sounded like a pale ghost of its former resonance. Bear, too, was dying.

"'And yet,' Gert continued. 'And yet, God has proclaimed suicide a sin. He wants me to go on. He commands it.' She looked at the dog, all black shaggy fur and huge brown eyes. 'But how can I without her, without them? It's like the devil came and scooped out my heart. Why go on? How? And, yet, I must.' She sighed heavily. 'You're the lucky one, Bear. God doesn't put such demands on you.'

"Bear whined.

"Gert dropped down beside the Newfoundland, into the same sagging, miserable position. 'There's nothing left of her, boy. I had to burn it all. Everything. Nothing

that holds her sweet, little smell. Nothing she clung to
with her pudgy little hand. Nothing to show she ever
existed at all.' She added carefully. 'Nothing left . . .
except you, Bear. The most beloved of all her things
remains. And yet . . . and yet . . . you, too, will soon be
gone.' Gert wrapped her arms around the warm dog,
and new tears managed to form, damp spots on the dry
fur. 'Bear you're all I have. If you go with her, I'm going,
too. Nothing in heaven or on Earth, nothing could move
me from this spot.'

"Bear's giant body trembled in Gert's grasp. He released a strange noise. His eyes drooped closed, and he
went limp beneath her.

"Gert could not believe anyone or anything could die
so suddenly. She loosed a sob, more like a howl, clutched
him tighter, and dropped her own lids, prepared to die
with him.

"Suddenly, Bear's eyes snapped open. He rose in gentle increments, careful not to dislodge Gert from her
embrace. Like a service dog, he led her blindly home on
a journey that she found impossible to remember later.
For the first time since Martha's death, they both ate;
they both drank. From the ashes of one fierce bond
came one even stronger. Gert regained her hope and
her strength, dying of natural causes at the age of
seventy-six."

The story ended too abruptly for Sarah and still did
not answer her question. She had to know. "What happened to Bear?"

"He pined on Gert's grave as he had on Martha's;
and, this time, no one saved him."

Sarah blinked, wildly confused. "How could he— How
old was Gert when she gave birth to Martha?"

Yvonne went directly to the question beneath the
question. "Bear lived fifty-three years."

"Fifty-three years?" Sarah had never heard of a dog
older than fifteen or sixteen. She would guess the record
was closer to twenty, and she had always heard that the
larger the dog the shorter the natural life span. "How
can that be?"

Yvonne shrugged. "Gert never questioned, never allowed herself to consider too long the blessing God had bestowed upon her for fear it might slip away. And the neighbors believed she deluded herself about the animal, finding new dogs to replace the old at intervals, always naming them Bear. Since she acted otherwise normally, they forgave her this one quirk. Bear was welcome in their homes, everywhere she went, in fact. Despite her terrible losses, Bear kept her quite happy."

Sarah tried to put the whole together. "I don't think I understand."

"You will." Yvonne stood up with a spry lightness. "When you visit dog heaven and see the little girl with the soul of a dog. For that day at the grave site, Bear made the ultimate sacrifice, trading his spirit for hers and giving his beloved mistress, and secondarily her mother, another chance at life."

Dog Gone

by John Zakour

John Zakour is a humor/science fiction writer with a master's degree in human behavior. In the past, he has done such diverse things as write zillions (well, thousands) of gags for syndicated cartoonists (*Marmaduke, Family Circus,* and *Dennis the Menace*) and comedians (for Joan Rivers' old TV show), ride ambulances as an emergency medical technician, work as a Web guru, and assistant-teach judo. His humorous science fiction books, *The Plutonium Blonde* and *The Doomsday Brunette* (cowritten with Larry Ganem) were published by DAW Books. His comic panel *Working Daze* (drawn by Andre Noel) debuted with United Media Syndicate in December, 2001.

MY NAME is Zachary Johnson, I'm the last freelance Private Investigator on Earth. All in all, it's a pretty good life. I get to carry a cool gun up my sleeve and get paid for snooping around. I may not always have work, but when I do, it's usually pretty darn interesting.

This case would prove to be no different. It was one of the dog days of summer, which happened to be very apropos. You've probably heard the expression "a boy and his dog." Well, this is the story of a big corporation and their investment that just happens to be a dog.

The day had not started well as my longtime girlfriend, Dr. Electra Gevada, was upset with me. I had forgotten about a personal appearance I was supposed to put in for the kids at her clinic. I often say (but usually not out loud) the only things greater than Electra's heart and beauty are her left hook and fiery Latina temper. To say Electra was a bit perturbed with me would be as much of an understatement as saying supernovas can get a wee warm. I claimed forgetting the event really wasn't my fault. After all, when you have one of the most powerful computers in the world wired to your cerebral cortex, that computer is supposed to remind you of important dates.

Problem was, I had just recently made the mistake of telling HARV, the holographic interface to that computer, that I could function perfectly well without him. In fact, I would probably be happier if I replaced him with a dog. Just to prove that I couldn't and wouldn't, he didn't remind me of my commitment to Electra. I pointed out to Electra that it was really HARV's fault for not reminding me. Of course, both Electra and HARV accused me of just using HARV as a scapegoat. Now, Electra was on her way to give a two-day seminar on Mars base, so I couldn't even apologize. Instead, I took my frustration out on HARV.

"HARV, I can't believe you didn't remind me to make that appearance," I scolded, as I entered my office on the New Frisco pier. I sat behind my real oak desk, popped my legs up, and waited for HARV to appear.

HARV appeared before me, in his English butler mode, at least the way HARV currently felt a proper English butler should look. Which today meant just a touch of gray in his gently-receding hairline, perfectly symmetrical little beady hazel eyes placed just under perfectly matching thin eyebrows, a long nose he considered regal and a little half mustache that always looked like it had just been trimmed. He had his arms crossed in the middle of his long lanky body and a total look of condemnation on his wrinkled, computer-generated brow.

"Sometimes I think you humans created computers solely so you could have scapegoats to blame all your troubles on! When things go right, you take the credit, but when things go wrong, I get the blame," HARV said. He straightened out his tux, though it really didn't need to be straightened. "If you had had me when you were five, you probably would have blamed me for your bed-wetting," he added. HARV may like to look like a proper butler, but he certainly doesn't feel obligated to act like one.

"Gee, HARV, I feel for you, I really do," I said, with as much sarcasm in my voice as I could muster.

"No need," he said with a dismissing little wave of his

hand. "I take comfort in knowing that without me, you would be totally lost."

I pointed my finger at HARV. "Listen, man's been around for five million years and we've only had computers for the last hundred. We survived just fine without you."

HARV threw his hands in the air and cast his eyes upward. "Whoop-de-do, you managed to survive without us." He looked me in the eyes and said, "You must be so proud. You and the amoebas."

Just as I was about to bombard HARV with a barrage of witty and oh-so-poignant counterarguments, or at the very least point out to him that his ears are so big they look like they could act as kites on a windy day, we were interrupted. The soft features of my receptionist and probable future niece (in-law) Carol filled my left wall screen.

"Tio, you have a call coming in thirty seconds," Carol said.

HARV turned to the screen. "I detect no incoming calls."

"That's because you're just a machine and I'm a psi," Carol said with a smile that was ever so slight but still managed to brighten the room.

"I guess she told you," I told HARV. Carol was one of the few people who could get the upper hand over HARV.

"The call will be from Mr. Lee Way, President and CEO of LoveClone," Carol said.

"Sounds like the title of an old B-holo-vid," I said.

"Oh, I thought it sounded like one of your dates before you met Tia Electra," Carol said with a sly wink. Carol was also one of the few people who could more often than not get the upper hand over me.

Carol's image faded from the screen and was replaced by that of a tall lanky man. He was fiftyish and had the look of a guy who alphabetizes his sock drawer and keeps a database on its activity about him.

"Mr. Johnson?" the man said, staring with wonder into my office. You could tell it was like nothing he had seen before. I was proud of the fact that except for the side walls of my office being giant computer screens and having holographic projectors mounted on the ceiling, my office looked like it was stuck in a hundred-year-old time warp. The mix of the latest computer technology along with a century-old real wood desk, chairs and lamps and coatracks that I had worked meticulously to obtain or at least simulate, made my office the perfect mix and match for these eclectic times we live in. With everything wired to everything else and news changing on the nanosecond, it's nice to have a place where I can sit back and escape the modern world. Still, it can be a bit much for some people to take at first.

"Yes," I said, coaxing the caller back into the conversation.

"I am Dr. Lee Way, President and CEO of Love-Clone," Way said, focusing on me again.

A message from HARV rolled across my eyes that read, *LoveClone has been cloning pets since 2048*. That's one of the perks of having HARV attached to my brain, he can give me very private messages.

"My company and I have been bringing back family loved ones for over a decade now," he said, in typical corporate zombie tones.

"In other words you clone pets," I said.

"We like to think of it as cloning love," he said, still in corporate zombie mode.

"What can I do for you, Dr. Way?"

He paused for a nano, contemplating what the right words should be. "My company and I need your services," he said. "We need you to find," he paused for a few seconds more, "something."

"I'm good, but you're going to have to be more specific," I said.

"One of our projects is missing. Our prize project to be exact."

"A pet?"

"Not just any pet, a very special animal."

"You're still going to have to narrow this down," I said.

Way made a gesture with his hand; the image of a German shepherd popped open in a little window that superimposed itself on part of the wall screen.

"This is Max-9," Way said.

I peered at the image of Max-9. He was a well-groomed, sturdy-looking dog, with a light brown coat. He didn't look like anything out of the ordinary. I knew there had to be more to this or LoveClone wouldn't be turning to me.

"Cute dog," I said.

"Oh, he's much more than that," Way said. "He's the world's most intelligent animal."

"Oh, I didn't know there was a contest going on."

"He has an IQ-2 of 157.9, which is far higher than most humans," Way said proudly.

"And this is good because?"

"He is meant to be the first of many companions for lonely people who have trouble dealing with other people."

"That's what ruids and computers are for!" HARV protested.

Way looked at HARV. "Perhaps, but our marketing research shows there are some people who are uneasy with intelligent machines."

"I can relate to that," I said, looking at HARV.

"So these people will be okay with a dog that is smarter than they are?" HARV said.

"We admit it's a niche market, but a profitable one," Way told him.

"You say he's missing," I said, trying to steer the conversation back my way.

"Yes, he's run away."

"How do you know he's run away?"

"He left us a message," Way said, very matter-of-factly.

"He can talk?"

"No, no," Way said, shaking his hands at the screen. "That would be unnatural. We would have had to surgically alter him besides making the biophysical augmentations."

"So how does he communicate?" I asked.

Way bent over and picked up a keyboard. He moved it close to the screen. It looked like a standard, old-fashioned keyboard with extra big letters on it.

"He uses this," Way said. "A type-a-talker."

"Oh, now that's much more natural."

"Here's his message," Lee said. He pushed a button.

"This is all I have to say to you stupid two leggers. I'm out of here. You can fetch your own DOSing smelly shoes from now on!" played from the talk-a-type.

"That's it?" I asked.

"That's enough," Way added. "Apparently we made him a bit too smart."

"Have you talked to the police about this?" I asked.

Way lowered his eyes. "The police are only interested in missing humanoids. Since Max has four legs and has been missing for less than twenty-four hours, they consider him neither. Besides we want to keep this as quiet as possible. That is why we have turned to you instead of one of those big corporations. If our competition ever found out about this, they would start doing it. Right now, we have the market cornered on intelligent dogs."

"So you want me to find a lost dog?" I said.

"A runaway dog."

"My rate is 5,000 credits a day plus expenses," I said.

"Pricey," Way said. "But we feel Max is worth it."

"You are now officially on the clock," I said. "Did you have any signs or warnings that Max might be planning to bolt?"

Way shook his head. "Not really," he paused for a nano or two. "Though, in retrospect . . ."

"Yes?" I prompted.

"His trainer, facilitator, and communicator, Ms. Gem Moon, said that over the last few months she had been picking up strange vibes from him. Like he was hiding something."

"Strange vibes. Is she a psi?"

"Yes, Class II, level 2. She specializes in dog communications. We call her the dog whisperer. She is how we communicated with Max while we were teaching him to type."

I just shook my head. This was a bit strange even by my standards. "Okay," I said slowly. "I'm going to have to check out the scene. Where are you located?"

"Here in New Frisco. At 1714 Bonds Avenue."

"I can be there within an hour," I said. "Please make sure Gem Moon and anybody else who has worked with Max is available."

"Very well, we will expect you then." The wall screen went blank.

Though today most people travel by airborne hovercraft I don't like them at all. When possible, I prefer to take my classic 2022 Mustang convertible. Sure it's old and stands out like a sore thumb on a brain surgeon, but this case didn't call for stealth. I figured I might as well travel in style. I always liked to tell HARV, *if man had been meant to fly, we would have been born with parachutes that shoot out of our butts.* Besides, driving the old-fashioned way, on the ground, gave me a chance to commune with nature and connect with my ancestors who lived in simpler, slower times.

As I drove and waxed nostalgic, HARV's face popped up in my dashboard's computer screen.

"Zach, I've been thinking."

"HARV, you're a computer. All you do is think."

HARV rolled his eyes. "I've been thinking about Max."

"Good, it's nice to know you're thinking about the case."

"The thing is, if Max is truly as intelligent as they claim, and he has run away from the lab, shouldn't we respect his wishes? Or does he have no rights because he's not human?"

As much as I hated to admit it, HARV had made a valid point. Just because LoveClone had made Max and held a patent on him, that didn't mean they could control his actions. Did it?

"You may be on to something," I said. "But my special PI sense is tingling here. Something is up. What if Max has actually been dognapped?"

"Yes, I do suppose it is possible Max has been taken against his will. Though I don't believe you have a special PI sense."

"So, let's just check it out and see what we find. And then we'll take it from there."

"Sounds fair enough," HARV agreed.

LoveClone headquarters was an unimpressive-looking, long, narrow, pale white, three-story building that looked more like a low-tech storehouse than a high-tech cloning house. Looking at it from the outside, there didn't even appear to be any windows. My guess was this was just some sort of holographic trick to help them maintain some privacy. When you are working with cloning, the less auspicious looking the better. There are a lot of people out there who are more than a little uneasy with all-too-human scientists making what many consider to be godlike decisions. Perhaps some anti-cloning group had taken Max to use him as an example?

I entered the building and was greeted by Dr. Way and a chubby older man in a blue uniform.

Way held out his hand, "Thank you for coming so quickly, Mr. Johnson."

"No problem, Mr. Way, and please, call me Zach."

"Dr. Way," he corrected.

Way turned to the older man and said, "This is Gus Lobo, head security guard."

Gus nodded to me. "I feel bad that the dog got out of here on my watch."

I put on my best business face. "Please take me to Max's . . ." I searched for the proper word, but the best I could come up with was, "cage."

Way was a bit taken aback by my choice of words. "I assure you Mr. Johnson, Max's quarters are mega-comfortable. In fact, most humans wish they were treated as well as we treat Max."

"Can Max leave whenever he wants?" I asked.

"Well, we take him for walks when he wants," Way said.

I decided not to push the point for now. I've learned from experience it's best not to bite the hand that pays you.

"Lead the way, then," I said.

Way and Lobo started walking me through the maze of corridors in the building. As we walked, I talked.

"How many people work with Max?" I asked.

"We had a team of well over one hundred work on his initial design, specs, and augmentations," Way answered.

Way pulled a disposable computer from his pocket and unfolded it. He touched a few sensor pads. "I've downloaded the names and vital info of the entire Max project team on this computer. Along with some other meaningful information on Max."

Way handed me the paper-thin computer. I looked it over briefly.

"He had filet mignon for dinner yesterday?" I said out loud even though I didn't really mean to.

Way shook his head. "Yes, he has filet mignon every day."

I looked over the list a bit more. "Only you, Gem Moon, and security have seen him for the last month."

"Yes, Max can pretty much take care of himself. His tutoring is done via computer," Way said. "He is very particular about who he lets into his pack."

I folded up the computer and stuck it in my pocket.

"When he goes out for a walk, he is either accompanied by me or one of my men," Gus said. "I run a staff of twelve security guards. There are always four of us on duty and we work eight-hour shifts."

"When was Max last seen?" I asked.

"Our computer records show him in his room last night at 23:55," Gus answered. "We were doing a routine restart of the security system. We shut the system down for five minutes and the next thing we knew he was gone."

This struck me as a bit odd. "You shut your system down completely yesterday?" I asked.

"Yes, of course," Gus said, very assured of himself. "We wanted to see how long it would take us to start the systems up again if one of our competitors somehow managed to sabotage them."

"I thought it was a great idea," Way said.

"Oh, okay," I said, though the logic behind it still escaped me. I have to admit I never quite understand what makes scientists tick.

After walking through two or three or five off-off-yellow hallways that pretty much all looked the same, we came to a big green metal door with a palm print lock on it. This door was thicker and more secure than the other doors that lined the walls.

"This is Max's room," Way said, as he placed his palm on the palm print.

The door popped open.

"How many people is the door programmed for?" I asked.

"Just myself, Gem Moon, and the security staff," Way said.

I was certainly starting to see a trend.

We entered the room. It might very well have been a cage, but it was a really sweet cage. The room was bigger than most people's homes. Though we were on the ground floor of a three-story building, the ceiling was much higher than I would have thought possible. It was also transparent, giving occupants in the room a crystal clear view of the sky above. I wasn't sure if this was a holographic illusion or if the floors above this room had actually been removed, but whatever the means the effect was quite striking.

The room itself was separated into two distinct parts. The side away from the door was the natural side. It was layered with thick green grass and had a pool in its center. The pool was dotted by an assortment of palm trees and fire hydrants. The farthest end of the room was simply a dirt area. HARV zoomed in on a sign on the wall that read: "designated digging space."

The domestic half was covered with nice thick shag carpeting. Big fluffy swivel couches, flanked by even more fire hydrants were positioned every 10 to 15 meters around the room. The entire east and west walls were computer screens that currently had simulated bunnies darting back and forth. My guess was if I was an intelligent dog, this would be heaven.

Way and Gus led me to a pleasant-looking woman with light skin and curly red hair. She was sitting at a long lab table in the middle of the room. The table acted as a sort of separator between the two distinct areas and it was covered with dog toys.

"This is Gem Moon," Way said as we reached her.

"Nice to meet you, ma'am," I said.

Gem didn't hear me. She appeared to be in deep meditation, holding a rubber chew bone to her forehead. A sparrow flew up and landed on her shoulder. This still didn't upset Gem's concentration. The sparrow looked around for a second or two, decided we were boring, and then flew back to its nest in one of the palm trees.

"Gem, Mr. Johnson is here to help us find Max," Way said, trying to break her out of her trance.

Gem lowered the bone and looked at me. "Hello, Mr. Johnson," she said politely. "This was Max's favorite toy. I was trying to see if I could pick up some vibes of where he might have run off to," she told me, answering my question before I could ask it.

"A dog with a 150-plus IQ has chew toys?" I asked.

Gem looked at me. "He may be smart, but he is still a dog, a dear sweet dog."

"I'd like to ask you some questions if you don't mind?" I said.

She looked at me and smiled. It was a warm, motherly, disarming smile. I could have sworn I could smell cookies baking.

"No, I don't mind," she said softly.

She locked her brown eyes on mine and her smile broadened a bit.

Thereupon something surprising happened. I heard Gem's voice inside my head saying, *Max has run away. You better go find him.* The words were meant to be an order, an order I wasn't supposed to hear but was supposed to obey blindly. She was trying to use mind control on me. Luckily, having HARV inside my head scrambles my thoughts just enough to greatly increase my resistance to mental domination.

Way and Gus, not having computers wired to their brains weren't so fortunate. Their eyes glazed over and they both said in perfect unison, "Yes, Max has run away. We must find him."

Not wanting to let on to Gem that I was on to her, I stared at her as mindlessly as I could and repeated, "Yes, I must go find him."

Gem's smile curled up ever so slightly. "Good. Now be good boys and run along."

Way and Gus turned like obedient pups and headed toward the door. I followed them. Sure, I had only been in the room for a few minutes, but I had seen enough.

As soon as we got into the hall, Way turned to me and said, "You will go find Max now."

"Yes, I will go find him now," I said.

"Good," Gus said, "we will escort you to the door."

We weaved our way quickly through the maze of corridors toward the exit. As we walked, we would occasionally pass a LoveClone employee. I noticed each of them had the same glazed look on their eyes that Way and Gus had.

The two escorted me all the way out of the building to my car. Apparently, they really wanted to make sure I was going to find Max. Gus opened the door to my car and motioned to it like a game show host showing a contestant what they had just won.

"Good luck finding Max who has run away," Gus said, as I got into my car.

"Yes, good luck," Way agreed.

Gus closed my door. I turned on the ignition and pulled away.

HARV popped onto my dash screen less than a second after I was away from LoveClone.

"So you picked up the message Gem sent me?" I asked.

HARV snickered. "Of course. It's not like you have so much going on up there that I could miss something like that."

"She turned Way and Lobo into obedient little pups."

"You would have been on her mental leash, too, if it wasn't for me," HARV said. "It was a powerful attack."

"No way that woman's a class II psi," I said.

"Agreed. She has to be a class I, at least level 5, maybe higher."

"She's obviously hiding something," I said.

"Maybe she's working for one of LoveClone's competitors?" HARV said.

"Maybe," I said, though I wasn't quite buying it. Somehow that didn't fit her vibe. "Can you get her address from the LoveClone db?"

"Already got it," HARV said. "She lives in the country about thirty K outside of the city. I'm feeding the information into the car's navigational computer now."

HARV churned for a nano more. "According to my info she lives alone,"

"Good, tell Carol I'd like her to meet us there. I want to fight mental fire with mental fire."

*   *   *

It didn't take us long to reach Gem Moon's home. It was a little light blue dome house with a finely-manicured lawn, all bordered nice and neat by a white picket fence. The neo-modern dome wrapped by an old-fashioned fence made for a very interesting look. While dome homes are all the rage these days, I can't help thinking they look like simu-plastic igloos with peep windows.

I hopped out of my car and headed toward the fence. Just as I was about to swing open the gate, three extremely large pit bulls came rushing out of the house door's doggie door.

"I don't think they are friendly," I told HARV, as I watched the dogs charge toward me. The three raced through the yard and leaped onto the fence, fangs showing and saliva flying. It was as if they couldn't decide if I was their next meal or if I had just stolen their next meal. Whatever the reason, they wanted to rip me limb from limb.

"They may be friendly, but not to you," HARV said.

"Nice doggies," I said, in a futile attempt to calm them down.

The dogs growled louder and snapped across the fence at me. It was as if they were offended by the fact I would try to befriend them.

"I don't suppose you brought any dog treats?" I said to HARV.

"I could make some holographic ones, but they would have no scent so they would not fool these dogs, unless by some off chance they all have head colds. I compute the odds of that being nine million to one."

I popped the gun from up my sleeve into my hand. "Well, I guess I can stun them," I said.

"Hold the ammo," Carol said, walking up to us from behind. Among the racket of the dogs barking I hadn't even heard her hovercraft land. "I don't want you hurting these nice little pups."

"Nice little pups! I think they're either rabid or in serious need of a doggie anger management program."

"Nonsense," Carol said. "They are just protecting their home."

Carol looked at the dogs.

"Time to be quiet, boys," she said. "We mean you no harm."

The three dogs looked at Carol and stopped yelping. I could swear they smiled at her. One by one they each rolled over calmly on their backs. They weren't sleeping, but they seemed as if they had found some sort of Zen inner peace.

"They'll be no trouble now," Carol said.

I opened the gate and stepped into the yard cautiously like the dogs were sensitive bombs and, if I rattled them, they would explode. The dogs just lay there as I walked past. They didn't seem to know or care that I existed. Carol followed me, giving each of the dogs a little tummy rub as she passed by. The dogs cooed and lay there even more content. They were now furry putty in Carol's hands.

"I didn't know you had experience using your powers on mad dogs?"

"I don't, but I do have a lot of experience with men," Carol said, as we walked onto the little patio that separated the house and the yard.

Just as I was about to reach for the door, a German shepherd popped his head out of the doggie door. This dog had a different look about him than the others. He seemed to be summing up the situation.

"Mr. Max, I presume?" I said.

Max nodded yes.

Carol looked at him and smiled. "Wow, his thoughts are incredible. So clear. So pure."

Max, figuring out the coast was clear, walked through the door and onto the patio. He was wearing a type-and-talk keyboard around his neck. Of course, with Carol around he wouldn't need it.

Carol looked at him. "He says he's glad we're here. Those three were keeping him prisoner."

"So Gem Moon dognapped you?" I asked.

Max shook his head yes.

"He says she used her psi powers to knock him out and to get past the guards."

"That explains why LoveClone decided to test their systems by turning them off," I said.

"Max says he didn't want to leave, he's no fool! He

had a good thing going there and he knew it," Carol said.

I turned to Carol. "How powerful of a psi would you have to be to influence an entire building of people?"

Before Carol could answer, she was cut down from behind by a stun blast. I turned toward the blast to see Gem Moon standing there holding a laser.

"I am a class I level 6," she said proudly. "Now put your arms up, please."

I did what I was told.

"How did you know I was here?" I asked.

"I'm clairvoyant," she said calmly. "As soon as you left the building, I got the feeling that my mental manipulation of you didn't work and that you would head to my house."

"So, what's your game here, Gem?" I asked. "Are you planning on selling Max to the competition?"

"No, of course not," Gem said. "I'm planning on keeping him here as my dear pet. What they did to him was unnatural. I'm going to give him a mental adjustment to make him a normal dog again. He'll be happier that way. Intelligence brings worries."

"Do you think the folks at LoveClone will just forget about him?"

"Actually, I do, Mr. Johnson," she said. "With a bit of help from me. I couldn't just completely erase Max from all of their minds, they have way too many records of him. But by convincing them he has run away, I can easily convince them that they can't find him, and eventually they will just give up."

"Ah. Not to be difficult, but what are your plans for me?"

"You are going to turn off whatever psi blocker you are using and let me erase him from your mind. I will give you a nice cover story. If you don't cooperate, I am afraid I will have to shoot you."

"I don't think you'd kill me."

"I will shoot you in the groin. Then that should make it easy enough for me to take over your mind. So you see, I am going to do it anyway. You might as well make it easy on both of us."

This was certainly a tight situation. I just can't pop HARV out. He is actually implanted via a lens on my eye that connects through my optic nerve to my brain. As much as I sometimes wish I could, I can't turn him on and off at will.

A message from HARV rolled across my eyes. *I think I can let her zap you and then I can unzap you when she lets her guard down.*

I looked at Max. He typed a message that said, "Gem, why are you doing this? I like my life!"

Gem looked at him and smiled. "Maybe, but you are both their toy and their prisoner. Trust me, Max. This will be a better, more natural life for you," Gem said. She turned her attention toward me. "Give me the psi blocker now!" she ordered.

That little delay was all I needed. I took an old 2004 quarter I keep for luck out of my pocket and tossed it to Gem. I figured I could use it as a decoy. These days nobody remembers what physical coins looked like.

"Here's my psi blocker," I said. "Now get it over with."

Gem caught the coin and looked at it. She seemed pleased with herself and how things were going. She locked her eyes on my mind.

The next thing I knew I was standing in a big grassy open field that rolled on and on as far as my eyes could see. The sun was shining and the wind was gently brushing against my face. I looked around a bit more; the field was dotted with fire hydrants. Suddenly a rabbit darted by. Then another. Then another. I had to catch those pesky rabbits.

I started after a rabbit, a chubby brown one who looked like he'd be an easy mark. I heard HARV inside my brain, "Oh, my Gates, she's turned you into a puppy!"

HARV's words snapped me out of my Gem-induced daze just as I had run past her toward my car.

"Woof," I said, not wanting to let on that I had broken free of her mental vise. I spotted Gem out of the corner of my eye. She seemed even more pleased with herself now. I stopped and sniffed the air, doing my best dog impression.

Gem bent down and picked up a stick. She tossed it toward my car.

"Go fetch!" she ordered.

I lunged toward Gem instead of the stick. I grabbed her gun arm, easily disarming her by twisting it behind her back. The gun dropped to the ground and I held her in an arm lock.

"I don't fetch sticks for anybody!" I told her.

"At least not for free," HARV said.

"I see this calls for plan B," Gem said calmly, too calmly.

I didn't like the sound of that. Gem looked back at me. Suddenly I felt as if the Earth was a giant magnet and I was a big steel rod. I crashed to the ground, pinned like a butterfly in a museum.

"Apparently she is a powerful telekinetic also," HARV said.

"Gee, do you think?" I said, as cynically as I could.

"Well, it is possible that the laws of gravity have changed only for you, but I compute the odds of that being greater than a trillion to one," HARV said.

I knew trying to force my way up would be futile. This called for a different course of action.

"It appears we have a standoff," I said to Gem.

She looked at me. "What standoff? I have you pinned helpless to the ground. I could kill you at any time."

"Semantics," I said, I would have shrugged if I could. "I know you won't kill me."

"What makes you so certain?"

"You're not a killer, I can tell."

"I've never needed to kill before because I could always use my powers to get what I wanted. But that doesn't mean I won't kill."

"Sure it does. You just want what's best for Max."

"That's true."

Max ran up to Gem and just looked her in the eyes. Gem bent down and petted him.

"Believe me, Max," Gem said. "I am doing this for your own good."

"Really?" I said. "For his good or your good?"

Gem turned to me. She tightened her mental pressure on me, making me feel like a lame fly under a swatter. "He is their prisoner!" she said. "I will love him!"

"We are all prisoners in one way or another," Max

said. "At least I know I'm a prisoner, and I have a really nice cage."

"Let me go, Gem," I said with great difficulty. "I am sure we can work this out."

"No!" she shouted "Those people at LoveClone are just playing god with his life!"

"So are you," I said.

"Perhaps, but I am playing god out of passion, not profit."

Gem looked at Max. A little tear formed in her eye. "What they did to you was wrong. With me, you will have a happy simple life. I will treat you well."

"But I will be your prisoner instead of theirs," Max typed.

"You will be happy. I will knit you little outfits. You'll look so cute!"

"This woman is in serious need of a hobby," HARV mumbled inside my mind.

"Think about it, Gem! What's your goal here? To make Max happy? He already is happy."

"Well, I also want to make myself happy," Gem said.

"You can both be happy at LoveClone," I said. "Max likes it there."

"I love it there!" Max typed.

"And you love Max. With you there, you can make sure Max is treated properly," I said.

Max looked Gem square in the eye. Or at least as square in the eye as a dog with such a long nose could. I could tell Gem was wavering.

"You can't keep me pinned here forever, Gem."

"Sure I can. I can use you as a scarecrow in my garden! I can let you move just enough to feed you so you won't die."

I had to give the lady credit for being persistent.

"People will come looking for me," I said. "And Carol."

"I will plant a story in her mind and send her away. Nobody will know you are here."

"Of course they will," I said. "My computer assistant will tell them."

She looked at the watch/communicator I wear on my arm. The watch lifted up into the air and floated toward her. It was a logical assumption on her part. After all, that is how most people communicate with their computers.

"I'll just smash your computer interface."

"It won't work. I don't have the standard computer assistant." My next statement was a bit of risk, but I figured I really had nothing to lose here. "My computer is not only more intelligent than the average computer assistant but he is hardwired to my brain. That's the reason why you can't control me."

HARV projected a hologram of himself from my eye lens. He bowed to Gem.

"Oh, that is just so unnatural," Gem said.

"I am alerting Zach's good friend Captain Rickey of NF police force of his predicament in ten seconds," HARV said.

"Let them come, I will make them all forget why they came!"

"Three seconds," HARV said calmly.

Gem was confused. She had the look of a woman who was going to snap one way or another. She had to release the tension built up inside of her somehow. She could either let it out slowly like air leaving a balloon, or she could snap like an old-fashioned rubber band stretched out too far. It that were the case, I could only hope she would snap without snapping me.

"I should crush you like a grape!" Gem shouted at me.

Gem clenched her fists and her eyes. Beads of sweat started to pop up on her forehead like bubbles in boiling water. The pressure on me increased, it felt like I was on Jupiter being run over by a steamroller. If something did not break the tension soon, I was going to be the one broken. My mind was frantically searching for some way out of this. I knew I had to calm Gem down, to reason with her. The problem was I had no idea how to go about that.

Max, however, did. He leaned over and licked Gem across her face.

My first instinct would have been to say, *Oh, gross, dog germs*. Gem smiled instead. You could feel the anxiety slowly ease from her body as she relaxed and hugged Max.

"Oh, Max, are you sure that's what you want?"

He licked her again.

"Yes. I can't imagine anything better than being at LoveClone in your care," Max typed.

I felt the pressure that was holding me down release. I sat up.

"You are doing the right thing, Gem," I said.

She looked at Max then she looked at me and said, "I know. Science may have given him intelligence, but nature gave him wisdom."

The next day I sat in my office recapping the past day's events with HARV and Carol.

"No ill effects from yesterday?" I asked Carol as she brought me a glass of ice tea.

"I'm fine," she said. "My ego took a bit of bruising by letting another psi get the drop on me, but I've learned to be more careful next time."

"I don't know if there'll be a next time for you," I said. "Your Aunt Electra is upset with me taking you into the line of fire. She really didn't buy my excuse that I didn't know there would be a line of fire."

Carol smiled at me. "Don't worry. I'll talk to her. I had fun."

"LoveClone was certainly pleased. Not only do they get their prize project back, but they learn they now employ one of the most powerful psi minds around. They offered to make her head of marketing," I said.

HARV gave me one of his patented (literally) condescending smirks.

"All in all, not the hardest five thousand credits you've ever made. Though if truth be told, you should share some of the fee with Max. If it weren't for his well-timed lick, not even I could predict how things would have ended."

I turned to HARV. Of course it was easy for him to imply it was an easy case. He wasn't the one being mind-handled by Gem Moon. Still, he had a point. Max had lent a paw to help make his rescue possible.

"You're right, HARV. Link with Max's computer and see if there is anything he wants?"

HARV flickered for a moment then grinned. "He says

he doesn't need anything, but if you know any nice bitches to send them his way."

Carol rolled her eyes and mumbled something about all men being alike no matter what their species.

I smiled. Now I was certain Max really was the world's smartest dog.

Life's a Bichon

by Bethlyn Damone

Bethlyn Damone currently resides in North Carolina but will always be a New Yorker at heart. When she is not writing or dodging hurricanes, she is focused on her work as an artist and jewelry designer. This is her first published story.

For Beast

FROZEN darkness tried desperately to smother the alleyway, but a full autumn moon pierced the blackness, casting eerie shadows. Moonlight exaggerated the falling plaster and paint from a sign marking a long abandoned business. Steam rose up from a vent on the ground. In the light it looked like a fine mist or fog had settled. A bead of cold sweat trickled down my back despite the temperature. Fear held me still. The crumpled paper bag clutched in my hand held my rapidly cooling dinner.

Angry animal voices echoed off the walls of the buildings. I stood pressed into a doorway, trying to be invisible. I counted ten or twelve dogs. Big dogs, not the mangy mutts that one usually finds running in packs, raiding Dumpsters for food.

The largest, a huge muscular mastiff, outweighed me by at least fifty pounds. Black as night with what almost reminded me of tiger stripes, he was the largest dog I'd ever seen. He stood out in front of the others, regal head held high, sniffing the air. Breath snorted like smoke from his nostrils. The rest watched him, frozen in place, waiting for his signal.

My body shuddered and not from the cold. Close to panic, I forced myself to think. Outrunning them was no option. I wouldn't get ten feet. I could hear my Uncle

Ed in my head, "Never run from a pack of dogs, Jeff. Food runs." I just molded myself tighter to the doorway, my eyes glued to the big dog. *He can smell me,* I thought. I heard good old Uncle Ed reminding me that a dog's nose worked much better than a person's even if their eyes didn't.

I cursed my own stupidity. Take the quick way home. I never should have ventured into the alley after dark. Now I was trapped. I reached up and tried the doorknob with my gloved hand. Locked. Of course it's locked. This is New York City. Who leaves doors unlocked? Even in old abandoned buildings.

An all-too-human scream cut the silence, echoing from deep in the alley. The sound froze my blood. I spun around, straining to see the source. The dogs took off running as one, led by the giant mastiff. They fanned out, cutting me off from the entrance to the alley, then moved out of sight. But it wasn't me they were after. I wasn't even sure they knew I was there.

The wailing voice sounded male, but I couldn't be sure. The screaming intensified, answered by growls and fiercer sounds. Oh, God! They'd attacked someone. Probably some poor homeless guy. I heard ripping and thrashing sounds. Vivid images flooded my mind. *Stop standing there! Get help!* My brain shouted at me. My cell phone was sitting on the dining room table two blocks away. I looked around. Shattered planks of old wood lay a few yards from my feet. How brave did I feel? Brave enough to take on a pack of angry dogs?

The screams were more muffled now. I cursed under my breath. If I was going to do something, it had to be now. That person was going to die. I set my bag down and crept over to the woodpile. I hefted the biggest piece I thought I could wield.

I made my way a few feet toward the sounds. What was I thinking? Wild thoughts ran through my mind. Fight or flight. This wasn't even my fight. My body didn't listen to my fears and I kept moving forward. Inside my head there was more screaming. My mind told me to run for it. But that person, his cries, he must be in such pain.

I crouched behind a crate and could see several of the dogs, their backs turned to me, hackles raised, hair on their backs prickled high. Growls reverberated, sending shivers along the back of my neck.

Straining to see, I leaned against the crate. It wobbled slightly. I looked up to see another piled on top. I was pretty sure I could topple it. If I made enough noise, maybe I could scare the dogs off of the guy and then call for help.

The growling suddenly intensified. What came next could only be a dogfight. I heard bodies being flung and the gnashing of teeth. Barking and yelping. My God, they were fighting over him.

Now was my chance, I decided. It's now or never. I stood and slammed my body into the refrigerator-sized crates. They fell over with the desired thunderous sound. I simultaneously jumped up and stood with the plank over my head, yelling like a madman as loud as I could. The tumbling crates shattered the old rotted wood across the paved ground. The dogs nearest me scattered, some whimpering.

I ran into the clearing swinging the plank like a club . . . and froze.

Only some of the dogs ran. The largest ones, including the mastiff, held their ground. Some looked in my direction but ruled me no threat.

The mastiff and the dogs closest to him blocked my view. The huge dog was on top of the guy, mauling him and trampling him with huge paws. I only got quick glimpses of the victim covered in blood, drool, and white fur. A homeless guy in a fur coat? Or was I witnessing a mere fight with some large white dog?

Again a very human scream rang out.

This was no dogfight. "Hey!" I shouted. "Get off him!" None of them moved. I tried to circle around them. The struggling intensified. The mastiff refused to release him. I caught a brief glimpse of the guy's head. More white fur . . . A person in an animal suit? Whatever it was, it was huge. The mastiff had the furry head in his powerful jaws and held it pinned to the ground, but only barely. The other dogs seemed afraid to approach yet wouldn't leave their leader. Two of the shepherd dogs paced, guarding.

Okay, where was the homeless guy? What was going on here?

The giant black canine snorted, his breath coming in steaming blasts. Foam and blood sprayed the ground near him as the thing under him thrashed. They rolled, revealing a long, lean body mostly covered in wavy white hair. The fur was thinning along parts of the body, showing hints of coat-lining. No . . . *skin*. Taut muscle stretched over bony joints. This was no person. It was the strangest thing I had ever seen. The face was hidden, but floppy ears lolled to the side of its head. The mastiff forced it back down, flattening it. The creature clawed at the ground with sharp . . . fingers! I saw fingers, but long curled claws protruded where fingernails should be. What was this thing? My imagination shouted something ridiculous. My mind argued werewolves were fiction, especially the fluffy white ones.

The thing thrashed violently, nearly toppling the mastiff, then flung itself toward me. I saw its face and screamed. A monstrous freak of nature stared back at me. Crazed black eyes sunk in a thick hairless brow with a bony ridge. A misshapen nose stretched impossibly over its short smooth muzzle. Its top lip was split and lifted, snarling at me with pointed teeth. Yet in all its horror, it looked undeniably . . . human. I could hardly comprehend or think, let alone move.

One of the shepherd dogs pushed me aside. I scrambled out of the way to avoid attack, but an attack never came. She put herself between the thing and me, protecting me. I didn't have time to wonder why. The mastiff grunted and flung his body upon the creature and clamped down his massive jaws on its neck. The mastiff tightened his grip and I heard bones crush. The creature whimpered a terrible almost-human sound, then fell still.

He had killed it. I stood for a moment that lasted forever, and then remembered to breathe.

The mastiff shook his head. Satisfied the thing was dead, he dropped it. The animal crumpled on the ground. The huge dog looked up at me panting, steam rising up from his mouth and I caught the glint of something shiny . . . his teeth. His teeth were metal . . . silver? I shook my head. What was going on here?

The animal on the ground moved again. I jumped. The dogs turned toward it. It wasn't alive. Fur and skin were folding in on top of each other. I thought the thing was melting. It was shrinking in size. Blood pooled on the ground. When it was over, the body of a small white fluffy dog lay there. A very dead small white fluffy dog.

Footsteps, the dogs turned to their source.

Out of the darkness a woman sprinted. She appeared young, late twenties maybe. Short, spiky dark hair stood out in contrast to blue eyes and pale skin. She wore jeans and a battered army jacket. She seemed winded and carried a rifle. A rifle?

The dogs ran up to her. She touched them with her free hand and moved toward the mastiff.

"You okay, big guy?" She didn't seem to see me. "You got ahead of me." He nuzzled her palm and she rubbed his furrowed head that came to well above waist height. She murmured something soothing to him then crouched over the dead thing.

"What," I stammered, ". . . what is going on?"

She looked up at me but didn't seem surprised. She knew I was standing there after all.

She poked at the dead dog with her rifle. The mastiff stood at her side. His head towered over her.

"The damn thing killed her owner and several others," she explained so softly I thought she might be talking to the dogs and not me. "We had to destroy it." She looked momentarily lost in thought but quickly snapped out of it. "It was just a dogfight. You can go home now."

No, she was not dismissing me. "Hell, lady, that was no dogfight. That was no dog." I stood my ground as one of the shepherd dogs walked up to me and sniffed my hand. "Exactly what is going on here?" I demanded and managed not to flinch with the proximity of powerful canine jaws against my fingers.

"You wouldn't believe me if I told you," she said wearily as if she'd done this before. But under her exhaustion was something else . . . perhaps a need to share something. I had this sudden desire to comfort her. She must have seen the look in my eyes because her eyes grew icy and she was all business again.

"Why don't you try me?" I said in a calmer tone. The copper-colored shepherd whined and nudged my elbow with her pointed snout. I hesitated, then patted her on the head. She sat down next to me so I could continue. The woman tried not to smile at the dog.

"Kelly prides herself in thinking she's a good judge of character," she mused, meaning the dog. "Remember, I told you so." I must have looked confused because she continued. She stuck her hand into the mastiff's mouth and lifted his heavy jowls revealing metal teeth. "Silver plated," she said and flashed me a wicked grin.

"What are you talking about?" Did she think I was an idiot? "You are not trying to tell me that was a werewolf . . ."

She smirked at me. "No," she chuckled, "more like a werehuman."

"What?" Was she messing with me? I clearly didn't believe her. In fact I was wondering about her sanity. I stopped petting the shepherd. The golden dog settled down at my feet.

"This," she tapped the head of the dead dog, "was a sweet little bichon frise that belonged to a little old lady. It got bit by another dog infected with the were-virus," she pointed to the moon. "When the moon became full, it turned into the creature you just saw and began killing people, dogs, and several cats."

Were-virus . . . Jesus! She believed it. This woman was clearly certifiable. "I think I better call the police," I started to move back toward the alleyway.

She rose to her feet, her expression shadowed with disappointment. It was plain on her face; she knew I thought she was nuts. I noted she left the rifle on the ground next to the mastiff. "You can call them," she said, then sighed. "But it won't do any good." Her tone was matter-of-fact.

"Who are you?" I asked.

"Dr. Rinna Lokken, veterinarian." She gave me an offhanded salute. She again looked tired. "This," she gestured to the big black dog, "is Beast, and the others, I guess, are my team."

I was standing before a crazed vet who plated her own dog's teeth with silver because she believed in shape-shifters. Dogs shapeshifting to . . . almost-human. I took a few more steps toward the street. "Yeah," I replied.

"Certifiable," I muttered under my breath. *Poor woman,* I shook my head and began walking out of the alley.

"Be careful on the streets at night," Dr. Lokken said after me. "Especially during a full moon." Did I hear amusement in her voice?

I tried to ignore her and walked home briskly. I almost stopped at the precinct down the street but I knew she was right. No one would have believed me. I could hear it now. "Um, excuse me. I'd like to report a dog fight . . . but not actually dogs, well one of them at least . . ."

I kept going.

I walked by a man leading an apricot poodle on a fancy leash. I gave the rhinestone-clad dog a look and it met my gaze. I crossed the street to the other side and picked up my step.

Keep the Dog Hence

by Jane Lindskold

Despite the impression this story may give, Jane Lindskold really does like dogs. Wolves have major roles in the four novels of her Firekeeper saga, and coyotes are central to *Changer* and *Legends Walking*. The author of over a dozen novels and forty-some short stories, Lindskold newest releases will include *The Buried Pyramid* and *Wolf Captured*. She is currently writing a contemporary fantasy. You can find out more at www.janelindskold.com.

I'M OUTTA HERE! was the man's sole exultant thought as he backed his car down the twisting driveway of the isolated farmhouse which had been his much-despised residence these last six months.

He was twenty minutes and thirty miles away before he remembered the dog he'd left chained in the backyard. He shrugged.

The dog had served its purpose. He'd have no use for it where he was going. He didn't think about the dog again.

The dog was a big, ugly bitch, part pit bull, part rottweiler, probably part Great Dane given her size and the stripes that marked her tawny hide. That hide bore stripes of another kind, too, long weals and scars from almost daily beatings.

The man who had fed her had feared the dog, so he had beaten her in the hope of making her afraid of him. Contrariwise and contradictory, the dog had sensed that the man had needed her, a need that meant the man kept feeding her, despite his fear. So the dog had taken the beatings, even when she might have fought back. She had protected the man, guarded his back though he beat hers. She was that kind of dog, a dog that had to be needed.

When the man stopped feeding her, the dog knew instinctively that she was no longer needed. She howled her protest and indignation, but no one came either to set her free or to give her food.

Sometimes the rain gave her water, but never enough, so that thirst became a continual torment. Her collar bound her throat like a strangling hand. And then, of course, there was the ever-present hunger.

As days passed, the dog grew thinner and thinner, her belly an aching torrent of emptiness, her body a jutting rack of bone stretched over with skin and scars. The collar around her neck grew loose, but the man had strapped the spiked leather monstrosity on too snugly for the dog to paw it off over the massive bones of her head. So the dog remained bound.

The only result of the dog's struggles to get free was that the skin on her throat became sore and lacerated. This didn't keep the dog from howling, though, only added sharp pain to her frustration and fear.

Eventually, the dog starved to death, but even in death she didn't cease her howling. Chains stronger than those that had held her body in that farmhouse yard kept her bound. She stood straddling the bones of her skeleton, howling her protest into the empty air.

One dark night her cries were heard.

The wind blew strong that night, its voice shrill and fierce, its screaming breath stripping the highest clouds into narrow white lines that barred the blackness of the sky.

It was the kind of wind that had forced primitive humans to huddle in cold stone caves. It had herded them, trembling and shrinking, backing away from the wind's howl. The howl of that wind brought with it a gut-twisting fear that made humans weak and afraid. In their deepest hearts, they knew this wind's voice was that of a predator more ferocious than any that had backed man or woman against tree or cliff, than any that had mocked the stone-tipped might of spear or arrow with the supple strength of fangs and claws.

When, in later times, human imagination gave that wind a form, they did not name it for those creatures that had preyed upon them in the distant past and who they now preyed upon in turn. They did not call the wind "wolf" or "tiger" or "lion." No, they named the wind for the dog, the one wild creature who hunted alongside them. In the cry of that wind they heard the baying of hunting hounds. It was an acknowledgment of a pact.

Later still generations of humans added a huntsman who directed the wind hounds. They told tales of cruel gods who chased men as men chased the deer. Later, when humanity became too wise for gods, they told instead of sinning hunters betrayed to the devil by their own evil natures, forced eternally to hunt across the night sky with their pack of fearsome hounds.

But whether the huntsman was god or man, the cry of the wind was always the hunting howl of the hound. Too late, some tried to replace the gut-twisting fear the wind invoked with pity, telling how the shrieking of the wind was that of unbaptized babies barred from heaven. Some tried to explain away fear with reason, calling the sound the shrilling of wild geese. But the human soul always knew, knew that the true voice of the terror wind was the howling of dogs.

This wind-running pack was the pack who heard the ghost bitch's howl. These were the hounds who swept out of the dark sky, shadow dogs, their breath panting fire, their eyes glowing like imprisoned stars.

These dogs broke the chain that held the ghost bitch to the ground. They shouldered her between them into the night sky, taught her how to run on the wind, how to catch the scent of their natural prey.

The bitch learned well and quickly. When she had learned enough, she went hunting.

The man stepped out of the club into the warm, humid darkness of November in Miami. Cupping his hand, he lit a cigarette, thinking about how the girl had said, "Hurry back, Henry," and the way she had looked at him. She'd said his name more Frenchy, "Henri." He liked that. He wondered if she'd remember to say it like that in bed.

He hoped she would. It would be a kick.

A few minutes later another man came out. He, too, lit a cigarette. They exchanged a few words, finished their cigarettes. Then the second man offered Henry a cigar, extending a very nice silver case in invitation.

Henry took the case, opened it. Inside were a selection of thin cigars. There were also a few folded bills with two zeroes following the numbers. When Henry handed back the case it neither held the bills nor one of the cigars, but it did hold several small plastic bags with interesting and illegal contents.

The second man did not even glance inside his cigarette case before he slipped it back into his pocket. They'd done this little dance before and neither had ever been dissatisfied.

"Light?" the man said.

Henry was about to agree, but he must have breathed in funny because suddenly his throat felt close. He'd have said his collar was too tight, but he was wearing an open-neck polo shirt. Maybe one of his gold chains had gotten snagged. He coughed.

"No, thanks," Henry said. "I'll save it for later."

The other man nodded, not really caring. He went back into the club. A few moments later, Henry followed. The girl pouted at him, asking how he could stay away so long.

Henry reassured her, patting her hand, but he was distracted. He tugged his gold chains down, making sure they were clear of his neck, but his throat still felt tight. He drank lots of beer, trying to soothe the closeness. The girl giggled and told him not to get *too* drunk.

Later, back in his fancy hotel room, the girl breathing softly beside him on the king-size bed, Henry reached for the water glass on the bedside table. It was empty. He tugged at the collar of his pajamas, realized he was naked, that there was no collar. He'd taken his gold chains off at the club, dropped them into his pants pocket.

He got up, shuffled to the bathroom, drank as much water as he could hold, went back to bed, then had to get up again to pee.

When at last he fell asleep, Henry dreamed of dogs.

*   *   *

In the morning, both the girl and the tightness about Henry's throat were gone. So were the folded bills he'd taken from the cigarette case.

Henry cursed ferociously but reassured himself that he was already ahead for the month. There was money in the bank. He made sure that the rest of his stash was safe. Finding it was, he decided not to hunt down the girl. He'd paid more for his fun in the past.

Over a breakfast that included fresh-squeezed grapefruit juice, organic bacon, and eggs from free-range chickens, Henry found himself thinking how far he'd come from those days when he'd had to hide out in that run-down farmhouse eating nothing but canned stuff, wondering if he'd be reduced to swiping the dog's kibbles. He'd been terrified to leave the place, scared less of the law than of former business associates who would rather see him dead than free to testify.

But Little Sammy had worked everything out and now Henry was living high in Miami. He wondered why stuff he hadn't thought about in months was bugging him now. Like the old man said, it wasn't wise to dwell in the past. It made you weak, put you off your food.

When Henry left the table, over half his expensive breakfast remained uneaten. Later that day, he vomited up the rest.

"I can't keep anything down," Henry explained as he had explained dozens of times by now to what was beginning to seem like hundreds of doctors.

This fellow was his last hope, a guy with more degrees than a thermometer. It had taken some doing to get the insurance company to agree even to a consultation, but Sammy had done the persuading and when Little Sammy talked even HMOs listened.

The gray-haired man sitting across the desk from Henry nodded absently while he reviewed the pages of Henry's file. Henry'd watched that file grow thicker and thicker over the past few weeks. Sometimes, weirdly light-headed as he was all the time now, he fancied that the file was putting on the weight he himself was losing.

"You can't keep anything down?" the doctor echoed, holding his place in the file with his index finger.

"Nothing but a little bit of water," Henry replied. "I've been getting intravenous crap, but even that's not doing much good."

"I see you've had a GI series," the doctor said.

"And an MRI and a CT scan and been X-rayed, given steroids, given vitamins, and everything else anybody can think of," Henry interrupted impatiently. "I've had so many blood tests that I think you doctors are vampires in disguise."

The doctor smiled a thin, polite smile that told Henry that he'd heard jokes like that one before.

"Don't you have any ideas, Doc?" Henry heard his own voice emerge in a pleading whine, but he was too desperate to care. "I've lost a hundred pounds. I'm skin and bones, but everybody says there's nothing wrong with me."

"It says in your file that you have complained of constriction about your throat," the doctor said.

Henry raised a pathetically thin hand to point to the raw skin that circled his throat. Ulcers that never closed oozed milky pus, but Henry couldn't tolerate even the lightest gauze bandaging over them, so they stayed open to the air.

"Look at these," he said. "Nothing helps them. Nothing! But your goddamned tests say nothing's wrong."

"Psychosomatic," Henry heard the doctor mutter, but he was too tired to fight.

"Are there any other symptoms?" the doctor asked in a louder voice. "Anything, no matter how strange?"

Henry couldn't tell him, not after that crack about the wounds on his neck being psychosomatic, but as a hospital aide wheeled him out of the doctor's office, off to another series of uncomfortable and undignified tests, he knew there was.

There were the dreams, dreams in which he ran through the sky, pursued by a pack of horrible slavering white hounds with red ears. The pack was led by a skeleton dog, its naked bones bare of every shred of flesh and fur, its throat encircled by a tattered spiked collar.

Tears of self-pity came into Henry's eyes. Bad enough he had caught some horrible disease, worse that he suspected he was losing his mind. He wondered what he'd done to deserve this torment.

No matter how hard he tried, he couldn't think of anything.

The man stumbled, fell, dragged himself to his feet, tottered a few steps, and fell again. This time he did not rise.

The bitch, heading the pack that had chased the man these many nights—one night each for each of the days it had taken her to starve to death—sniffed his body. There was no breath in it. He was dead.

The pack swept around her, running the wind, their howls gradually fading as they vanished into the distance. One man run to ground didn't end their hunting, for their hunting would continue as long as humans lived and breathed and betrayed.

This was what the primitive humans had acknowledged when they heard in the terror wind the voice of a hound pack in full cry, a thing their descendants had forgotten.

There is an ancient pact between humans and dogs, a pact based on shared responsibilities. Dogs agreed to hunt with humans, to herd their beasts, to guard their lives and homes. In return, humans would share their food and shelter with dogs, give them a warm place beside the fire, and a new pack around which the dogs could twine their hearts.

As humans grew more sophisticated, dogs became the guardians of a new thing—the oath—and oath-breakers became their rightful prey. No man or woman or child with the least guilt stirred outside when the terror wind howled lest those they had wronged invoke the pack's aid in gaining revenge.

As this bitch had done. Now her hunt was ended. The wrongs done to her and to many others had been punished.

She stood, slowly wagging the skeletal bones of her tail. She shook and the spiked collar dropped from her neck. From somewhere not too far away she heard a

call, the welcome summons she had always yearned to
hear throughout her lonely life, the loving call denied to
a dog who was big and ugly and mean-looking.

As she turned to answer that call, more distantly she
heard the howling of the terror wind as the pack caught
the scent of someone else in need of hunting.

The bitch shook herself, trotted a few steps toward
where a loved voice still called her home, then listened
again to the wind. She remembered her own rescue and
knew where she wanted to be.

She barked promise of her return to the loved voice
and stretched out in a loping run that would carry her
never-fail to join the pack. As she ran, her body filled
out, muscles rippling beneath a coat as white as snow.
Her eyes brightened with stars. Her long red ears
flapped with the speed of her running. She raised her
voice, strong and full, and the pack answered gladly.

She might be big, she might be ugly, but she knew she
was that kind of dog, a dog that had to be needed.

Snow Spawn

by Nancy Springer

A novelist, Nancy Springer is the author of thirty-eight volumes of mythic fantasy, realistic fiction, children's literature, mystery, short stories, and poetry. Recent fantasy works include *I Am Mordred* and *I Am Morgan Le Fay*, both retelling the Arthurian mythos from a villain's point of view. Springer is to be found most mornings writing on a laptop computer at a diner near her home in East Berlin, Pennsylvania. The divorced mother of two grown children, Springer now mothers various rescued animals: four cats, an honorary cat (Chihuahua), and a white mouse named Fang. When not writing or being bitten, Springer can often be found walking, fishing, hanging out with her fiancé, or otherwise indulging in her principal hobby, which is the cultivation of household dust.

"BEWARE, beware storm, snow, you don't *know* what's out there. Maidens fair, beware, beware, don't give your heart to a dog to tear. Come all ye maidens, stroke the hair of the dog that bites the hand in marriage. Beware, beware. . . ."

Jake shook his head against the singsong annoyance of his wife's nonsense. There she sat rocking and droning while the blizzard romped so wildly it shook the cabin, wind howling in the pine woods all around, snow clawing the windows. Odd how snow in the night looked as black as sin, even though a man knew it was white. Maybe because of the gas lamp's uncertain light. No electricity way out here. Better hope the bottled gas didn't give out. The cabin felt vulnerable tonight. Damn rampaging blizzard stampeded right over the usual sounds, the fire mewling in the wood stove, the lamp's mantle fizzing and stuttering, the wife's rocker creaking on the pine floor. Too bad the storm didn't blanket her babbling.

". . . dog who is a friend of man, or with his claws he'll dig it up again! Mad dogs and stingy men go out in the midnight snow. Storm dogs storm dogs go go go. . . ."

A blast that must have gathered speed clear from the Arctic rammed the cabin so hard the glass rattled in its narrow casement, and the wife skipped a beat to look. "How much is that doggie in the window?"

To shut her up, Jake ordered, "Get me a beer."

She did not move a muscle except the ones that ran her mouth. "Lassie, Lassie, fetch, Lassie. Wife, wife, it's a dog's life."

Normally Jake paid no attention to her stupid talk. As long as she did her work, who cared? It wasn't his fault if women were too weak to stand the solitude out here. He gave her a roof over her head and food in her belly, and her job was to cook his dinner and set it in front of him, scrape the skins he brought in from the trap lines, submit to him in bed, and do as she was told.

Which she generally did. So what the hell had got into her now? Stupid female, she knew better.

It must have been something about the howling night, the snowstorm whipping the windows. Jake felt on edge. He hated being shut in the cabin, which was why her dog this and dog that was annoying him. Ever since he'd killed that damn dog of hers, she'd been yammering.

He clenched his teeth and spoke through his beard. "Woman, get me a beer," he commanded again, his voice darkening in warning.

She became silent, pressed her lips together, then obeyed. Or started to obey. She got up and walked toward the propane-gas refrigerator.

Something thumped the door so hard Jake jerked erect in his armchair.

The wife turned toward the door as if someone had knocked. Which didn't happen often. Least of all at night in a blizzard.

But Jake heard the thump again, then a scratching sound, like claws on wood. The wife gasped. She darted toward the door.

"Don't!" Jake yelled, heaving himself up from the armchair. "Don't open it, idiot, you don't know what's out there!" It could have been a cougar, a wolverine, anything.

But as if she didn't care what he said she flung the door wide open, and the snow dog bounded in.

Amid a swirl of snowflakes he leaped into the cabin, as big as a wolf but unmistakably a dog, with his big eyes and blunt, puppyish head. Panting, grinning, he shook himself, and white light seemed to fly from his wild white fur—or hair, rather, long and flowing like sleet. Right then, Jake felt a chill, partly due to the blast of arctic air from the open door, but mostly due to— something about the dog. It was too white. Every white animal Jake had ever seen looked piss yellow in snow, but this all-white dog made the snow drifting on the floor look dingy.

Jake felt chilled to the marrow. He barked, "Shut the door, for God's sake!"

The woman closed the door, then folded to her knees and put her arms around the dog's neck.

"Are you *crazy?*" Jake yelped. But she just hugged the dog, and the dog just sat shining white and massive, giving Jake a black-lipped smile and letting the wife hug his ruff. Damn dog let his tongue hang, panting, and Jake saw with a shock that his tongue was blue, dark blue like new jeans. One of his eyes was blue, too, but lighter, ice blue. And the other eye—at first Jake thought it had to be brown, but then he saw it was really green. As green as poison.

In that moment Jake realized he should never have let her close the door with the snow dog still in the cabin. "Get that animal out of here," he ordered. The woman knew he wanted no damn dog in the cabin. What did she think he'd got rid of the first one for?

But she didn't move to obey him, just knelt there with her face in the dog's long white mane. "Oh, my white angel snow boy," she crooned. "Come to my arms, my beamish boy."

Jake shouted, "I said, that animal goes *out.*"

But the woman just lifted her head and cocked her face up like she was howling to the moon. "Let it snow, let it snow, let it snow," she sang, "as long as I love you so, oh barefoot boy with cheek so white—"

Running out of patience, Jake headed toward her to give her a well-deserved blow and throw the dog out of the cabin himself. But as he strode forward, the dog looked at him and growled. Just a low rumble deep in its chest. You wouldn't even think a man could hear such a growl with the blizzard snarling around the eaves, the snow rasping at the window. But Jake stopped short, feeling the hair on his neck prickle as if he'd heard river ice crack under his feet. Maybe it wasn't the growl so much. Maybe it was the eyes, one blue ice and one green, their mismatch giving them a trickiness so he couldn't quite tell whether the dog was looking at him or through him. That stare sent ice lizards scampering down his spine.

The wife looked at him yet past him, her gaze just as skewed. She started singing a babyish song. "Oh where, oh where has my little dog gone, oh where, oh where can he be? With his tail so short and his ears so long, oh where, oh where is he?"

She knew damn well where her little dog was. He'd told her what he was going to do if she didn't keep it out of the cabin and away from his pelts, and he'd done it. He hadn't even bothered to waste a slug on it, just clubbed it and left it lying in the snow, far out on the trapline.

She kept singing. "Oh joy, oh joy, oh my little boy's here. Oh joy, oh joy it's my snow angel boy . . ."

Jake eyed the dog and knew it had his ass caught in a trap, for now. Big, strong, but the main thing was, something not right about it. Too white. And those weird eyes. The old trappers hunkered on the bar stools in Furtown liked to tell tales of creatures that spawned in the snow, but Jake had always figured they were cracked. Maybe it was happening to him now, maybe he was imagining. . . . No. There was something strange going on, and he needed time to figure out how to deal with it.

"That dog can stay till morning," Jake told the wife sternly, as if he were in charge, as if the dog hadn't made up his mind for him. "Not a minute longer." He slammed another log into the wood stove, then strode back to his chair, his shoulders steely with tension.

The wife squeezed the dog, then got up and danced to the fridge, singing her stupid song. "Joy, joy, it's my boy, boy, boy . . ." That was what she'd called that damn pooch he'd killed, BoyBoy. "C'mere, BoyBoy," like it was a goddamn human child. Ugly little brown mop. Wouldn't keep its stinking teeth off his furs. Now what, was she getting the big white monster something to eat?

It wasn't until after they'd gone to bed and she was asleep that it hit Jake: she never did bring him his beer.

Jake didn't sleep much. All night the blizzard howled around the cabin, but that wasn't what kept him awake. Blizzards he was used to. Damn freaky white snow dogs he was not. He wondered again whether he was imagining things, whether he'd been alone too much, whether he was going crazy. He spent half the night stroking his beard to help him calm down and think. At first light, before the wife was awake, he got up, figuring he'd get that damn dog out of his cabin before she knew a thing about it. He'd use a club to drive it out if he had to. Or a gun. Most stray dogs will run at the sight of a gun. Barefoot, he padded toward where they'd left the dog sleeping on the braided rug near the wood stove—

Jake gave a yell fit to wake the dead.

Certainly it awakened the dog.

Only it wasn't a dog. It was a boy.

Buck naked, adolescent, and skinny, he lay on the floor looking up at Jake as calm as snow, and there was no way for Jake to try to tell himself this was a normal kid who had wandered in somehow. This boy's skin was blue, denim blue. All over. His lips looked black. His hair, shaggy and hanging to his shoulders, was pure snow white. And his eyes, one ice blue, one green, stared at Jake yet through him, as if one eye watched out, but the other watched eternity. And Jake would never know which was which.

From behind him came his wife's singsong voice, placid and glad. "Oh barefoot boy with cheek of indigo, shall we run and play in the snow?"

Jake spun to glare at her standing there in her flannel nightgown, her chenille bathrobe, her old brown slippers. The weird boy got up, walked across the cabin and helped himself to a hunk of bread from the loaf on the table. Without a word. Maybe he couldn't talk. He walked on his hind legs, all right, but he took the bread straight into his mouth, gnawing at the loaf, using his hands like paws.

"Get him out of here," Jake ordered his wife. *"Now."*

But she didn't even look at him to acknowledge the command. Acting like she hadn't heard him, singing, "Snow, snow, beautiful snow," she sashayed right past him, opened the door of the wood stove, and started building up the fire.

Jake opened his mouth to roar, but closed it again without making a sound. No use roaring and wasting his breath. She had him by the short and curlies, and she knew it and *he* knew it. Throwing a stray dog out of the cabin was one thing, but putting a human being out the door in a blizzard was different. Likely to bring the law down on him. Sheriff wouldn't know the person wasn't really human. Wouldn't know he was denim blue. Any dead body would be blue when they found it.

Besides which, he had to be going crazy. None of this could possibly be happening.

Still singing, with her bathrobe swirling, the wife waltzed over to the propane gas stove to make breakfast, patting the naked boy's silky snow-white hair as she passed him.

Jake burst out, "God's sake, put some clothes on him." He didn't care if the boy froze, but the sight of the damn kid's navy-blue groin offended him.

She made no move to obey him. "Ring around the clothesies, pocket full of nosies," she sang, placing a plate full of scrambled eggs and toast in front of the boy. "Here, boy," she cooed, and he put his face right down in the food. Disgusting. But as if she loved the sight of him, she sat down across from him with her own breakfast.

Still standing there in his long underwear on the braided rug, for a moment Jake felt so stunned he couldn't move or speak. Then, with a wordless bellow of rage, he leaped. How dare she serve food to this intruder, and to *herself,* before him? He would give her a black eye for that.

But as quickly as he leaped, the strange skinny boy

moved faster, vaulting lightly over the table and landing
on his bare blue feet like a cat, in Jake's way. Jake heard
a sound like hissing snow as he snarled, teeth bared.
And his teeth were sure as hell not a boy's normal baby
teeth. They were frost-white fangs.

Jake stood a head taller than the boy, and knew himself to be no coward. He'd taken on his share of fights—
but with *men,* not with—not with freaks. That snarl froze
him to the floor. Right to his icy bones, sure as sin, Jake
knew that dog-boy would rip his throat out if he moved.

It was real. It was happening.

And the woman sat there eating her breakfast.

Goddamn everything, it was her dog, or boy, or freak,
whatever, weird brute that had spawned in the snow,
and she'd better damn well call it off. "Wife! Get him
away from me," Jake commanded, his voice coming out
hoarse.

She glanced up briefly, as if she had heard some sort
of a strange noise amid the sighing of the wind, the patter of snow sifting through the cracks of the doorframe.
Then, losing interest, she took another bite of scrambled eggs.

"Woman!" Jake roared. "Dammit, come here!" His
raised voice ought to bring her scurrying, or he would
have to beat the nonsense out of her. Once he got this
snarling dog-boy out of his way.

The wife swallowed her last bite of breakfast, laid
down her fork, wiped her hands on a dishcloth, then
stood. Taking her good old time. He would knock her
silly—

Christ, she still wasn't obeying him! She just stood
there looking at him.

"Come *here,* stupid!"

She looked him straight in the eye. She never did that.
He didn't like it.

She spoke. For the first time in years she spoke a
direct sentence to him. Four words. She said, "What is
my name?"

"What?" Flabbergasted anew, and preoccupied by
keeping an eye on the growling dog-boy, Jake truly did
not understand the question.

She repeated, "What is my name?"

Her name? Stupid twit, her friends—back when she'd had friends, before he'd taken her away—they used to call her Witchie. For Witch Hazel. Her name was Hazel.

She wanted him to say it for some damn fool reason.

And he'd be coated in cornmeal and fried in lard like a walleye pike before he did anything *she* said. What the hell was she trying to do, order him around?

Anger made Jake twitch and clench his fists. The boy crouched to spring, his growl escalating to a snarl to a roar.

"What is my name?" the woman demanded for the third time.

Jake felt himself shaking with righteous rage, such fiery wrath that it consumed his fear. To hell with the blue boy; he turned on his wife, fist raised. *"Bitch!"* he screamed. "You—" He was going to tell her to shut her fat mouth, but the minute he called her a bitch, she smiled.

That smile made Jake want to club her down the way he'd clubbed the little brown dog, beat her into the snow and let it bury her. Kill her. He would have done it, too—but in that instant, her smiling lips went black. She opened her mouth to speak, and her voice came out a fay, gay yowl.

"Bitch . . ." Jake's voice came out a hoarse whisper this time. Blinking, he staggered back and almost fell. His breath seemed to turn solid in his throat, choking him as he gawked.

The woman's nightgown and bathrobe lay in a heap on the floor, and the creature that had been his wife stood over them, settling from its hind legs to all fours, another goddamn snow dog. Big. Blue-tongued, panting, grinning. Gleaming with its own eerie light. But not just like the first one. This one's sleety white fur shimmered with an ice-blue tinge. And its eyes gleamed almost yellow, that yellow-brown color, what was the name of it . . . ?

Hazel.

The blue dog barked loudly, wildly, and dashed to the blue boy. Joy! Joy! Joy! it barked, rearing to place its great paws on his shoulders.

With indifference like weather changing, the blue boy turned away from Jake, no longer snarling. But Jake just stood there, still too staggered to do anything. With a black-lipped smile the boy patted the tall blue dog. It slurped his face, then jumped away from him to paw at the door.

"Hey! Where you think you're going?" Jake yelled, getting his breath and his voice back. By God, she might be a dog now but in a way she always had been and anyhow she was still his possession. "You're not going anywhere!" He jumped to grab the rifle from its elk-antler rack on the wall. He'd shoot her before he'd let her run off on him.

But as he raised the rifle and turned, a blast of icy air swirled into the cabin through the open door. There stood the blue boy like a naked butler, holding the door open; it seemed he knew how to use his hands after all. And the hazel-eyed dog bounded out the door, romping into three feet of snow.

Jake still had time for a shot. Rifle to his shoulder, he took quick aim.

The boy turned and stepped into his way. Too furious to care anymore whether the blue freak was human, Jake squeezed the trigger—

Crack, like the crack of doom doubly loud in the cabin, the shot sounded, and Jake knew the bullet had to have gone right through the boy, couldn't possibly have missed at that range—but the weird boy just stood there. He snarled, pointed at Jake, and a blast of snow slammed Jake's eyes with the force of water from a fire hose, bowling him over, blinding him.

He heard a sardonic, youthful male voice say "Bye-bye." Or was it "BoyBoy"? He heard the door close.

After a moment Jake got his eyes cleared, but he still couldn't see a thing. It was like a whiteout in the cabin, snow fogging the air, like being blind with white rather than with night. Leaving the rifle, Jake crawled toward the window. His hand encountered something lying on the floor—a bullet. It had bounced right off the damn freaky kid.

There. Faint light from the window, from outside, shone through the blizzard going on inside the cabin. More snow was flying inside than out, by the looks of things; the storm seemed to be over out there. Jake reached for the windowsill and pulled himself erect, swaying on his feet as he looked out. But the woods loomed close around the cabin, and already the runaways had disappeared between the towering pines.

Jake utilized his stash of whiskey and drank his way through that day. But the next day at dawn he groaned, cursed the woman who had left him to fix his own breakfast, got up, and despite his hangover he got into his gear and headed out on his snowmobile to run his trapline.

At the first trap he stood stroking the ice from his beard with one gloved hand, just looking.

There had been a fox in it. Tracks. Orange smudge of blood on the snow. But the jaws of the trap grinned toothily up at him, sprung and empty. And there—human tracks in the snow.

Barefoot.

His? Hers? Jake couldn't tell.

But he saw clearly enough that those human footprints didn't lead up to the trap or away. Only canine prints did.

Floating over the snow from somewhere deep in the forest came a singsong voice: "But when he got there, the cupboard was bare, and so the poor doggie had none . . ."

Jake whirled, rifle to his shoulder, but he couldn't spot her.

"Beware, beware!" the voice sang. "Don't give your heart to a dog to tear."

Even snug within his top-of-the-line snowmobile suit, Jake felt cold.

But he tried to act normal. He bent over the trap, reset it, baited it, and went on. Nothing else he could do.

The next trap was like the first. Dog tracks, bare human footprints, and the mink long gone. Jake wondered whether it was the woman or the boy who had released it. Or both. He wondered whether she had mated with him yet. Whether in dog form or human. Or both. He felt his mind begin to crackle like thin ice.

In the third trap he found a wolverine caught by the head, dead the minute the trap was sprung. But its pelt had been torn to ribbons by sharp teeth.

The next three traps showed only dog tracks, and

human tracks, and had been sprung before they could catch anything.

At nightfall Jake returned to the cabin with an empty belly, no pelts, no supper waiting on the table, and in his mind an uproar like a glacier calving.

All night he lay awake stroking his beard.

The next day he went out again. Didn't know what else to do. Told himself maybe they'd get tired of tormenting him.

Zooming up to the first trap, he smiled, because, yes, he saw something brown and furry lying in the snow. Some animal.

But as he approached, it stood up, shook itself, and yapped happily at him.

Jake stopped the snowmobile with a jerk, and seemed to feel his heart stop at the same time.

It was not in the trap. And it was not a fox or a mink. It was a little brown bobtail dog with floppy ears and moppy hair.

It was BoyBoy.

But it couldn't be. Unless he had hit a new low and was seeing ghosts.

Bright-eyed, the little dog panted at him with all the joy in the world.

Jake felt his whole body shrink with cold. Hands shaking, he fumbled for his rifle.

The little brown mop of a dog turned its head and leaped from joy into ecstasy, frolicking over the surface of the snow with its stubby tail waving.

Jake turned to see the ice-blue bitch trot up and lick the little dog's face.

Sitting in the snow, she faced him, and the little dog sheltered under her belly like a pup.

Jake jammed the rifle to his shoulder and leveled it at her. Even though his hands shook so badly he couldn't get the crosshairs centered on her, still, he knew he couldn't miss at that range. He fired.

She sat there giving him a black-lipped grin.

He fired again, and again. From under her unflinching belly the little dog yapped at him, and there was nothing more infuriating to Jake than the yap yap yap of a useless lap dog. He blasted half a dozen rounds rapid-fire.

BoyBoy barked on, and the blue bitch panted as if she were laughing at him.

A soprano voice spoke, seeming to chant right inside Jake's mind. "Beware, beware! Snow, snow, you don't *know* what's out there."

"Shut up," he whispered.

But she did not shut up. "Beware the dog who is a hand in marriage, or with her claws she'll dig it up again."

Jake let the rifle drop right into the snow. He revved the snowmobile and got out of there. Back at the cabin, he didn't even pack a bag, just grabbed the keys to the 4X4 and went.

He headed out of those snowy woods and kept going, fully intending not to stop until he reached someplace where snow never fell. Never.

Improper Congress

by Elaine Quon

Elaine Quon has been writing since her first crayon. Her exploits include bad poetry, journals filled with emotional tripe, short stories her peers called "weird," using method acting techniques to create fictional characters, and a stint as a developmental editor for a sex education magazine. These days, she's working on a novel about a bodyguard, but dabbles in short stories so she can actually finish something. With a bachelor's degree in physics, she takes great pride in decreasing entropy locally and contributing her share to the heat death of the universe. A perpetual daydreamer, she'd view a stint in solitary confinement as a creative opportunity and a good chance to evade her chores. She lives in a no-dogs-allowed apartment (sob!) in California with her domestic partner of sixteen years, who spoils her rotten.

I MET THEM on Coalinius 19, the armpit of the region. Actually, the entire region was an armpit. There was just barely enough work for an itinerant lawyer that I had a dim hope of earning enough to return to somewhere more hospitable. In between contract gigs, I needed two things. Food. And entertainment. Of the female kind.

Anyway, I was walking back to my bartered rooms with a large box of hazah. The smell of the eelwort was making me salivate.

The lowlifes here still used automobiles for transportation. It was like going back to the Age of Destruction. I suppose I should have been grateful they weren't still using organic byproducts for fuel.

The human eve and her dog were walking the other way. She was a thirtysomething with a head of short strawberry-blonde fuzz. Not exactly a looker, flat-chested, built rather like a boy, strong jawline . . . a look that was popular in another era, but I couldn't recall which one.

Walking beside her was a little dog. I hadn't seen a dog of any kind since Bakaan 2. This one was a little mutt, mostly tan with some black patches. One ear stood up straight, the other folded down in a triangle.

I'm not really a dog man. And, in my experience, the little ones tend to be teeth-grindingly hyperactive and obnoxious as a horny morthon. Although this one seemed calm enough.

The redhead approached me eagerly, as her dog growled at our feet. "Time for dinner," she announced with an inanely happy expression on her face. She wrapped an arm around my waist and rested her head on my shoulder.

Her little pet began to bark.

"Not now, Muff," she said impatiently.

I was frozen by her odd behavior. But her scent had all the right pheromones, so maybe this was entertainment falling into my lap.

It would be nice not to have to work for it for a change. Coaline females expected to be courted, even for a quick one. A lot of bother for a basic biological function, in my opinion.

Observing my hesitation, she ran her fingers down to my crotch and rubbed. Charlie responded right away. There *was* enough hazah for four, and we could pick off a few pieces of eelwort for her pup.

So ignoring the obviously pissed dog, I ventured, "Dinner *and* IC?"

How "eye-see," improper congress, became the buzzword for sex, I'll never know. There's probably a good story there, if you knew a linguistic historian to ask.

The strange woman nodded vigorously. "Dinner first. Dinner first." She leaned toward the box, inhaling frantically. The gleam in her eye suggested that she was about to snatch it from my hands, but she didn't.

Odd eve. And very hungry. I'd have thought she was space trash, but there was plenty of meat on her.

So, the eve was really weird, but she was ready to go. And so was Charlie. Why not, then?

"Okay," I held up my free hand, in a feigned surrender. "C'mon."

As we headed toward my apartment, the little dog followed. *After dinner, you're going in the bathroom, Toto.*

"So what's your name?" I asked, as we headed up the tube to my unit.

"Louise," she replied, pressing her hands against the door of the tube, as if she couldn't wait for it to open.

She didn't ask my name. "I'm Peter of Methan."

She tilted her head at me in a curiously uncurious way. The dog gave a short bark that sounded like a reprimand.

Louise of planet-unknown said blandly, "Nice to meet you."

When the tube finally opened, we stepped into the lobby. It's more than a little shabby, but unlike some previous dates, she didn't demur, just marched through the lobby at a high rate of speed.

I started to wonder just what she was so eager about. I've got so little cash on me that I wasn't worried about being robbed. There was nothing in my apartment worth stealing.

She seemed to like me a great deal, though I could not fathom why. She didn't know anything about me to like. I didn't look like wasteport refuse, but I wasn't what anyone would call handsome.

I chalked it off to gamma radiation poisoning. A lot of the new downsiders are non compos mentis for a few days.

It was going to be a weird evening, but I didn't really mind. Maybe she'd be kinky in bed? One could only hope. As far as I was concerned, the more improper the congress, the better.

Inside my apartment, I put the box on the table and went to the plumbing module for water. When I returned, she'd gotten the box open and was chomping down the hazah like a hungry morthon.

It was a good thing I'd gotten a full platter.

Well fed she might have been, but this eve was *hungry*. I had a feeling she could have eaten the whole thing.

She gave me only a fleeting glance as I scooped off a large piece for myself. Tossing a slab of eelwort at the mutt, I took a bite.

The dog allowed the meat to land on the floor, sniffed it suspiciously, then lay down again, resting his chin on a paw. His tiny shoulders seemed to slump.

"Is your dog okay?"

Louise glanced at her pet. "Yeah, sure," she said around a mouth full of food.

My guest consumed the entire rest of the hazah in the time it took me to take three bites. Then she downed a full glass of water and rose to get more. Drinking that, she glanced around the kitchen, as if she was looking for more food.

Spying a box of Flavor-Over-Nutrition brand chocolate-and-smeek carbohydrate crunches, she reached for it.

The dog barked, again sounding very critical. Definitely going into the bathroom for the IC. I didn't need to hear about my technique from a zorned dog.

Louise looked at it and gave an exaggerated frown. Then turning to me, she asked, "Uh, okay?"

"Sure, go right ahead." Good thing food was cheap on this planet.

Louise inhaled the box of crunches. When there was only one left she eyed it covetously, but instead of eating it, placed it down on the floor. After a careful sniffing, the mutt took a modest bite and whined.

Louise looked at me. "Do you have any milk?"

"Low fat Morthon milk?"

"She won't drink that." She shook her head. "Sorry, Muff."

Muff gave a disgusted chuff, but nibbled delicately at the cookie.

Rising again, Louise came over to my side of the table. Although I was still finishing the hazah, she sat on the floor next to my chair and started nuzzling my crotch.

"Hey! Let me finish eating first, baby." I gently pushed her head away.

This eve must have had the patience genes deleted. Though I couldn't think why anyone with a cerebellum would do that.

Louise whimpered a bit, but put her head back on my lap and nosed around my groin while I consumed the last of the meal.

After finishing the cookie, Muff started exploring my apartment.

I nudged Louise. "Is it house-trained?"

"Oh, yeah. Most definitely." Nuzzle. Sniff.

My experience with eves has been that they mostly don't appreciate the way men smell, but this eve was all over me.

Done eating, I wiped my face and hands, passing a napkin to Louise, who had hazah on her face. She blotted it halfheartedly.

My gonads were fully primed, so on the way to the bedroom, I shut the door to keep out the pup.

Louise's appetite for sex was every bit as strong as her hunger for food. I felt about twenty years older when she was through with me. On the other hand, I hadn't felt this . . . well IC'd in many cycles. Afterward, she slept quietly on the bed, curled up in a ball.

Unable to sleep, I pulled on a pair of pants, exited the bedroom, and headed for the bathroom.

Muff greeted me with anxious barking, standing over the com station.

Ignoring the beast, I stepped into the bathroom.

Zorn, I *looked* well-IC'd. Hair standing up on one side. Face extremely relaxed. She was weird, but she was zorned good fun in bed. Very oral. And not afraid to let me do some barely legal things to her nimble, athletic body.

Stepping to the toilet, I saw that someone had been there before me. Someone very small. Who couldn't reach the disposal button. I almost wished I'd seen that. Even the eve's dog was strange.

When I left the bathroom, the little dog started barking again. It scurried over to me and then ran back to the com station.

Well, it was a talented dog. Maybe I had an important message.

The only message on the viewer was one being composed. But I hadn't written any messages. I sat down and took a closer look.

You IC'd my dog, you space weevil!
I'm Louise. *She's* the mutt. Glasmine Station was hit by traackle radiation and we were remolecularized inverted. If you could get us to Beezek Engineering in the 18th Sector, I can get this straightened out.

I glanced down at the furry thing. "Uh-uh. No way. You did not enter this message. You're just a dog."

It jumped on my lap, growled menacingly at my crotch, then hopped onto the table. Using its nose and a paw on the data pad, it slowly entered, "Yes, I did."

Well, IC me!

I did *not* IC her zorned dog! Louise, or whoever that was sleeping in my bedroom, was not a dog. She *tasted* all woman. *Human* woman. Nothing peculiar at all.

So she had a very smart dog? That was telling me lies?

This evening had turned out a lot weirder than I had anticipated.

The dog rubbed the data pad again and tapped out, "Take us to Beezek Eng."

I met the mutt's gaze. "I don't think I should get involved. I don't even know if you're telling the truth." Using a molecularizer for anything besides transportation was illegal. *Uh-uh. No way.*

"I'll pay you."

"How much?"

The little furry face gave me a dark look. "Five thousand dren."

Enough to pay for second class fare to Paradisso 7. "I'll do it. But I need a down payment."

"Funds scans only work on *my* retinas."

Which were sleeping in my bed. Hmm . . . "I'll ask Lou—, uh, her to do the scan."

Muff exhaled slowly, then squeezed out, "She likes being human."

My mouth twitched before the guffaws came. I swear the little mutt glared at me.

If it was true, it was funnier than a morthon at a

bar mitzvah. Louise trapped in the body of a small dog. The dog happy to be in the more versatile human body.

The mutt growled.

Zorn, if it was true, I *slept* with it.

Ew.

All humor in the situation had evaporated. "So she won't . . . cooperate?"

Head shake.

"Seven thousand dren."

"Mercenary." It gave me the look it gave the scrap of eelwort. "Fifty-eight hundred. Final."

"Done."

Half an hour later, the bedroom door whooshed open. Louise darted out of the room and bounded onto my lap.

Oh, zorn, it *was* true.

She planted slobbery kisses all over my face.

IC me. I just IC'd myself.

"More food? Can we have more food?"

Think. Gotta get her to Beezek Engineering.

"Uh, I don't have more food here, Louise, but we can go get some."

She pouted, glanced around the apartment, then replied, "Okay."

Tugging at my arm, she pulled me to my feet. I grabbed a shirt and boots, then we all headed for the door.

Just like being back on Earth in the 2100s, I hailed a taxi. Louise didn't pay any attention when I whispered our destination to the Lumonian driver. Yep, the little dog had the brains.

The trip to Beezek Engineering would take most of my cash, but I could replenish that with the 5,800 dren the mutt was going to pay.

To keep Louise from coming unglued, we stopped four times for food. I made sure to get a small quantity of whatever would take the longest to eat. She was quite happy with anything I got. At least until it ran out.

It took most of the night to get to Beezek. A select slab of dried eelwort got Louise through the front door without asking any questions. Inside, we were greeted by a frail service rep.

Louise sat on a chair, gnawing the tough eelwort.

I gestured to the clerk to move away. The mutt followed and listened as I explained the situation. We had a brief, pithy conversation about the laws in this system, which ended as soon as Muff agreed—with a nod—to pay a further bribe to the rep.

Good thing it's a rich dog, or it would be playing fetch with the eve of great appetites for the rest of its little furry life.

We joined Louise just as she had polished off the last of the dried meat. "More food?" she queried, ever hopeful.

"Soon, Lassie," I said, rubbing her shoulders vigorously. Maybe petting would keep her copacetic. She seemed to like it.

I still couldn't IC'ing believe I IC'd a dog. At least it could have been a more respectable-looking beast. Xaniask hounds are very clean and comely. *Oh, zorn! What am I thinking?*

The elderly man led us through a hangar and past the universe's largest pile of spacecraft refuse. When we got to the reaction chamber, the dog skipped into the room, barking pleasantly.

Oblivious, Louise stepped to the door, tugging me along, a hand reaching for my crotch. No, not bright. Or maybe it wasn't a lack of intellect, it was more a matter of *values*.

Food. Sex. These *were* the really important things. It kinda makes you wonder.

But, no, Louise-doggy, I'm not going into the chamber. I'd have probably come out as the mutt and no one would have had to cough up the 5,800 dren. "Sorry, I have to . . . uh, go to the bathroom."

"More eelwort?"

Playing the role of bait with gusto, the dog came to the door, barking and extending her two front paws.

Louise grinned at it, then gave me an uncertain look.

"I'll get some and bring it back with me."

She nodded, then turned around, dropping to the ground to romp with Muff.

Food. Sex. And play? Maybe she's the *smart* one.

As soon as I stepped outside, the attendant closed the door and turned the sealant lock key.

Louise's puzzled face appeared briefly at the window, then she shrugged and disappeared again from view.

The procedure took only a few seconds.

As the elderly man pressed the lock release, I wondered how I'd know if it worked. Or maybe they'd pretend it didn't, so they wouldn't have to pay me.

The door opened and Louise stepped out, with a very bland expression. She approached me slowly, then smacked me across the face with the back of her hand.

It worked.

Ow.

The mutt offered a vicious bark to my ankles. Good thing I was wearing boots.

"Very bad dog," Louise muttered in a low tone.

Muff tilted her head and gave a little yip. A perfect picture of innocence. Though false.

Louise shook her head, closed her eyes, sucked air into her recently reacquired lungs and regained her equanimity. The service rep led us to a funds machine. The transfer went flawlessly. I was half surprised she didn't try to stiff me. A dog-woman of honor, I guess. Once she'd paid me and Beezek Engineering, she scooped up her little dog and headed for the door.

I wouldn't be able to catch the shuttle until tomorrow morning. I wondered what *she* was like in bed. It's not like I hadn't already been there . . . more or less.

I made it to the door, just as she stepped onto the street, stopping her with a hand at her shoulder. "Hey, you wanna—"

Abruptly, she turned to face me, blue eyes filled with ire. "Not after you had IC with my dog, you morthon-faced lice carrier."

I guess that was sort of a . . . disincentive.

I manufactured a smile.

Muff yipped at me, and I patted her on the head. She was a good IC after all.

Louise put her on the ground and strode away at a

brisk pace. The little dog trotted happily after her. Short memory.

With any luck they were both up to date on their antireproductive inoculations. Didn't even want to think about . . . *puppies*.

Huntbrother

by Michelle West

Michelle West's novels include *Hunter's Oath, Hunter's Death, The Broken Crown, The Uncrowned King, The Shining Court, Sea of Sorrows,* and *The Sun Sword,* all published by DAW; she also writes a book review column for *The Magazine of Fantasy & Science Fiction.* As Michelle Sagara, she is the author of *Into the Dark Lands; Children of the Blood; Lady of Mercy;* and *Chains of Darkness, Chains of Light.* She has also written under the name of Michelle Sagara West, and has published over forty pieces of short fiction. She lives with her family in Toronto, Canada.

KINGDOM of Breodanir.

An old story: Girl who must marry for duty falls in love with boy who cannot fulfill that duty. The boy goes away to war, and war takes him; he never returns.

But this story was slightly different. The boy was given leave to return, in the casement of his god's flesh, and the girl, leave to spend one night with him. The night was glorious.

The morning was terrible.

And after?

The mirrors were covered in cloth; dust nestled in the folds made of tarpaulin's fall. The chandelier, likewise covered, hung above the great table and the fine, old chairs, casting shadows; it had offered no light in the outer chambers of these rooms for months.

Nor should it. Cynthia had refused all guests, and all visitors; had adorned herself in the colors of mourning, the deep black, with edges of green, brown, and gray. She wore a veil when it suited her, and it suited her this day.

Too old to be sent to her room, she had nonetheless chosen to retreat there, for Lady Maubreche, her mother, was in a mood that was just shy of fury. Her proper, brittle voice had fallen into ice, and the space between each of her evenly pronounced words was an attempt to maintain the facade of a civility she certainly felt her daughter did not deserve.

As Cynthia had made her way up the grand staircase, its finery almost too ostentatious for the nobility of Breodanir, she had met her father, Lord Maubreche. His hair had grayed only over the last half year; his beard had turned white. The hunting injuries he had sustained during the Sacred Hunt would never leave him; he had neither the youth nor the vigor to fight their slow decay.

He had had very little to say. His daughter's condition, the doom that had been placed upon her slender shoulders, had robbed him of wrath. Of hope.

But not of affection.

It was the affection that was hardest to accept, for it was couched—and offered—in a hesitance born of pain. He expected her to reject him. She wanted to.

But she knew that death waited, and soon, for this man who had once been the pride of the Master of the Game, the King as Hunter. He had been offered the rank of Huntsman of the Chamber, and he had taken his dogs into the Sacred Woods by the King's own side.

He would never do so again.

And the certainty of that made her want to rage against the resignation she saw in a face that had once defined strength. This man had taught her to handle his dogs, although she would never love them so dearly as he; this man had brought her the books that she craved, and given her the horses that even his stableboys had difficulty taming. He had given her every freedom that a daughter could be granted, and some unwisely, as her mother had often told him.

But he could not give her more. What was left her was duty, and he *could not* ask her to fulfill it. Except in this way, eyes rounded and narrowed, hand upon the banister.

"Lady Eralee will come at the end of the twoweek with her son."

She nodded; she did not trust herself to speak.

"Your mother bids me remind you."

And you are to run Mother's errands now? But she did not say it. Instead, stiff, she nodded and mounted the stairs that led to her only privacy.

She rocked a while on the bed, her arms crossed against her chest, her head bowed. The tears that she had shed at the death of Lord Stephen of Elseth were gone; gone because she willed them gone. As he was. She had seen his corpse, and even the ceremonial dressing that bound him together, that made him whole, could not disguise how terribly his body had been mauled.

By the Hunter. By the Hunter God.

Aie, but it was not the savagery of the death she hated, for it was a death that every Hunter Lord, every huntbrother feared—and faced—within the Kingdom. Only by death was the Hunter God assuaged; only by such a death were the lands made fertile, and its people fed.

It was simply the death itself. Stephen had left her on the evening of her debut; Stephen had promised to return. And in some sense he had; the God himself had brought what remained: spirit, soul, ghost.

She had taken what he offered, desperate, pathetically grateful for the moments, the hours, that were hers. But in the end, Stephen of Elseth had no way to return to the mortal land; he would travel to the Halls of Mandaros, there to be judged for his life, and his life's deeds.

And she, Cynthia of Maubreche, returned home.

Returned home.

Lady Eralee was not a predatory woman, and it was for this reason that Cynthia found her presence a comfort.

She greeted Cynthia in the chambers reserved for the most important of dignitaries; the servants nicknamed it the King's room, although it had another, older one.

The older woman was dressed simply. She wore high collars and a gown that fell from shoulder to floor. This was not the current fashion, but Lady Eralee was old enough that elegance counted for much.

"Lady Cynthia."

She noticed the dark colors of mourning Cynthia chose to wear; she was no fool. But she did not respond to them, did not offer anything but the silence of sympathy.

"Lady Eralee." Cynthia's curtsy was perfect.

"I trust you remember my younger son. Corwin, please, Lord Maubreche has promised you inspection of the kennels and the runs. Attend us now before he arrives."

Lord Corwin of Eralee was, by Hunter standards, a handsome man. His hair was dark and thick, and his eyes bright and wide; his lips were full, and were often turned up at the corner in a smile. His nose had been broken at least once, but it didn't mar the line of his face.

He turned from the windows and bowed.

Cynthia was impressed in spite of herself; the bow was perfect. She wondered what dire threats Lady Eralee had made to ensure such perfection and decided she didn't want to know.

"And my son's huntbrother, Lord Arlin."

She curtsied again, but when she rose, she met Lord Arlin's eyes. They were nothing at all like Stephen's. Lord Arlin was not as dark as Lord Corwin; his hair was a brown that would pale in sun and darken in winter, and his eyes were an odd shade of green. His skin was dark with sun, and the creases around his eyes would deepen with time. He wore a beard, where Stephen had worn none.

Nothing about him reminded her of the dead.

And yet, there was something about him that spoke to her in a way that no one but the dead had.

She had met no less than six Ladies who had made the offer to Maubreche on behalf of their Hunter sons. And of the six, Lord Corwin had the two strongest advantages: His mother, with her obvious affection for him, and his huntbrother.

"I must apologize, Lady Eralee, for my conduct during the Sacred Hunt."

"No, Lady Cynthia, you must not." Her eyes were kind. "It is I who must apologize. I understand that mourning must take its course. Believe that time heals all but the fatal wounds. Believe that, in time, the memories will be gentle.

"And forgive me, for I do understand this truth, at my age, but in spite of this understanding, I am here, with my son. Corwin," she said, her voice taking on some of the steel that *must* be hidden beneath the kindness of her words. "Attend us."

He came.

Arlin had never left.

"My son is a Hunter."

Cynthia offered a conspirator's smile. "I've lived with a Hunter Lord all my life."

"With a Hunter of the Chamber, Lady Cynthia."

"Honor or no, he would rather be with the alaunts and the lymers than within the confines of the manse." She smiled.

Corwin smiled as well. His smile was a Hunter's smile, but it was not shorn of kindness.

"I would not hold him," Lady Cynthia said. "And I hear my father's heavy tread upon the stair. He will join us soon, and he is *most* excited to have a visitor who will appreciate the value of the Maubreche kennels. We have had many, many Ladies visit over the last six weeks and only two have troubled themselves to bring the sons they hope to marry."

"My thanks, Lady Cynthia, for your understanding," Lord Corwin said. Almost before the door to the hall was open, he was through it. He paused, one foot on either side of the doorframe. "Arlin, are you coming?"

"I would prefer to sit; I have not yet recovered from last week's hunt."

Corwin's brows drew down in a single thick line. But the retort he might have made was killed in its entirety by the fixed smile on his mother's face. He left.

"I have never envied the life of a huntbrother," Cynthia said softly.

"And I," Arlin replied, "have never envied the life of a woman who will sit in judgment upon the seat of her lands."

It was not what she expected to hear, and she rewarded the words with a hesitant smile. "It makes us hard," she said. A warning.

"It makes you human, I think. I am aware that there is a difference between a mask that is worn and the face beneath it."

"And mine, Lord Arlin?"

"Yours?"

"Do I wear a mask now, or do I expose the face beneath it?"

He laughed. "It is true, what is said of you."

"Arlin," Lady Eralee said.

"No, Lady Eralee, I am not so easily offended. Gossip—where it is checked and informed by affection—is a simple fact of the life of *any* house. I am aware of what is said of me in *this* house—but I admit that I am less aware of what is said beyond these walls.

"What part of what is said is true, Lord Arlin?"

"That you are as bold and direct as a Hunter, Lady Cynthia."

"But hopefully not as . . . distracted."

He laughed. She was surprised that she could like the sound of his laugh, although she could not quite bring herself to join it. "Lady Cynthia," he said, rising, "I have taken the liberty of bringing something of value to me. It is not a gift, for you have not accepted our suit, and I would never burden you with an obligation. It is a . . . loan."

She was curious.

He reached into the folds of his jacket, and drew from the pocket a small book. Bound in leather, she saw that it was much read; the leather itself had cracked and chipped in places.

A book. She took it in hands that shook. Opened it gently. There was an inscription so faded that she could not read it, but above it, the title of the book. It was called, simply, *A Life*.

"I haven't read this," she told him.

"Very few have. It was written by a young man who once apprenticed to Omaran the Maker. It says much about Makers, but more about art, and although it has little in common with my life in Breodanir, I have found that it speaks to me."

A book. "I thank you, Lord Arlin, for lending me something you so obviously value."

Thinking, as she said it, of all of the days she had met
Stephen while she hid from the young ladies of the court
in the quiet stacks of the royal library. Another life.

"Lady Eralee, I am honored to have seen you again.
You are always such a joy. I find your youngest son the
epitome of a Hunter Lord, and I believe that—should
my parents approve—he would make a fine Lord
Maubreche."

Cynthia rose then, the ghost of Stephen of Elseth
painful in his sudden presence. "I am called away, but
Lady Maubreche will join you shortly." She turned her
head to one side.

Arlin rose as she rose, and he stepped toward her; she
shied away when he raised his hand. "I apologize, Lady,
if my gesture has caused offense—"

"No," she said, meeting his eyes although her own
were heavy with water, "no offense at all, Lord Arlin."

Six months passed in peace. After Lady Eralee's
visit, Lady Maubreche entertained the noblewomen
who had come, aware that no formal engagement had
yet been announced; she had not, however, required
her daughter to be in attendance for such meetings. In
her severe fashion, Margaret, Lady Maubreche, could
be kind.

But after six months had passed, that kindness had
changed to something harsher: fear. With fear came
anger, for the Lady Maubreche had no easy way of containing the things that were beyond her control, and she
could see—anyone who thought to look could now see—
that Lady Cynthia was with child.

If her mother was surprised—and outraged—her father was not. And perhaps that was why he dwindled.

But when Lady Maubreche chose to confront her
wayward daughter, he intervened. He often intervened
in the affairs of his Ladies, especially when those affairs were tainted by raw fury. He had always been a
brave man.

"Cerle," his wife had said, offering him a rare warning.
But he had simply shaken his head, forcing his shoul-

ders to stretch to an almost forgotten height. "Margaret.
Come. I have something to show you."

"What can you have to show me that cannot wait?
Your daughter is in disgrace. All that we have done—
all that we have arranged—will be *undone,* and publicly;
Lady Eralee will see this as a betrayal of her trust. And
it *is.*"

"Our daughter is not the only woman whose heart has
overruled her head; she is young, Margaret. You were
young once, and I have always been aware that I . . .
would not have been the husband of your choice."

That silenced his wife a moment, and it surprised Cynthia, for Margaret, Lady Maubreche, was the epitome of
Breodanir nobility. "Come," he said again, quietly. "If
Andrew were here, he might have shown you what you
must see. He is not, and I must accept that duty."

Andrew, huntbrother to Lord Maubreche, and taken,
these many years past, by the Hunter God in the Sacred
Hunt. But his name still had power.

For that reason, it was seldom invoked.

Lady Maubreche hesitated a moment before she took
the arm her husband had offered her.

"Cynthia," her father said. "If you would accompany
us?"

What her mother accepted, she could not refuse. She
nodded, although no like arm was offered to sustain or
guide her, and she trailed after her parents as she had
not done since she was considered a child in Maubreche.

They wandered, of course, into the gardens. There was
not a room in the manse that did not have the ears of
the servants, and some dramas were best played out on
a private stage. But the gardens were not their destination; what lay beyond them, in the heart of the Maubreche responsibility, was. The maze, the hedges of the
Master Gardener.

On a day like this one, the sun half-veiled by passing
clouds, the maze cast scant shadow; what drew the eye
was the life of the hedge. Not the greenery, although
there was no finer hedge in the whole of Breodanir, but
rather the details contained in the clipped command of
shears. There was, about the hedge, a mystery and a

grandeur that had silenced even the most voluble of Maubreche's many guests.

Perhaps it was because the maze grew. It changed. It seemed a thing of life in a way that even the living were not. Among its hedges, one could see the hesitant face of a doe, her child, leaves carved and cut in a way that suggested wide eyes and delicate face, beneath her forelegs. One could see the flight of birds, suggested by the rustle of branches that did not, in fact, rustle; could see the little signs of captive life.

But beyond them, beyond these living miracles, these growing statues that changed as the days changed, lay something that was hidden from the eye of the casual visitor: the hedge-wall.

It was to the wall that Lord Maubreche now went.

Lady Maubreche was still silent, but the quality of that silence had changed. Cynthia knew it well; it was kin to her own, and contained an unspoken dread that was not—quite—fear.

The history of Maubreche could be seen here, and unlike the outer hedges, there was no sense of life's urgency in the living carvings. Year after year Cynthia had seen the men and women who had earned a place upon this hedge, and they did not move, did not seek to break free of the confines of the branches and roots that told their story.

She could see the eyes of Hardann the Black as he stood upon the cliff's edge, gazing out upon the vast hills and forests of his domain; could see the savagery of the expression of one of the earliest of the Maubreche Hunters. She could see dogs—Aswaine, the finest that Maubreche had ever produced—holding a crazed bear at bay; could see the sundered horn at his feet, the wounds—green, but gaping—in his side.

More. More, and she knew it all.

But her father did not seek to offer her a lesson from the history of the oldest of the Breodani families; the time for that had passed, with childhood. It was the first time he had truly acknowledged that her childhood was over.

The distant past gave way to the near past.

It was almost over.

As if he could hear what she did not say, her father turned; the line of his shoulders had fallen again, and he walked with a pronounced limp, gifted him for his valor at the King's side in the Sacred Hunt.

"No, Cynthia," he told her gently, "it has only just begun." He lifted an arm, and Cynthia could see her mother's hands rise, although she could not see her mother's expression; Lady Maubreche's back was turned toward her daughter in the stiffness of what had, a moment ago, been fury.

Cynthia walked around her father and came to stand by his side.

To see, upon what had once been the unshorn, unsculpted branches of the last stretch of the wall itself, the image that had caused her mother to raise hands to mouth.

She saw herself.

Saw herself, in formless robes that she had never worn, and by decree, would *never* wear: they were Priest's robes. Their color was green, as the hedge was, but their form and shape was unmistakable.

Is that what I look like? She approached this woman, this other Cynthia, and found that they were of a height; the maze was tall. But this woman's expression was one that Cynthia had never seen upon her own face. Not peaceful, not exactly, but free of the misery and the pain of loss that had guided the last half year.

Yet it was not this that stopped her mother, nor the fact that beneath even the trailing robes of a Priest, her pregnancy was so advanced it could not be hidden, could not be denied.

It was the hands upon her shoulders, the head above her head.

Her eyes rose slowly.

Above her image, carved as the statue in the maze's heart was carved, was Breodan, Hunter God.

She had seen him. She had heard his voice. She knew that the statue no more captured his essence or his truth than this clipped and tucked artistry.

But she knew, also, that that statue was known. That the face it wore was the face that the Hunter God presented to his people in effigy.

She turned away then.

She had not seen this. She had not come here since she had left, six months ago.

She swore that she would never come again, but she swore it in silence, for words spoken aloud had power and exacted a price, and she was not willing to expose herself to the wrath of Breodan.

"Cynthia!"

Her mother's voice. She ignored it for another ten steps, but when it came again, she turned like a beast brought to harbor.

The fury was gone from her mother's face, and with it, the color.

"Why did you not tell us?"

She had nothing to say. For just a moment, nothing. And then, cheeks burning, she met her mother's eyes defiantly. "He came to *me*," she said, voice soft because there was no other way to force the words out. "He came to me as Stephen. Stephen of Elseth.

"For one evening. Just one."

Her mother looked stricken.

"And in return, he asked of me one thing. He did not command it. He did not compel it. But he *asked* it, and who of us have ever refused what the *Hunter God* has asked?"

"We—we—must call the Priests."

"No." Her voice was louder now.

"Cynthia, the Priests *must* know. If you bear the son of the Hunter—"

"I bear Stephen's *son*," she said, the words raw, the lie rawer.

But that was not what the god had promised. He had offered her no lie. He had offered her no comfort. *The child will be mine; I contain the spirit of Stephen, but the flesh is gone.* It hadn't mattered.

Her mother released her father's arms and crossed the perfect grass. "Cynthia," she said, her voice a voice that had not been heard in Maubreche since Cynthia was a girl.

"Don't pity me. I don't want your pity."

Cupped hands caught the sides of her face. Warm hands. Her mother said nothing at all.

* * *

Not that day. But later, when the awe and the compassion had once again taken its place in the depths of Lady Maubreche's shuttered heart, words came.

"Cynthia."

Cold words. "Lady Maubreche."

"What do you think you're doing?"

"I am dressing," Cynthia said coldly, "to meet Lady Eralee and her sons."

"You are not a child," her mother replied. "That dress will *not* be acceptable. Look at you."

"I chose this dress for a reason."

"You look as if you might bear a child at *any* minute, and you've months before your time."

"I will bear a child," Cynthia said, with a calm that fooled neither. "Am I to dress as if that child is the product of grief and histrionics? Am I to hide him?"

"Lady Eralee is not, as you well know, apprised of your . . . situation." It had been a bitter point of contention between the elder and the younger Ladies. "I should have overruled you. Your recklessness—"

"I am *not* reckless!"

"You *are*." Her mother's hand rose, palm exposed, as if it were weapon, or worse, as if it were all of her rage. Rage, Cynthia accepted with a bitter grace. But what lay beneath that rage, and that urgency, she could not force herself to closely examine.

But her mother did not strike. The hand fell, and with it, the line of her mother's shoulder. Lady Maubreche looked *old*.

"The healers are not certain that your father will survive to see the birth of your child." Just that.

Her mother's face was a wall now.

Cynthia stood, but the blood left her face, and her knees bent toward carpet and hard floor. She did not accuse her mother of lying. Could not. "But—but he—"

"The infection that came of the wound weakened his heart. I confess I am not a healer; I do not understand the whole of the details, and I have heard them time and again. Your father," she added bitterly, "will listen to no one."

"Why did you not tell me?"

"Because I am old and foolish," Lady Maubreche replied. "And because I raised no fool; I had hoped you might notice it yourself."

Cynthia's words slipped away from her, water through cupped hand. She stared at the lines around her mother's thinned lips.

"Yes," her mother said, sparing her nothing. "We have no time to wait, and none to waste. When Lord Maubreche at last succumbs to his stubborn—" she turned her head a moment, lifting a hand in warning. "When that happens, there must be a Lord Maubreche to take his place.

"Think, daughter. Think of what you choose to do. I cannot turn Lady Eralee away; two weeks of travel separate our territories, and the winter is already approaching. If she does not come now, we will have to wait until the spring."

"Margaret, are you shouting at the poor girl?"

Lady Maubreche turned as the door creaked open upon the face of her Hunter Lord.

"I am discussing the duties of the afternoon with the woman who will one day continue the work that I now do," she told him, the chill in her voice more of a threat than the winter.

The argument might have continued; in truth, it might have had no end.

But that day, that day the dogs had come in from the runs, leaving their kennels like a stream of muscled flesh and glistening coat. They were silent, the alaunts; silent and determined. But they came.

Through the runs, over the fences that served to mark their territory, out of the huts and houses that were tended with such care. Black bodies, brown bodies, white and gray; sable, with patches of lighter colors. They had run up the path to the main house, and they had thrown themselves against the doors with deafening thuds until Sartay had chosen to open them.

The dogs had run *into* the hall, nudging the door wide to allow themselves free passage. They had run unerringly up the stairs, Hasufel at their head, and Onma, the best of the lymers, a leap behind. They had come to

Cynthia—herself no great champion of theirs—and laid themselves, almost on top of one another, at her feet.

"Hasufel! Onma!" Lord Maubreche said, the command in the words undeniable.

Hasufel, the pack leader, raised his muzzle. He uttered the first sound the dogs had made since they had gained entrance into Cynthia's chamber. He whined.

And then he rose. Rose and placed his great forepaws gently against the swell of pale blue cloth, beneath which lay flesh and child. His paws were not perfectly clean; they left a mark against the fall of fabric; a dog's footprint. A signature.

Lord Maubreche met Hasufel's eyes; the whining grew in pitch. Cynthia saw the peculiar expression that spoke of Hunter's trance cross her father's face. More than that was lost; she could not take her eyes off his alaunts. There were reasons that they were not kept in the house, and not all of them had to do with the strict demeanor of the keeper of the keys.

Perhaps because the dogs drew her attention, she missed the subtle shift of her father's expression; what was left, when she turned to face him, was something akin to surprise. He walked across the room, closing the distance between them, and then, as Hasufel before him, he lifted a hand and placed it gently against the crest of her belly.

To his wife, he said, his intonation low, his words a growl, "Let her be."

Just that. And Lady Maubreche bowed her head, wordless.

In the face of Hunter business, the greatest of Ladies could not be judged weak for leaving the arena.

Thus dressed, thus marked, Lady Cynthia of Maubreche met the mother of her future husband for the seventh time.

That Lady had taken the trouble to arrange her skirts upon the settee in the King's room. She looked up as Sartay opened the doors to announce the presence of Lord and Lady Maubreche; her smile was pleasant, the expression that Cynthia remembered.

She wished, for just a moment, that she had taken

her mother's bitter advice. For the smile froze on Lady
Eralee's face so completely Cynthia wondered if it would
ever return.

"Lady Eralee." Cynthia executed a curtsy that would
have made her mother proud in any other circumstance.

"Lady Cynthia." The elder woman's smile was pinched
and forced. "You look well."

"Lady Eralee," Lady Maubreche said quietly. "Lord
Corwin. Lord Arlin." She offered them a full curtsy.
"You honor us with your presence. I assume that Lord
Corwin would like to inspect the kennels?"

But for once Lord Corwin's attention did not seem to
be upon the kennels, the alaunts, the Hunt. Where his
mother's face was pale and hard, his was unschooled;
his mouth was open in what seemed a wordless parody
of shock.

"Forgive us," Lady Eralee said coolly, "if we came at
an awkward time." Beneath the surface of her chilly
words, her meaning was plain. She desired an explanation. Now.

Cynthia could have let her mother speak. It was Lady
Maubreche's right, and responsibility, in such an uncomfortable situation. But instead, she lifted a gentle hand.

"Lady Eralee," she said, with a calm she did not feel,
"Please accept my apologies."

"What I accept, Lady Cynthia, has yet to be decided."
Her frown was now pronounced. Cynthia could not recall a time when she had seen Lady Eralee so furious
that her anger could not be contained behind a civil
facade.

"I bear a child," Cynthia continued. "And I *will* bear
the child to term."

"That much, Lady Cynthia, I can see. We were not
informed of this . . . development. And I can be certain
that the child is *not* my son's."

"No," Cynthia replied gravely.

"Had you no desire to accept my son's suit, you might
have chosen to be more forthcoming and less insulting.
May I ask whose child you carry?" It was not a polite
question.

Cynthia was silent. She looked to Lady Eralee,

straightening the line of her shoulders. And then, she looked to Lady Eralee's son. To Lord Corwin. To Lord Arlin beside him. She studied their faces, and if what she saw there did not bring hope, it did not destroy it. Hope was a bitter thing.

Lord Corwin met Cynthia's eyes. Held them. "Lady Cynthia," he said, drawing toward her. "How long have you known that you carry a child?"

"I knew," she told him, "the night of his conception."

"Why did you see fit to hide it from me?"

Not from you, she wanted to say. But she was of Maubreche; she chose her words with care. "I deemed it too great a risk."

"A risk?"

Was tired of choosing them with care. "Yes, Lord Corwin." She knew she should speak with Lady Eralee, for in the end, the decision would be hers. But Lord Corwin now stood close enough that she could see no one else.

"And that?"

"Of the six men who have made the offer to my mother, you are the only one I wished to accept. I am aware that my situation is tenuous; I am aware that I *must* marry. I am aware that for the sons of lesser families than Eralee, or of greater ambition, my condition— no matter what its apparent cause—would be no obstacle. If you choose to withdraw, we will begin again with one of the others. But—"

He reached out, slowly, as if she were an injured alaunt, and placed his palm against the curve of her belly. His hand was warm; beneath the multiple layers of cloth, she could feel the heat.

"My apologies," he said, his unblinking eyes the peculiar windows of a Hunter Lord's face. He bowed head. "I did not mean to interrupt."

"I had hoped—I had hoped that you might forgive me."

"But you did not speak."

"No." She closed her eyes a moment.

"Why?"

"We—" She could not speak of her father's death. Could not.

"So . . . if I accept your hand in marriage, I am to be the keeper of another man's child." His face was shuttered now.

She looked for condemnation in it; found nothing at all to hold on to. Was surprised at the pain this caused. "I know what you must think of me—"

"No, Lady Cynthia, you do not. Arlin?"

Arlin rose from his place beside Lady Eralee on the settee. He bowed to Lady Cynthia, his face concealing more than Lord Corwin's. She closed her eyes. Heard his words in the darkness.

"I told you," he said softly, "that she was wounded."

"And this?"

"What do you think, Corwin?" Impatience, in the words. Sharp impatience. "When the alaunts are wounded by boar or bear, they do not lightly suffer anyone's touch. Look," he added, "at your left hand, if you require proof. You bear the scars. But the alaunts serve you, and you alone."

She could end it. She could tell them the truth. But . . . but there was something she *had* to know. And because of it, she bore the humiliation of their assumptions.

"And you would accept her, after this?"

"You know my answer. But it is not, in the end, my decision. She is not like many of the other Ladies we have met."

"No, indeed. Not one of the others would risk her future and her fortune in such a fashion."

"Yes. Because they are careful; because they are calculating. Were she different, there would *be no child*. She will also be a good deal more powerful than the others you have met."

"Speak plainly, Arlin. You seem to love words."

"She has too much heart, and she has too much will; what she feels, she feels strongly. Yet I believe that if we accept this, she will give you what few of the others *could* give."

"And that?"

"In time? Love." He looked at Cynthia then, and she met his dark eyes; saw a compassion in them that she wanted, desperately, for her own. "And a son."

"True. Maubreche is not known for fecundity; perhaps

this can be seen as proof that *my* line will be established here."

"Lord Corwin—"

But Lord Corwin turned to Cynthia's father. "Lord Maubreche," he said quietly.

"Lord Corwin."

"It would honor me greatly if you would allow me inspection of the kennels that will one day be mine." His smile was sharp.

Her father's brow's rose; for just a minute, Cynthia thought he would growl. Instead, he laughed. "The alaunts are in the runs, but they have been forbidden the forest stretch for the day, for it seems they thought it acceptable to charge *into* the manse."

"Into the manse? Why? Was there some danger to you?"

"To me? No." The old Lord Maubreche turned the most gentle of gazes upon his only child. But he did not speak of what had happened. Instead, he said, "If you care to view a pack of hostile, unhappy running hounds, the honor would be mine."

"As I said, old man," Corwin said, with a wolf's sharp grin, "I desire to see what will be mine."

Her throat was tight. She felt tears at the edge of her eyes, her open eyes; felt breath desert her. She closed them, and again, in darkness, heard words. This time they were her own.

"Lord Corwin?"

"Lady Cynthia."

"The child I bear is Breodan's."

Later, when the engagement had been announced and the agreement written, signed, sealed by wax and the crests of the two families, Lord Corwin looked up from the table. His Hunter eyes were bright and keen; he was on the hunt, even surrounded by furniture, carpets, long curtains, and thick windows.

"Why did you not just tell us the truth? It would have spared you much."

Lady Eralee placed a thin hand over her son's; the contrast in color was the difference between their responsibilities. "If you do not understand, ask Arlin."

"Arlin doesn't understand it either."

"Ah, well. Arlin *is* a man, even if he is the finest of huntbrothers."

Corwin looked annoyed. It was an expression that only the Lady Eralee could easily provoke.

"Forgive them, Cynthia," she added, using the family name. "I am proud of them both; for a Hunter, Corwin is a fine person."

"Truly there is nothing to forgive, Lady Eralee."

"Call me Amanda."

"Amanda, then. There is nothing to forgive. Lord Corwin's question is a reasonable one."

"Very well. Since you are so keen to be charitable to the man who will be your husband, I must assume that your kindness is an act of loyalty, and such loyalty is always balm to a mother's heart, even if it is in this case misplaced."

"You tell us, then," Corwin snapped.

"Is that the neatest signature you can make?" His mother said with a sniff, greatly enjoying herself. "Very well, I will take it upon myself to answer your question. There are very few among us who do not desire to be loved. Or to be trusted.

"If she could appear thus before you, with no word and no explanation, and you could offer acceptance, could believe that some extenuating circumstance drove her to this situation, you would prove—to her—that some trust exists. You accepted her for *herself*."

"Well, who else would I accept her for? She's no one else." He was annoyed.

"Lady Eralee—"

"Amanda, dear."

"Amanda—really, I think Lord Corwin is correct. I was foolish."

"Besides, it proves no such thing," Corwin continued. "I could have accepted it if I wanted a house of my own, lands I could claim and rule. My acceptance might have been a matter of practicality. And greed."

His mother sighed. "Did she not say, of the six, she chose you for a reason?"

He rolled his eyes. "Do not," he said to his wife-to-be, "spend too much time with my mother. I would not have her infect you with her wordplay."

One month later, they were married. The ceremony was not small, but Cynthia allowed her mother to choose the dress, the veil, and the accoutrements in which she would be seen. She no longer cared if her pregnancy—which was well advanced—was hidden to the best of the dressmaker's capabilities. All that she wanted, she had achieved.

She was nervous.

Corwin was not. But Arlin made up for his composure.

Breodani weddings were not a simple matter of two people; they were a binding of three. The bride and the groom might stand together, but in the procession, it was the huntbrother who led the way, and when they arrived before the Priest, it was the huntbrother who gave over the symbols of the joining of their houses: the chalice, the rings, and the key.

Lady Eralee had obliquely threatened poor Arlin with six different torments if he dropped anything, stepped on Cynthia's train, or worse—much worse—allowed the dogs to disturb the ceremony.

For the dogs had their role. They were as much part of a Hunter's flesh as wife would be. Perhaps more.

But Corwin's dogs were silent throughout. They stood in the room at the top of the nave, waiting; they watched, heads raised, ears peaked, as the Priest began his incantations. Cynthia was certain they were thinking of food, but one glance at her husband's face said otherwise; he was deep in trance. She hoped the Priest would not be too offended.

Iversson had performed many Hunter marriages; if he noticed this breach, he spoke above it.

But when the joining was done, when the chalice had been filled, first with wine and then with the blood of the three supplicants—Hunter, huntbrother, and wife—the dogs rose as one, as if called. They walked quietly, and with a processional air about their movements, until they stood before Lady Cynthia. Then, as one, they lifted heads, elongating throats; they bayed.

Even she, born to Hunter but not to Hunt, understood
what they offered, and she was moved by it.

Corwin, however, was not, and they were kenneled
for the twoweek after the ceremony was concluded.

When Cynthia's child was born, he was born in silence, and his wide, golden eyes, crouched in the red
wrinkles of a newborn's face, looked out on the world
with curiosity. Corwin and Arlin haunted the room that
the midwives had grudgingly allowed them to enter, and
it was Corwin—not Arlin—who had taken the babe from
the arms of the midwife; Corwin, and not Arlin, who
had lifted the child with an awe and an open expression
of wonder that Cynthia would never forget.

He had taken the long, soft squares of swaddling cloth,
and with shaking hands—huge hands, in comparison
with the babe's—he had swaddled him tight. Then, before the midwives could stop him, he bent and placed
lips upon that wizened brow.

"This child," he said softly to Cynthia, although he
could not take his eyes from the babe, "is your son. But
allow it, Cynthia, and he will be mine; I will raise him,
and I will teach him the ways of the Hunt."

She wept, then, because he was Hunter Lord, and almost incapable of lying. She said, for the first time, the
pain and exhaustion of hours of labor loosening her
tongue, "I love you, Corwin of Maubreche."

And his eyes had widened further, his sun-darkened
skin still capable of reddening.

Arlin had come to sit by her; had taken her shaking
hands in his. His smile was gentle.

She had been happy, then. In truth, she would have
remained happy.

But from the moment her son could walk, he had been
drawn to the maze.

Although she was tired after the baby's birth, as the
midwives had warned she would be, she was calm; she
felt graced by the absence of pain and the absence of
burden. The babe slept—the midwives also assured her
that this would not continue—and she herself passed
from waking to sleeping with ease.

But on the third day, her father woke her at twilight. He entered the room with a swinging lamp in hand, and held it aloft, pressing one finger firmly against lip. It was both a request and a command, and Cynthia, for the first time since the baby was born, rose from the birthing bed. In the darkness, she dressed, and then she joined him.

He walked slowly, and he paused several times. She heard the rise and fall of his chest as he labored for breath, but she did not injure his dignity by offering him aid.

They walked, together, toward the heart of the Maubreche maze, and there, in the darkness, they paused before the statue of the Hunter God. The moon did not cast his shadow, but it lit him softly; he looked less forbidding in the evening than he did during the height of sun's light.

"There is something you must know," he told her quietly. "About Maubreche. About the Hunter."

She nodded, understanding fully what he meant by this: his time was almost past.

"The first of our line was, like your first son, born of the God. I do not know how; I have not had the ability to ask him. You, I fear, have spoken with the Hunter far more often than even his Priests; there is little that I can teach you that you do not already know.

"But this place is the heart of his worship. This is what I was told by my father before his death, and what my father was told by his; it has passed in an unbroken line to all of the Maubreche blood.

"The hedge-wall," he added quietly, "is almost complete."

She nodded.

"You have seen yourself in its leaves and the cuttings of the Master Gardener. What you do not know is this: when the last of the hedge is complete, the task of the Gardener is at an end."

Her brows rose.

"The Gardener is older than the Kingdom," he added quietly. "And he swore his oath to the Hunter when Maubreche was a man and not a great family. He has labored for centuries upon this work."

"What is his work?"

"The history," he said quietly, "of Maubreche; the history of the first—and the last—of the Hunter's chosen family." He bowed his head. "I did not understand it, Cynthia, when I was told. It was not clear to me. My father was taken by the Hunt, but he *knew*, before that Sacred Hunt, that he would not return to these estates. I asked him how he knew, and he told me he couldn't say. I realize now that this wasn't a matter of choice.

"Because I know, and I don't know how, or why. It doesn't matter. When I . . . found you here, on the hedge, I understood. The Hunter has waited centuries for another child; birth was the beginning of our line, and birth, in some fashion, is closure to that tale.

"Your son will fight an enemy so terrible that he is not named. But it is in preparation for that fight that Maubreche has stood, these centuries; it is for that fight that the Hunters have waited, that their oaths have been given and taken.

"My son is—"

"Yes," her father said, his face grave with pity and horror. "He is a babe. I've held him, even though my arms are so weak they can barely keep a lamp aloft. I know how slight he is, how vulnerable.

"But he is Breodan's Hope," he closed his eyes. "In this garden, in the Heart of this maze, he is safe. But if he stays within its confines, he will have failed not only Breodan, but all of Maubreche and its ancient history.

"We've waited for your son, Cynthia." He bowed his head.

She stared at him, sorrow and anger blending until they were inseparable, a weave she would wear for the rest of her life.

"But waiting or no, we have had no way of discerning his worthiness. He must take a huntbrother," he added.

"Of course! He's Breodani, Hunter-born."

"Yes. And he must learn what Hunters often fail to learn: the value of the people he must protect. Without that knowledge, without that guidance, he will fail us all."

She swallowed. "Let me do it," she whispered.

He frowned, but it was gentle. "So has every parent said since child was born, and not only within Maubreche. But we cannot protect our young in any way

save this: We can teach them the value of love, of trust
and trustworthiness. Not more, and not less."

He bowed. "Your son's road will be strange and difficult. He is of the Hunter God; we cannot forget this.
But he is *also* mortal; he is still a child. What a child
needs, he needs." He walked to where she stood, and
leaning down, kissed her upturned brow.

"I am proud of you, daughter," he said quietly.

Two weeks after the birth of his first grandchild, Lord
Maubreche passed away.

Lord Corwin became in name, Corwin, Lord Maubreche, and Lady Cynthia, Cynthia, Lady Maubreche,
heir to its vast responsibilities. Her mother had promised
her that she would grow to meet the needs and demands
of Maubreche, and as often was the case, her mother
had been correct.

When Stephen was well into his seventh year, the arguments began.

"He needs a huntbrother, Cynthia. He is our oldest
son. He will be eight in six months; he will be expected
to take the green and the gray of the page; he will be
expected to make his vows. Iverssen is waiting."

"I know."

"Then give me leave to find a suitable boy. The streets
of the King's City are full of them. Let me hunt there."

"Not yet," she answered softly. The answer would become less soft with time.

"You cannot coddle him!"

"He is not like other Hunters. He has the eyes of
the God."

"He has the eyes of the God, yes. But he *also* has the
duties of the Breodani! Would you deny him the heritage of his people?"

"No! Nor would I force him to take vows that he is
not yet capable of making."

"The Hunter's Law—"

"The Hunter's Law guides Hunters," she said, and it
pained her. "But our son—"

"You mean *your* son, is that it?"

His anger was sharp; the words were harsh. What he

had promised, from birth, he had lived up to. He loved
Stephen. Had always loved him. Because of it, she knew
that he could not let it rest; he was Hunter, after all.
But she said, "It is not yet time, Corwin. Be content."

"Content?"

"Breodan has bid us wait."

Her husband fell into a grim silence. He would break
it, again and again, as the years passed, for he felt her
refusal as a wall between himself and the child of his
heart. And it was.

If Stephen had not been so adept with the dogs, perhaps the argument would have—like so many of their
arguments—been left to wither, growing the cold edges
and hidden barbs of all such unresolved pain.

But the dogs adored Stephen. At least it seemed so
to Cynthia; to Corwin it was much, much deeper. When
an alaunt appeared, sidling out of the runs, to sit by
Stephen's feet, it seemed natural to her; to Corwin, it
was not. Because the dogs, in all things, had their hierar-
chy, and the dog that was also first to abase himself in
the joyful abandon of an anxious pup was no pup. It
was Hasufel.

With the death of Cynthia's father, he had—with initial reluctance—become Corwin's dog.

But he was Stephen's liege.

He would take his portion from the hands of the master of the game, but he would often take it *to* Stephen,
and Stephen would quarter it for him, feeding him from
hand as if Hasufel were an imperial falcon and not the
finest of the running hounds Maubreche boasted.

The truth of this allegiance could not be denied. The
awe it caused, among the Hunters, even less so.

Corwin's anger simmered, boiled, simmered, and boiled.
In the end, they could barely speak of Stephen. Only
Arlin stood between them, and it caused him some bit-
ter pain.

Aie, they waited. Stephen passed his eighth birthday,
and his ninth. On his tenth, Corwin's anger knew no
bounds, and he left—without Arlin—to hunt the dogs
made wild by the temper he could not contain.

When he returned, he was subdued, but the anger and

the helplessness of the situation did not leave him. His son, his oldest son, was not yet allowed entrée into the world of Hunter Lords.

It would have been natural for him to turn his attention to Robart, his youngest. And he did, for Robart was now seven, and fast approaching the first of the many ages of majority within Breodanir. But his success with Robart, and the introduction of Mark—a scarred young boy with an unruly tongue and a rough sense of loyalty—as the first huntbrother of the Maubreche kin, had not calmed his anger.

Because the anger was based in fear. Fear for Stephen of the golden eyes.

She hated his fear, but she loved him for it. She accepted his rage as if it were weather, a storm that she could predict but could not deflect. Was it not her own?

But the day finally came. It was a day much like any other, but it was punctuated by the presence of guests—guests who were as much kin as people could be who did not bear Maubreche blood. Gilliam, Lord Elseth, and his unearthly, wild wife, Espere. They had come on a social visit, or so Gilliam said—but there was about him a tenseness, an anger, that she had not seen since they had first met, and Stephen of Elseth had stood between them, loved by both.

Her Stephen, her own son, was called to the house from the runs. But he failed to arrive. And after an hour had passed, Lord Corwin had looked up, bleakly, at his wife.

She closed her eyes. "Yes," she told her husband, her voice subdued and quiet but without any hint of gentleness, "I will go and fetch him."

Lady Cynthia lifted her skirts and began to walk, with purpose, toward the maze. Purpose was required. She knew that today the maze would give way to the land that the Hunter God opened on occasion for those of his blood. Knew that grass and hedge and flower bed would become gray and insubstantial; they were mortal, things not meant for the odd landscape of the world Between the realm of the gods and the realms of man.

She turned the corner, following the line of the wall by the shadow it cast upon tended grass. When that shadow changed, lengthening into something slender, she looked up.

Met the silver-gray eyes of the Master Gardener.

She bowed at once. In no other garden was a gardener afforded such a genuine gesture of respect.

He returned that bow gravely. "Lady Cynthia."

"Master Gardener."

She did not speak his name because she did not know it. Had never known it. When she had been younger, she had asked it of him, as she might ask it of the other children she met. His answer was a stiff, cold silence—an indication that she had breached social protocol. She had not asked again.

"I—I come looking for my son."

"He is at the Heart of the maze," the gardener answered. He raised his hands; they were empty. He carried no shears, none of the tools of his life's work.

She did not ask him why. But he stood before her, immobile, as if he were a gate, locked and barred against her passage. "Am I to be forbidden the maze now?" Her voice was cool.

"No, Lady. But it would be prudent if you chose to return to your guests."

"My guests wait upon my son," she told him quietly.

"He will come," the gardener replied. "But he speaks, now, with his father."

She felt the cold, then; the sun could not pierce it. Gathering her shawl about her shoulders, she stepped forward.

"I was never terribly prudent," she said quickly. But her voice shook. At a decade, memory slept. But it had never died.

"Then I will not stop you," he replied. But his eyes were cold.

The mists rose at last above her face, obscuring the maze, with its intricate, secret hedges, its indictment and its promise.

She bowed her head; felt the sweet air of the Between in her lungs. This was the Heart of Maubreche. She had come to understand it in a way that none of her predecessors had.

She could not see Stephen.

But in the shadows that no sunlight cast, she saw the Hunter God.

As always, she turned away from the sight of him, steadying herself. The God was not a man, although he bore form similar to one; he was not a beast, although the great tines of antlers rose from the perfect smoothness of his forehead. He was not a giant, although he was tall; he was not simply beautiful in the way men can be.

But he suggested all of these things, as if mortality were a dim and tarnished echo of his glory, and when he turned his eyes upon her, they were of gold and fire.

"Lady Cynthia."

"Lord." She bowed. She bowed deeply.

"You have waited," he said gently. "And by the reckoning of my people, you have waited long."

For what? But she did not ask.

"For the time when your son is able to hear my voice without the crutch of Maubreche and its hallowed ground; for the time when your son is able to make himself heard across the wild of the mortal plane. He has my gift," the God continued. "The oldest and the greatest of my gifts: His is the power of the oathbinder."

Oathbinder.

"Honor," the God continued, his voice the multitude, the crowded murmur of young and old, of man and woman, of sorrow and joy, anger and peace, birth and death: a song; a God's song. "What is given, as oath, to my son, will be binding. Only death will end it."

What does that have to do with the Hunt?

"He will take his place among his people," the God said, speaking as gently as a gale could. "I have watched our son. I have spoken with him. I have judged him, where judgment is possible. What he is, he is. What he will be . . .

"It is time."

"And his huntbrother?"

For just a moment an expression solidified upon the God's face. Compassion. Or pity.

"You have defied convention before."

She closed her eyes. "When?" she asked, without opening them.

"Today. Today, Cynthia, and believe that had we any other choice, we would make it."

"We?"

"The Enemies," he answered, after so long a pause she thought he might not offer words, "of the Lord of the Hells."

She was Lady Maubreche now. In her youth, she had been another girl—but the Between was a funny place; it existed outside of time.

And outside of time, in her heart, she was Cynthia. The Hunter's gaze moved her to a bitter fury.

"Have I not given enough?" she whispered, through clenched teeth. "This boy, *this* Stephen, is mine; he is all that remains to me of—of—" Her hands were fists; they shook.

"You have given," the Hunter God said quietly, the multitude fading, "what only Maubreche can give."

"Then do not ask more of me!"

"It is not of you, in the end, that all will be asked." Pity.

She hated pity.

"You will find your son," he said quietly. "And he will be with you some little while yet."

Stephen was golden-haired. Golden-eyed. His skin was the pale white of a Northern clime, unusual among those born to the heat and the sun of the Hunt. His face was slender, his chin pronounced; his cheeks were high, and if color was to be found in his face, it was there. He was tall, or seemed tall, for his age, but that was simple illusion; he wore his height well because of his slender build. Only his eyes spoke of his parentage, and no craft on her part could dispel their truth.

Those eyes were round now, and unblinking; they had been touched by the God, and they burned brightly. Even when they narrowed in confusion, as they did now.

"Mother?"

"Lady Maubreche," she said, correcting him automatically.

He grimaced. "We have guests?"

"Yes. We still have guests."

"How long was I gone?"

"Not . . . not long," she told him quietly.

"I'm sorry." They were probably his first spoken words; they were certainly his most common ones.

His wince brought her no pleasure; no sense of the superiority of experience or knowledge that separated them. His eyes lost a hint of their brilliance, and none of their color, as his vision turned inward.

"Why did you leave, Stephen?"

"I heard the Hunter," he answered quietly.

Answer enough. "Are you finished, then?"

He nodded quietly. Offered her his arm, as if he were already past childhood. She accepted it with gravity.

"Mako is angry," he told her.

"Mako is always angry." Although Stephen had not taken the first of the Hunter's Oaths, and was therefore not legally allowed his pack, his pack had nonetheless formed. It was one of the few facts of Stephen's life that made Corwin happy, and Cynthia accepted it gratefully.

Of Stephen's alaunts, Mako was the wildest. She had no fondness for him, nor he for her; everything was his rival for Stephen's affection. She smiled briefly. "I can't imagine what he's going to be like when you finally take a huntbrother."

His arm tightened. "Mother?"

This time, she offered no correction. "Yes?"

"Are you ready?"

It was an odd question. An honest one. "I don't know." She didn't. This son, this Stephen, was far more like a huntbrother than a Hunter in temperament, and if something would slowly transform him into a Hunter, she wasn't sure she wanted to see it. Although the dogs were indisputably his, they had never robbed her of his company or his attention; they were not his obsession, not the signal truth by which he might claim, in the end, his title and the fullness of his power.

She was afraid to lose him.

Afraid to see Corwin or Gilliam when she gazed upon her son's face; afraid to lose the very little she could see of the man she had once loved, and at such cost.

Afraid, because in the end, if he was Hunter Lord, she would surrender him to the Sacred Hunt that might claim his life.

"No," she told him, pensive now. "I'm not. But I'm not certain I will *ever* be ready."

When they reached the lawns, Cynthia stopped. She reached for Stephen's shoulder, gripping it tightly enough that his breath came out in a hiss.

Lord Gilliam stood, and by his side, bristling, stood Espere, his truly wild wife. Her lips had come up over teeth, and those teeth, long and white, were bared. He had taken her as wife over his mother's muted objections, and she had never been given the full duties of a Lady of Breodanir. Instead, his mother, Elsabet, continued to fulfill the Elseth duties.

At Gilliam's side, Corwel, the third of his dogs to be so named, crouched, belly low to ground, throat vibrating with growl. He was not cowed; he was tensed to leap.

And only his Hunter Lord's command restrained him; Cynthia knew it, although she had not been witness to the command. She might have picked up her pace, then, for it was one of a Lady's many duties to ease tension and hostility; the Hunters could often be like their dogs when matters of implied territory broke the thin veneer of civility.

But there were no other Hunters present.

There was a Priest, or perhaps a mage, someone of medium height who hid behind the folds of a voluminous robe. The robe itself was strangely dyed; its cloth was of a deep blue that suggested midnight rather than darkness. The cowl of that robe obscured the stranger's face.

But Gilliam's expression made Cynthia wary.

"Oh, no," Stephen muttered. "Mother, let's hurry."

"Do you—do you know this man?"

"She's not a man. And I know of her, but I've never met her before. I'm sure she's met me."

"Stephen—"

He placed a hand upon the hand that restrained him, and gently pried himself free. But instead of hastening to the distant tableau, he turned to his mother, offering her the expression that reminded her of his namesake. "You don't have to like her," he said softly, "but for my sake, don't judge her. You've paid all the price the Hunter demands, but nothing that you—or I—will ever pay will be as harsh as the burden she carries."

"Who is she, Stephen?"

"She is the Wyrd of Mystery," he answered, his eyes glowing softly, as if he were looking at something that she would never be able to see. "And she carries a God's burden. But she's not a God, Mother, no matter how powerful, or how distant, she seems. Remember that, if you can." He hesitated a moment, and then said, "And remind me, when I forget."

Not if, but when. Cynthia nodded.

"Come," she said, hearing the Hunter's voice. "Let us greet this unexpected guest."

The woman—and she was a woman—turned before they reached her. Her face was as pale as Stephen's, but where his hair was golden, hers was the color of pitch, with a hint of snow's frost about its edge; where his eyes were golden, hers were the colour of winter violets, housed and grown in glass.

"Lady Maubreche," she said, inclining her head.

"Don't speak to her, Cynthia," Gilliam snapped. Anger there. Tension in the line of his jaw.

Lady Maubreche replied. "She is a guest, Lord Elseth; I can hardly fail to tender her the hospitality due a traveler."

He snarled. Like an alaunt, as tense as Corwel beneath his feet.

"It was because of *her* that Stephen died."

Cynthia froze. Stephen of Elseth. Stephen.

Gilliam was Hunter; Gilliam did not lie. Had he learned that trait, she would still have heard truth in his words; they were raw with pain and the loss of more than a decade. That loss, more than any other thing, bound them.

Before she could ask, the stranger said, "It is true.

It is because of me that Stephen of Elseth traveled to
Essalieyan. Because of me that he met the Hunter God
on the day of the Sacred Hunt."

Cynthia struggled to remember the words her son had
just spoken, but they passed through her mind like water
through cupped hands. She had no words to offer.

"It was because of his oath," Stephen of Maubreche
said into the terrible silence. "If you helped him, if you
guided him, the truth of his oath was offered by Stephen
of Elseth alone, and he chose, in the end, to abide by
it. You accept much, Evayne a'Nolan. But I am Breodan's kin, and I will not allow you to dishonor Stephen
of Elseth's memory. He chose."

Violet eyes widened. Beneath the slender point of stiff
chin, the glinting silver of metal caught light; she wore
a pendant, shaped like a small flower. It seemed odd to
see it there; Cynthia had expected a medallion, some
emblem of office or rank.

"Fair words," she said at last, and her voice was all
of midnight. "But tell the whole of the truth, if you will
use truth, Stephen of Maubreche."

"I have."

"No. You have not. Stephen of Elseth was *oathbound*,
yes. But he swore his oath when he was barely eight; he
offered a child's promise. He did not understand the price
he was expected to pay—either to carry out the oath,
and have peace, or to reject it. Can a man truly be said
to have made a choice when he is doomed by words that
he does not have the experience to understand?"

"Yes."

"You are your father's son," she said bitterly.

"Both of my fathers. And he understood his oath before the end."

"Would you have killed him, had he failed?"

"No. I am not the God."

She closed her eyes. Closed them, and it came to Cynthia that this stranger, this Evayne, had known Stephen
of Elseth. And had loved him, in her fashion.

She felt a pang, something akin to pain or jealousy.
But she was Lady Maubreche. "Evayne a'Nolan," she
said quietly, "you have come today for a reason."

"Yes, and it was not to be corrected by a boy." But she smiled as she said it.

The smile was heavy. "You look like Stephen of Elseth," she told the young Maubreche Lord. "And you have some of him within you. I . . . had not expected that."

Stephen approached her, passing Gilliam and Espere, passing Corwel. He stopped a foot from her, well within the sphere of personal space that was never breached in polite society.

"I'm sorry if it makes things harder for you." He meant it.

The stranger's eyes widened again, and then they narrowed. "I am not so young a girl as I was then. I will never again be that girl."

"I haven't had your experience. If the gods are kind, I will never have it. But . . . my mother is your age, and she still remembers what she was, and what wounded her. Some wounds never become scars," he added, "because they never heal."

"You are, indeed, of the god-born," the stranger said. "Or I know little of boys."

"He has always been quick to speak, and subtle," Cynthia said at last, with quiet, uneasy pride.

"My apologies, Lady Maubreche. Time is of the essence, and I am needed elsewhere."

"But you came upon some urgent business?"

"Indeed." And she lifted the folds of her cloak, opening them wide. Cynthia caught a brief glimpse of what lay within, and she blanched, although later she could not say why. "Come," the stranger said quietly. "Come, Nenyane."

From out of the swirl of midnight, a young girl emerged.

She made Stephen look ruddy; her skin was the color of snow. Her hair was so pale it was silver, and a silver that was unkind; it was not the pale of blonde, but rather the color of platinum, of age, cold and harsh. Her eyes were wide in the white of her face, gray as storm.

Cynthia went forward immediately, hand outstretched as if the girl was in danger of breaking. She could not know what experience had scarred the girl, but the color of her hair could not be natural. Had she thought Stephen was slender? Not compared to this child. She was knife thin, all bones and angles.

"Nenyane," Evayne said, "this is Lady Maubreche. And this is her son, Stephen. We spoke of him while we traveled. Stephen of Breodan, Stephen of Maubreche, what have you heard of Nenyane?"

Stephen barely heard the question. His eyes were golden, round, clarity to storm. He lifted a hand, palm out. The girl stepped out of the lee of the storm of robes, and the folds of cloth fell at once. She had eyes only for Stephen, and when she lifted a hand, it was the mirror image of Stephen's shaky gesture. Their fingers touched.

In the bright clarity of daylight, shorn of the mystery of night and the shadows of twilight, Cynthia thought she saw a light flare where their fingers made contact. It was brief; she could not be certain that she had seen it.

Or would not be.

"Nothing," he said at last. "Except that I'm her Hunter. And she—she's the huntbrother I've been waiting for."

"Yes," the stranger said quietly. She turned, took a step toward the gardens, and disappeared. But the girl she had brought forth remained.

What she expected from her husband, not even Cynthia could say, and she knew because she tried to give it voice. Throughout the speech of the stranger in her fell robes, throughout the speech of the son that was not his son, he had waited in silence.

Nor had he spoken when the girl had come forth from robes that should not have hidden her, no matter how thin and gangly she was. But when Stephen spoke the single word *huntbrother,* Lord Maubreche had risen, the silence a shield and a cloud. He meant to storm off, but before he reached the edge of the green, he turned.

Cynthia met his gaze; saw in it an equal measure of shock, and a terrible bleak anger, before he continued on his way to the kennels. She would have followed him; she started across the green to do just that.

But two hands touched her.

Arlin's.
And Stephen's.
She let him go.

Gilliam of Elseth was silent. Brooding. It was a state
with which Cynthia of Maubreche was acutely familiar.
She had seen him thus for the better part of a year after
his return from the far East; had seen him thus at every
Sacred Hunt thereafter. Only when he was soothing the
temper of his wild and inexplicable wife did that darkness leave him, and for that reason, if no other, Cynthia
placed some value upon Espere of Elseth.

For Lady Maubreche and Lord Elseth had come, over
time, to an unspoken understanding. Of the bereaved,
they were the two who felt the loss most keenly. Stephen
of Elseth was gone, and only in memory was anything
of him retained. That was their responsibility, Cynthia
and Gilliam: the memories.

Cynthia had given Stephen a son. Had insisted upon
naming the boy after the dead. The name was a compul-
sion, for Gilliam of Elseth, and he had undertaken some
responsibility for his huntbrother's namesake, even when
he knew that in form, in truth, the boy was son to the
creature that had killed him.

But this, this was difficult.

"Lord Elseth," Cynthia said quietly.

He turned his glance briefly upon her face. "It can't
be done," he told her. "You know that."

"Is there law against it?"

"Hunter law," Gilliam answered. "I know that his
eyes mark him, Cynthia." No formal title offered in return for the use of his; he desired no distance. Probably
didn't understand why she would. "I know it. But Breodan's law is Breodan's law."

"He is as close to Breodan as any Priest who has ever
undertaken to follow the Hunter God," she replied, with
a calm she did not feel.

"She's a girl."

"I had noticed that."

"There is a reason they aren't called huntsisters."

"She is not a Hunter Lord," Cynthia replied. "She
will never lay claim to that title. Not for her are the

dogs, or the trance; not for her the claim of lands, and the responsibility that goes with it. She will be what Stephen was—a child that is forgotten. A child in need of a home. Would you have me deny her that?"

"A home? No. Give her a home, by all means. But what you desire, you cannot give her. She is *not* Breodani. She is not—"

"No huntbrother has ever been blessed with the gift of the God," she continued, offering reason, logic, the persuasion of a woman who sat upon the seat of judgment. "A huntbrother has always been the human face of the pairing; a huntbrother, trained to the peak of his abilities, has at his disposal only ingenuity, loyalty, and affection. Does it matter, in the end, whether she is a boy or a girl? She does not have to *be* a Hunter. She only has to offer the Hunter her support and her oath."

"And will she swear the oath?" he snapped. Espere turned, although she stood some fifty yards distant. He cursed, but quietly, and forced himself to quiet.

"She is to be huntbrother. She will swear the oath."

He closed his eyes. "Lady Maubreche," he said, finding the formality and the distance that had, moments before, eluded him. "He *is* Stephen's son, to me. I don't care about the color of his eyes. I don't care about the Priests. I don't care about the Hunter. I heard what he said, and I know what I heard.

"If not the girl, then no one. He will never be a Hunter."

She had him, then, but it brought her no sense of triumph, for what he heard, she had heard.

"He knows, Cynthia," Arlin said. The lamplight shone at her back, reflected in twin circles on the curve of the high ceiling above her. Before her, curtains drawn and sheers hooked aside, the widest and longest of the windows reflected some of that light; she moved closer, losing reflection. The night was clear.

"I know," she said bitterly. She pressed her head against the cool glass. It would get colder still before winter's end. "I know, it." She bit her lip. "Arlin—"

"He has to deal with it in his own way."

And what of me? She wanted to cry. She said nothing.

He came to stand behind her, his hands upon her shoulders, light as a feather, as a bird wing. "You've waited," he said at last, acknowledging the bitterness she could not put into words.

But such acknowledgment was often the key to what lay locked in silence. She closed her eyes. "Yes," she said at last. "I've waited. I've waited through all the arguments, all the anger, all the pain. I've waited for the moment when Stephen would finally find a huntbrother and make his vows. I want—"

"I know." Arlin was more generous with words than she. Not really like Stephen at all. "Peace," he said. "An end to the fighting."

"I wish Corwin could speak to the Hunter."

"There is only one way that he will ever have that chance. Do not wish for it, Cynthia."

She bit her lip again. A girl's gesture. She hated it. "I do love him," she said at last. "I still love him."

"And he loves you."

"As he can."

"And he loves his son. Both of them."

"Yes. But it shouldn't be like this, Arlin. It shouldn't. All that love, turned inward like a weapon, turned outward in anger—all that love, a growing divide. It shouldn't be."

She lifted her hands. Caught his gently and disengaged them, turning to face him. "And you, between us, trying to heal the rift."

"I love you," he said quietly. "Both of you."

"And Stephen?"

Arlin's turn to stare beyond the panes of glass. "Yes," he said at last. "But, Cynthia, Nenyane is not . . ."

"Not?"

He shook his head quietly. "I don't know," he said at last, with a marked hesitation. "But I think it best for Maubreche that Robart not be neglected."

She felt the cold then; winter coming early.

Mark, Robart's huntbrother, was not kind to the newcomer. He himself, newly arrived, was not yet comfortable in his position—as if the rank of huntbrother could somehow be snatched from him, and his life be returned to the streets of the city from which he had come. He knew that, among any pack of children, there must be a victim, and he did his best—in subtle and not so subtle ways—to make sure that it wasn't him.

She found it hard to forgive him this, although she understood it; it had not been long enough since he had been the hunted, in his own way.

Robart did not go out of his way to welcome the girl either, and this, too, Cynthia understood, although she accepted it less readily. Robart was his father's son, and his father's most vocal supporter, and he knew that Corwin was not pleased with her presence.

She also knew, although it pained her more, that Robart stood both in awe and in envy of Stephen's strange position within Maubreche: Stephen was the Hunter's son. His golden eyes marked him, as did the loyalty, slavish and inexplicable, of the alaunts and the lymers. Stephen was not allowed near Robart's hounds; Stephen was not allowed near Corwin's pack. They were brothers, and although it happened in some families that brothers held little affection for one another, she hated to see it happen in hers.

If Stephen felt pained by this enforced separation, he was careful not to show it—but although he was marked in all ways by his birth and his blood, Cynthia knew that he was a boy, with a boy's sensitivities. In that, he was like his namesake.

The girl herself was more of a difficulty.

She spoke rarely, as if words and their use were foreign and achieved only with struggle and a deliberate attempt to remember their use. When she was willing to speak with Cynthia—and that was seldom—she became instantly mute when any questions were asked about her past. Cynthia had encountered some of the same resistance from Mark, but she found Mark's silence less threatening; he had not arrived in the dark clouds beneath the folds of an enchanted robe.

Nenyane ate little, slept little, and often disappeared for hours at a time; Cynthia could find her only when she asked Stephen for his aid.

And Stephen himself?

He was entranced by the girl. He deferred to her in too many things. He called her out to see the dogs, and he tried to teach her what he himself had not, in theory, been taught. He protected her.

And that was not, in the end, the role of the Hunter.

Three weeks after Nenyane's arrival, the first of the snows fell.

The letter that Lady Maubreche sent to the Queen herself had made it to the roads before the snows; the reply would not be tendered—without the use of the mages the Order of Knowledge granted—before spring.

She could not honestly say what the reply would be, for it asked permission to break the most ancient of the laws of the Breodani. Winter was therefore cold and unpleasant in the Maubreche house.

But Nenyane had found a use for the time.

"Cynthia."

Cynthia looked up from the desk at which much of her work, for the winter, would be done. She looked up a little too quickly, and perhaps a little too eagerly, for Corwin seldom entered her study. Or her bedroom, these days.

But the hope died when she met his gaze, and she composed herself as only a Hunter Lady could. She rose stiffly, setting quill aside. "Lord Maubreche."

"I want you to see something."

"Is something wrong with the alaunts?"

"No." He held out a hand—or started to. But the gesture was aborted; the hand fell to his side. "Come."

The tone of his voice brooked no refusal.

She walked with him, leaving the large room in which she worked, leaving the halls that led to their separate chambers, leaving the towering heights of the second story.

The descent led her to the great hall, and the great hall passed by, mirrors and tapestries unheeded; her husband's stride was wide, and she had to step quickly to match the pace he set.

She wondered where Arlin was.

Stopped wondering as she heard, in the distance, the sound of metal against metal.

Her eyes rounded, her brows rose and fell. This much

she could not keep from her face, and Corwin noted it in silence. Too much silence, these days.

The sound grew louder; much louder.

She knew where it came from: the training rooms that were, at the moment, empty. Robart was eight; not until he was nine would work with swords begin in earnest. And Stephen was not a Hunter—not a page, not a varlet; the room was closed to him.

He *knew* this.

But it was Stephen's voice she heard, Stephen's sudden curse, from beyond the closed doors.

Without another glance at her husband's face, she placed hands firmly on the doors and pulled them wide in a single motion. They did not move silently, but the noise they did make was lost to the louder crash of blow and parry: Stephen was upon the floor, and at his side, gray eyes flashing, Nenyane.

She looked, to Cynthia's eyes, like a dancing blade—all angles, all lean, cold steel. Her white hair was bound tight, pulled from her face and her eyes. Stephen's, shorter, fell across his forehead in a sweaty, damp patch.

The blades, to her measured but inexperienced eye, were not sharpened; they had the weight of true swords, but not the edge.

Still, weight of that kind, carelessly handled, could cause death or injury less cleanly than edge, and she drew a single sharp breath. "What is going on here?"

Not even the din of this practice battle could dampen the force of her words. Nenyane froze at once, and Stephen jumped back, lithe and quick, from the reach of her still blade.

"Mother!"

"And Father," she said coldly. "Stephen, what are you doing?"

"Sweating," he replied. "And bruising a lot."

Her lips thinned. "There is no weaponmaster in this room."

He snorted. It was not the reply she expected.

"Stephen?"

"You haven't seen her fight," he said darkly. "She's— she's—"

"Nenyane."

The girl turned her narrowed eyes upon the Lady of Maubreche. She bowed.

"Are you teaching my son swordplay?"

The girl nodded. There was no hesitance in the motion; none of the reticence that Cynthia had come, with experience, to expect.

"And you are qualified to be his teacher?"

Stephen knew better than to answer his mother's question. He knew her mood well.

But he answered anyway. "She is," he said. His voice was subdued. "She's better with the sword than—than she looks like she should be." The words had the force of wet paper. But he spoke steadily, and without cringing.

"You know that this room is forbidden you," Cynthia said. She felt her husband's shadow presence at her side. Did not turn to him for support.

"Yes."

"Then what are you doing here?"

"It's the only room that's big enough, and empty enough. We could have used the ballroom, but—"

Her brows rose. "Stephen!"

He bowed his golden head, closing eyes that were nearly the same color as his hair.

Corwin stepped past Cynthia. It was not what she expected, and it was *not* what she desired.

"Girl," he said, for he called her nothing else.

Nenyane looked up. Her pale face was smooth and dry; her eyes were startling. She put up her blade, but she did not drop it or lay it at her feet, as Stephen had done.

"My son is not a boy who has seen much swordplay. His opinion is therefore suspect. Mine is not." He walked to Stephen's side, but he did not so much as meet his son's eyes. Instead, he bent and retrieved the blade the boy had set aside. "I would spar with you."

It was not a request.

"Corwin—"

"Now."

"I am not here to teach you, Lord Maubreche," Nenyane replied, but she began to move carefully in what was an obvious circle around the Hunter Lord.

"You are not here to teach *anyone*," he snapped back.

"But if you will do so, you will first convince me that what you have to teach will not be harmful—or incompetent."

At that, the girl's eyes widened.

In the pale, gaunt lines of her face, the expression was sharp and bright.

"Nenyane—" Stephen began.

But his father waved him to silence, the motion so abrupt, it, too, was a command.

Stephen was well enough trained that he obeyed. But he came to stand by his mother's side, and his right hand tugged a moment at her elbow. A child's gesture. Her child's.

She looked down. But in truth, it was not far down; gone were the days when she bent just to place her ears close enough to his mouth that she missed none of his words.

What she saw in his face gave her pause.

"I'm not good enough with a sword," he said, the words hushed enough they were clearly meant to carry only to his mother. "And I'm old, she says, to start training."

"Old?"

"If it were up to her," he said with a grimace, "I'd have started when I could walk."

"It is not up to her."

He winced. "Mother—"

She looked across the floor at her husband's face. "Only Arlin," she said quietly, "could stop him now."

"If I call *Hasufel*—"

"Do not call *Hasufel*."

Stephen swallowed. And then, in a bitter voice that was years beyond his age, he said, "He's never going to accept her, is he?"

And she heard what lay behind those words. *He's never going to accept me.*

She placed one hand upon his shoulder; the gesture was not gentle, but the ferocity behind it was born of her desire to protect.

"He has always done what he feels is best for you," she said, punctuating the words with a shake. "But he is a Hunter Lord, and the only thing he understands is what he *is*. He loves not the title, but the life. And he cannot conceive of a crime worse than this: depriving you of your place in that life." She paused, and then added, "And depriving you of Arlin, of a huntbrother, is the greatest measure of that life."

"Then the Queen—"

"It is not in the Queen's hands," Cynthia replied coolly, "as you well know. If she chooses to grace us with her support, she may make her pleas on our behalf. That is all."

Stephen swallowed. Then, just before the first of the clashes of steel robbed them of words, he said, "I'm sorry."

But steel had the whole of her attention.

Corwin was not an indifferent swordsman. He had had years with which to hone this skill, and if it was not Hunter's trance, if it was not the use of spear, it was still an important part of his early training.

But Cynthia could see, from his stance, from the first strike that came out of that peculiar stillness, that he intended to take Stephen at his word; his eyes were light, his movements quick, his breath quicker. He had called Hunter's trance, and he resided within its preternatural speed.

Nenyane did not seem to notice. She bent into her knees, and when Corwin charged, she snapped to the side, dodging the strike by the simple expedient of being above the crescent it traced in air. Her limbs, like the limbs of a bird, remained hovering for just long enough. When they touched down, she was in motion. Her blade was in motion.

Corwin parried, but the parry was clumsy; the strike had come at his back, and he had only enough time to deflect it, no more. He was forced back three steps. His eyes widened. His lips thinned.

He growled.

Stephen, by Cynthia's side, flinched and covered his face.

Corwin struck again. Nenyane was gone before the motion started. She did not press him; she was simply not there when he chose to strike. But by allowing him the attack, she chose not to end the evaluation. There was no fear in her.

Corwin gathered speed. The shape of his shoulders changed; he bent into his knees, approaching with caution, but still approaching. He had passed beyond game; the Hunter's trance informed the whole of his vision. She was his game.

Cynthia was grateful for the absence of the alaunts. She watched, because she could not—as her son had—look away.

And she saw Nenyane in flight. Saw the girl's sword respond to her arms as if it were an extension more natural than limbs or hands. She parried every blow, but the blows were heavier. If Corwin had remembered that she was a child at the start of their bout, he forgot it.

"Stephen—"

Her son peeled fingers from eyes and met his mother's gaze.

And while she looked at the golden flash of her son's eyes, she heard the crash of steel against steel in the background; it was followed by silence.

She looked up.

Corwin held the jagged remnant of the practice blade in his right hand. His left was empty.

Nenyane waited.

"Corwin!" Cynthia shouted, as her Hunter began to circle the girl again. "Enough!"

He shook himself then. Struggled with the hunt, with the Hunter's imperative. Slowly, too slowly, he looked at what he held.

He stepped back.

Nenyane remained where she was.

The Hunter Lord bent slowly and placed the ruin of blade against floor. He rose, stiffly, and bowed.

"Your son," Nenyane said quietly. "May I teach him?"

His only answer was silence, and he did not stay long to offer it. He swept past wife, past son, past training room.

Cynthia watching his retreating back. "Yes," she said softly. "Yes, Nenyane, you may continue to teach him."

*　　*　　*

That day marked a turning point, although it was subtle, and only in retrospect did Cynthia note it.

Corwin was no friendlier than he had been—but he was suddenly present, a shadowy grim figure, taller than either his son or his son's chosen huntbrother. He often watched while the two practiced in the training room, and after a week—only a week—he began to offer Stephen his own observations. Nenyane herself did not seem to notice this intrusion; she spoke only when she thought Corwin in error, and thankfully, that was seldom.

"She's too damn skinny," Corwin said at dinner two weeks later, winter piled against the windows in faces of snow. He still did not choose to speak the girl's name, but Nenyane looked up anyway.

"Am I?"

"You've no weight behind you," he replied. "You can lift the sword—Hunter alone knows how—but you can't lift a simple chair without straining."

"I have no need to lift chairs."

His brow rose. Cynthia's surprise was more easily masked; Nenyane had spoken more at this meal than she had at any other.

"You don't know what you'll need to lift," he snapped back. "Can you lift a boar, when it falls? Can you help Stephen to lift it? Can you help him to drag a deer to its resting place? In your duties—in the duties you think you will earn—you will need *strength*."

She raised a white brow.

Stephen, hearing the question she didn't ask, nodded.

"How am I to gain this strength?"

"Eat," he said. "Eat more."

She looked at the food on her plate with a vague air of suspicion.

Again, Stephen nodded.

"But Lady Maubreche eats, and surely she is no stronger than I?"

Arlin was taken by a sudden coughing fit. Robart snickered. Mark was sullen. But Cynthia herself smiled. "I am not allowed upon the Hunt," she said quietly. "And I can, indeed, move chairs when the necessity arises."

Nenyane shrugged.

But she began to eat, and throughout the winter, the gaunt contours of cheek, the sight of skin over bone with little flesh to cushion it, began to recede into memory. With weight came color; a blush to the cheek, a pink to the tone of skin. Her hair was white, and would remain a winter color, but her eyes lost some of their silver light, their edge of hungry intensity.

The only chore that winter required of those who had not yet taken their title was the cutting of wood. The wood itself, dead, had dried over the course of the summer and the autumn, and required only the gentle urging of an ax blow to split.

When Corwin was not called away by the duties of the winter hunt, his voice was often raised in the woodshed.

"How is it," he snapped, "that you can handle a sword with such ease? You've almost lopped your feet off *twice* in the last half hour!"

"An ax," Nenyane snapped back, "is not a weapon. And these," she added, nudging the logs with what looked suspiciously like an ill-humored kick, "are hardly *foes.*"

"The cold is a foe," Corwin countered, taking the ax in hand. "It is always a foe. Fire prevents it from claiming lives, and without wood, we have no fire. Come, Nenyane."

Cynthia forgot to wrap her shawl more tightly around her shoulders; for a moment, the only sound that entered the shed was the howl of wind outside the crack in the door that had granted her entry.

She could see Nenyane's unusual hesitance.

"And foe or not, your enemies won't care where you took your wounds. If you have no feet, you can't run. If you cannot run, you will *never* be given leave to take the ceremony and swear the oath."

Nenyane glared at Corwin. It was . . . a young girl's glare. Corwin came to stand behind her. "Your feet," he said sharply. He would always speak sharply, but the fact that he spoke at all was precious. "Do what I do. Plant them apart like this. And here," he added, his arms above hers. "You must hold the ax with your hand here, and here. Do you have it?"

She nodded.

"Good. Stephen? The log."

Stephen shuffled a log onto the stump upon which it would be split. It teetered a moment, and he righted it. "Try again."

In the winter, the hay in the lofts of the alaunts had to be changed with care, for the dogs were often restless. They wore winter coats, of course, and their kennels boasted the warmth of fireplaces. The pages were to tend to those fires, and although Mark and Robart had attained that rank and Stephen and Nenyane had not, Corwin suddenly decided to order them to see to the comfort of the alaunts that served Stephen.

Here, too, her husband was often an unwelcome presence—to Nenyane. To Cynthia, he was something entirely different, although it was not her duty, and would never be, to tend the hounds.

She had a mother's visceral fear, a mother's joy, and it was balanced between these two that she made her way to the kennels. Villagers often crept into the kennels in the late winter to sleep with the hounds, and the hounds, accustomed to this intrusion from the time they were puppies, bore it with arrogant grace.

But the winter had not yet grown so cold, and the wood supplies not yet so squandered, that these villagers were witnesses to Corwin's harsh lessons. "Nenyane, attend!"

Like an insolent hound, she drifted to stand by his side, her gaze touching Stephen's first, as if for reassurance. He nodded. Words seldom passed between them, although the Hunter's bond had not yet been established. Their language was a language of gesture and expression that would serve them as well as the bond the God blessed.

Nenyane was taught to turn the hay, and was taught to tend the fire. The last always fascinated her, and Corwin came close to blows in his frustration, for she failed to hear him when she was given to the spark and sputter of cracked, black wood.

But he had grown cunning; he refused to allow Stephen to stay by her side. She had to learn to listen to the Hunter Lord, and if the lesson was slow to take, it came with time.

"Corwin, what are you doing?" Arlin's voice. Cynthia, shivering, turned.

Her husband held the chains and leather bindings used to couple the lymers. "What," he said, through clenched teeth, "does it *look* like I'm doing?"

"It *looks* like you're trying to teach Nenyane how to couple the lymers."

Nenyane glanced up. "He is."

"Thank you, Nenyane."

"Is he doing something wrong?"

"You will find, with experience, that Hunters are almost *always* doing something wrong. It will be your duty, as huntbrother, to ensure that they do not suffer for that wrongdoing. Or that they aren't caught."

Her frown was a child's frown. It came easily to her face, and often stayed for hours.

Stephen laughed, and his laughter caused her eyes to narrow. "She's afraid of the dogs," he told Arlin casually.

"I am *not* afraid of the dogs!" she snapped, heated now. So many words from a girl who had initially offered none. Cynthia might have hoped she could learn less of Corwin's intonation, but she was simply grateful to hear them at all.

Corwin snorted. "You are," he said. "And they know it. They're not as skittish as horses, but they're a good deal more devious. You have to learn to hide your fear."

"I've got nothing to hide!"

He smiled. For just a moment, the chains idling in his hands, his expression was warm. "Then come, and try again. Leave Mako; take Cebran and Rain, and bind them."

Stephen started forward, and his father said, without looking up, "If you do that again, I'll throw you out. This will be her duty. She *must* be able to handle the dogs."

"Mark didn't have to go *near* the dogs until after the ceremony."

"Mark is a boy," his father replied, the smile quenched. "He has nothing to prove."

When Corwin came that night to her chambers, Cynthia was surprised. But his expression was grim and shuttered as she set quill and paper aside.

"You work late," he said.

"There is work."

"You waste light."

She smiled. "You sound like my mother."

His brows rose for a fraction of a second, and then his face thawed. "Or mine," he said, almost rueful. He stared at her for a long moment, and then he stood and he crossed the distance—all of the distances—that lay between them and took her in his arms; his clothing and skin were cold with winter.

He did not apologize in any other way. She didn't expect it. But she found the hollow beneath his shoulders that best fit the curve of her cheek and stood there until the bit of winter had vanished.

"She is difficult," he said, speaking into her hair. "I thought she was slow or addled. But she is no fool. She is *not* a hunter."

She said nothing.

"But there is already a bond between them that I do not think can be broken. I know," he added, with grim amusement. "I've tried."

"Corwin—"

His arms tightened. "He's my son," he said quietly. "What man wants less for his son than he himself enjoys? Cynthia—the girl can stay by his side. She has to. I understand that now."

For just a moment, Cynthia thought she could see a glimmer of the peace that had eluded them both for so many years.

"But let me find him a *legal* huntbrother. A true huntbrother will understand what they have and accept it—"

She pulled herself free from his arms and turned away.

"He's not what I expected."

Cynthia nearly dropped the books she was carrying

when she heard the words; they were Nenyane's. She looked around quickly; there was no one else in the study. No Corwin, no Arlin, and most significant of all, no Stephen.

With care, she righted the books by their spines. With Nenyane, it was best to appear to give no more than half one's attention.

"I'm not sure that you're what he expected either."

At that, Nenyane offered a smile. It was slight, but it was there. "You love him," she said, after a pause.

"He *is* my son," Cynthia replied.

Nenyane nodded. Her gaze was distant, but it was not sharp, and the harshness of the early days had left it entirely. "Corwin loves him, too."

"He is Corwin's son," Cynthia said. She set the books upon her desk and turned, leaning against the wooden lip.

"But he's not."

"He is in any way that matters."

"Do you believe that?"

"Yes."

Nenyane frowned. "He is Breodan's son."

"Is that why you came?"

For just a moment, Nenyane lapsed into a familiar silence. Cynthia expected her to leave, but after a while, the girl nodded.

"We can't afford to make any mistakes," she said quietly. "We have so little time."

"We?"

Nenyane shook her head, and Cynthia let the question drop.

"But he's young, younger than I thought he would be."

"You're not that old, Nenyane."

"Aren't I?"

On impulse, Cynthia took the girl by the hand and led her to her dressing room. There, she paused in front of the mirror, hands on either of Nenyane's shoulders. "Look," she said quietly.

Nenyane did. Her eyes widened as she stared at herself. She shook her head a moment, and white hair spilled out of her loose braid.

But she did not say anything else. After a while, Cyn-

thia left her there, staring as if everything about her
image was foreign to her.

It came to Cynthia, as the snows melted, that Nenyane
was afraid.

They were *all* afraid. The roads would be open within
days if they were not already open from the capital. And
the road would carry the Queen's message. Although
the Queen did not make Hunter law, her advice would
carry its weight; in such a way, warning could be given
to noble families without the legal censure the King's
words would, by nature, carry.

But such a fear was not Nenyane's.

She came to visit Cynthia while Cynthia busied herself
with the seedlings that would eventually find their way
to the garden. It was not real work; the Master Gardener
would, no doubt, dispose of most of the results of such
labor. Still, it kept her hands busy, and she required that
busyness. The silence was difficult.

She became aware of the girl after some time had
passed, and rose, hands wet with dirt.

Nenyane's eyes were wide and almost haunted. "Lady
Maubreche," she said.

"Nenyane?"

"You must come. You must gather your—your family. *Now.*"

"My family?"

"Everyone. Everyone in the House."

Cynthia rose, wiped her hands on her skirts, and *ran.*

She found Stephen in the kitchen arguing with the
cook and his assistants. Her presence stilled the harsh
flow of incredulous words.

"Ellias," she said, bowing. "You are *ordered* to leave
the kitchen. Take what you need for warmth."

Her son shook his head.

"But come *now.*"

"Come? But where? What has happened? Is there a
fire?"

"Worse," she said softly, seeing the color—or the lack
of it—in Stephen's face. "Go at once to the maze. Wait
for me there; I will lead you to its Heart."

He paled, then, and he bowed instantly, obedient for the master where he had been truculent with the son.

She met Corwin and Arlin as she raced up the stairs. Corwin's face was grim, his lips set. His eyes were already the peculiar color they took when he had summoned a light trance. "The dogs," he began.

She shook her head. "It's not just the dogs. Empty the household, Lord Maubreche. Send everyone to the maze, and do it *now*."

He did not question her. But he glanced at the face of their son.

"Where are Robart and Mark?"

"In the kennels," he said.

"Good. Tell the alaunts to get them to the maze."

"The alaunts will—"

"Corwin," she said, her voice rising.

He nodded again. She loved him then.

She had no time to take a head count; no time to take a tally. But she thought—and prayed—that she had not missed anyone. They gathered, some shivering in the cool of early spring, and they waited upon her word.

Nenyane and Stephen stood beside her.

Robart and Mark stood with Corwin, and she could see from Robart's excited bounce that he knew something *big* was happening.

"Forgive me," she said, raising her voice so that it carried. "But we are in some danger, and we must harken now to the Hunter in the maze. Follow me, and if you get lost, follow Stephen; we know the way, and if we lead you, you *will* arrive in safety. Do *not* touch the hedges. Do *not* disturb the gardens."

They nodded. She was proud of this obedience, and grateful for it. She turned, skirts still dark with new dirt, and began to walk as quickly as she could without breaking into a panicked run.

Corwin's voice rose and fell at her back; she did not turn to see why; she trusted him.

The maze opened before her, and she followed its twists and turns, its broken walls, as if they were the halls of her childhood. They were. She felt safety in their

presence, although she was exposed to sky and the brisk
bite of wind.

But she stopped, once, at the hedge-wall. People
bumped into her, driving her forward a step; her hands
brushed branches that were only beginning to bud.

She did not come here in winter. She expected to see
only bare branches, the skeleton of bush. But even in
this exposed state, she could see what the Master Gardener had carved. Could see where her place upon the
hedge was. Could see, clearly, that something else had
begun to take shape and form in the wall.

It wasn't human. It wasn't even close.

No, she thought. This is old. This is part of my
other life.

But she *knew*.

She picked up her skirts and she began to run. At her
back, her servants now followed in utter silence, for they
had eyes, and brains besides; they had seen exactly what
she had seen.

They did not name it. They did not pray. Instead, they
sought the shelter that only Maubreche could provide.

She broke into the Heart of the maze, her eyes raised
to meet the eyes of the stone Hunter God.

Something spoke.

"Well, well," he said, turning, his long leather wings
unfurling in an expanse that seemed to go on and on,
"you took your time. We were beginning to think that
we would have to hunt you."

In the Heart of the maze, three creatures stood. She
had seen their like only once in her life, at the side of
the long dead Stephen of Elseth. And she knew how
kind her memory had been, because this reality was so
much worse.

She found voice before she found weapon, although
she reached for both at the same time. *"Sanctuary!"*
she cried.

The creature laughed. "It only works if we're on the
outside," he said.

But she felt some distant answer to the single word.

"Your God has ascended," the creature continued.
"He has left you here, to the mercy of *our* God. And

our God has chosen to make this realm his home. There are always a few . . . difficulties . . . in such an arrangement, and we have been sent to smooth them out."

He lifted a taloned hand, a slender arm; they were the color of night. At a distance, he might have been beautiful, in the way predators are. But there was no distance here.

Fire flew from the tips of his fingers.

At her back, the household staff began to scream.

But the fire did not reach them. It lapped against the old, wet grass that had been blanketed by snow for months. The grass burned anyway, tracing the edge of a circle that began at Cynthia's feet.

The creature frowned.

With a confidence she did not feel, she said, "You are in the Hunter's domain. Go, now, and you will be spared."

His eyes widened. He turned to his companions. "Kill them," he said. "Kill them all. If the boy does not fight, spare only him. Do you understand what you are being offered, boy?"

She knew who that boy was, but she did not turn to look at him; instead, she drew knives, one in either hand.

But the boy—her son—replied. "Yes," he said quietly, his words drawing her glance where the demon's could not, "I do. My first test."

He was ten. Almost eleven. He was a child.

But he stepped out from behind the broad girth of the cook, shaking himself free of that man's large hands. In his own, he carried a sword.

She had not seen it when she had summoned him. Had not seen it in the kitchen, nor at the edge of the maze. But it was there, and it was not the only sword drawn.

By his side, her eyes a pale silver to Stephen's gold, stood Nenyane. She, too, held a sword.

The creature laughed, but the laughter was short and sharp, and it died quickly. Where he was oddly compelling, his laughter was simply ugly.

"Kill them all," the creature said, and pushed off the

ground, seeking the vantage of height in which to do battle.

Cynthia turned to face Ellias, the man who had tried to protect her son. "No matter what it says," she told him, "no matter what it *does*, do not try to leave the Heart of the maze. If it is not safe here, it is far, far less safe anywhere else in Maubreche."

Ellias nodded grimly, and said, "All right. But we're going to have a discussion about my salary after this is over."

The faintest of smiles tugged at her lips and was gone.

Nenyane leaped to the right as the creature dove; Stephen stayed his ground, the tip of his sword tracing flat, brown grass.

The creature did not, however, attack them; instead he focused the whole of his attention upon Cynthia.

She threw her knives. It was a skill, and one that she had been taught in lieu of sword. One dagger skirted the underside of the leathery wings; the other sank into flesh.

The creature snarled.

But he was one; there were three.

Stephen's sword came up as the second creature took to the air; there was a clang, as of steel against steel, and talons came away without leaving a mark. Stephen was driven back by the impact; the cook caught him, righted him.

He almost paid for the interference with his life, but the winds in the maze's Heart rose, sudden and terrible, and the creatures, airborne, were driven back.

"This is the work of a lifetime," a familiar voice said. "I will not have you carelessly damage it."

She turned at the sound of the voice, and then looked up. *Standing* upon the thin branches of bushes that should never have supported his weight was the Master Gardener of Maubreche.

In his hand was a blade that seemed to be made of blue fire. Gone were clippers, shears, trowels; gone was the nondescript clothing in which he worked, day by day and year by year. He wore something that must have been armor, but it conformed so perfectly to his slender frame, Cynthia thought she must be mistaken.

"Lady Maubreche," the Master Garden said, "you once asked my name, against all convention, and I did not choose to answer you. I am sorry to answer you now, and perhaps you will better understand why I chose silence when you have my answer.

"I am Caralonne." He lifted his left arm, and a shield suddenly graced it; it was of the same metal as the sword, burning brightly in the daylight.

The creature upon the winds shrieked in fury. *"Caralonne?"* it spat. *"But you are dead!"*

"I see that you are as observant as you always were," the Master Gardener replied coldly. "But you are *not* in your element here. Choose the air, and it will devour you."

Wind swept across the clearing of the maze's Heart. It forced the creatures back, and they dove to earth, finding purchase against the unnatural howl.

But the gale did not touch Cynthia or her people.

Instead, a different howl did.

The alaunts were coming.

Stephen and Nenyane *moved*. Before Cynthia could stop them—and she would have, and knew it was wrong—they crossed the flat ground, blades flashing in the sunlight. No blue burned those edges, but the glint there told her that these were not practice blades. Her son was wielding a man's weapon, and at his side, his huntbrother wielded one, too.

First blood: Stephen's. It fell when talons raked his arm, splitting the thick winter fabric as if it offered no resistance. His blade replied, and the creature snarled; it had extended its arm too far in an attempt to deal a fatal blow.

Nenyane's blade bit to bone; second blood was a good deal more dear than first had been.

The creature sprang up; the wind battered it and it came down at once.

Cynthia turned to look at the Master Gardener. He was watching, his gaze intent, his sword readied. But he did not leap down from the hedge-wall; he did not choose to join her son.

As if he could hear her, he said, "Stephen is correct. This is his test."

But it was not a child's test; to fail was simply to die.

"You have your responsibility, Lady Maubreche. Do not desert it."

He's a child, she wanted to scream. *I'm his mother!* But she was silent. Her weapons were gone; her responsibility remained. But she could not turn away.

The dogs came through the maze, snapping at the servants who stood in their way.

At their head, horn in hand, was Corwin; at his side, spear readied, Arlin. They were like, and unlike, Stephen and Nenyane, but they moved with a single purpose.

Cynthia could not interfere with Stephen. She could not—had no desire—to call Corwin back. But she *did* reach out to grab Robart and Mark by their collars; enough was enough.

Robart snarled, but Mark went limp instantly. He was terrified; he had come this far because his duty and his loyalty lay with his Hunter. She loved him for both his loyalty and his fear, and she drew them both close.

"If you do not still *this instant,* I will hand you to Ellias," she said, into Robart's ear.

"But Stephen's there, and he's not even a page!"

"Stephen is Breodan's son. This *is* his place." Driving the wedge between her sons more deeply into place and regretting it, she spoke.

"Mother—"

"I would have stopped him," she said, mouth by her youngest's ear. "But I can't. You're *eight*. He's *eleven*."

"He's *ten!*"

"Enough. I need you here. If they fail, there will be no one to protect us. Do you understand?" She shook him to punctuate the words.

But they had their desired effect.

The battle raged. Everyone moved so damned quickly it was hard to take it all in, but Cynthia bore witness. She bit back a cry when Arlin fell, and did cry out when he rose, bloodied, his hand upon the haft of his spear. The dogs leaped past him, snapping at the demons, and she knew that they would lose at least one of the hounds.

But she was unprepared for that hound to be Hasufel.

He was the link between father and husband, between husband and son, and he was older now, too old to be pack leader. But not too old to be Hunter's hound; not too old to give his life in the defense of his many masters.

He did not even cry out when talons sliced through his windpipe, felling him in a single blow; his jaws still gripped tight about the leg of the demon, and Arlin and Corwin used this momentary pause to time their attacks. The Maubreche spear pierced the creature's chest, lifting him an inch off the ground.

Nenyane and Stephen were besieged by the two remaining demons; if there had been any question who their target was—and there hadn't, but there had been hope—it was dispelled.

Stephen was cut again, and this wound was deeper, but he did not lose his footing; instead he leaped clear of the strike that would have ended his life, and returned it, taking the wing at pinion. The wings of these creatures were as much a threat as their talons; he had crippled it for the moment.

Nenyane removed its head and turned, shouting Stephen's name.

He flattened; something passed over his head. Something red and bright. A sword. One of the demons had drawn sword in the maze.

Nenyane screamed at the demon in a language that Cynthia did not understand. The demon froze an instant and then turned to stare at her, incredulous. It was a costly mistake, for she did not pause, and in her wake, her Hunter was also moving.

But Nenyane took the first of her wounds in that meeting; Stephen escaped unscathed. The creature did not.

The dogs gathered around Stephen were his own. Rain and Cebran snarled, but they did not leap, and it took Cynthia only a moment to realize why: He had given them orders. Hunter orders, in the silence of a trance that she knew he had not yet learned.

They traced a circle around the creature, snapping and growling, but they bounded out of his way when he brought his sword to bear.

And then the creature was attacked from behind;

Arlin had managed to remove his spear from the chest of the demon, and he had found an opening in the space between the great wings.

It was not over in that instant, but Cynthia drew breath, for it *was* over.

The Master Gardener stepped lightly down from the hedge. He landed just beyond Stephen, gaining his feet with a nimble grace that did not suit a gardener.

"Breodan-kin," he said, and he bowed. "You pass."

Stephen, bleeding and breathing heavily, looked up at the face of the Master Gardner as if he did not understand his words.

"It was a simple test," the Master Gardener continued.

Stephen glanced at the bleeding body of Hasufel and said nothing.

"You will lose much, much more than Hasufel before this is over," the Master Gardener said, but his words were oddly gentle. "Do you understand what the test was?"

Stephen frowned. "We killed them," he said at last.

Nenyane, by his side, and bleeding just as profusely, rolled her eyes. "He's not really stupid," she said to the Master Gardener. "But this is his first real fight."

Stephen turned on her. "If you're so smart, you tell me."

"He offered you your life," she said, "if you left."

Stephen's frown spoke clearly.

Nenyane laughed. "You don't remember?"

"Of course I remember. But—"

"But?"

"Not much of a test," he said. He set his sword down then, and walked over to Hasufel. He lifted the alaunt with as much care as a slender boy could; Hasufel's blood darkened his shirt, mingling with his own until they were one and the same.

"No," Nenyane said. "But I never said demons were *smart*."

But Stephen didn't hear her. He was crying.

In the somber silence of the Maubreche spring grounds, they buried Hasufel. The standing stones that existed upon any Hunter Lord's domain still bore the trace of ice from winter's passage, and the ground was barely thawed; Stephen and Nenyane had to *work* to dig the grave in the lee of the ceremonial stones.

The healers, accustomed to Hunters, kept their outraged complaints to a bare minimum; Stephen's wounds were not healed, and he was in no way whole enough to undertake such an arduous task.

But he did the work. Nenyane's months of eating and training had indeed given her the muscle necessary to move chairs—and earth. She did not complain about wielding a shovel to fight with dirt.

Instead, she glanced at Stephen as she worked; he did not meet her gaze.

Cynthia watched in silence. Her hands were balled fists at her sides; she had attempted to offer Stephen comfort, but she knew that he would take none. Time would give him what he required, or nothing would; he had never lost a hound before.

Corwin and Arlin bore witness as well. They offered their help, but only obliquely, and neither man seemed surprised when Stephen curtly—even rudely—refused them. They *had* suffered the loss that Stephen now suffered, and they accorded Hasufel the respect of their open sorrow.

It was the only thing they could offer Stephen.

Three days later, the Queen's letter arrived, carried by a man who wore the livery of the Master of the Game. Hunter Green, the darkest of colors. Cynthia recognized him immediately.

She took the Queen's letter and retired at once to her chambers, followed by Corwin and Arlin.

They waited in a hushed silence as she broke its wax seal. The silence grew as she read; she did not speak the words aloud.

But these two, they knew her. They knew the subtle nuances of her expressions well. What had been written was there in the stiff lines of her face.

She looked up; met first Corwin's and then Arlin's eyes before handing them the news.

Corwin did not read the letter. Instead, he cursed roundly.

"I'd better go," he said quietly. "Arlin?"

Arlin looked up from the Queen's response, his expression bleak. "Where?"

"To the King," Corwin snapped. "Where else?"

"The King has spoken," Arlin replied, lifting the letter. "Through his Queen, he has made his decision. Will you challenge the Master of the Game?"

"Yes."

"And his Priests?"

"Even if the only forum we're given is the Sacred Hunt, then *yes*, damn you. They didn't see what we saw," he added. "They weren't there for the fight in the maze. If they *know* about it, they'll change their minds."

His huntbrother offered him the loyalty of silence.

"You saw her," Corwin continued, speaking to his wife. "You saw Stephen. They *are* Hunter and huntbrother. Without oath, without ceremony, without any bloody *training*, they are what they are.

"And I'll be damned if my son is denied his life because of a set of stupid laws."

Cynthia's eyes widened. "They're the Hunter's law," she said, muted.

"No," he said quietly. "I thought that. But I know what I saw, Cynthia. I know what I felt. Will Lord Elseth stand as witness to a ceremony that does not have the King's blessing?"

She was almost shocked. But she gathered herself quickly. "I believe," she said, choosing her words with care, "that Lord Elseth would die before he would fail Stephen of Maubreche."

"Good. Write to Lord Elseth. I will write to my mother and my brother. Stephen doesn't know the horn calls; he didn't sound the hunt. But he *hunted*. He's earned his title.

"And we'll give it to him. If we have to break the Priest's laws, we'll break them. He's *Breodan's* son. What the Hunter God accepts, I'll shove down the throats of everyone else."

She reached up and placed her hand against his mouth, stemming the flow of his words with regret. It was seldom that he spoke this freely. "He is *our* son," she said, with a quiet pride.

"Cynthia—"

She shook her head. Walked into the circle of his arms, although he had not—yet—lifted them. She was careful to touch him gently, and after a moment, he bent his head and kissed the top of her hair.

"Yes," he said at last. "He is. Our son. And if I come to an understanding of things less quickly than you, Lady Maubreche, I *am* a Hunter Lord. I will fight for what is mine."